Burying the Dead

by

Kerry Blaisdell

Book Four of The Dead Series

Burying the Dead

Cover Art by *The Wild Rose Press, Inc.*

The Wild Rose Press, Inc.
PO Box 708
Adams Basin, NY 14410-0708
Visit us at www.thewildrosepress.com

Publishing History
First Edition, 2023
Trade Paperback ISBN 978-1-5092-4581-9
Digital ISBN 978-1-5092-4582-6

Book Four of The Dead Series
Published in the United States of America

"I—we need your help. And more to the point—*Geordi* does."

Rina frowned at that. "What do you mean? What are you talking about?"

Nico also leaned forward. "Spit it out. What—you think you can demand a ransom for him?"

I gasped in my outrage, and suddenly those hard blue eyes bored into me. And then they faded to black. He stood, towering over me.

"And *you*—you think you're owed some of the Dioguardi pot, because your sister squirted out Nick's son? We're done here. Give us Geordi, or I'll do worse than call the cops."

The whole room crackled with demon energy—three pairs of eyes were now black, and I shot to my feet.

"No—wait—everyone calm down. I—we—aren't here for money. Geordi's in danger—that's the help we need."

That brought them up short. Rina narrowed her gaze. "Go on."

"It's true," Jason said. "Paolo made a deal to host a Hell Demon. He kidnapped Geordi, and we don't know where he is or how to get him back."

Hearing the words, spoken so bluntly, brought back all the fear and anguish, and from her expression, they had the same effect on Rina. She went whiter than the coffee table, staggering back, grabbing at Nico's arm to keep from falling.

"*No…*"

Nico's eyes, just fading to blue, snapped black again. "You lost him? To a Hell Demon?"

"Yes," I managed. And then I burst into sobs and collapsed onto the chair.

Praise for Kerry Blaisdell

PRAISE FOR BOOKS 1-3 IN THE DEAD SERIES

"The supernatural mystery and suspense elements drive the fast-paced plot forward, combined with enough romance to add sentimental flair between the characters. Balanced with a sense of fun and quirky situations, Debriefing the Dead is excellently imaginative and hard to put down. "

~ Reader's Favorite

"Fans of television shows like 'Constantine' or 'Supernatural' will absolutely love [WAKING THE DEAD]…The main character, Hyacinth, is phenomenal and develops so much in this book."

~ InD'tale Magazine

"If you're a paranormal reader, pick up DAMNING THE DEAD. If you're looking for an addictive series to binge-read, you'll want to read the whole Dead series."

~ N.N. Light's Book Heaven

"Ms. Blaisdell is a master storyteller…So many twists and turns will have you sitting on the edge of your seat!"

~Still Moments Magazine

Dedication

For my husband, Tom. Best. Minion. Ever.

Chapter One

"Confront the dark parts of yourself, and work to banish them with illumination and forgiveness. Your willingness to wrestle with your demons will cause your angels to sing."

~August Wilson, American Playwright
(1945-2005)

I picked an invisible speck of lint off my maroon tights and tried not to fidget with the hem of my black pencil skirt.

Jason gave me the side-eye. "Relax, will you? Everything will be fine."

"Easy for you to say—you're one of them. They *have* to listen to you. Me, not so much."

In fact, at best, the "they" in question probably wished they'd never heard of me. And at worst—well, let's just say my current outfit could easily be accessorized with concrete boots and a deep ocean dive, to make sure I never resurfaced again.

If you're wondering, I'm Hyacinth Finch, former graverobber turned "art dealer" for a certain select clientele who like to steal from each other for fun. I'm also a former dead person, with a brand-new third career as Assistant to the Angel of Death, otherwise known as Archangel Michael. His job is to shepherd souls Up or Down, depending on their life choices, and my job is to "presort" said souls, so he can attend to other business, like stopping Satan's escape from Hell. Which I also help with, by tracking down rock shards that contain both his and Satan's powers, left over from a big battle they had, eons ago. If Satan gets enough of these, he can use them to break out of his prison, and I'm the only "rock senser" Michael's ever met, so…lucky me.

But I'm on a temporary hiatus from the day job, so I can grovel to my dead sister Lily's ex in-laws, Niccolò and Caderina Dioguardi—the aforementioned "they"— in hopes they'll help me save my nephew, Geordi, from the Hell Demon who kidnapped him. The slight hitch being that they're also demons—although not from Hell—and they want Geordi for themselves. He's their only grandchild, and has incredibly strong supernatural powers himself. Which is why he was kidnapped in the first place: to be used as a bargaining chip by various factions who want his powers for themselves. Including Satan.

I shivered, and Jason took my hand. "Hey— seriously—it will be okay. Marchosias won't hurt him. Geordi's far too valuable to be damaged."

The vast marble-columned foyer in which we sat, awaiting an audience with Nico and Rina, felt cold and unwelcoming, and I wanted nothing more than to burrow into Jason's side and let him keep lying to me that this would all be okay.

Jason is *also* a Dioguardi, and a demon, but a "good one." Supposedly. He uses Jones as his surname, but even so, it's hard to separate him from the larger family sometimes, especially since he's got the signature Dioguardi "look": wavy black hair, baby blue eyes— when they aren't demon black—and a hefty six-foot-six height. Which seven-year-old Geordi, who is technically his cousin, is well on his way to achieving.

But things are complicated between us right now, so instead of caving to my instincts, I removed my hand and tugged at my skirt again, and Jason sighed and sat back.

"Look," he said, "I get how much it cost you to do this. Hell, Rina and Nico get it, too. I know you've viewed them as the Enemy for months now. And I admit, you're probably not their favorite person."

In spite of it all, I laughed, and a smile crept onto Jason's face.

I blew out a breath. "I don't trust them. I know you think there's another side to the story, but Nick didn't happen all by himself. His abusive nature was augmented by their nurture, and he meant everything to them. And I…"

Jason grimaced. "It's not your fault their only son—"

"Their only *child!*"

"—died. He brought that on himself. But you're right. They do blame you, in part. Still, they'll take into account that you came to them. The family as a whole has done terrible things. But they're honorable. If they give you their word, you can trust it."

His eyes were dark and unreadable—not black, thank God, so his demon powers weren't surging, or whatever it's called. But…did he count himself among the "whole" who'd done "terrible things"? Did I want to know?

At this point in our relationship, probably not. Not that we're *in* a relationship—far from it. In fact, I have a boyfriend. Sort of. Assuming his spirit recovers.

As though reading my mind—an annoying talent he

has—Jason said, "Eric will also be fine. If anyone can save him, Nadezhda will."

Eric Guilliot is a former French police officer killed by the Dioguardis the same night I died, and Nadezhda is a woman we met in Turkey who, like me, walks among the Dead. She *had* saved Eric once before, by making him Full Dead, but this was different. He'd been damaged, possibly beyond repair, when he appropriated a fresh corpse, to gain a living body again. He'd succeeded for a time, but then the man's body began absorbing Eric's spirit, and kept those bits behind after Eric got ejected.

The nausea roiled, and I shoved it down. "How can you be so sure? About any of it? How can you stay so positive?"

What I really wanted to ask was, *Why are you always so damn nice?* The words stuck in my throat, and he looked away. But not before I saw the suppressed emotion in his blue eyes—rage, but not at me. And fear—but not for me.

"I have to," he said quietly. "It's the only way through."

The double doors in the silk-paneled and gilt-accented wall across from us opened, and Caderina Dioguardi stepped through, wearing a cream wool pantsuit and strappy high-heeled sandals that clicked like claws on the marble floor. She had to be in her sixties, though the Dioguardi genes—and a bottomless bank account—made her appear younger. Her hair was glossy brown, a shade lighter than most of her cousins' black locks, and her eyes were gold and cat-like.

It was actually a bit jarring. Now that I knew she, like Nico, had also descended from the priest who'd introduced the demon blood into the Dioguardi family eons ago, it seemed weird that she'd broken the black-haired, blue-eyed mold. But a Dioguardi is a Dioguardi, and I'd best not forget it. At least her eyes weren't black...yet. They would be, once she heard the news.

She reached us, her laser focus on me. "Hyacinth. So good of you to *finally* grace us with your presence. We've been scouring the world for you. But then, you knew that, or you wouldn't have been hiding in the first place." I rose, opening my mouth to reply, and she faced Jason. "And you must be Jason. We've heard *so* much about you—and your extracurriculars."

I guess he'd told the truth when he claimed not to be in "*le cercle rapproché des Dioguardis,*" as Eric calls it.

Jason's jaw ticked, but he only unfolded his impressive frame from the bench and planted himself at my side. "Thank you for agreeing to see us. Where's Niccolò?"

"Where's my grandson?"

That confirmed what we'd suspected: They hadn't learned of the kidnapping yet. If they had, I wouldn't be standing here. The concrete boots would be joined by iron bracelets and a two-ton weight, and the bottom of the ocean wouldn't be deep enough. At least, that's how I'd accessorize anyone who "lost" Geordi. And now, I had to confess that *I'd* lost him.

Jason put a reassuring hand on my shoulder. Or maybe it was a warning. We'd discussed this: Yes, we needed Nico and Rina's help. But Jason didn't think I could remain calm and rational where they were concerned, and cautioned me against just diving into the details before we'd taken the temperature of the room.

I drew in a breath, then exhaled slowly, glancing

around the foyer while I pushed my fight or flight instincts down. But that just made me antsy in a different way—*so* many priceless paintings and *objets d'art*, practically begging to be, er, borrowed. Most were probably stolen anyway, so who'd even notice if a few fell into my over-large purse on the way out?

I glanced back at Rina to find her watching me, unblinking. She'd notice, that's for sure. And I didn't need *another* reason for her to hate me.

I smoothed the silver-gray cashmere sweater I'd borrowed from Lily's closet and said as calmly as I could, "Is there somewhere we can talk? Privately?"

A few servants had wandered past while Jason and I cooled our heels, and I had no doubt security cameras recorded our every breath. But what we had to say shouldn't be said in a hallway, however grand and richly furnished.

Rina watched me a moment longer, but I refused to give her the satisfaction of flinching. Her gaze flicked to Jason, and then without a word, she turned and walked back toward the doors through which she'd entered.

Jason said, "That's all the invitation we're likely to get. After you…"

I picked up my purse, telling my queasy stomach this would be over soon—one way or another—and followed Rina farther into Dioguardi Central than I'd been since Lily left Nick a year ago. At least Jason literally had my back—the most constant, reliable demon I knew.

Even if he was a Dioguardi.

We passed through the open doors, which closed silently behind us, two servants having apparently been standing at attention, waiting for just such a purpose. I didn't hear a lock click, but then, I was on their turf, unarmed and outnumbered, so who needed locks?

Rina walked ahead of us through a long narrow gallery, filled with artwork, statuary, and royal-quality jewels. A wall of sheer-curtained windows to our right let in the late-November sunshine, while a richly embroidered runner cushioned our feet from the cold marble floor, and I tried not to wobble in the heels I'd thought would best complete my outfit.

If you haven't guessed by now, I'm not a skirt-and-heels kinda gal. But when facing one's grotesquely wealthy Mafia in-laws, it's probably wise to wear your Sunday best. Jason put a steadying hand at my waist, and I tried not to dwell on my feelings for him, or my guilt over Eric. Since leaving Germany four days ago, Jason and I had avoided any and all discussions about "us." This might be consideration on his part, or maybe he'd just had it with my indecision, but either way, I needed to sort out my emotions once and for all.

I'd returned to Lily's Paris apartment with a contingent of my "minions"—men who'd thrown their lot in with me over the past weeks—while Jason went back to his own place across town. He could have bunked at Lily's, but again, by unspoken agreement, we'd avoided the whole question of *where should I sleep,* by removing the possibility of "together" entirely.

The thing is, I missed him when he went home. It's crazy, and in general, I'm a loner. But Lily's place, even with the minions, felt empty and sad, and I wanted to lean on Jason for comfort. I mean, he was only a phone call—and a few neighborhoods—away. But I couldn't ask that of him, when I still had feelings for Eric, and I couldn't resolve *those* until Eric recovered.

He has to—he can't *leave me.*

I shuddered, and Jason's hand pressed more firmly into my back, offering his strength and support. Which felt *so* good, and at the same time, *so* wrong.

With Geordi, and everything else, was it any wonder my emotions were a mess? I swiped at my eyes as Rina passed through the doors at the far end of the gallery. We followed her down another short hall, also lushly furnished and artistically decorated, until we reached a door near the end.

She opened this, gesturing us into what appeared to be either an enormous study or a midsize library. The high coved ceiling was quartered by gilded buttresses, with copycat classical paintings in each quadrant. Thick carpets covered the floor, and three sides of the room, including the one we'd entered by, were floor-to-ceiling recessed shelves, filled with books of all sizes and apparent ages, protected by sliding glass that moved in either direction for easy access. The fourth wall, to our right, sported French doors opening onto an expansive garden—impressive, as we were in the heart of Paris. On either side of these, two Medieval suits of armor stood sentinel, their closed helmets and battle axes doing nothing to lower my anxiety.

I looked away and came face to face with Niccolò Dioguardi, regarding me impassively from his seat at a heavy ebony and leather desk near the back of the room. I'd been invited to a few family events after Lily's wedding, before we realized these were *the*—not just "some"—Dioguardis. But I hadn't spent quality one-on-one time with Rina or Nico.

He bore a striking resemblance to his son, Nick Junior: close-cropped black-grey hair, piercing blue eyes, hard jaw. He was older than Rina, maybe early seventies, but also aging well, due to the demon blood—an unadvertised perk, keeping them all young and beautiful.

I glanced at Jason. Yeah, that applied to him, too.

Nico rose and came around the desk, but didn't offer his hand or acknowledge us with a greeting. He was shorter than Jason but taller than Nick. Also beefier: He wore a dark blue blazer over a white t-shirt, the fabric straining over his muscles as he moved. He resembled a bear in clothing, big and knowing full well he could smite me in an instant, not even counting his demon powers.

Experimentally, I checked for Jason's shield but didn't feel it. Since the battle at the cave, when our threads connected without physical contact, my "reception" of him has been spotty. Sometimes, I can sense him from several rooms away, his thread warm and strong in my mind. At others, it's like a dead radio: no static even, to indicate fine-tuning would produce a clearer frequency.

Nico leaned against the desk, studying me, and I suppressed a shiver. All jokes aside, he's a very powerful *capo*, in a very dangerous branch of the Sicilian Mafia, *and* a demon. My only hope was that they'd recognize they needed me, to get Geordi back.

Rina moved to his side, also regarding me like a messy knot she'd rather not unravel, and I straightened my spine.

"Thank you for seeing us," I said as steadily as I could.

Neither of them responded, and I wondered—should I offer sympathy for their loss? What *were* the social norms, when I was at least partly responsible for Nick's death? But…did they know that? What story had Paolo—Jason's cousin who, unbeknownst to me, had been there the night we all died—what had he told them? I hadn't thought to ask him, or for that matter, Jason.

Oh, what the hell. Anything I said could hardly make this situation *worse*.

"I'm, uh, sorry about Nick. Did Paolo explain what happened?"

Nico watched me a moment longer, then exchanged an unreadable glance with Rina, before answering. "He said Nick came to your shop to retrieve *his son*, from your sister."

All true so far, though I noticed the lack of reciprocal sympathy for *my* loss.

Rina added, "And he was shot during an armed robbery, by two of Satan's top Hell Demons, before you escaped with Geordi. What a *miracle* you survived."

"Erm, yes."

Of course, Paolo hadn't known back then that I *didn't* survive, but eventually came back to life, thanks to my new boss, Michael. But it would be better to avoid that scenario in favor of delivering the Geordi news, and from Jason's frown, he thought I procrastinated.

"Okay. So, yeah, I escaped with Geordi. And I know you've been searching for him. And me. Obviously. Look, can we at least sit down? This is important, or I wouldn't be here."

My heart raced and my palms were sweaty. This was a mistake—Jason and I should just go. We'd get Geordi back another way—we *had* to.

Except, we'd been trying. In my desperation to avoid indebting myself to the Dioguardis, we'd spent the last four days frantically doing everything we could to find Geordi, or learn what Marchosias's plans for him were, or make *any* progress on getting him back.

Trying, and failing. Miserably.

Even my dead minions—long story—couldn't come up with anything, nor could the contingent of "my" Dead and Living who'd remained in Germany, where he'd been taken. It was like searching for a specific drop of water in the whole wide ocean, and after this many days, with no sleep and no leads, I had to admit we just didn't have the resources.

But Geordi's Demon Mafia grandparents did, and I couldn't let a little thing like my fear-slash-loathing get in the way of saving Geordi.

Jason gripped my arm, preventing my panicked flight. "We should *all* sit down. You may not want to be standing when you hear what we have to say."

Two pairs of eyebrows shot up at this, but no eyes changed color, indicating they didn't suspect just how horrible our news was.

"Of course," Rina said smoothly, ever the perfect hostess, no matter how much she might want to, literally, kill her guests. She indicated a brocaded sofa and two wingback chairs, grouped around a gilded white coffee table in the center of the room. Nico planted himself on the sofa and she joined him, while Jason and I took the chairs. I set my ginormous purse on the floor and tried not to fidget with my skirt again.

"Well?" Nico asked, and Jason opened his mouth, but I caught his eye.

"No, I should be the one to say it." I inhaled and exhaled, before facing them. "You want me to relinquish Geordi to you. I understand that. I don't agree, but I get

11

it. And I also understand your anger over what happened to Nick, and because I hid Geordi from you. But I—we—need your help. And more to the point, *Geordi* does."

They exchanged another look. I couldn't tell if my candor surprised, impressed, or had no effect on them, but after a moment, Rina faced me again.

"Fair enough. He's your nephew, and you think he's better off with you. But you didn't come here to state obvious facts, or to deliver him to us. So why *are* you here? What help does my grandson need, that you'd crawl to us? Make it quick and forget the bullshit, or I'll have you arrested for Nick *and* Lily's murders."

So much for the gracious hostess, or my stalling. "I really wish you wouldn't."

Jason leaned forward. "Yeah, not a good idea. You need us as much as we need you."

Rina actually frowned at that. "What do you mean? What are you talking about?"

Nico also leaned forward—Dioguardi Demon pissing match?—saying coldly to Jason, "Spit it out. What—you think you can demand a ransom for him?"

I gasped in my outrage, and those hard blue eyes bored into me. And then they faded to black. He stood, towering over me.

"And *you*—you think you're owed some of the Dioguardi pot, because your sister squirted out Nick's son? We're done here. Give us Geordi, or I'll do worse than call the cops."

Rina also rose, as did Jason. The whole room crackled with demon energy. Three pairs of eyes were now black, and I shot to my feet.

"No, wait—everyone calm down. We aren't here for money. Geordi's in danger—*that's* the help we need."

zThat brought them up short. Rina narrowed her gaze. "Go on."

"It's true," Jason said. "Paolo made a deal to host a Hell Demon called Marchosias. He kidnapped Geordi, and we don't know where he is or how to get him back."

Hearing the words, spoken so bluntly, brought back all the fear and anguish, and from her expression, they had the same effect on Rina. She went whiter than the coffee table, staggering back, grabbing at Nico's arm to keep from falling.

"*No...*"

Nico's eyes, just fading to blue, snapped black again. "You *lost* him? To a *Hell Demon?*"

"Yes," I managed. And then I burst into sobs and collapsed onto the chair.

Chapter Two

"There aren't demons flying around with horns, people are demons."
~Chuck Schuldiner, American Singer-Songwriter
(1967-2001)

Even Jason didn't know what to do with a sobbing Hyacinth. I mean, I'd cried on his shoulder before, but not like this. Until now, I hadn't comprehended the tight rein I'd been keeping on my emotions. I'd tried to act normal, hoping to *make* things normal. But coming here—admitting to *these* people that I'd failed Geordi so horrifically—that I couldn't even be sure he still lived—opened a dam, and I shook with uncontrollable fear and loss.

Rina clawed Nico's arm, going through her own crisis, and Jason dropped down next to me. "Hey, it's okay. We *will* get him back."

"You're goddamn right we will," Nico snarled. He made an impatient gesture, trying to shake Rina off, but she only clung harder.

"No…" It came out a whisper, and she cleared her throat, strengthening her voice and steeling her spine. "No. Nico, even you can't blame Hyacinth for this. If Paolo—" She swallowed. "—if he made a deal, and with *Marchosias*—" She glanced to us for confirmation.

"Yes," Jason said flatly.

Nico included us both equally in his rage. "How the *hell* did he get out?"

"We don't know," Jason answered. "But there's more. Dito's dead and Bala's in the hospital. They were protecting Geordi when Paolo—Marchosias—attacked them."

"*What?*" Rina sat down hard, looking more haggard than I'd ever seen her.

Bala is a distant Dioguardi cousin, who, according to Jason, only pretends loyalty to the inner circle, while actually working with Jason's Super Secret Sect against them. But apparently, her act is so convincing that both Nico and Rina view her like a favorite niece. By contrast, Dito, though adopted as the "spare heir" in case something happened to both Nick and Geordi, had never been tight with the family, as no one thought the unthinkable would happen, until it did.

Still, close or not, it had to be a blow for Rina, losing her son, grandson, and adopted heir, in short order. Although if she hadn't learned of Dito's death by now, days later, her grief might be short-lived after all.

As though reading my thoughts, Nico said dismissively, "Dito's not dead. If he died, we'd hear about it. For all we know, Geordi's fine, too, and they're just fishing for money."

I started up at this, but Jason tugged me back down, saying to Nico, "I thought you might have doubts. I took this from Dito's effects at the morgue in Germany. I assumed you'd want it back." He pulled something from his jeans pocket and held his closed fist out to Nico.

Nico automatically lifted his hand and Jason dropped a small gold object onto it: the Dioguardi signet ring, its hefty head bearing the family's falcon crest. Dito wore it daily, as had Nick before him. Now it would pass to Geordi, although at seven, he could fit *two* fingers into it.

Nico stared at it uncomprehendingly. We could have gotten it some other way, but at this point, even Nico had to realize that the obvious answer was the correct one: Dito was dead, Geordi'd been kidnapped, and somehow, we all had to work together to fix it. He closed his fist over the ring, then sat next to his wife and bowed his head.

For her part, Rina had calmed down. She took a tissue from the covered box on the end table nearby, delicately blotting her tears without disturbing her makeup—even her mascara. She didn't offer me one, but with a wry smile, Jason passed me a handful. Luckily, I never wore makeup, because it would be smeared beyond repair at this point.

I blew my nose loudly, and Rina eyed me distastefully. "You say we need you. Why? What's to stop us from retrieving Geordi on our own, without your supposed help?"

This was the tricky—well, tricki*er*—part. Because in truth, they didn't need us. Or at least, not me. And if I couldn't convince them otherwise, I'd lose Geordi forever, even if—*when*—we found him.

"Because," I said, "if you do that, I'll never stop trying to get him back. I'll sue for custody, and keep you tied up in court as long as it takes. And in the process, stuff might come out—things you'd rather not have dragged into the legal system. But if we all cooperate…"

My throat closed over the words, and Jason squeezed my arm reassuringly. I blew out a breath. "If you agree to this, I won't fight your involvement in his life."

Oh God—I couldn't. They were *demon Mafia*—

Jason sensed my panic and broke in. "Sort of a shared custody agreement. Hyacinth won't actively prevent your seeing him, and will *consider* sending him to school in Massachusetts, but you'll share decision-making until he's eighteen. *Equal* sharing, that is."

This last was likely for my benefit as much as theirs, and I choked back my knee-jerk reaction. Realistically, I didn't have much power in this situation. I knew it, and so did they.

But I hadn't been making idle threats about "stuff coming out." During a bout of tidying at Lily's, I'd discovered a stash of documents, cleverly hidden in the pages of Geordi's earliest picture books. She'd known as well as I that the Dioguardi business dealings were suspect at best. Or at least, we'd figured it out after realizing exactly *who* she'd married.

More to the point, she knew that any hope she had of winning custody of Geordi, or keeping herself alive after the divorce, rested on her having a hold over them. But she must not have had time to grab the papers when she took Geordi and fled to me, before dying after all.

I shoved *that* guilt away and took my phone from my purse. Jason frowned—this wasn't part of our planned strategy—but I ignored him, scrolling through the photos until I found what I needed. Facing the phone outward, I showed the pic to Nico.

"Does this mean anything to you?"

He scowled but leaned forward—then jerked back, first turning pale, then red with rage. He shot up. "*Where did you get that?*"

He reached for my phone, but I snatched it back.

"The originals are somewhere safe. And they'll stay there, so long as you work with us, and don't have us arrested—or worse—for murders you know damn well we didn't commit."

I'd kept my voice steady, though I'll never know how I managed it, and I saw I'd at least impressed Jason with the move. Nico's brows furrowed, weighing my words and the documents I had, against his inclination to shoot me on the spot.

I willed myself not to blink. I'm an okay poker player, but beyond that, I'd realized one of my strengths lies in handling rich assholes who want to get their way all the time, for no good reason. That describes half my former clients: members of the Marseille elite, who hired me and my now dead partner, Vadim, to steal priceless *objets d'art* back and forth from each other, until their collections were evened out. Silly, and petty—and right up Nico's alley.

Rina tugged his arm. "What is it? What has she got?" Nico murmured in her ear, and she sucked in a breath, eyes going wide. "You wouldn't *dare*..."

"Try me. And in case I haven't been clear, I have lawyers with instructions to, er, bring to light any information that might be *helpful*, should I suddenly wake up dead one day."

Ha. Little did they know, I woke up dead every day. But I doubt Michael would keep bringing me back to life, were I to die again, and either way, I'd rather not find out.

Rina's uncertain gaze flicked from me to Jason, who shrugged. Now *he's* an excellent poker player, and smart enough to pretend he knew my plan all along.

Nico stood and planted his hands on his hips,

preparing to call what he perceived as my bluff, when abruptly Rina stood. "Agreed."

Nico's shock was comical. "What the *hell*—"

Rina cut him off. "Enough! My grandson has been kidnapped by a Hell Demon, and I want him back. If that means working with *them,* then we'll do it." She faced us again. "Let me be clear: I don't like you. And we *will* raise Geordi as a Dioguardi. But as for his demon blood, he—"

"*Rina.*"

Her gold eyes met Nico's iron-black ones. What had she been about to say? I already knew Geordi's powers were incredibly strong. It's why everyone wanted him in the first place. But something in her tone made me think she'd been about to disclose something different.

A moment later, with no apparent weakening of her stance, she faced me. "I assume your people have been unsuccessful at tracking him down?"

"Er, yes."

She wrinkled her nose. "Hmph. We'll start our own investigation and get back to you."

"Regularly," Jason interjected. "Even if you have nothing to report, you'll check in. And so will we. We'll work *together* on this."

The room crackled again, her eyes darkening. After a tense moment, she said, "Fine. Where's Bala?"

"Hôpital de la Pitié."

Without another word or a backward glance, even at her husband, Rina walked to the door and left.

Nico glared at us. "Find your own way out."

Then he left, too.

My knees wobbled, and it's good I was already seated. Jason looked at me questioningly, but I said, "Not here."

I stood and grabbed my purse, then led the way out. I'd achieved my goal: Enlist the aid of Geordi's Demon Mafia relatives, in saving him from the Hell Demon who'd kidnapped him. But I'd also agreed to the one thing I swore would never happen: their influence in his life.

I couldn't decide which to do first: throw up, or cry with relief.

****

I drove Jason to his place, both of us silent during the car ride. But when we arrived, rather than getting out, he said, "What scared Nico so shitless?"

I turned off the Peapod. "You tell me."

He frowned. "Jeez. I thought we were past this. You know you can tell me anything."

"No, I *am* telling you. I don't *know* what I have on him. I found some papers in Lily's apartment, and they had Dioguardi written all over them. Literally. I couldn't make sense of them, and I didn't have a lot of time, so I snapped the pic, in case I needed it."

Jason stared at me. Then he burst out laughing. "You were *bluffing*? Christ, Hyacinth—what if they were for legitimate business dealings? Or Nico's dry cleaning?"

A smile crept onto my own face. "Guess *some* of my ability to lie is coming back."

"Maybe. And it worked—this time. But you took a big risk. Before, you were just Geordi's aunt, who Nico and Rina despised but weren't afraid of. Now…" He shook his head. "Fear makes people desperate. And they were already dangerous. That's a bad combination."

"I know. But I couldn't think of a way to make them work with us. They have all the cards—you know they do. What's to stop them, even now, from just going off on their own, getting Geordi back, and taking him from me? Forever? I *had* to make that play."

He regarded me thoughtfully. "They don't have all the advantage, and they don't know everything. Like I said, they think you're just Geordi's aunt. They don't know you're...special, in your own right."

His voice was low, his gaze heated, and I looked away, lots of wildly inappropriate—yet equally pleasurable—responses to his words—to *him*—igniting a battle between my rational mind and my totally irrational body. Not to mention my heart.

I cleared my throat. "*I* don't even know what makes me 'special.' "

"Maybe. But that doesn't change the fact that you have abilities—ones they know nothing about. That's a huge advantage."

I wanted to believe him, but since my so-called "abilities" felt rather random, I wasn't reassured. So I changed the subject. "What do you think Rina wanted to say, that Nico didn't want us to hear?"

"I honestly don't know. From what Paolo and Dito both have said, there's been tension in their marriage for a while. Maybe even before Nick came along. Rumor has it Rina's less enamored of the whole demon blood side of things." He saw my expression and gave an ironic smile. "Don't get too excited. She's still a Dioguardi, by blood *and* marriage. Whatever her and Nico's personal issues, they'll stick together against the Enemy."

"Meaning me."

"Meaning anyone who crosses them. But in this case—yes, you."

I sighed. Even so, knowing she might have *some*

doubts about the whole demon-Satan connections in the family gave me hope. Not that it mattered. Even without the blood, they were Mafia, and headed for Hell, one way or another.

Jason got out of the car, then leaned back in. "I'm going to go visit Bala today."

My gut clenched, for a variety of reasons. Bala—Dito's friend and partner, and a trainer at the demon academy in America, where everyone but me expected Geordi to go—had barely survived the attack that killed Dito, when Marchosias took Geordi. She'd been in a Paris hospital since then, recovering from her injuries: broken bones and other physical wounds, as well as internal "supernatural" ones the doctors were at a loss to explain.

Either way, the guilt weighed on me, because I'm the one who put her in danger in the first place. Never mind that she and Dito came to France specifically to evaluate Geordi, and Jason himself had expected them to protect him.

But on top of that, Bala had been…something…to Jason, at some point. It shouldn't bother me, because Eric is…something…to me, *now*. However, emotions not being tidy—especially mine—it bothered the snot out of me. But Jason stating his intentions sent a message beyond mere words. He'd repeatedly said they were just friends, so being him, he shared his plans with me, to prevent me hearing about it later and getting mad.

Annoyingly mature of him, and very limiting to my own inclinations.

I nodded. "Okay. Tell her…I hope she's feeling better."

He gave a lopsided smile and closed the car door,

giving it a "drive on" *thump-thump*.

Back at Lily's, I dumped my purse on the entryway table and headed to the guest room to change into jeans and a sweater. Then I went back to the sunken living room and flopped on the cushy couch. The weather had been mild, but now a winter chill drifted in. Plus, it had started to rain, so it seemed like a good day to fall asleep watching a movie.

It was not to be.

The moment I hit the cushions, Torben and Ulrich emerged from the back of the apartment. They're two of the living minions who returned to Paris with me. Both are blond, German, and what most women would call "hunky." Torben's stockier, while Ulrich is taller and thinner, but neither's a slouch in the muscle department. In fact, most women would be thrilled to be living with two such manly men. However, I'm not "most" women.

"*What?*"

I didn't quite snarl, but I came close. Luckily, my minions know me, and Torben only said, "Have you eaten any meat recently? The fridge is getting low, but we can do some shopping later."

I compressed my lips. As a longtime vegetarian, I continue to struggle with the idea that, apparently, being brought back to life has made me a carnivore. "I'm fine. Is that all you came to ask me?"

"No. We discovered something interesting."

I sat up, fast. "Will it help find Geordi?"

"Maybe. It's more informational. So, it could help in the long run, just not immediately."

I tamped down my disappointment. "Okay. What is it?"

"You said when you were on Malta in September,

you ran into a demon in a farmer's field, and he attacked you, correct?"

I'd told my minions every detail of this whole mess, from the moment I met the Rousseaux—the High Demons who killed Nick, Lily and me—onward. I'm not usually this forthcoming, and in this case it's even weirder, since both men recently worked for the Burkes, a pair of Devil worshippers who forced me to raise an Army of the Dead, then tried—but failed—to free Satan and usurp his powers. Many of the Burkes' former minions were happy to see them go, and the ones who defected to my side had repeatedly proven their loyalty, so I'd taken the plunge and put my trust in them.

Torben said, "Turns out the stone mound in that field is a Hell Gate. The locals avoid it—rumors of animal attacks and the like, but really, it's a portal. And…it's where Marchosias escaped. In early September."

I stared at him. "*That* was Marchosias? You're sure?"

Ulrich interjected, "Absolutely. We verified it, and I can show you what we found."

"Not necessary. I know how thorough you are."

He glanced away, shamefaced, and I thought, crap. I hadn't meant to remind him of Geordi's loss, so I said as gently as I could, "It's not your fault—really. If Marchosias escaped when we were on Malta, he must have planned to take Geordi long before you came along."

His expression filled with guilt and remorse. "If not my fault, then whose? He was under *my* care when Marchosias struck. And then I ran off and left Dito to die. Maybe Bala, too, if she doesn't recover. I could have helped them. I—"

"No, you couldn't. If you'd stayed, you and your cousin both would have died. She's an innocent civilian. You did the right thing, saving her."

"No, I didn't."

What could I say? He'd had an impossible choice to make: save his cousin or stay to fight with his team. I didn't blame him for protecting her instead, but he clearly thought he could have done more. I opened my mouth, but he stood and walked to the en suite elevator, punching the button and avoiding my gaze.

"I'll go get you some meat."

He kept his head down as the elevator doors closed on him, but Torben saw my dismay. "Leave him be. He knows he made the 'right' choice, but it still had terrible consequences. He has to live with that, and it gets worse every time we fail to find a lead on Geordi."

"Maybe I shouldn't have let him come to Paris with us."

He gave me an ironic look. "Not your decision. You think after abandoning your nephew—" He lifted his hands defensively. "I know *you* don't think that, but it's how *he* sees it. He won't desert you now, no matter what. Give him time. He'll be okay."

But would I? Would any of us? I didn't blame Ulrich for not fighting off a Hell Demon with bio-demon-enhanced powers. But I could relate to feeling responsible, since I'm the one who put Paolo-Marchosias into the mix in the first place.

I cleared my throat. "So Marchosias had literally *just* escaped from Hell, when we saw him? Or rather, when he saw us?"

Talk about dumb luck. Jason, Geordi and I go for a

stroll after breakfast, right past the portal where, at that exact moment, a powerful Demon makes the jump from Hell? I'd love to know the odds on that one.

"There's more," Torben said. "It's possible he escaped, *because* you were there."

"Say…what now?"

"We-ell, we've also been researching your situation."

A touchy subject, because I hadn't asked them to do anything of the kind. But it could be useful in finding Geordi, so I made go-on motions, and he continued.

"It's possible the combination of you plus two demons acted as a sort of…magnet."

"You mean we *pulled* Marchosias out?"

"It's likely. At the time, you didn't know Jason was a demon, but you felt his shield. Think about it. If you— untrained, and unaware even—sensed his powers, then a Hell Demon would definitely notice, especially before Jason activated his shield. Marchosias could simply latch on, like a skier to a boat. Once out, he likely recognized Geordi's potential immediately, and followed you to Turkey."

Unfortunately, it made sense. I thought we'd "defeated" that demon, but obviously not. And if he'd ID'd Geordi as a primo catch, to either make nice with Satan, or use as a bargaining chip while overthrowing him, of course he'd pursue us.

I said, "And by the time he caught up to us, Nadezhda had given Geordi the scarab."

The "trinket" we all believed to be gift shop bling, which had been shielding Geordi all along—until he gave it to me, for my own safety. So not only had I pulled Marchosias from Hell myself, it was *my* fault he took

Geordi. Doubly so, because I was the one who'd insisted "Paolo" tag along on the ill-fated mission to hide Geordi at Bala's island home.

Torben nodded. "Jason thinks Marchosias made the deal with Paolo shortly after he—Paolo—also came to Turkey. Jason managed to meet up with him behind your back a few times. They had a prearranged meeting place—he didn't want to just text or call, in case you checked his phone."

How thoughtful. Whatever. I'd gotten over the anger that Jason infiltrated my life specifically to spy on me. Mostly. It's a work in progress.

Torben continued, "Jason said Paolo seemed antsy at the first meeting, but he didn't think much of it, and put it down to Paolo having been traveling all night. But it's likely that's when Marchosias moved in. By the time Jason took Geordi to him, Marchosias had absorbed more of Paolo's memories, and acted more like his—Paolo's—old self."

I suppressed a shudder. Even lesser Hell Demons could pretty much jump into any human they wanted. But a willing host made it easier for the demon to access their memories, and essentially *become* that person, with no one the wiser. A creepy thought, with creepier implications. Like, what if my own minions were possessed?

So much for mushy trust circles.

I said, "But if Marchosias had already moved in when we came to Turkey, why couldn't Paolo see Eric in Trier, months later? Didn't Paolo do it, specifically to enhance his powers?"

"Yes, but most likely, Marchosias wouldn't let him, because if Paolo saw Eric too soon, it would've raised a bunch of red flags. By the time we came back to Paris, Marchosias must have decided it was safe for Paolo to use his powers. Probably so Marchosias could use them, too. Essentially, by limiting Paolo, he limited himself."

My cell rang from the depths of my purse in the entryway. Torben dug it out, checking the number before bringing it to me. "Jason."

What would make him call so soon after I dropped him off? I pushed down my instinctive dread and swiped to accept the call. "What now?"

I thought he'd rib me for being grumpy, but instead he said, "We have a problem."

Merde. "What's going on? Is Bala okay?"

"She's fine. It's Dito. He's here, and he won't leave. I think he's…drunk. He's shouting about joining the cause and keeps trying to pick things up and throw them. I'm afraid he'll hurt Bala. Unintentionally, but still. I thought, you know, because of your day job…"

Shit. "I'll be right there."

Chapter Three

"So when the devil says to you: do not drink, answer him: I will drink, and right freely, just because you tell me not to."

~Martin Luther, German Priest
(1483-1546)

Jason waited for me when I got off the elevator at l'Hôpital Universitaire Pitié-Salpêtrière, in the Thirteenth arrondissement, near his apartment. It's France's largest hospital, providing the best care, but I couldn't suppress a stab of *how convenient that he can walk over to see her any time.*

His face was creased with worry and I sighed inwardly. Of course he'd visit her often. Number one, that's the kind of person he is. And number two, *she's* a good person. In fact, they'd both be better off with me out of the picture.

"This way," he said without preamble and led me around the nurses' station and down a cramped, equipment-strewn hall, toward a corner room at the end.

Even before we reached the door, I heard slurred male shouts mingled with muffled thumps. Luckily, Dito was newly dead, so none of the nurses, doctors, or other patients could hear him. But to me and Jason, it made a pretty good racket.

"Why is he here?" I asked. "On Earth, I mean."

"Don't know. He's not exactly coherent, but my guess is he wanted to see Bala, and it either took him this long to find her, or he had to fight his way back after he died."

I sneaked a peek at his profile. His jaw had set in that hard line it gets when he's really pissed about something. So maybe he did have feelings for Bala, and Dito's arrival pushed him into realizations he'd avoided before.

If that were the case… A wave of sadness swept through me. Guess that's a realization of my own, about how deep *my* feelings go. I swallowed hard and faced the door.

Jason took a deep breath. "Ready?"

"Yes."

He paused. "Hyacinth—I know I brought you here and all. But, if you can, do you think you could avoid calling Michael down? It's just…"

I understood his dilemma. "Of course. I don't think Michael could or would do anything against you or Bala. I honestly don't know about Dito. A dead demon? I just don't know if the good he's done is enough. Either way, I'm with you—I'd rather not find out."

His Adam's apple bobbed as he swallowed and nodded his thanks. Then he opened the door.

The scene inside was…odd, even for my new normal. Bala lay propped up in a hospital bed, attached to various IV bags and vitals monitors, her pale skin covered in bruises and her right arm in a cast to her shoulder. Beneath her cotton gown, bandages wrapped her rib cage for support, and she had stitches everywhere from the several surgeries it took to repair the damage done to her internal organs.

She was lucky to be alive, and a wave of guilt washed through me. First, because I sent her into Marchosias's path to begin with. And second, because I couldn't be entirely sure my motives were pure. Subconsciously, I'd wanted her out of the picture, and maybe I hadn't considered the danger too closely as a result.

I don't know if my mixed up emotions showed on my face, but she gave me an ironic smile by way of greeting. She seemed more alert than when I'd visited her in the ICU a few days ago, but then, having a drunk dead demon in her room probably perked her right up.

A crash came from near the window, and Jason, Bala and I all looked in that direction. Dito leaned one-handed on the wall, staring blearily at a shattered vase on the floor. Fractured glass mingled with two dozen red roses in an impressive puddle of water. A card lay face up in the center of all this, *Jason* printed on it in bold handwriting I'd recognize anywhere.

I swallowed the lump that rose in my throat, but before any of us could react, a nurse bustled in, having heard the commotion.

"*Qu'est-ce qui c'est passé?*" she demanded, before noticing the vase. She glanced at what she perceived as the unattended bench by the window, where the vase had previously sat, then at me and Jason. She opened her mouth to berate us, but Jason smoothly cut her off.

"Guess we put it too near the edge. Must have been top-heavy."

She processed this, still doubtful, then nodded. "I'll go get something to clean it up."

"No—leave it!" Dito shouted drunkenly, but of course, she didn't hear him, and left.

Although, if he could already move objects, then making himself audible—and visible—couldn't be far behind.

Jason had similar thoughts. "We have to do something, quick. Who knows how long before he bleeds through and scares the crap out of someone?"

Bala said to me, "Can you do anything? Without, you know, involving your boss?"

"I don't know. How did he even get here? And how did he get so drunk?"

I'd never seen a dead person eat or drink anything, ephemeral or otherwise. But Dito gave every indication of having imbibed his body weight—living, that is—in alcohol: He appeared ready to slide down the wall at any moment, his clothes were dirty and torn, and he seemed in worse shape than Bala. Not surprising, since he was *dead.*

He swayed, caught himself just in time, then noticed me. "Hya—*hic*—cinth! You're here—*finally.* Been sayin' y' sh'd be here. Y' c'n fix it—y' c'n let me stay. Please lemme stay. Wanna help—*hic*—the cause."

He pushed off the wall just as the nurse returned with a broom and dustbin. Unable to stop himself, he passed through her just as she stooped over to sweep up the broken glass. They both gave identical shivers of distaste at the sensation, which would have been comical, except Dito's momentum pushed him right into Jason.

Unlike the nurse, Jason *could* see—and fully feel— Dito, so he *oomphed* and stumbled back, trying unobtrusively to stop Dito from careening into Bala on the bed. The nurse frowned in their direction, but Jason faked a coughing fit. Brilliant, except her frown deepened.

"*Êtes-vous malade?* You'd better leave. An infection could kill her."

"I'm fine. Just allergies—from the flowers."

Her expression cleared. "Of course. They were so beautiful. And so kind of you to bring them, in spite of *vos allergies*. Let me see if I can find something to put them in. *Je suis sûr que votre petite amie* there would like to salvage them."

Bala and Jason reddened at the assumption that they were romantically attached, but before they could "protest too much," the nurse's words penetrated Dito's drunken haze. He straightened—as much as possible—and shoved out of Jason's hold, rounding on him and lifting his arm, poised to swing.

"*Fottuto stronzo!*"

I noticed several things in the fractions of a second that followed. First, Jason had a choice to make: either duck and make the nurse remove him on grounds of mental instability, or take the punch and try not to react. Dito's shorter than Jason, but he's strong—solid muscle everywhere—and at the moment, he was filled with a righteous fury.

And secondly, both Jason and Bala weren't far behind. Every demon-blue eye in the room abruptly went black, leading to the third thing, which was that instantly the room *crackled* with demon energy.

Merde. Shit, shit, *shit*.

I'd only truly experienced Jason's powers a few times: when we pulled Eric free at the Rousseaux's villa, and again in Germany, when fending off other *worse* demons. But on the whole, I've been able to ignore the fact that he *is* a demon.

33

Not today. I stared in shock-induced slo-mo as Dito's fist headed for Jason's face. Jason's eyes went black, and then I felt...*something*...that made what he did in Turkey seem pitiably insignificant. Bala struggled to sit up, her own eyes black, but she was hampered by all the attached medical devices. The nurse, oblivious to all of it, rose from sweeping up the broken glass and put herself right in the middle of Demon Testosterone Central.

Jason raised his palm, cupped toward Dito, as if about to hurl a ball at him. I *felt* the energy in the room being drawn into his hand, coalescing into something explosive and deadly.

I stepped forward, trying to stem the disaster, when the door flew open and Nico and Rina rushed in. "What the—" Nico began, when Rina cut him off with a shriek of joy.

"*Dito—you're back!*"

Dito stumbled, the punch going wide, and Jason automatically dodged it, dropping his hand. Bala fell back, dazed, and the nurse used her free hand to scoop up the fallen flowers, then faced the newcomers.

"There are too many people in here. *Seulement la famille proche.*" Her glance fell on Jason. "And you, of course. Dito, is it? *Je ne pensais pas que vous étiez italien.*"

Nico watched the real Dito, who'd staggered through the nurse again, bumped the bed, and sank to the floor in a heap. But instead of Rina's unbridled joy at their "spare" returning—sort of—from the dead, Nico's face twisted, and he let out a roar, making the nurse jump.

"Wait!" I yelled as Nico started toward Dito,

obviously with the intent of doing him severe bodily—ghostly?—harm. "Stop! Everyone calm down."

Nico ignored me, but Jason stepped in his path. "She's right. We all need to calm down and talk about this." He said to the nurse, "Please, will you excuse us? This is a family matter."

The nurse sniffed. "That is what I have said. Only *family* can be in here."

I said quickly, indicating Nico and Rina, "They're her parents. And I'm, uh, her sister."

Jason had said Bala's actual parents were both dead—as the youngest of eleven siblings, they were older when she was born—so I felt relatively certain the nurse wouldn't know the difference. Bala's eyebrows rose, but she and the Dioguardis played along, Rina nodding like a well-coiffed bobblehead doll, and even Nico grunted assent, while still eyeing Jason as though assessing how to plow through him to get to his quarry.

The nurse sniffed, stepping on said quarry to adjust some of Bala's monitors that had loosened during the ruckus. Then she left, giving us a *you'd better be gone when I return* look as she shut the door.

"Move aside," Nico growled. Jason didn't budge, and the room crackled again.

Rina raised a hand toward Nico. "*Please*, don't hurt him…"

Obviously, I didn't have all the facts here, because only Rina seemed happy about Dito's return. And her joy was tempered by concern for her husband's intentions. Nico's stance widened, Jason's palm opened again, and Bala made a futile gesture from her prison on the bed.

I blew out a breath and dove into the fray, addressing Nico. "Yes, please, just wait a sec. Whatever beef you've got with him, he's newly dead, and drunk off his ass."

Jason's gaze shot to me, and he made frantic *stop* motions with his hand, but I ignored him. I had to soothe Nico, before he destroyed the whole hospital in a fit of rage, so I continued, "He doesn't know what he's doing, and whatever's going on, it wouldn't be a fair fight."

Rina gasped in shock, and Nico seemed about to turn his fury on me, for having the audacity to interfere, when his eyes widened and he jerked away—from *me*.

What the hell?

And then Bala said from the bed, "They didn't know." I frowned at her, and she gave one of her *you're a dumbass* eye rolls. "About *you*. They didn't know you could see the Dead, but now they do, so you know, they're processing."

Merde.

On the floor, Dito started to giggle. If you've never heard-slash-seen a dead drunk demon giggle, it's quite jarring. He looked at Nico, and laughed harder. "Y' picked the wrong sister. Shoulda picked *her* instead of Lily!"

Nico's mouth worked soundlessly, and Rina sagged against the door.

What the *hell?* I rounded on Jason, the only possibly sane person in this mess. "What's he talking about?"

Before he could respond, Rina recovered. "You see the Dead."

Too late to pretend otherwise, so I nodded. This only made Nico act more like a dying fish, but Rina's brain processed faster than a super computer.

"All of them? And touch them? Like us, they're solid and real for you?" I nodded again, and she snapped, "How? Why?" And then her eyes widened. "You were there—the night our son died, you were *there*. The High Demons killed all three of you. Nick and your sister passed on to the Afterlife, but you came back. Why?"

What should I tell her? What *could* I tell her? They'd figure it out eventually, at least parts of it. But did I share everything—the rocks, Michael, being a sorter? As noted, I'm a cards-close-to-the-vest kinda gal, especially where scumbag Nick's family is concerned.

On the other hand, I needed their help to get Geordi back. I caught Jason's eye, and he shook his head, as if to say, *Your call, and I have no idea what that call should be.*

Rina said sharply, "Answer me, or you'll never see Geordi, ever again."

I felt like she'd punched me in the throat—my whole body reeled and fear iced my veins. "No! Okay—I'll tell you. I did die, but before Michael processed me, he—"

Rina gasped again, and Nico's jaw snapped shut and he eyed me with severe distaste. Guess they viewed an archangel, who spent his days eradicating anything Hell-related from the world, as an enemy. Oh well—too late now.

"Anyway. It's a long story. But basically, I work for Michael now, helping him sort souls, and…other stuff. But I swear, he tells me all the time he can't do anything against humans until they die. Even, uh, ones like you, with, uh, demon blood in them."

I stopped and held my breath, waiting to see how they'd respond. I'd been upfront—mostly—especially in acknowledging their demonhood. It was risky, but I had limited options. On the one hand, they could decide my job made me a huge liability, and chuck me out the window, to fall to my second death many stories below.

Or maybe they'd feel more comfortable sharing Geordi with me, since I not only knew of his supernatural abilities, but had some myself. Which still felt weird to think, let alone say, but whatever.

"You *bitch*," Nico snarled. So much for option two. "You fucking—"

"Nico," Rina said.

She hadn't raised her voice, but her cool tone cut through his fury. This morning, I'd gotten the impression that he called the shots, and she mostly let him. But right now, she'd clearly told him to *shut the fuck up and back off*.

He glared at her, more belligerent than ever, but she only faced him down. "I've lost two sons *and* my grandson—not to mention Paolo—in four months."

"I know," Nico growled, transferring the scowl back to me. "It's her fault—all of it. I'll end her, and we'll get Geordi back where he belongs, with *us*."

Jason made a defensive motion, and even Dito frowned, like the idea harshed his buzz. But Rina focused only on her husband.

"It's not *all* her fault."

Another husband-wife moment passed between them. Now that I knew she might not be *totally* onboard with all the family demon-ness, I wondered if she blamed Nick's death on it? Like, if the Dioguardis weren't linked to Hell, her son would be alive today? Of course, Nick wasn't a demon. But she might think even being demon-adjacent put him at greater risk.

"It's more her fault than anyone else's," Nico shot back, "and she deserves to die for it."

Rina said, "I have a better plan."

That brought us all up short. Nico's eyes bugged out

with the effort not to "end" her first, then me, but Rina faced me calmly. "We won't harm you, and will honor the deal we made, that after we get Geordi back, you can be involved in his life. On one condition."

I got a bad feeling deep in my gut. "What?"

"Bring Nick back. And I don't mean his ghost. Bring him back, *alive*, the way you are. If you agree, our deal stands. Disagree, and Geordi is ours, solely and forever, and Nico can do whatever he wants with you and your little friends."

All the blood left my extremities, including my head, and I swayed. "No...I can't..."

"Yes, you can. You're resourceful. Figure out a way to bring my son back to life, or..."

She shrugged, her smile the rictus of a demon mother who'd lost everything, and saw me as a way to get some of it back.

And then Nico smiled, too. "Excellent plan. Nick's life for yours. You have until tomorrow to decide. Now get out, and take him with you."

He shot Dito a scowl of utter contempt, and both he and Rina walked to the bed, where Bala appeared almost as dazed as me. Jason dragged Dito to his feet, then took my arm.

"Come on. We'll figure it out. I promise."

Even Jason couldn't fix this one. Helplessly, I let him lead me out of Bala's room and down to the ground floor. And all the while, I kept thinking, *I can't do it. Even if I wanted to, I don't know how...*

Chapter Four

"Nothing in his life
Became him like the leaving of it."
~William Shakespeare, English Playwright
(1564-1616) – Macbeth, 1.4.7-8

"I can't do it," I repeated for the gazillionth time. "I send souls *to* their final destination, through Michael. I don't even know how I'd pull anyone back on my own, and it's not like I can go to my archangel boss and ask him to do me a solid."

"Actually," Jason said slowly, "there is a precedent. You called back the Dead at the Moselle. And Leopold—you woke him up again. Both times without Michael's involvement."

We sat on Lily's sofa, with Torben, Ulrich, Liam and Jun spread out across the remaining furniture in her living room. Liam is from somewhere in Britain, with ruddy hair, freckles, and green eyes. He's tallish, and was around thirty when he died last week. Jun is of Asian descent, mid-twenties, and has been dead a little over three weeks. Both of them also worked for the Burkes and chose to stay on Earth after dying—Liam because he's an atheist, and Jun because he just didn't want to leave. This creates a bit of a wrinkle for me with Michael, as Jun should have been passed to him for transport to the Afterlife. But I hid him from Michael, and so far, he's managed to stay under the radar.

Speaking of souls, upon returning from the hospital, we'd deposited Dito on the floor of Lily's bedroom to do the ghostly equivalent of sleeping it off. Even with this being the penthouse suite, I had limited space, and I refused to put anyone in Geordi's room, so I compromised. The bed would've been okay—I know Lily wouldn't mind—but he fell in a heap on the floor, and even Liam and Jason together couldn't get him back up, so that's where he stayed.

"I didn't do that 'on my own,' " I pointed out. "Both times, the Burkes had me use the two shards they'd found—Satan's and Michael's—to enhance whatever power I have."

I shuddered at the memory of what I'd done, and the Devil-worshipping psycho couple who made me do it. Satan had annihilated Heinrich Burke, body *and* soul, but his wife, Rachel, still existed out there somewhere. Not as a ghost, but as a slimy cold fog that oozed away before we realized what had happened. Yet another terrifying item on my to-do list—but one I couldn't face until we got Geordi back, *without* relinquishing him to the Dioguardis.

"Plus, they aren't technically alive. Rina wants Nick back as living, breathing flesh, not as a ghost."

"Okay." Jason leaned forward, elbows on his knees. "But…you're alive. So it *can* be done."

"But not by me."

We were going in circles. I could raise the Dead without Michael's help, but not into true Living form. Michael could do that, but for obvious reasons, wouldn't. Especially in Nick's case.

Liam spoke up. "Why not by you?"

41

"Because I've never done it before!"

"Had you ever done *any* of this, before you had to do it?"

I opened my mouth, then closed it again. "No, but this is different."

"How?"

I wrinkled my nose. "I know what you're doing. You're trying to make me see that anything is possible, blah-blah-blah."

He grinned. "Is it working?"

"No, because this isn't a musical from the fifties!"

Right on cue, Dito warbled from the bedroom, which he'd been doing every five minutes since we got here. This time he'd chosen "Almost Like Being In Love" from *Brigadoon*, which was weird on many levels, not the least of which being I wouldn't have pegged a twenty-something demon Mafia goon for a Gene Kelly fan. But he had a lovely, if loud, baritone, so we all waited until he lost his train of thought again and dozed off.

But then Liam suddenly assumed a vaguely Scottish accent, saying, " 'I told ye if you love someone deeply enough, anything is possible…even miracles.' "

I rolled my eyes. "Yeah, yeah, I get it. Life is simpler in musicals. But we're not in one. Or if we are, it's *The Rocky Horror Picture Show*—all chainsaws and cannibals, not magical worlds where life is perfect."

He shrugged. "You love Geordi, right? Seems to me that love has made you do a whole mess of shit you never thought possible. Can't hurt to try."

Jason lifted an eyebrow at me, indicating, *We both know it* could *hurt, but…*

I blew out a breath. "Even *if* I agree, I wouldn't

know where to start."

"I do," Liam said, "We find more rocks. Two of them—one of each kind."

Torben grabbed his tablet off the coffee table. "On it."

"Wait," I said, "even if we get two—without Michael finding out, which is *another* big if—I don't know what to do with them. The other times, Rachel did all the prep work. She located the souls she wanted and had at least some idea how to raise them. I don't know what she did, or how to harness those powers without her…help."

I shuddered again. There had to be another way. Like not bringing Nick back at all. Jason took my hand and gave it a reassuring squeeze, and I sent him a grateful look. Whatever lay between him and Bala—or me and Eric—I needed his support. I couldn't deny it, so for now, I'd take it.

Ulrich leaned forward, thinking. By the time we got back from the hospital, he'd returned as well, seeming calmer. So maybe he did just need some space to process and accept the outcome of a failed mission.

"Look," he said, "I know you don't want to do this, and you think you can't. And maybe you're right about that—"

"Gee, thanks."

"Didn't say *I* thought you were, just it's a possibility. But part of your job is to hunt the rocks, right? So, let us do that, and if we find any, you can decide what to do with them later."

Faced with such irrefutable logic, I gave up. "Fine. But either way, I don't know where to find Nick. I mean, I know *where* he is. But I don't exactly have card key access to Hell."

I looked at Jason, and his mouth twisted. "Hyacinth, I know you think all Dioguardis have Satan on speed dial, but we don't. Not even Nico. It's been centuries since the original priest got the blood. Even then, the idea was for demons to live in this world, not hop in and out of Hell." I opened my mouth, and he cut me off. "If we did have access, wouldn't Nico and Rina have *used* it by now, to get Nick out themselves? Why ask you, if they can do it instead?"

I blew out another breath. "Still. You have more of an in than I do. Do you have *any* idea where to search? Is there a two-way mirror? You must know *something* about it."

Jun spoke up. "I might be able to help with that."

He'd been a shaman before joining Rachel's Band of Merry Mercenaries, but claimed to be *tongji*: able to communicate with spirits, but not control them. However, I'd learned to not immediately dismiss my minions' seemingly crazy suggestions, so I said, "Okay. How?"

He smiled, likely reading my expression accurately. "Rachel had me research my abilities, in case I could do your job, which I can't. But I came across several rituals that allow a shaman to cross into the spirit world. Now I am dead, I believe I may cross even more easily. I could slip into Hell and scope it out for you."

"But…what if you can't get back?"

As far as I knew, the Dead I'd raised in Germany, who hadn't left with Charon, had chosen to stay on Earth. I assumed that, once a soul passed the veil, they stayed there. So how would Jun manage it?

He shook his head. "I am not worried about that. I

am meant to stay here. I would be visiting the spirit world only, and can return when I am done."

"But we're not talking about the Good Place, and Satan won't care where you 'belong.' If he decides to keep you, I can't have that on my conscience."

Jun said simply, "I am willing to take that risk."

Jason took my hand again. "It's not your decision. And Jun has a point—he's uniquely qualified for this. At least let him try. He might come up empty-handed, but it would be good to get the lay of the land, if we can."

"But the 'land' is *Hell*. You've felt Satan's pull— he's bound to notice Jun poking around. What if that gives him a pipeline back to us, and he sucks you in, too? Or me?"

Jason squeezed my hand once before letting go. "Do you have a better idea?"

I opened my mouth, then closed it. I shook my head. "That's your job. Remember?"

"I'm fresh out. If your team wants to help, I say let them."

My "team" had already begun organizing themselves. Torben and Ulrich were better able to utilize tools in the real world, such as computer keyboards and search engines, so Liam opted to help Jun prepare for the first ritual he needed to perform, to get himself ready for the trip to Hell.

I rose and tried one last time to talk some sense into all of them. "Even *if* we find Nick, and figure out how to resurrect him, where am I going to pull him out?"

Jason said simply, "The Plutonium."

Duh. Like the one Marchosias used on Malta, gateways to Hell exist around the world—weak spots where Satan can push his powers through, or his demons can cross over. But this particular gate's also an entrance to the realm of Pluto, God of the Underworld, making it doubly powerful. Plus, it's in Turkey, where Nadezhda tried to heal Eric.

I don't know if Jason had thought of that—probably yes—but either way, it made sense. I sighed. I couldn't stop them, so I said to Jun, "Can I at least help somehow?"

He thought a moment. "Can you find something of Nick's? Something personal, or with a strong family connection—maybe passed down through the generations?"

"Like for a police dog? You need an item with his scent on it, to pinpoint his location?"

"Something like that."

"Okay, I'm sure Lily kept some family heirlooms, for Geordi's sake."

"I'll help," Jason offered, and we headed to Lily's room.

I switched on the light and we stepped over Dito, snoring just inside the doorway. The room hadn't been touched since the day of Lily's mad flight to Marseille with Geordi, after snatching him from the Dioguardis on the courthouse steps. Which is to say it was in serious disarray, because I hadn't been able to face going through her stuff yet. Clothes were strewn everywhere, drawers hung half-open, and her jewelry box lay upended on the bed.

Jason took it all in. "So what's your best guess?"

"You'd know better than me." He opened his mouth, and I raised my hands. "I'm not starting a fight. I just mean you're more likely to recognize a Dioguardi heirloom. I know valuable old stuff, but we need *specific* valuable old stuff, and I can't distinguish purely art pieces from anything more personal."

He exhaled. "Okay. You might be right about that. But I keep telling you, I'm not part of the inner circle."

"Still. You've been around them—you know things."

"Not much more than you. Seriously—we need someone with *lots* of time on the inside."

Dito burped loudly and rolled onto his side with a groan.

We stared at him.

"Any chance throwing cold water on a ghost will sober him up? Or ghost coffee?"

Jason said, "Doubtful. But I have another idea."

He disappeared into the hall, and I heard him enter the kitchen. Cupboards and drawers banged open, and then he returned, holding something in his fist. He squatted in front of Dito and lifted his eyelid, and Dito groaned again, batting him away.

"Lea'me alone. I'm dead. Can'choo see that? Jus' lemme sleep."

"Not today," Jason said. "Today, we need your help. Sorry to do this to you, but…"

He uncurled his hand, revealing some type of dried herb mixed with coarse white granules. In one quick motion, he pressed his palm over Dito's nose and mouth and kept it there, using his other hand like a vise on the back of Dito's head. Dito's eyes bugged open and he gagged, his face going from red to white as he fought like a madman, clawing at Jason's hand.

Jason's bigger than Dito, but fear—and a surge of ghost adrenaline—gave Dito extraordinary strength. He thrashed harder, and Jason grunted at me, "*Stand back—*

"

I jerked away as Dito heaved himself up, using his powerful legs as leverage against his attacker. Jason had been forced into an awkward angle and fought to maintain his balance. Dito took full advantage, shoving with his legs, twisting to the side, and yanking his head out of Jason's grasp.

They fell in opposite directions, and Dito pushed onto his hands and knees, coughing and breathing hard. "*Shit*—it burns. What the fuck did you do that for?"

His eyes and nose were red and watery, like he'd been pepper sprayed. He grabbed a hank of his ghost t-shirt and rubbed his face, then spit onto Lily's lush wool carpet. Luckily, ghost saliva doesn't leave a mark, but even so—pretty gross.

He cleared his throat a few times, then crawled to the foot of the bed and rested his back against it, glaring at Jason. "What the hell was that?"

Jason also righted himself and sat, leaning against the dresser. "Sage and salt. Turns out those supernatural TV shows got some of it right. Welcome back."

Dito scowled harder. "I don't want to *be* back. Not without…" He reddened. "Anyway. I wanted to forget. If I can't be *in* oblivion, at least let me *be* oblivious."

Jason frowned. "What are you talking about? Didn't you want to stay here?"

Dito's gaze slid away. "Kind of."

This did not fill me with sunshine and rainbows. "What does *that* mean?"

He blew out a ghost breath. "Okay, I had a good reason for staying here. Or, I thought I did. Guess I was fucking wrong on that score."

The belligerence was back, so whatever Jason had

done, it'd only mostly sobered Dito up. He dropped his head in his hands, and Jason raised a questioning eyebrow at me.

"You of all people should know. But I'll spell it out for you: he has feelings for Bala."

The shock on Jason's face would have been comical, except Dito took it as confirmation that Jason also had feelings for her, and he pushed himself up in a huff. Damn it. As usual, we didn't have time for this. Luckily, his coordination was crap, and he hadn't made it far. I grabbed his arm and pulled him back.

"Hey—wait a sec. Can you at least tell us what happened? It might help us with Geordi."

He sat back down again. "Fuck. I thought maybe you'd found him." He scrubbed a hand over his face. "I'm so sorry I couldn't protect him."

"Not your fault," I managed. "Marchosias took over Paolo a long time ago. Plus, none of us knew it, but Geordi's scarab was protecting him, and he left it for me when you all took off. But now we have a plan—sort of—and you might be able to help."

He shoved a hand through his hair. "Yeah, okay. What do you want to know?"

"First, how did you get back?"

"I didn't. I never left."

"No one showed up to guide you?"

Dito, like most of the Dioguardis, is Catholic, despite being a demon. From what I'd gleaned, being born into it, not created by Satan, gives one the ability to survive things like Mass and other Catholic Rites. Plus, I mostly believed Jason when he said not all Dioguardis were evil. Either way, Dito should have gone *somewhere* after he died, whether Up *or* Down.

Jason said to me, "Isn't it automatic? Can souls really just stay if they want?"

"I don't actually know. Michael has said that for souls who don't believe in him, it's a nonissue. And others—like Eric—are just supposed to stay here. Which sounds like a cop out. I mean, either everyone who 'believes' has to move on, or they don't. But you keep saying the Dioguardis are 'good' Catholics, so…"

He compressed his lips. "I go to Mass more often than you do. We all do."

He threw a look at Dito, who shrugged. "Sure—I'm devout. Maybe they just missed me?"

I narrowed my eyes. "What are you leaving out? You know, I can call Michael down right now. I don't feel like I need to guide you anywhere, but he sure as hell"—*ha!*—"will."

That did the trick.

"Fine—someone showed up. I think. I was pretty out of it. But people came to help Bala, and then one of them headed right for me. I didn't want to go, so I ran and hid."

I stared at him. "A sorter showed up—and you *evaded* them? How?"

A whole mess of new questions popped into my head. Like, would I now start being called to find a newly deceased soul, instead of them finding me by accident during my daily routine? And could they really hide, forcing me to hunt them down? If any of this were true, my day job had just gotten even more complicated.

Jason said, "Where did you hide? Where have you been all this time? Bala's been in the hospital here for days—they life-flighted her in. If…" He cleared his throat awkwardly. "If she's the reason you stuck around, why didn't you come to Paris sooner?"

"I had to do something first. I didn't want to go to the Afterlife, but not just because of...well, you know. When Marchosias attacked, I could *feel* his power—but not just his. Paolo wasn't strong on his own, but Marchosias amplified what he had, and vice versa. And similarly, when I realized I'd died, I noticed..."

He paused, framing his words, as though uncertain how to explain. "It's like I felt suddenly *alive*. I know that's crazy, right? How can I be more alive, when I'm dead?"

I said slowly, "No, I get it. I felt that way after I died, at least some of the time." Especially after eating meat, though as noted, I hated to admit it.

Jason said to Dito, "So it's true? What Paolo surmised, about a dead bio-demon having enhanced powers?"

"I don't really know yet. I found a soul—a woman—who accepted me as a demon, and still agreed to make me Full Dead. It took a few days to set everything up, and then I came here."

Jason asked, "What made you drunk?"

"The woman said my injuries were so bad, I wouldn't be full strength again for weeks. But I wanted to leave right away, so she gave me something for the pain, and to help with traveling long distances on my own. She called it ghost lavender. I only used a little for the trip, saving most of it until I got here. But by then, I was in a lot of pain, so...I used a lot of it."

I considered what he'd said. "You've sealed your deadness—you're committed to staying here?"

He nodded. "Absolutely."

So, in theory, I didn't need to call Michael down.

But though Jun had set a precedent for this very situation, hiding another soul—especially a demon Catholic one, from an archangel who was also my boss—seemed like a Very Bad Idea.

He said, "Honestly, I don't know if I can help, or if it makes a difference. But I thought, since it's my fault Geordi's gone, it's worth a shot."

I remembered what he'd said, about finding his place and his purpose with the Super Secret Sect of Dioguardis, of which Jason and Bala are leading members. Or something. Maybe someday I'll understand how it all works. But for now, I couldn't look a gift horse in its proverbial mouth.

"It's not your fault. But maybe you *can* help. Jun is going into Hell to locate Nick. He needs something to guide him. Can you think of anything Lily might have, that could work?"

"No," he said promptly.

"Nothing at all? She must have *something* of Nick's."

"I doubt it. After she left, she wanted nothing to do with him or any of the Dioguardis, and gave everything back, except the apartment. She wouldn't have anything of Nick's that would work for our purpose." He pushed off the floor to a stand. "But I bet his girlfriend does."

Chapter Five

"I will have but one mistress and no master."
~Elizabeth I, Queen of England and Ireland
(1533-1603)

It didn't surprise me that Nick had a little side action going on. Probably more than one. But I did wonder that he hadn't taken better care of her. I would've expected him to put her up some place at least as fancy as Lily's. Instead, she lived in a rundown building in the Nineteenth Arrondissement, one of the poorest areas in Paris.

"Are you sure this is the right place?" I asked Dito as we parked the Peapod and got out.

"*Si,*" he said, thanking Jason for opening his door. Being made Full Dead improved his functionality in our world, but so far, dematerializing still took too much out of him.

He led us down the block to a side alley between two older tenements. It smelled of days' old trash from several dumpsters lined up on one side, and recent rains had left the gutters clogged with moldy leaves and other offal I'd rather not examine too closely.

Nick's girlfriend, Flore, lived in a first story apartment—second, if you count American style— accessed by an exterior iron staircase so rusty, I feared it would collapse. At least Dito didn't weigh anything, but

Jason and I together had to be at least three hundred pounds. The first step creaked but held, and we made it to the landing, then located her door and knocked.

It opened, revealing a much younger woman than I'd expected: mid-twenties at most, but I guess that shouldn't surprise me, either. Nick was too dumb to be more than a stereotype, and she fit the "young mistress" bill to a T. Plus, he obviously had a type: petite and blonde, although unlike Lily's, her highlights came from a bottle.

She'd pulled her chemically fried hair back with a scrunchie, the resulting high ponytail ratted into a wild mass that haloed her head. She wore a lime green sparkly tube top under a long black cardigan, and shiny silver capri leggings. She'd applied heavy makeup, like she planned an evening out, including pink rouge, bright red lipstick, and buckets of mascara. Her fingernails were long, fake, and clearly cheap, varying in color and level of bling, but we couldn't see if her toenails matched, as her feet were stuffed into old fleece-lined slippers that were ugly beyond belief, but cozy on a chill winter day.

She frowned at me and Jason suspiciously, but didn't seem to notice Dito, confirming her non-demon status. Of course, she could have been "demon lite," like Paolo, or even Jason, before he took the Rousseaux's powers. But by now I deemed Dito trustworthy, and besides, why would he lie about this?

"*Quoi?*" she demanded. "What do you want?"

Dito said to me, "Tell her you're here about the porcupine."

I exchanged a glance with Jason—he clearly didn't know what that meant, either—then said to her, "*Nous sommes ici pour le porc-épic.*"

She jerked back in surprise, then chewed her lip, deciding. Finally, she widened the door and stepped back, and we entered.

Inside, the apartment looked as depressing as on the outside: dark, dreary, and untidy. Flore flopped onto an ancient sofa covered in clothes, papers, and fast-food wrappers. Everything smelled greasy and stale, and I wrinkled my nose, wondering what she could possibly have of Nick's that might help us? Surely if he gave her anything of value, she would've hocked it by now and upgraded the furniture, or paid for a cleaning service.

I started to say as much to Jason and suggest we leave, when she grabbed a cigarette from a pack on the battered coffee table and lit it, saying, "I figured someone would come for it eventually. But before I give it up, I want something from you."

My brain whirled. She at least thought she had something someone would want. Maybe we'd get lucky after all.

Dito said to me, "Tell her that wasn't part of the deal."

I repeated what he said, and Flore glared back. "*Je m'en fiche!* If you want it, you'll get me what I want."

I lifted an eyebrow at Dito, unable to hide what I did from Flore, who scowled harder. We probably should have hashed this out before coming here, but maybe Dito had thought she'd just give "it" up without a fight. Apparently not.

He said, "We need it. And before you ask, yes, this is probably the only thing of value to Nick that might work. Nico and Rina have tons of his shit from his childhood, but I doubt his third-grade math test will do the trick. Especially with his scores. And no, I don't know what it is, just that he left it with Flore, figuring no one would believe he'd hide it in such a dump."

That might be the only thing Nick ever got right. I faced Flore. "I'm not agreeing to anything yet, but what do you want?"

"I wanna be a Hell Demon."

All three of us stared at her, open-mouthed.

She took a deep drag, blowing it out between her teeth. "You heard me. I know you all are demons—Nicky told me all about it, even though he wasn't one. Make me a demon, and I'll give you the porcupine. Otherwise, I'm dumping it in *la Seine.*"

I pinched the bridge of my nose. "Look, I can't just make you a Hell Demon. And he can't either." I glanced at a very dazed Jason, who managed a confirming nod. "But..." Man, I must be really desperate, to even consider this. I blew out a breath. "I might know someone who can."

Jason shot me a puzzled look. Then realization dawned, and he gripped my arm. "*Hyacinth.* You can't! Think about it—"

"I *am* thinking about it! I'm thinking about Geordi, and Marchosias, and what Nico and Rina are making me do, and this is it. I'm out of ideas. And besides, if she wants to do something that dumb, let her. Like you said about Jun, it's not our decision."

Dito grimaced and said to Jason, "She's right. Besides, Flore's not going to the Good Place, no matter what. I could tell you some stories."

Oblivious to Dito's assassination of her character, Flore took another drag. Jason released my arm, and I wondered if I'd finally crossed some invisible demon line for him. Too bad. I *had* to get Geordi back, and I couldn't see any other way through this.

I said to Flore. "Give me the porcupine, and I'll ask my, er, guy, to grant your wish."

"Right here, right now."

It was a demand, not a request, and I nodded. "I can't guarantee anything, but…I'm pretty sure he'll do it."

Why wouldn't he? Any self-respecting Hell Demon would jump at the chance to add to their Army. The only hitch being that I didn't know if he would—or could— come when I called. We still weren't sure who had survived the battle at Sennelager, but this particular Hell Demon had the survival skills of a cockroach, so I felt confident he'd made it out intact.

Flore stubbed out the cigarette and took a second from the pack. "*Before* I hand it over."

Damn. Not quite as dumb as Nick. "Yeah, sure. Gimme a sec."

Jason tugged my arm, saying to Flore, but also for Dito's benefit, "We'll be right back."

She lit the smoke. "Take your time. I'm in no hurry."

Jason pulled me outside and a safe distance down the steps, into the alley, before rounding on me. "Are you crazy? I mean seriously—have you fucking lost it? If you call Claude back, who *knows* what he'll do to you. You've gotten in his way, time and again. Do you really think he'll do you a *favor*, instead of just exterminating you?"

Not unexpected, but a blow nonetheless. He'd been there for me from the start—he *had* to see this was the only way. But even if he didn't—even if this is what made the irrevocable break between us and sent him back to Bala—even with all that, I'd still do it.

I took his hands in mine, the electric warmth of his

thread immediately coursing through me. He felt agitated—more so than I'd ever known him to be. Maybe that should have scared me, but losing Geordi terrified me more.

"Nico and Rina want Nick. Jun needs something to find him. Dito thinks this is the only thing that will work. And Flore wants to be a demon before giving it up. If I knew what it is, or where she keeps it, maybe I'd just take it. But I don't, on either score, and I don't have time to agonize. Because more important than *any* of those things—including whatever happens to me—is getting Geordi back."

He compressed his lips. "I agree. I just don't know if this is the way to do it."

"I *have* to try. Nico and Rina want an answer by tomorrow. I need to know by then if it's even possible to do what they ask. I need Jun for that, which means I need Flore, and also Claude. He might even be willing to guarantee Jun safe passage in and out of Hell. Unless you know any *other* Hell Demons who can do this for me?"

"You know I don't. But that's not even the point. Do you understand what you'll be doing to Flore? She has no idea what it means to be a demon. But *you* do—and not just a bio-demon. Becoming a Hell Demon is a…process. Can you really do that to another person? Even someone like Flore, and even for a 'good' reason?"

"I—"

Nothing came to mind. No words to make him understand—no justification to make *me* understand how I could do something so vile to another person, even if they thought they wanted it, and even if, as he said, I had good reasons.

He gently removed his hands and stepped back.

"Okay. Your call. But regardless, have you considered—I can't be here for this. You're not the only one who pissed him off, and I…"

He shook his head helplessly, and took another step back, and sudden pure fear and loss ripped through me. "No—wait—"

"Hyacinth." His voice was quiet. Calm. But resolute. "I took their powers—*stole from High Demons*. I can't be anywhere near here, if you insist on calling him back. Remember the deal you made with him the last time?"

"Of course." I knew it wouldn't work, but on some level, I thought if I just kept him talking, he'd stay. "He said he'd forgive our transgressions, including that you stole powers from him. And that the forgiveness extended to Jacques as well. So he can't do anything to you—you said even High Demons have to honor the deals they make."

"True. But do you really think that what happened in the forest, when you and Vadim's Dead—when *we* defeated Claude's Demon Army—that he'll take it philosophically? He said the forgiveness would not extend to future transgressions. I'd say that's a pretty big one, right there."

I opened my mouth, then closed it, because he had a point. Claude Rousseau might not act against Jason about the stolen powers. But the defeat of his army gave him an excellent excuse to flex his rage for other reasons. And Jason still had those powers in him, making him a "Hell magnet." I couldn't ask him to stay. But I couldn't bear him leaving me—maybe for good.

"I'm sorry. I…"

He swallowed, his bobbing Adam's apple the only

sign this *might* be hard for him, too. He lifted a shoulder, then turned and walked up the alley, away from the car—and from me.

I took a half-step after him, then scrubbed my eyes. Whatever happened next, I couldn't take it back. If—when—I did this, I'd be committing a living person to demonhood, whether she understood the consequences or not. And then I'd be sending an innocent—mostly—as far as I knew—soul into Hell on a highly questionable mission, to retrieve a banished soul who *should* burn for all eternity. None of which aligned with my own morals, iffy though they might be, or fit my job description as assistant to Archangel Michael.

But worse than that, I'd decided to make *another* deal with Claude Rousseau. Jason was right to call me crazy. But if this is what it took to get Geordi back, I'd do it.

I breathed in, then exhaled. *Claude—where are you? I have a new deal for you.*

Sudden heat smothered me and the stench from the dumpsters grew. A rustling came from behind me and I turned slowly, dreading facing him, even though I'd called him forth.

However, it wasn't Claude who'd returned from whatever pit he'd holed up in after the battle. It was his brother, Jacques, oily as ever, his black hair slicked back, his bulk amplified by one of the white suits he and his brother both favored. He almost glowed in the grungy alley, and I experienced another bout of mild hysteria, because—though actually Bael, a Great King in Hell—outwardly, at least, he resembled an angel more than my boss usually did.

"Mademoiselle Finch," he said, voice hoarse and

filled with darkness. "I did not expect to hear from you again—and so soon."

Thinking back, this might be the first time I'd heard him speak out loud, since he normally left the talking to his brother. Oh God—*had* Claude been obliterated in the battle? If so, Jacques probably wanted revenge, not to make a deal.

I fisted my hands at my sides. Too late now—I'd better get it over with. "I, uh, need a favor. But I think it will benefit you, so…" I swallowed, telling my conscience I'd make up for this some other way. "I know someone who wants to be a demon. Can you make her one?"

He took that in, then said, "I assume that is the benefit to me. What is the favor for you?"

I tightened my fists, willing my heart rate down. "I need to find someone in Hell. One of the Dead thinks he can help, and I want you to guarantee him safe passage."

Surprise flickered in his eyes before they reverted to their normal empty blackness. "Why? What is so important to you, that you would ask this of me?"

"I…"

What should I tell him? The truth? Not really my style, and probably not best practices with a Demon King in any case. If only Jason were here. I glanced around, hoping he'd lurked in the bushes after all. But neither he nor bushes of any kind were visible in the dank alley. I could've asked Dito, but I probably shouldn't alert Jacques to his presence, either, as like Jason, he might get sucked into Hell, simply from being a demon himself, bio or not.

"I think you already know," I said at last.

"Ah. Your nephew. Marchosias has been very bad,

oui?"

A sudden thought occurred to me, and I blurted, "Can *you* get him back?"

Merde. What had I done? Jason would *know* this was a terrible idea, something my own gut confirmed as soon as the words popped out.

But Jacques only said with mock regret, "Even if it were possible—which it is not—you could not afford the price." He chewed his fat lower lip and studied me impassively. "Who are you attempting to retrieve?"

"Geordi's father," I said before I could second-guess myself. Odds were that Jacques could figure it out anyway, so I might as well tell the truth. For once.

"Ah. I cannot get him out for you, either. I cannot set foot in Hell for the time being. You understand—it is complicated."

Yeah. Complicated. Because he'd escaped from Hell with the help of his brother, but without Satan's blessing, in part to oust Satan from power. And since Satan himself remains trapped, it's a touchy situation.

"I'm not asking that. Just for safe passage for my guy to go in and poke around. You can do that, right? I give you a new demon convert, and you instruct your demons on the inside to help my guy through. *And* back out again."

I may be dumb enough to keep making deals with Hell Demons, but I was at least learning to be *very* specific about the terms.

He studied me, and I wiped all thoughts from my mind. Not that I had anything to hide, as far as I knew. But better to be safe, and all that.

"Very well," he said at last, and some of the tension eased out of me.

"We have a deal? You'll help Jun—my guy—get in and out of Hell, and I'll give you your new demon?"

He nodded. "Yes. That is our deal. There is no going back."

I swallowed, and nodded, too, wondering when the other shoe would drop. Which turned out to be *right now.*

He said, "I could make Flore—yes, I know who she is—a demon without your introduction. But I will enjoy the opportunity to help remove one of Satan's most precious souls out from under his nose."

"I don't understand…"

"Nicholas Dioguardi holds a position of honor at Satan's right hand, for being such an effective soldier of Hell on Earth. Removing him will *not* go unnoticed, and it will not be easy. But if I can play some small part in Satan's further destruction, I am more than happy to oblige."

He held out a hand, and I shook it, feeling the burning heat of his evil energy—darker even than his brother's. What had I done? Bad enough, making Flore a demon. Far worse, sending Jun into Hell. But asking him to go *deep* into Hell, right *to* Satan—and then stealing Satan's favorite plaything out from under his nose—wasn't just crazy. It was suicidal.

But even worse than all that would be letting *Geordi* wind up in Satan's clutches.

"Okay," I said. "What next?"

Chapter Six

"I never know sadness, but only a madness that burns at the heart and the brain."
> ~Jack Parsons, American Rocket Engineer
> (1914-1952)

I took a long hot shower when I got back to Lily's place. At some point, I'd have to start calling it *my* place. But not today.

The shower could never cleanse me of my sins, or wipe the memory of what I'd done, but it reminded me that just surviving the encounter with Jacques was enough for now.

I shuddered and grabbed my towel, but scrubbing myself dry didn't help, either.

Apparently, even High Demons—a *Great King* in Hell—can't just snap their fingers and make someone a demon. If Satan were free, possibly. But his imprisonment limits his demons' powers, especially those who escaped without his permission. Or so Jacques claimed, and I couldn't see why he'd lie about this. So I took him at his word, and we trooped up to Flore's rooms—the staircase *really* protested under his enormous bulk—to deliver the good news.

Dito was MIA, so he must have sensed Jacques and skedaddled. I get why he, like Jason, would avoid a Hell Demon, but it still gave me a pang. Guess I'm finally learning not to be a loner all the time.

Flore was slumped on the ancient couch, a fresh cigarette in her hand. She scowled at me, but one look at Jacques deflated some of her bravado, and one look *from* him told her she'd made her choice. So she stubbed out her smoke, rose, and disappeared into a back room, emerging moments later with a musty wooden box, about the size of a thick book and secured with a tiny padlock. The carving on top depicted a porcupine, tiny quills erect and so intricate, I couldn't imagine the patience it took to create it.

She handed it to me. "*Alors,* it's all yours now, and good riddance."

I really wanted to peek inside, but one, I was still pretending I already knew, and two, Jacques seeing it likely wouldn't be prudent. It didn't have a key, but it would be easy enough to break the lock off later, so I tucked the box in my bag as Flore faced Jacques.

"*Bon—faisons ça.* I'm ready."

Jacques gave her the once over, as though assessing her potential. "*Très bien. Alors*—do you consent to the process of becoming a demon?"

"*Ouais.*"

"And do you agree that I owe you nothing for this— that you are asking freely, for your own benefit and gain?"

"*Ouais.* Just get on with it." She sounded nervous, but the time for regrets was long past, for either of us.

"And do you agree to the *whole* process—to doing whatever it takes, for however long, in order to receive the gift of eternal life and power from your new master, Satan himself?"

She nodded. "Yeah, whatever, just do it."

His grin widened. "Excellent…my pet."

He waved a hand over her face, and she…left. Not physically, but the spark went out of her eyes, her shoulders slumped, and her hands, which she'd been twisting agitatedly, fell to her sides, loose and still.

Despite my better judgment, I rounded on Jacques. "What did you do to her?"

"What she asked—what *you* requested for her. *Quoi*—you think becoming a demon is like cutting your hair? Poof—instant change? *Non*. There are steps that must be followed, in order, before she will be ready. If she lives that long."

"And the first step is…?"

"Becoming a demon pet, *bien sûr*. If she is good, and survives what I ask of her, she will be a demon in, oh, five or six hundred years. *If* Satan wants her. It is not actually up to me. I will, of course, prepare her. But it will be up to her, and to Satan's whim, what the end result is. If she pleases him, he will use his powers to complete the transformation. If not, he will give her to his Hell Hounds for supper."

I gaped at him. Then I shut my mouth. Flore should've asked more questions. Me, too. But she'd agreed to everything Jacques asked. Was it my fault she hadn't thought it through?

My conscience, inconveniently vocal at the best of times, piped up that, yeah, I might be at least partially responsible.

Jacques placed a hand at Flore's elbow, then paused. "Earlier, when we discussed your nephew, you asked the wrong question. I cannot help you retrieve him, but there is something you should know. Kimaris survived the battle at Sennelager, but Satan is angry with her."

I frowned. "Why? I thought she wanted to free him."

Kimaris—Kim—is a Hell Demon who claimed to be helping us protect Geordi from detection by various *other* Hell Demons running around Germany and France. But in reality, she was working for Satan the whole time, and acting in her own self-interest more than ours.

Jacques lifted a shoulder. "Who can say? Satan's whims are…capricious, at best. But again, that is the wrong question."

He clearly toyed with me. But I was desperate for *anything* that might help us find Geordi. "Okay…where is she now, and what is she doing?"

His wolf's teeth flashed in the light slanting through the broken blinds. "Better. She is on the outside, searching for your nephew. I believe she is very close to locating him."

Hope and fear shot through me in equal measure. "How do I find her?"

He made a *tsk*-ing sound. "As I said, Satan is angry with her. Though Satan exhibits a…preference…for you, he would not like Kimaris interfering in his business. She, like Marchosias, is assessing the best route to take, for her own continued well-being."

Oh God—did she now *also* want Geordi? Panic clawed at me—my whole body shook and I wanted to throw up. I shoved it all down, trying to think logically by brute force.

"Why are you telling me this?"

His eyes glinted with amusement. "Because, Mademoiselle Finch, the players are lining up on the chessboard. And your nephew is the pawn who could one day become a queen—the most powerful piece in the game. You will need to choose which side of the board to play on—the side where Satan is King, or...the side where he is not."

"Meaning your side."

"I believe you would prefer Satan remain trapped in Hell. He has other plans. Perhaps allying yourself with those who wish to prevent his escape would be in your best interests, *and* your nephew's. Should you choose Kimaris instead, well, who knows what will happen?"

With that, he and Flore vanished, and I hightailed it out of there, adrenaline, nausea—the works—roaring through me, so that I stumbled down the stairs and out to the street. Dito waited by the car. He didn't ask where Jason went, or what happened to Flore, and I didn't offer details. With luck, I'd never have to *think* of it again, let alone speak.

Back at the apartment, my minions were in the dining room, discussing matters of state. I plunked the box on the table in front of Jun and Liam, then moved toward the hallway.

Liam said, "What's inside?"

"Don't know, don't care."

Jun spoke up. "We just needed something of value to him. It does not matter what is inside—the box alone might suffice."

I said, "Good. Hope it works. Oh—and I made a deal with Jacques Rousseau. Jun, you should have safe passage into and out of Hell while locating Nick. But be careful. Jacques said Nick is tight with Satan, so you might have to go pretty far in to find him."

My minions—living, dead, or demon—stared at me.

"Yeah, you can yell at me later, when I'm done yelling at myself. And Jun, if you've changed your mind—"

"I haven't."

"Great. Jacques also said Kimaris is still around, and she might know where Geordi is, but she won't tell us, because she's on the outs with Satan, and needs the leverage."

Without a word, Torben picked up his tablet, and I turned and headed to the bathroom.

In all my dealings with the Rousseaux, Claude had been my primary point of contact. Decidedly creepy, but he had an elegant air reminiscent of my wealthiest clients, which, if not exactly reassuring, at least felt familiar. Jacques was…not like that, at all.

I felt raw, exposed. As though, by making this deal with him, I'd opened myself to a new level of *something*, and like Flore, I'd glossed over the details. Jason, however, had known it from the start, and now I knew it, too: I'd made a huge mistake, and aligning myself further with the Rousseaux would be even dumber. But…

Geordi.

As Jacques himself said, Geordi *was* a pawn: small, helpless, the chaos around him bent on chewing him up and spitting him out. But which "side" would be better for saving him? If only I knew more of our family history—where Geordi's powers actually stemmed from. Then I might have some idea who to trust, or how to carve out a third path instead. Despite everyone constantly referring to Geordi's powers as his "demon blood," Jason insisted my parents weren't demons. So…what were we?

I finished drying off and shoved my clothes into the hamper—I should probably just burn them—then went to the guest bedroom and dragged on sweats, a t-shirt, and a hoody. I also found a pair of old slippers, but they reminded me too much of Flore, so I opted for wool socks instead.

Somewhat restored, I returned to the front of the apartment, to find my minions circled around Jun at the table, his hands resting on either side of the now-opened wooden box. The inside was lined with pale blue satin on which lay a small black disc, about the size of an American silver dollar, except thicker, with a bluish-gray porcupine carved on its surface.

Mystery solved, though I didn't know the significance. But what difference did it make? Either it worked, or it didn't.

Jun sat silently with his eyes closed, so I asked, "Are we ready?"

All four of my other minions looked at me sharply and said, "*Shhh!*"

Liam added in a whisper, "He's already gone."

I opened my mouth, but they all put fingers on their lips and glared at me. I keep forgetting they're a well-oiled machine. And Jun didn't need me for this, anyway. I'd done my part, conscience be damned—maybe literally—so I pivoted and went to flop on the pillowy sofa instead.

Liam came to sit in a chair nearby, saying in a low voice, "We did all the prep work while you were gone. We think the porcupine is a coin, like the ones used to pay the Ferryman for safe passage to the Underworld. So once you said Jacques's demons in Hell would also help with that, Jun decided to leave right away. He's been gone a little over five minutes. You need to give Nico and Rina an answer by tomorrow, and he doesn't know how long this will take."

"But...he's still here." As a ghost, I'd assumed his spirit would actually travel *to* Hell, but apparently not.

Liam said, "I don't know much more than you. But I've learned a few things, both before I died and after. Remember, Hell isn't a physical place. It's more a state of mind, but not really that either." He made a frustrated gesture. "Sorry. Jun couldn't explain it either, but basically, his spirit walks in Hell, while the shell of his spirit—what we see here—stays put."

I wondered how he felt about that on a personal level. I mean, in my case, the "shell" everyone sees is my body. But this was levels of spirithood—literally, layers of existence. Like Eric's appropriation of the body that absorbed him. Maybe only Eric's outer spirit had broken apart, and his core remained intact. Not much better, but it gave me a little hope.

I said, "Thanks. I just wanted to talk with him first. He really didn't have to go, and—"

"Yes, he did. No one else could do it, and maybe if Nick knows what his parents want, it will pave the way for whatever you have to do later, to pull him out."

My minions were annoyingly logical, almost as often as Jason. Thinking of him sent that pang of loss through me again, and as though reading my thoughts, Liam said, "Where's Jason? I would've thought he'd want to be here for this."

"Gone. Maybe for good."

The tears welled up, and I twisted away. Liam cleared his throat awkwardly, but I made *go away* motions, and after a moment, he quietly returned to the dining table.

What had I done? I *had* to get Geordi back. But at what cost? Not since Lily died had I felt this alone, despite being surrounded by minions. Jason had always been my touchstone—my conscience—a giant cartoon cricket, demanding I think things through, fighting to keep me whole, before I careened off the boat into the ocean. Without him, I felt shattered—broken by my deal with Jacques, and the prospect of pulling someone from Hell who was *so* evil, he'd become Satan's favorite in mere weeks.

I couldn't do it—I'd get Geordi back, but I'd lose my humanity in the process. If only Eric were here—*someone* to reassure me and hold my hand and say we'd figure it out, together.

But he wasn't, and I couldn't save him, either. I shoved my face into the pillows and wept in earnest, praying my minions were too busy watching over Jun to notice.

****

I must have fallen asleep, because when I came up for air some time later, a weak gray dawn broke through a gap in the floor-to-ceiling drapes. Memory flooded back and I sat up fast, peering at Jun, who remained entranced, while my other minions variously worked on laptops or tablets—the living ones—or talked quietly—the dead ones.

I rose. "Is he still gone? It's been hours. Shouldn't we pull him back or something?"

Liam shook his head. "He said not to. He said he'd know when to leave, and if we wake him or interfere in any way, it could disrupt the ritual and actually trap him there."

Ugh. Now I felt even worse, and it being Jun's choice made no difference. As the so-called leader of this oddball troop, anything that happened rested squarely on me.

Liam said, "It's not your fault. And you need coffee." He moved toward the kitchen, then froze sheepishly, abruptly remembering he was dead, and unable to caffeinate me.

Torben set down his tablet and pushed back his chair. "I'll do it."

"I can make my own damn coffee," I said. I sounded testy, but I couldn't help it. Torben ignored me in any case and filled the coffee pot at the sink.

Ulrich said, "Let him do it. I can update you on the rock progress."

"Fine." I ungraciously pulled out a chair and plunked down on it.

Ulrich also ignored my grumpiness. Which I secretly appreciated, but it also made me grumpier. I wasn't accustomed to having so many people, alive *or* dead, in my face all the time, *doing* things for me. I'd been living solo for over fifteen years. I didn't need their help.

Except I clearly did. I might not like it, but I couldn't do this—whatever *this* was—alone. They each had skills and expertise far different from my own, and if nothing else, were extra hands, allowing me to multitask in ways I otherwise couldn't.

I blew out a breath and opened my mouth to apologize, but Ulrich cut me off. "Not necessary. Listen, this is what we've got so far. We wanted something close by, in the interest of time. This seemed a good place to start."

He handed me the laptop he'd been working on, opened to a web page titled *The Paris Rock & Mineral Show*. He seemed okay now, but maybe his eagerness to help stemmed from his feelings of failure at not being able to protect Geordi. I could totally relate.

I skimmed the page, then handed the computer back to him. "It's going on now? That's a stroke of luck. But other than there being a bunch of rocks in one room, we have no reason to think any of them are Michael's. Or Satan's."

That was another aspect of all this I'd prefer to ignore. It's one thing to accidentally find Satan's relics during my lawful pursuit of Michael's, but quite another to deliberately seek stones possessing remnants of the Prince of Darkness's powers. Plus, in this case, I wanted the shards not to restore them to Michael, but for my own nefarious purposes. So it didn't really matter whose I hunted. Either way, I'd be screwed if we were found out.

Ulrich said, "Come on—we have to give it a shot. Even if none of the sellers pan out, one of them is bound to know someone who might."

"Okay, I'll go later today."

He gave me a sympathetic look. "Wish we could do it for you, but…"

"You're doing what you can. Until someone else can sense the vibrations, I'm it."

Torben came from the kitchen, bearing a tray loaded with three steaming mugs of coffee and a selection of piping hot breakfast muffins, including one that smelled deliciously of cheese and bacon. I reached for blueberry instead, and he swatted my hand.

"You need meat. You're not eating it enough, and you're wearing down. Now is *not* the time to choose principles over your health." He placed the meat muffin on a plate near my mug, then returned to the kitchen with the empty tray. "Eggs and sausages, coming right up."

I glared at his back, but took the muffin. It tasted savory and amazing, and I *felt* my energy surge at the first bite. When, a few minutes later, he passed me a plate overflowing with meaty-eggy goodness, I didn't even put up a token protest. I did need meat, and denying it only hurt me and potentially put everyone else in danger.

I dug in, stifling a moan of pleasure, while Torben sat and picked up his tablet. "If the rock show's a bust, I've been searching the dark web for off-the-books auctions. There are some coming up that could be…interesting."

I swallowed my latest bite. "What does that mean?"

He exchanged a glance with Ulrich, Dito and Liam, and I set down my fork and folded my arms.

Torben raised his hands. "Fine, fine. Not trying to hide anything from you. It's just kind of…icky…stuff."

I should've known. Obviously, anyone collecting relics belonging to Satan probably wasn't Monsieur—or Madame—Good Citizen. But I'd rather not know what an "interesting icky dark web auction" entailed. Unfortunately, I might have to at some point, since no one could locate the shards for me, and I couldn't do it remotely.

However…Geordi could. It's one of his powers we'd discovered in Germany, which made him so valuable to Satan, or to anyone currying his favor *or* trying to overthrow him.

So essentially, to everyone.

The greasy sausage sank in my gut, and I pushed my plate away. "Okay. We'll cross our fingers for the mineral show. But it's good you're finding alternatives, if we need them."

He nodded, still troubled.

"It's fine," I said. "Really. Besides, maybe we'll catch a break this time."

Ulrich surreptitiously rapped the wood table three times with his knuckles, and I thought, why the hell not? I did it, too. We needed all the luck we could get.

"Speaking of icky stuff," I said, "*if* we manage to pull Nick out, we need to figure out how to—I don't even know—recreate his body, I guess? Rina said she wants him alive, like me. But his corpse has been buried for three months now."

Liam said, "With embalming and an expensive casket, he's probably in great shape—good as new, even." We all stared at him, and he shrugged. "My father owned a funeral home. A skilled embalmer and a tightly sealed bronze coffin can make a body last for years. And I'm guessing the Dioguardis spared no expense on their only son's eternal bed."

"But…wouldn't his organs have been removed?"

Liam grimaced. "Maybe in the old days. But modern embalming just sucks out the blood and gases, adds the embalming fluid, and *voilà*. Unless they did an autopsy?"

"I doubt it—bullet to the brain. Pretty straightforward. Except I'm not sure what shape his head is in."

I shuddered at the memory of Nick lying on the floor of my shop, in a pool of coagulating blood. I hadn't paid too close attention at the time, but I thought the bullet hit his left temple, with most of the damage from the exit wound in the back of his skull, leaving his face intact.

Liam said, "Not a problem. A good mortician can reconstruct just about anything. And one more time— I'm sure Nico and Rina paid for the best. Only thing is, he might have to wear a hat—or a wig. His hair won't grow back over the reconstruction site, even if it does elsewhere. But it probably won't be noticeable to anyone who doesn't know."

Okay, then. If we got him out, it appeared he had a "home" to return to. Of course, he'd have to be exhumed, but Nico and Rina could damn well figure out *that* part of all this.

Suddenly Jun sucked in a huge ghost breath, startling all of us. His eyes flew open and he shoved away from the table, knocking his chair aside as he stumbled backward into the living room.

"I found him. But I don't think we can get him out."

Chapter Seven

"Through me you pass into the city of woe:
Through me you pass into eternal pain:
Through me among the people lost for aye…
All hope abandon, ye who enter here."
                    ~Dante Alighieri, Italian Poet
                    (1265-1321) – Inferno, III.1-3; 9

I made Jun repeat the story of what he'd seen in Hell until he recited it by rote.

Essentially, he'd taken the ghost equivalent of peyote, with the goal of opening his mind to the paths of Hell. I didn't ask where he got it. He definitely had his own way of doing things, so I landed on gratitude that he had it and knew how to use it.

"What's the first thing you saw?" I asked again.

"Jacques's demons, waiting for me as promised."

"What did they look like? What did they do?"

"As I said, they resembled…nothing. Empty, evil voids, not in their human suits. I showed them the porcupine coin, and a path appeared, with fire and heat on either side, but the path itself felt neutral to the touch."

"And you think the *porc-épic* represents the long line of Dioguardis bearing Satan's blood?"

He nodded. "Each quill symbolizes an individual ancestor. The porcupine has many, many quills, showing there are many loyal descendants of the original priest, leading down to Nick, and possibly explaining why he is such a favorite of Satan's already."

"Okay. What happened next?"

He sighed, but recognized I needed to hear it all again. "I followed the path with Jacques's demons on either side of me. The noises of Hell surrounded me, but nothing could touch me, so I went deeper and deeper down, until we came to an open space. No lava pits or fires, just burning hot air, with a throne of grayish-white metal in the center."

At this point in the original recitation, Torben had interjected that the metal was likely tungsten, which evidently has a very high melting point, but a very low "vapor pressure." So Satan was a practical bugger, valuing function over form: no easily meltable gold for him.

Jun continued, "I stayed hidden at the edge of the room, far away from the throne. Something large and dark sat on it, but I couldn't discern any details, and Jacques's demons were frightened of being caught helping me. They wouldn't set foot inside, but even from that distance, I could see a man—Nick—handcuffed to the Dark Presence."

I inhaled and exhaled. "One more time—you're certain the thing on the throne is Satan, and Nick's handcuffed *to* him? Not to the throne, or a ring in the floor?"

"Who else would sit on a throne in the middle of Hell? But yes, whoever it is, Nick is handcuffed to him. I couldn't alert him to our plan, and I don't see how we can take him, without first convincing Satan to uncuff him. So, I left."

Damn. I'd pictured Jun cozying up to Nick and

basically saying, *Hey—friend of your parents. You down with coming back to Earth? Great, back in a jiffy with your ride!* And then we'd whisk him away, with a moderate head start before Satan even noticed. But with Nick chained directly to Satan, there'd be no hiding his disappearance. And I couldn't just ask Satan to do me a solid. He might not have killed me, but that didn't mean he wanted to *help* me.

Dito said, "What if we broker a deal?"

We all stared at him, and he cleared his throat, saying to me, "You're good at that. You've basically set up a domino surgery here—you know, those ten-way transplants, where I'm a match for your kidney, and your friend is a match for someone, with a friend who's a match for the person I'm connected to, and we all exchange extra kidneys at the same time. You're already partway there, with doing Flore her favor, to get Nick's thing, to help Jun through Hell, so Nico and Rina can get what they want, to save Geordi, which is what *you* want."

It was possibly the longest speech Dito had ever given. Certainly, the most he'd volunteered since I knew him. And I got his point. But…

"This is *Satan* we're talking about. Even if he'd listen to me, I have no idea what to offer, in exchange for his new Best Friend."

"I think I do," Jun said slowly. "We just have to find her first."

I started to ask who he meant, and then I got it: Rachel.

On the one hand, her plan to steal Satan's powers had enraged him, and he thought he'd destroyed her on Barnacken. If he knew she'd survived, the urge to finally end her might outweigh the giddy good feelings Nick gave him. But on the other hand, finding her could be dangerous. She was capable of *anything*. Including, perhaps, besting Satan himself.

I mulled that over. What had the least potential to annihilate all of us? Working with Satan, to destroy Rachel, or hoping *she'd* destroy *him*? More to the point, which option would give us Nick, and therefore, Geordi?

Liam spoke up. "I don't like it—too dicey. For one thing, if Hyacinth gets near Satan, it brings him that much closer to Geordi. We don't know if Marchosias has approached him yet, but if not, reminding Satan of Geordi's existence seems like a really bad idea."

"I'll do it," Dito said, and we all stared at him again. He lifted a shoulder. "I'm a dead demon. What have I got to lose?"

I shook my head. "No. *Because* you're a demon, you're at higher risk of being sucked into Hell. Maybe not as much of a Hell magnet as Jason with his Rousseau powers, but still."

"If I bring Rachel to Satan, he'll let me go, and give us Nick to boot. Of course, you'll have to figure out how to bring Nick out of Hell, back to Earth. I doubt Satan will be *that* generous. But if we play it right, he might at least uncuff Nick for us."

"That's a lot of ifs," I pointed out, but Torben leaned forward.

"It's worth a shot. We need to do something about Rachel anyway. We can't just leave her loose in the world. Might as well find her, and like the rocks, you can decide what to do about her later."

I started to protest again, and Ulrich said, "Better to find her before she finds us. She's probably pissed, and now she knows Satan has some regard for you, she might try to cash in on that. It's better if we're proactive, instead of waiting for her to pop up when we least expect it."

Yet again, they were right. If nothing else, maybe having a tentative—if insane and impossible—plan would take the pressure off and we'd think of something better.

"Fine. We search for Rachel and rocks, and go from there. But if we come up empty…"

"We won't," Torben said. "Just let us do our thing, while you do yours."

He meant the gem show. According to the clock on the dining room wall, early bird access started in an hour. I might as well get that out of the way. And who knew? Maybe we *would* catch a break, and I'd find everything we needed, all in the same booth.

Yeah, right.

****

Jun accompanied me. He's not a Super Senser, but he had silenced the key shard, which is more than anyone else could do. Dito also tagged along, since as a Dioguardi demon, he could help negotiate if we encountered a seller on the shady side. Plus, he'd known about the *porc-épic*, and might spot something I missed.

When I paid admission and entered the venue, followed by my freeloading ghost buddies, my heart sank. Though smaller than an American convention center, it was still big: comparable to one and a half football fields put together, with row upon row of booths. Just walking the perimeter would take thirty minutes, let alone perusing the aisles.

"There are a lot of tables here," Jun said. "Do you sense anything?"

"No."

Even after all this time, I didn't know how close I needed to be, to feel the vibrations. Once, at the Plutonium in Turkey, I'd noticed them from the outside, but the rock couldn't have been more than a couple hundred meters in. Plus, it was just one rock in a tunnel. Maybe being here, in the presence of so many minerals, gemstones, and the like, created some type of signal interference. I couldn't make a definitive call one way or another, without at least getting closer to the middle.

Dito said, "Might as well get started."

He headed to the left side, Jun aimed for the right, and I went to the center. Despite them not being "sensers," we'd decided to split up, figuring if none of the vendors had anything resembling the original slab, it would save time. Plus, with me starting in the heart of things, I might pick up on something laterally that I'd miss from the outer aisles.

At least we'd come early, before the crowds. The downside to this being that we—or rather I, as the only visible one—stood out. Since most sellers at these events like to chat, I had a hard time going through quickly. Besides, I wanted to curry favor with them, in hopes they'd drop some useful intel. Like that one of their comrades loved Satan and had a magic rock. Or even just a clue of where to search after we left here. Anything to dodge the whole Dark Web Auction situation.

Unfortunately, nothing leapt out at me, and the closest I came to anything "unusual" was a vendor who had a feather carved from black onyx, about the size of my thumb. It looked so different from the polished tiger stones, jade eggs, and such on the table, that I picked it up. Like the porcupine box, the details were extraordinary. I'd brought both box and coin with me, and I pulled them out now, comparing the coin side by side with the feather.

At first I'd thought the porcupine and its base were two different pieces, glued together, but now I saw they'd been carved from a single material. So the mineral used had multiple layers, which the artist had skillfully peeled back to create the raised gray carving on top of the darker disk.

I'd also brought Geordi's scarab with me, and I took it from my pocket. All three items—scarab, coin, and feather—were roughly the same size, and of similar colors, with the black base of the coin appearing nearly identical to the black onyx of the other two.

The seller—a rotund man in his early sixties, with wispy grey hair and a bright pink complexion—smiled, indicating the feather. "Ah, *mademoiselle*. It speaks to you, *oui*? It is a dove feather—a message from a loved one who has passed on, or from an angel, perhaps."

My pulse quickened. I'm not superstitious, I swear. But... Had I picked up the feather unconsciously, because of Eric? He always called me "*mon ange*"—his angel. And even dead, he could hold Geordi's scarab, exactly as a living person would. But if it *was* a message from "beyond," did that mean he was gone-gone, and I couldn't save him?

No. I would *not* go there. And anyway, Nadezhda would tell me if anything happened.

"I don't believe in that stuff," I said and the seller's smile widened.

"It matters not what you believe. Dove feathers bring clarity. You are struggling with something, and it will open you to the truth. That it is from a dead black dove is doubly significant. There is a great transition—possibly a permanent separation—ahead of you."

He must have seen my unease, because he added, "This is not always a negative. Perhaps the separation is from something that has limited you, holding you or your loved ones back. The feather represents the release from those bonds—a new freedom from the past."

I couldn't help it—I'd been sucked in by his belief in all this. "Obviously I can see it's a black feather. But how do you know it's from a dead dove specifically?"

He leaned forward, pointing with a beringed stubby forefinger at the feather's bottom. "See here? The shaft is broken and jagged, bent to one side." He lifted it off my palm. "And see the back? Those droplets are not ink—they are blood." He replaced the feather on my palm, closing my hand over it. "It has chosen you. Even if you do not buy it, the damage is done."

I couldn't stop a shiver from creeping up my spine. But then my rational side kicked in. Objects like this only have power over people who *let* them.

And yet...

"I'll take it," I said.

If nothing else, I'd find Geordi and give it to him, with his scarab and the coin, so he'd have *three* stones protecting him. Not that I'd let him out of my sight, ever again.

The vendor took my money and handed me a small paper bag, containing the now tissue-wrapped trinket. "*Merci beaucoup, mademoiselle.* May it bring you luck and fortune."

I noticed he omitted the qualifier "good" from either wish, but probably he was being economical with his speech, not cursing me for eternity. *That* happened the day I made my first deal with the Rousseaux, and I'd been sealing my own doomed fate ever since.

"Thanks. By the way—can you tell me what this is made from?"

I handed him the coin, and he examined it, before handing it back. "This is also onyx."

"Really? But it's not pure black."

"Onyx comes in many colors, some with lighter bands throughout. This one is niccolo onyx. It has a thin upper layer which, when carved, reveals the bluish colors you see here."

Huh. So maybe the *porc-épic* originally belonged to Nico. Or it was a coincidence that the stone's type bore his name, and the seller's superstitions were getting to me.

I thanked him, put the coin back into its box, and dropped it, the scarab, and the bag with the feather into my purse, then went to find Dito and Jun. They'd finished traversing their aisles without finding anything I needed to check out, so we headed down the elevator into the garage and aimed for the car.

Which is when an icy wall slammed down around us, like metal fire doors in a museum, and I turned to find that Dito'd gone white, muscles straining like he grappled with something heavy and unwieldy. I followed his gaze to a man in a tan suit walking toward us, who had an average build, short brown hair—and black voids where his irises should be.

He stopped a few yards away and said to Dito, "Relax, man. I'm on your side."

Dito said to me, "He's a Hell Demon. Not a very powerful one, but still."

The demon grinned. "Better to use a little power

wisely, than waste a lot unnecessarily." Dito kept his shield up, and the demon shrugged and faced me. "Marchosias sends his regards."

Adrenaline rocketed through me—first as fear, pounding my heart and slicking my palms. But then it coalesced into pure rage. "Where the *hell* is my nephew?"

"Safe. For now. Marchosias has not revealed himself. Your nephew sees only that he is with Paolo, a favorite cousin."

The relief at that almost eased my rage. One of my biggest fears was that Geordi knew he'd been taken by a Hell Demon. I'd pictured him alone and terrified, not knowing if we were coming for him. This wasn't much better, but at least he didn't comprehend the danger.

I said, "Who are you?"

"I am Chrétien Lacroix." At my obvious disbelief, he lifted a shoulder. "*Est-ce ma faute* that the only meat suit I could find on short notice had devoutly Christian parents? Didn't want to waste my powers"—he lifted an eyebrow at Dito—"creating a temporary body. And devout or not, this guy jumped at my offer, so here I am."

I'd calmed down somewhat. He didn't seem bent on harming us, and I'd been desperately awaiting a message or sign of what Marchosias wanted. This appeared to be it.

"What does Geordi think is happening?"

"Marchosias told him Hell Demons attacked Bala and Dito, and that he, as Paolo, saved Geordi. They are 'hiding' until it is 'safe' for you to retrieve him."

He made the air quotes, and I thought, even demons? Really?

"What does Marchosias want?"

"I think you know. Power. All he can get." I shuddered, and Chrétien bared his teeth, a demon rictus of a smile, enjoying my fear. "However, your nephew is raw—untrained. Marchosias needs powers that are more…refined, shall we say. Polished, through centuries of use. So…"

Nausea roiled my gut, and the two dead men behind me move subtly closer, backing me up. I was grateful not to be alone, but it didn't change the horror at what Chrétien hinted. Pretty much what we expected, but being forced to face it was nightmarish in the extreme.

I said flatly, "He's offering Geordi to the highest bidder—someone willing to give up a huge chunk of their current powers, to invest in Geordi's future potential."

Chrétien grinned again. "*Oui.* But there is no great bond between Marchosias and Satan. And Satan is stingy. He will want Geordi for himself, but he will not wish to give up too much power to get him. So Marchosias is…inclined…to accept other bids, if they are of greater value."

"Who?"

The question surprised him. Maybe he thought I'd just cower at the news, but I needed to know what we were up against. And I was damn tired of everyone dropping hints and smirking at me, instead of just getting to the point for once.

"Marchosias is exploring his options. But if Geordi's relatives were to make a solid offer, he would consider it." His glance flicked to Dito. "A *very* solid offer, mind you. Chat soon."

He walked away, and when he was out of sight, Dito's shield disappeared. "You okay?"

"Mostly. Let's get out of here."

****

Back at Lily's, I updated Torben, Ulrich and Liam on the gem show being a bust, and on Chrétien's message. Strangely, I felt mostly okay about it now. I'd been operating on an underlying current of terror, but getting even one small piece of information took the edge off. A good thing, because my minions hadn't made much progress on their end.

It was almost noon. What if we had no concrete leads on rocks or Rachel by the end of the day? I had to agree to Nico and Rina's demands no matter what. I'd just hoped we'd have *some* idea of how to proceed—or if we even could—before then.

Liam said, "Why don't you go lie down, or read or something?"

"I can't. I need to *do* something."

I considered cleaning, but my minions know I dislike clutter, and had adopted a "tidy as you go" MO, so the place didn't really need it.

At least, not the front portions.

I sighed and headed for Lily's room, pretending I'd just "look around." I told myself she'd died, and didn't need her stuff anymore, but a pernicious voice in my head whispered, *If Nick can come back, why not Lily?*

I would never do it—really—but… If souls could return from beyond the veil, why should it matter which veil? I'd assumed Michael could restore me to my body because I hadn't been gone long or moved on to the Afterlife. Now that I explored Nick's resurrection—however repugnant—it opened up a new set of questions, about what had happened to me, and *why*.

For instance, why did Lily and I go straight to the

landing pad, instead of Michael—or one of his sorters—finding us on Earth? Or why had Lily passed on without a fight? But that's probably a therapy issue, not a Resurrection one.

I gave myself a shake, deciding to tackle the closet first, since it mainly held fancy dresses and things she'd purchased after marrying Nick. To me, at least, they didn't represent the "real" Lily, and would be easier to sort and get rid of. I hoped.

I pulled back the bi-fold concertina doors, revealing an untidy jumble of dresses, shawls, pantsuits, and the like. On the shelf above the closet rod were boxes of shoes, stacked three high. At least she'd never added walk-in closets, or this would take days. I mounted a nearby step stool and grabbed a box on top that didn't appear integral to the structure. But as I tugged it forward, its neighbor slid out so fast, I had to duck as it *whooshed* past my head and thumped to the carpet. A few more items rained down in rapid succession, including a sharp-edged triangular cribbage board and half a dozen hat boxes.

A moment later, Dito poked his head in through the open doorway. "Everything okay?"

I hopped off the stool. "Yeah. Just finally clearing out some of Lily's stuff."

He nodded. "Company?"

Why not? Probably better not to tackle this alone. "Sure."

He came in, and I opened the box I'd grabbed, which held a pair of insanely high-heeled sandals with bright red soles. I tossed the box over by the door, then bent to retrieve the first fallen one. It *was* heavy, and when I lifted the lid, I saw why. Instead of shoes, it held a locked box made of iron. No key in sight, but I'm handy with a straight pin, so I grabbed a brooch off the dresser and a minute later, the padlock surrendered, and the lid swung open.

Dito examined the papers inside. "Shit. That's Rina's handwriting."

Now *that* was interesting. I picked up the first item, a letter dated a month before Nick and Lily's wedding and started reading.

Nicky—

I am so pleased that all is going according to plan. Davide is correct—her family goes way back. Not as far as ours, but acceptable. When he presented her, I had my doubts. Her ignorance of her lineage is so improbable, I thought she must be lying. But she really has no idea, which is infinitely better, because she'll have no reason to question us or make unrealistic demands.

And when she gives you a son, Nico will have to reinstate you. He can't disinherit you, once he knows your son has Michaud blood in him. I wish it could be otherwise, but it can't, and this is the best means to our end.

For now, destroy this note. It would be terrible if our plans were known before we're ready.

Your loving,

Mother

I dropped the letter back in the box. It implied that the Dioguardis—or at least, Rina and Nick—knew of mine and Lily's heritage and *chose her for it*. But—and this was the real hashtag-dumb-luck kicker—apparently Dito's earlier drunken ravings were based in reality after all: They'd chosen the wrong sister.

I choked down my hysteria, then gave up and hooted

with laughter, startling a glance from Dito, who'd nobly refrained from reading over my shoulder. I tried to explain, but I couldn't stop laughing at the terrible— *terrible*—and not at all funny—irony of it all.

My other minions tromped in, expressions wreathed in concern, which only made me laugh harder, clutching my aching sides. Tears streamed from my eyes, and I gasped in a breath.

"It's...nothing...fine...I'm *fine*. It's just—" I sat on the bed, scrubbing a hand over my face. I inhaled, then exhaled, and my cell buzzed with an unfamiliar number. I managed another restorative breath, before asking, "Anyone know which country code 90 is?"

"Turkey," Ulrich said promptly.

I shot up off the bed, shaking fingers barely hitting the button to accept the call. "Hello?"

"Hyacinth? Is Nadezhda. I haf news about your dead friend."

Chapter Eight

"Art is not what you see, but what you make others see."

~Edgar Degas, French Impressionist Artist (1834-1917)

I found Nico and Rina at the hospital with Bala—and Jason. Not surprising, though the knowledge stabbed me in my gut. But Jason and I weren't together, and likely never would be. The episode with Flore no doubt pushed him too far, and he and Bala obviously had a history together—*and* I was leaving him to go help Eric. So jealousy would be pointless. We are who we are.

Rina looked up avidly from her seat at Bala's bedside. I hadn't had time to read anything else in the iron box, but just that one letter put a whole new spin on Dioguardi dynamics. Clearly, there were secrets. And maybe less love lost between Nico and his son than I'd thought.

Nico himself rose from the window seat and stood, hands on hips, scowling. "Well? What's it going to be?"

So much for the pleasantries. I smiled a greeting at Bala, then peeked at Jason, sitting across the bed from Rina, expression unreadable, and the pang worsened. Even in the most dire circumstances, I'd felt some empathy from him. It hurt to know how far he'd shut me out—and that I'd forced him to do it.

I swallowed and faced Nico. Rina rose and joined him, presenting a united front, the happy couple, stronger together. But now I noticed she watched me with an anticipation her husband lacked. He was clearly pissed, whereas her face shone with a desperate hope.

"I'll do it," I said. "I know where Nick is, and I'm working on a plan to extract him. It's complicated, so you'll have to give me time, but finding Geordi can't wait. So the deal is, you get him back, I get Nick back, and when they're both, er, back, the arrangement starts. I'm part of Geordi's life—equal input—without worrying I'll wake up dead one day."

"Agreed," Rina said immediately.

Nico shot her a dirty look. But he only rolled his shoulders and cracked his neck. "Fine. But you'll update us regularly—no dicking around. If you think you can pretend to *try* to bring Nick back, you're wrong. We'll know you're faking it, and the deal will be off. Understood?"

No point in defending my professional honor— better to appease him and move on, so I nodded. "One more thing. *If* I get him back, he's going to, uh, need a place to stay."

Nico growled, "What are you talking about? He can stay with us. Just because your *whore* of a sister got the apartment doesn't mean he's homeless."

Typical. I ignored his nasty words, but Jason started up defensively. I made *sit down* motions at him and addressed Nico calmly. "Not that. He needs a body—*his* body. I assume you can get him dug up, and figure out an explanation for why—*how*—he's back?"

Nico's eyes bugged out. Guess he hadn't thought this through. But Rina interjected, "We'll take care of all that. We'll say he went away on a secret undercover mission, and now he's back, we can stop pretending he died. And of course, he shouldn't have a grave if he's alive, which is how we'll explain digging up the coffin."

Her husband regarded her like an alien who'd landed in our midst—like he'd just realized he had *no* idea who he'd married. She ignored him, focusing on me.

"We're already searching for Geordi. Of course we wouldn't wait. But Marchosias is too smart to damage anything this valuable. We'll find Geordi, and you'll bring Nick home, and if you deal fairly with us, we'll deal fairly with you. I swear it."

I almost believed her, if only because Nico was so clearly pissed she'd made the promise.

I said, "Speaking of Marchosias, one of his lackeys came to me this morning. He said Marchosias is willing to talk with you, but didn't give specifics. He said he'd be in touch."

Rina's eyes closed in obvious relief. "Thank you. That gives us a starting point." She cast an unreadable glance at her husband, then said to me, "As you know, we'll pay *any* price to get him back. Marchosias is walking a fine line. If he gives Geordi to anyone who is against—"

"*Rina,*" Nico said, but she continued undeterred.

"—Satan, Satan will unleash all the armies of Hell on him. But if he gives Geordi to someone Satan considers more…friendly…"

She trailed off, her meaning clear: Satan might leave Geordi alone if we returned him to the family fold—because the Dioguardis were pro Satan. Apparently even Rina, despite Jason's hints to the contrary. At least in regard to getting her grandson back.

Forget Marchosias. *I* walked a fine line. I'd already agreed to work with the Dioguardis, but now I might have to essentially *become* one, if I wanted Geordi in my life. Without stating it directly, Rina had reminded me again that they held all the cards, and as favorites of Satan, might be the one thin veil of protection, keeping Geordi from spending the rest of his life in Hell.

I swallowed my fear and loathing and nodded. "I understand."

"Good."

Jason rose and came around the bed. "Hyacinth— can we talk outside for a sec?"

"Sure," I said, trying to ignore my anticipation at the prospect of being alone with him. In a crowded hospital, but still—away from prying Dioguardi eyes, including Bala's.

"Look," I said once we were out in the hall, "I know you think this is a bad idea, and I'm a terrible person, but I *have* to get Geordi to safety, and, like Rina, I'll pay any price to do it."

He blew out a breath. "I know. I'm sorry. Flore made her choice, and if not you, she would've found someone else to do it. As for working with the Dioguardis—I've done stuff I'm not proud of, like spying on you, and…other things. And you managed to forgive me, so…"

I nearly staggered with the relief. But then my conscience twinged. "Before you make nice, you should know that Liam and I are driving to Marseille for a few days."

He stared at me blankly. "Now? In the middle of all this?"

I nodded, tamping down my anxiety yet again. Jason

was the last person I wanted to discuss this with, but I owed him the truth. "I have to go. Nadezhda thinks Eric never passed on to the Afterlife because he has unfinished business here, and reminding him of it will save him."

"Let me guess. You have no clue where to start, and you're going anyway."

I nodded miserably. "I'm sorry. I *have* to."

The muscle in his jaw ticked. "Do you have *anything* to go on?"

The advantage to one's minions being former techsperts for various Special Ops units is that they can track down almost any detail in the blink of an eye. "I have his home address, and what branch of the *Police Judiciaire* he worked out of. Not much, but it's a start."

He watched me for a long moment. "I'll go with you."

"You can't." He opened his mouth, and I touched his arm. "Bala needs you here."

Oh, God—this was so messed up. Touching him—even as I reminded him of another woman, before heading off to save another man—sent waves of longing and sadness and *need* through me. Similar emotions warred in his expression, and I thought, *At least I'm not alone in this.*

He took my hand, lacing our fingers together. "That's different. There's nothing…romantic…between me and Bala."

And yet there *was* something "romantic" between me and Eric, but it didn't change my feelings for Jason. Everything would be so much easier if it did. Plus, I didn't entirely believe him. He might think he spoke the truth, but I knew all about denying my feelings. Maybe with me gone, it would help us both figure things out.

"She still needs you, whatever your relationship is. Dito died—her best friend and partner. And she couldn't save him. That's got to hurt. She needs you now, more than ever."

He gazed down at me, eyes dark, for a long moment. Then he tugged me forward. I thought—hoped?—he'd kiss me, but instead he wrapped his arms around me, holding me close, his chin resting on the top of my head. "I hate it when you're right."

A laugh bubbled out of me. "It has to happen sometimes."

He leaned back, expression serious. "Hyacinth—I know you can't make a decision until Eric's condition improves. And I can be patient until then. After that..."

He shook his head helplessly, and I nodded. And then he did kiss me, slow and gentle at first, then deepening, running his hands over my back and sides, not *quite* getting to my breasts, but damn close. I couldn't help it—I leaned into him, running my own hands over his chest and up, cupping his face, kissing him harder, an unconscious moan mingling with his groan.

At last he broke away. "Sorry. I know I shouldn't keep doing that, and I should wait until you've decided, and...I just..."

I took a breath, trying to slow my pulse. "Thank you." He grinned, and I glared at him. "*Not* for the kiss. I mean—it was great—and, um—"

"Hyacinth. It's okay. We don't have to talk about it. Just know that, when you decide, there'll be a *lot* more of that."

Implying I'd choose him. But...what if he chose Bala?

And I hadn't even told him of Rina's letter. Maybe he knew all along that she and Nick pursued Lily on purpose. What if he'd even helped them? He might not be in the Dioguardi inner circle, but he'd have to maintain his cover, to hide his involvement with the Super Secret Sect working against them. So… Would that have made him fight to save Lily, or…not?

Messed up didn't begin to cover it.

****

The drive from Paris to Marseille takes seven hours without stops. With Liam being dead, and me on a mission, we kept potty breaks to a minimum, and arrived by late evening. I hadn't been home—whatever that meant these days—in over three months, but I'd been auto-paying my rent this whole time. What I hadn't done was replace the keys I lost on the day I died. Oops.

I'd also never canceled my lease on the Switzerland place, and since Nick had given Lily her apartment as a wedding present, once probate concluded, I would own it outright. I didn't need *three* residences, so probably I should ditch this place, too, and settle in Paris.

Or America, if that's where Geordi ended up, *when* we found him.

Shoving worry over him aside yet again, I parked half a block from my building and killed the engine. Liam had been silent during the drive. He didn't seem bothered by his deadness, but *I* felt guilty over it. Especially since we were here to, essentially, save his killer.

I unbuckled and got out, and Liam followed, minus the unbuckling, of course. He'd mastered dematerializing, so I didn't need to get his door, and we walked to the landlady's apartment on the ground floor.

It was almost ten, but her lights were on, so I knocked and waited for her to peer through the peephole, process her surprise at seeing me, and unlock the deadbolt.

"Hyacinth? Oh, thank Heaven—I thought you'd left for good! *Comment ça va?*"

Her effusiveness surprised me. Not that we disliked each other. I just never got that close to most people in my life, and I experienced a disconnect that she might have missed me.

She's not tall, but has what's called an "ample" figure. She wore a pink floral-patterned muumuu and pink feathered mules that showed off her hot pink toenails. Her hair looked glossier and darker than I remembered, pulled up in a loose knot, and though she's in her sixties, her skin looked great, too. I should be so lucky—assuming I make it that long, which is doubtful.

"Jeannette," I said as warmly as I could, eliciting a puzzled grunt from Liam, as I hadn't been "warm" to anyone in our entire acquaintance.

She couldn't hear him, of course, and only smiled back. "Come in! I imagine you're here for a key."

She moved to a narrow table near the door and pulled out a drawer, overflowing with keys, pens, papers, and other junk. Liam waited on the stoop, while I followed her inside.

"Yes, but how did you know?"

She rummaged in the drawer. "Well, after the break-ins, the locks had to be replaced."

"Break-ins? As in—plural?"

She glanced up, clearly confused. "I thought you knew. I forwarded the police reports to the postal box you gave as your new address. Did you not get them?"

Oops. My fear of the Dioguardis had been tempered

by my responsible nature, so I'd concocted a series of mail forwarding orders I hoped would at least marginally conceal my whereabouts. Guess I forgot to have my Swiss mail sent to Paris. The sad thing is, if I'd mentioned it to my minions, even in passing, it would've been quietly handled without me even knowing about it.

"Ah—here it is." Jeannette held up a shiny new key on a ring, attached to a paper tag that had "HF" printed on it in spidery handwriting. She passed it to me, continuing her narrative. "The first break-in happened right after you left, as near as I can tell. Late August, right? Then again in mid-September, and twice more last week."

Now that surprised me. I could understand the first two—most likely the Dioguardis, trying to get a bead on where I'd absconded with their High Prince. But why now, three months later, when I'd already resurfaced?

And if not the Dioguardis, then...who?

Through the open door, I saw Liam reach for his pocket before remembering he could no longer phone my other minions and ask them to investigate. He made a frustrated gesture, so I thanked Jeannette for the key and left, before she could ask nosy questions. Like, where had I been all this time that I hadn't even known my place was burgled? Which, as a professional burglar myself, is annoying.

"I don't like this," Liam said once we were alone.

"Me, neither."

When we got to the second floor, everything looked both exactly the same, and wildly different. The building is a six-story rectangle, four apartments per floor, with a breezeway down the middle, and my door's the first on the left. It used to be the same orange-painted wood as my neighbors', but apparently the whole thing had to be replaced, because now it was unpainted steel.

Speaking of my neighbors, the lady in the apartment across from mine must also be away. The flowerpots on her stoop were dry, the wilted chrysanthemums a sad gray-green in the weak light from the breezeway's overhead fluorescent bulbs. I should probably water them for her, though Jeannette usually does that. But maybe she forgot?

I inserted my new key into the new lock on my new door. It worked much better than the ancient deadbolt I'd had before, and the door swung inward on oil-silenced hinges.

I experienced yet another déjà vu moment: This felt like when I came home dead the first time, to find my door open and Jason lurking inside. Except at the time, I'd thought him the demons, or the Dioguardis—which he actually *was*—on both counts—but whatever.

Liam followed me in, glancing around curiously as I switched on the light. I dropped my bag on the floor, then surveyed the place myself. It'd only been a few months, but it was totally bizarre to be back—to see the sock I'd dropped near the couch while packing, or the cupboard doors open in the kitchen, just as I'd left them while hunting for food to take on my journey to Turkey with Jason and Geordi.

Liam frowned. "I thought your landlady said there were multiple break-ins."

"Yeah. So what?"

"If that's the case, shouldn't your place be ransacked? At least a little?"

He had a point. The place was messy, because that's how I'd left it. Which just goes to show my abnormal state of mind at the time. But if someone broke in, they had to be searching for something, or else…why? Yet everything appeared to be as I'd left it: no knifed cushions, emptied drawers, or removed baseboards. The painting hung undisturbed above the couch, covering my wall safe, and when I checked inside, everything seemed untouched.

"Maybe they cleaned up after?"

Liam grunted. "If the door's so busted that the break-ins are obvious, why bother? And if the door wasn't busted, then how did your landlady know anyone broke in? It makes no sense."

Again, all good points, but at the moment, I couldn't think straight. "Let's sleep on it. We have a lot to do tomorrow, and sadly, this is low priority right now."

"Fine," he said, which I knew meant he'd keep mulling it over, while I wasted time asleep, but hey—he'd volunteered to be a minion, so I should let him do his thing.

I opened the futon for him and retreated to my tiny bedroom. Another surreal moment, sleeping in my own bed for the first time since having been, quite literally, transformed into a different person.

I wondered what Eric would have thought of me, if we'd met before all this. Assuming we hadn't. I've been hassled by the cops now and then, thanks to my questionable business dealings. But it's unlikely Eric picked up any cases having to do with me.

Still—an odd thought, made even more so because Liam and I would be invading Eric's former life tomorrow. What would happen when our worlds collided? I probably didn't want to know, but as with most things these days, I had no choice.

I rolled onto my side and prayed for sleep, though I doubted I'd get my wish.

Chapter Nine

*"A man's dying is more the survivors' affair than
his own."*
~Thomas Mann, German Novelist
(1875-1955)

My phone rang at an ungodly hour the next day. I'm a morning person, and it wasn't *that* early—almost eight—but when I'd finally drifted off, I'd slept deeply, making me disoriented. Plus, waking up in my own bed made the last few months feel like a dream.

But when I picked up my phone, I saw Yvo's number on the screen. Nope. Not a dream—a waking nightmare.

Yvo is a twenty-something German guy who, like my other minions, worked for the Burkes. He switched sides right away, but when I left for Paris, he stayed behind to maintain operations with Sabine Vezinet. She's extremely capable, and could have done it on her own, but she's dead, so Yvo does the "living" stuff, like making phone calls, while she directs from behind the scenes. They've been working to determine who lived, died, or got obliterated at the Demon-Dead battle at the cave. I really needed a catchier name for it. Now that I'd been in two Supernatural battles—the one on Barnacken, and this one—I needed a way to distinguish them. They'd never show up in history books, so it's really just for me, but still.

Anyway. Sabine worked intelligence for the *Résistance Belgique* during World War II, and Yvo's a general can-do guy, so they're an excellent team. Especially when it comes to tracking escapees from Hell. I swiped to answer the call, and Yvo greeted me cheerfully.

"Goot morning, Frau Finch. How *ist* everyzink goink in Paris?"

Yvo has a thick German accent and insists on "showing respect" by not using my first name, so he's a bit old-fashioned. Which might be another reason he works well with Sabine. Although he does use her first name—interesting to note, if-slash-when I had time to think about it. Which I never did.

"Hi, Yvo. I'm actually down south, in Marseille. What's up on your end?"

"Vell, ve haf news. Not wery goot news, unfortunately. It *ist* about Rachel."

I sat up. "What?"

"Vell…ve zink she escaped Germany altogezer."

Crap. But not exactly unexpected. After her death, she'd appropriated one of *her* minions, Sieg, as a "safe room." But then Eric also "borrowed" his corpse, not realizing she was in residence, and later, they were both ejected by a *third* spirit trying to move in. I'd hoped any damage she sustained in the process had impeded her ability to travel far, but apparently not.

"Where do you think she went?"

Yvo hesitated. Most likely he—or rather, Sabine—had a good idea of her whereabouts. So his unwillingness to state it must be the "not wery goot" part of the news.

"Just tell me. It's better I know."

"Of course. Sabine's scouts tracked her to ze border of France, but zen...ve lost her."

"What does that mean?"

He sighed. "She vas in anozer person. Ze scouts found ze corpse inside ze northeast border of France, but no Rachel. She must have ditched zat person and found anozer, or else a vay to travel on her own. Giffen ze direction she vas headed, she may haf gone to Calais, and from zere, to Dover. She could be anyvhere by now."

He clearly thought he'd failed me, which is the most challenging aspect to having minions. At least when I screw up on my own, I don't have to make anyone else feel better about it.

"It's fine. I figured she'd turn up somewhere. And on the plus side, if she went to England, it likely means she's not after Geordi. I just wish we knew her actual location. In fact, now we *need* to know."

I told him of the plan to offer Rachel to Satan as a bargaining chip. If it shocked or repulsed him, he didn't let on. Instead, the news gave him renewed purpose.

"I vill tell Sabine, and ve vill find her for you. And Geordi—I svear it."

Which reminded me of Chrétien's message, and Rina's promise-slash-threat, regarding the Dioguardis' connections to Satan. "Thanks—I know you're working on it. The Dioguardis have started their own investigation. If there's *any* way we can find him first..."

If I reneged on our deal, I'd live the rest of my life with a giant target on my back. But if it saved Geordi from being under their thumb—and by extension, Satan's—I had to try.

Yvo said, "Ve vill double our efforts."

"Thanks," I said again, and we hung up.

I dragged myself out of bed and into the bathroom for a quick tooth-brushing and ponytail touch up. Then I dressed and moved to the front of the apartment.

In the living room, Liam was already up. Probably he'd never slept—a ghost thing I wished I could manage. I'd get much more done, not spending a quarter of my life unconscious. It should be a third, but I'd given up on that long ago.

In the kitchen, I discovered coffee in the cupboard, and the drip machine appeared functional. I added grounds to a fresh filter, saying to Liam, "I'd offer you some, but…"

He gave an ironic smile. "I keep forgetting I'm dead. I don't mind—mostly—but it's frustrating when I go to do something that used to be automatic, and now I can't. And it's weird, because I still crave coffee, even though I'm not thirsty, or hungry, or anything else."

"Michael told me once that when we pass on to the Afterlife, all our 'earthly wants' vanish. But when a soul stays here, that doesn't always happen. Or it takes more time, maybe? I'm not really sure, and what happened to me isn't the same anyway."

He shrugged. "Guess I'll find out, one way or another. For now, I can live—er, exist—vicariously, by watching you drink yours."

I lifted my mug in salute, then took a swig before updating him on Yvo's report, though he'd gleaned most of it from hearing my side of the conversation. My apartment is very small, and the walls are far from soundproof, even the one separating me from the neighboring unit.

"Good," he said. "Sabine has a lot of scouts—they should come up with something. Far more than Torben and Ulrich could, even with help from Jun."

"That was my thought."

Just talking with Yvo, and being reminded of Sabine and her capable team, gave me the first real hope I'd had in the week since Geordi'd been taken. Like maybe I *could* find Rachel, and get Geordi back, and make it work with the Dioguardis.

Meanwhile, I hadn't come to Marseille to sit around drinking coffee. I stood, and Liam recognized my intent to act.

"What about breakfast? You need food—meat specifically, and—"

"I know, but there's nothing to eat here. I'm afraid to open the fridge—I doubt Jeannette emptied it after the break-ins." Which we also needed to investigate, but not now. "There's an *épicerie* around the corner. I'll get something there. And another coffee, just for you."

He grinned, and we headed out, locking the door behind us.

****

Marseille in the morning is a bustling place, even in late fall. I'd lost track of time, but my phone said we'd made it to November twenty-third. Being on the Mediterranean, it never gets truly cold here, but today it rained, and the temp had dropped into the fifties. At least I'd left all my cool weather wear in my closet here, when I ran off to Turkey in August. And like all souls I knew, Liam wasn't affected by the weather. Even the rain just passed through him, unnoticed.

Eric had resided in the Quartier Malpassé near central Marseille, about twenty minutes from my place, which is in the Quartier Saint Louis to the north. Torben and Ulrich couldn't determine who lived there now, as the lease still bore his name, but the only other info they'd uncovered was his place of employment. Having been investigated by various police departments around town, I didn't like the idea of walking right into headquarters, so we'd decided to start with his personal life.

Malpassé itself didn't fit my image of Eric. The area's been the site of "urban redevelopment," but not everyone is happy about the older buildings being torn down and replaced with higher rent options, and there have been protests and other bureaucratic altercations. By contrast, Eric presents himself as "put together": well-dressed and composed, for lack of a better description. Malpassé just seemed too chaotic.

But I trusted my minions, so we parked and headed up the elevator to the ninth floor. Inside, the building appeared well-kept, with clean, light-colored carpeting in the halls, and no paint peeling from the walls. There were even potted plants near the elevators and by some of the apartments.

Eric's door was flanked by two such offerings, a prayer plant on the left and a snake plant on the right, making me wonder if the tenants chose their own, or the building manager did it. I'd never pictured Eric as a "plant person," but then, I really knew very little about him.

Now it came down to it, I hesitated to knock. I'm not a fan of worm cans, in case you haven't noticed. And this one could be huge. Did I really want to pry it open?

Liam sensed my dilemma. "The woman helping him—Nadezhda?—said you have to figure out what his unfinished business is, right?"

I nodded. "That's the problem. What if it's

something terrible?"

Eric has always been clear that, while he *was* a decorated detective, he'd carved his own path to get there. Including deciding for himself what "justice" meant, and how to execute it.

Liam lifted a shoulder. "I know you'd rather not know. But you want to help him, so…"

I blew out a breath. "You're almost as annoying as Jason sometimes." I lifted the brass knocker and rapped smartly twice, before stepping back to wait.

At first I thought no one was home, and experienced a brief relief that I could hide from the truth, whatever it was, a little longer. But then a muffled voice came from within, a man calling out, *"Un instant, s'il vous plaît."*

A couple of *"instants"* later and someone fumbled the lock, before the door swung wide and my jaw dropped to my chest.

Before us stood a near carbon-copy of Eric himself. A decade or so younger, but even so—the resemblance was uncanny. I knew he had an older sister, but he'd never mentioned a brother. Eric is in his late thirties, and this guy couldn't be more than mid-twenties at most, barefoot and dressed in sweatpants and a faded merch shirt for a band I didn't recognize. He'd painted his toenails purple, and tattoos snaked up his arms and peeped from his neckline. He had several piercings, including in his nose and lower lip, and the plugs in his ears looked painfully large.

But even with the total absence of Eric's well-dressed neatness, he had to be a relative, and a close one at that. Even Liam, who'd only seen Eric's ghost once, briefly, in a very dark cave, did a double-take. Of course, the guy couldn't see Liam. But he *could* see me staring, and frowned.

"*Puis-je vous aider? Qu'est-ce que vous voulez?*"

I snapped my jaw shut and regrouped. "Uh, I'm looking for Eric Guilliot. Does he live here? I'm a, uh, friend of his."

I hadn't planned this out, expecting a random stranger to be living here, or maybe Eric's ex—current?—wife. A close relative threw me for a loop, and I couldn't decide what to reveal.

Unfortunately, the guy picked up on my hedging and his scowl deepened. "You must not be a good friend. He died a couple months ago."

He started to shut the door, but I reached out a hand. "Wait, you're right—he died—that's why I'm here. I really do know—*knew* him. I just have a few questions. Please, can you help me?"

"Why should I? He never helped me when he was alive—not once. The *only* good thing he ever did was leaving me this apartment."

Well, if I needed Eric's unfinished business, it seemed I'd found some.

"I'm sorry," I said, noting he hadn't actually shut us—me—out yet, so he must be a *little* curious, despite the outward scorn. "Might I come in? Just for a minute?"

He glanced at the smart watch on his wrist. "Sure. Why the hell not? But I'm finishing my yoga before I go to work, so you'll have to be fast."

He retreated, and we followed him into a setup not much bigger than mine, but definitely higher class. The entry hall opened to a living area with floor to ceiling windows giving expansive views of Marseille spread out below. A smaller hall to the left likely led to the bedroom and bathroom, while a galley-style kitchenette lay to the right, outfitted with high-end stainless steel appliances and glass-paneled cupboards. The tasteful leather furniture in the main room fit Eric's style, but items obviously belonging to the new resident were strewn everywhere, including bongs and other drug paraphernalia, fast food wrappers, and clothes. On the floor lay a tie-dye-patterned yoga mat, on which our host now performed a credible downward dog.

I assumed his quasi-invitation extended to sitting, so I pushed some of the detritus off the sofa and made myself comfortable. Meanwhile, Liam snooped around, checking out the bookshelves and such, and I thought, there are advantages to having a dead minion in tow. In fact, it's exactly what Eric used to do for me.

Once settled, I said, "Do you mind if I ask who you are? You look a lot like Eric. Are you his younger brother?"

He made a scoffing sound. *"Non. J'suis son fils."*

Luckily, he was head down in the yoga pose, and so missed the utter shock that must have showed on my face.

Liam whistled. "Shit. Weren't expecting that, were you?"

Even more fortunately, the guy couldn't hear Liam, but I still struggled to process. "His...*son?*"

Eric Junior broke the pose, flipping over and sitting on the mat, elbows on his knees. In the light from the windows, I saw his eyes were the exact shade of jade-grey as Eric's, his golden hair limned by a ray of sun, in the same way I'd seen Eric's hair lit, many times.

"Ouais. His son. *Now* I believe you knew him, or you wouldn't have been so shocked. Or rather, you would have pretended better that you *weren't* shocked."

"I don't understand..."

"He wasn't exactly proud of me. No one knows I exist, because that's how he wanted it. If I'd told you, and you'd said, 'oh sure, now I remember,' I'd know you were lying, because he never talked about me. To *anyone*."

His tone was thick with resentment—but also hurt. I racked my brain, trying to come up with anything Eric might have said, to hint he had a son.

An adult son.

"Do you mind if I ask how old you are?"

His lips twisted ironically, another near replica of Eric's—his *father's*—expressions. "*Encore une fois*— this just proves that you knew him. Because yes, I am too old to be the son of a man Eric's age. Unless he fathered me in his teens, which is precisely the case. He was sixteen when he knocked up my mother."

The resentment was back, the "knocked up" illustrating who he blamed for *that* event. But if Eric had gotten anyone pregnant, at any age, I couldn't imagine him not stepping up and taking responsibility for the child, and most likely the mother, too.

I wouldn't get anywhere with that line of reasoning, though, so I said, "I'm Hyacinth Finch. What's your name?"

He hesitated, mistrust warring with some other unnamed emotions in his eyes, but at last he relented. "Stefan—Guilliot, but I don't use it. My mother named me. She should have put her surname on the birth certificate, but she wanted his paternity on record, so..."

He trailed off, and I detected a vulnerability he tried to hide. He might be angry as hell at Eric— understandable, if Eric *had* abandoned him—but I'd lay odds the anger stemmed from wanting a relationship with his father, however messy and complicated it might be.

Except...Stefan thought he'd missed his chance. I knew better—or at least I *hoped* better—but I couldn't broach *that* subject yet, either.

Stefan rose and folded the yoga mat, then tucked it away in the hall closet, an oddly tidy gesture in a decidedly untidy room. "I have to change and get to work."

I stood also, thinking fast. He hadn't thrown me out, and he'd been mostly willing to talk. I took a chance. "Can I come back later? Or meet you after work somewhere? I'd really like to ask you a few more questions. Your father is—was—very important to me."

He swallowed, his Adam's apple bobbing, before he slowly nodded consent. "Give me your number. I'll text you when I get off."

.

Chapter Ten

"Your future needs you. Your past doesn't."
~Anonymous

After we left the apartment, I decided to face Eric's work life after all, since Stefan's shift wouldn't end until mid-afternoon. He was a barista at a coffee shop in Les Docks Village, a shopping area surprisingly close to the warehouse where I store miscellaneous things that won't fit in my shop. Including Vadim's crates, which started this whole mess.

Eric operated under the auspices of *la Direction Centrale de la Police Judiciaire,* which handles anything in France related to "financial misconduct," aka organized crime. Since his mission in life was to take down the Dioguardi Mafia specifically, and anyone like them more generally, this made sense. Of course, he worked out of a regional office here in Marseille, in the First Arrondissement, a fifteen-minute drive southwest from his—now Stefan's—apartment, with Stefan's café about the same distance away, but to the north.

In fact, only another ten minutes separated either place from my warehouse. Odd, when I put it all together. Who knows how long Stefan had been a barista, but Eric started his career as a cop decades ago. And I've been in Marseille awhile—far longer than anywhere else. It's just bizarre to think we all might have crossed paths—maybe more than once.

And…did Eric ever drop in for a coffee at Stefan's café? If so, did he acknowledge his lookalike son? Try as I might, I couldn't picture Eric ditching *any* of his responsibilities, but especially not this one. And I had *no* doubts about Stefan's paternity. Outside of the tats, piercings, and age difference, he couldn't resemble his father more if they were identical twins instead.

So why had Eric abandoned him? And *was* this the unfinished business Eric needed to deal with? It seemed likely, but in the meantime, I needed to complete the picture, so I parked in a garage near his office, and Liam followed me out to the street. The rain had stopped, and the sun peeked out from the ominous clouds, but not enough to banish the dreariness of the day. Or maybe it was only my mood after meeting Stefan, further dragged down by the prospect of what we might find in the building before us.

"You sure about this?" Liam asked.

Having been a Special Ops minion for the Burkes, he understood my hesitancy to voluntarily enter any place related to law enforcement. At least this branch's focus on mob crimes made it unlikely anyone here had ever investigated me. But still.

"Not really, but let's get it over with."

We entered the lobby, found an elevator, and headed up to Eric's department. When the doors opened and we stepped out, I experienced another déjà vu moment, because on the wall across from us hung a life-size photograph of Eric himself, in full dress uniform, including the peaked cap, gold badge, and various arm patches and medals. His piercing green eyes stared directly at me, a slight ironic twist to his lips, and my heart clutched.

I *had* to save him, whatever it took.

I stepped closer to read the brass plaque below the picture, which had "Gone Too Soon" etched on it, followed by his full name: Eric Stefan Guilliot. I wondered how Stefan felt about that? Or maybe he didn't know. But his mother, at least, had been really on the nose about it. In fact, it surprised me she hadn't named him Eric Junior after all.

The last line of the plaque gave his birth and death dates. Doing the math, if he hadn't died, he would have just turned thirty-nine in October. Also, he's a Scorpio, if that means anything to you.

A reception area lay to our left, and I approached the tall counter. I'd come up with what I deemed a reasonable opening gambit, so I smiled at the woman seated behind the desk at an older model computer. She appeared to be somewhere around forty, with honey blonde hair and hazel eyes, dressed in what must be her daily uniform: dark blue polyester shirt and pants, wide duty belt, serviceable shoes, and no hat. I couldn't discern her rank, but she was clearly a police officer, not a civilian, and I stifled my nerves.

"You got this," Liam said loudly, making me jump, and I made shushing motions behind my back.

I said to the woman, "*Bonjour, madame.* I need copies of the police reports filed on some recent break-ins at my apartment."

She looked puzzled. "*Je ne comprends pas.* We do not handle petty crimes here."

"It's a long shot, but I think the break-ins are mob related. I've been out of town, and my landlady just told me about them. I was in the neighborhood, so I thought

I'd at least try."

I gave her my most winsome Innocent Upstanding Citizen smile, and tried to wipe my mind of any lurking criminal thoughts or urges. She gave me the once over, then pulled her keyboard closer. Guess Jason's not the only one who can charm his way in when needed.

"Ah—I see. Name?"

"Finch. Or maybe Lavigne—that's my landlady. Jeannette Lavigne."

She clicked noisily on her keyboard, then waited for her search to process. She skimmed the records returned, then faced me. "I'm sorry. There's nothing under either of those names."

Now it was my turn for puzzlement. "Are you sure? She told me about them last night—four in all, the first two in August or September, the most recent ones last week."

"I can try to search by date range instead. It's possible the names were misspelled or something." More clicking, and then a few moments later, she shook her head. "Address?" I gave it to her, and she repeated the process. "There's nothing here."

"Oh well—I'll try somewhere else."

"Actually, the databases are linked. Wherever a report is filed, it should show up here."

"Really? That's...odd."

She lifted a shoulder in the general French gesture for *I don't know anything about it, and it's not my job or my problem, so go ask someone else.*

"Very odd," Liam said behind me, at full volume, making me jump again, and the woman shot me a confused look. At least Eric murmured his comments. If Liam kept startling me like this, it could be an issue.

This was supposed to be a quick in, to get her talking, so I could casually ask about Eric. But it had fast become another item on my *Figure Out What the Hell Is Happening* list.

I tried again. "I'm at a loss. My landlady said she forwarded the reports to my new address, but I never got them. And now you're saying they were never filed?"

"That is correct—no report exists. If you'd like to file a new report now, I can see if someone is available to help you. Or you can do it at your local precinct."

I can take a hint, so I said, "Thanks. I'll do that later. But before I go—I couldn't help noticing the portrait across from the elevators. Eric Guilliot, I think it said?"

Her expression, open and curious a moment ago, suddenly shuttered. "What about him?"

Her tone had also cooled, and all sorts of radar signals started crackling—or whatever radar does—around me. "Uh, nothing. He's just so young. What happened to him?"

"Life. That's what happened."

"Did he die in the line of duty?"

She compressed her lips at the portrait, just visible around the corner by the elevators, and her eyes glinted with malice. "No. He got robbed. They shot him, then stole his car. The department just put that up because it's what they do—honor the fallen, even when it's their own fault they died."

This made no sense, since Eric really had died on the job—maybe not technically *on* duty at the time, but he'd been investigating radio chatter about the Dioguardis being nearby, and got caught in their gun battle. But even if she thought herself correct, her reaction seemed harsh.

"I don't understand. How is being carjacked his fault?"

"Because the only reason he was in that neighborhood is that he was a cheap bastard, who wouldn't pay for his own son to get a better apartment."

I stared at her. "You know about Stefan?"

She sat up abruptly, eyes narrowed, expression furious. "*Mais bien sûr que je le connais*—I'm his mother. How the fuck do *you* know about him?"

****

When we were back outside, Liam said, "You okay?"

I nodded, though I'm not even sure how we escaped. I have vague memories of hemming and hawing, and eventually admitting I knew Eric, and that I'd met her son. This did not improve her opinion of me, but being at work, she refrained from cussing me out and instead suggested—*not* politely—that I should leave, immediately. Which we did.

"That's fucked up," Liam said. "He has a kid with her, abandons them, then winds up working with her—and he *still* doesn't acknowledge his son?"

I shook my head. "Something's off, here. That's not the Eric I know, and I'm betting she's the one who requested the transfer to his department. She clearly wanted to rub his face in it. And besides, Eric couldn't have completely abandoned Stefan, if what she says is true, and he came to Stefan's neighborhood the night he died."

Unless he *hadn't* known. Had he been so ignorant of Stefan's whereabouts that he only went there that night in pursuit of the Dioguardis? Or had he been driving *to* Stefan's, when he heard the Dioguardis were nearby?

With Stefan's mother—I'd finally peeked at her name tag, which read Elaine Archambault—working in the same building as Eric, surely she would have dropped some broad hints, if not direct orders, telling him to visit their son, and adding the particulars for good measure. So he had to know, and most likely had been en route when the shooting happened.

This made me feel somewhat better. At least if he'd *tried* to connect with Stefan, however late in life, it was better than believing him so callous, he'd shut out his own offspring.

Talk about unfinished business.

I took out my cell phone and found Nadezhda's number, pressing the button to connect the call. Turkey is two hours ahead of Marseille, making it early afternoon there. I didn't know her habits, but I pictured her as a night owl. Even so, she should be up by now at least.

She answered on the third ring. "Hyacinth. Is good you call. You haf news? He not well—we must find way to help him."

It still felt surreal, chatting with her over modern technology. When we first met, I thought her one of the Dead, largely because she lives *with* them in a necropolis, or City of the Dead, at the ruins of Hierapolis in central Turkey. I guess all the ancient crypts and marble-columned structures, combined with the hardened-limestone natural-wonder "waterfalls" cascading down the nearby cliffs, just didn't scream "smartphone user" to me.

"He definitely has unfinished business," I said. "But what am I supposed to do about it?"

"What is it?"

I told her, and she cackled.

"*Da*—that would do it. Okay. Here is plan. You bring Stefan here, to his father. I make so Stefan see Dead—see him. He see Stefan. Reminds him why he want to stay, so—he stay."

I pulled the phone away and squinted at it, before placing it next to my ear again. "Say what now? I can't just go to Stefan and say, 'Hey, I just met you, but let's go to Turkey. Remember your dead father, who you hate? His ghost is there and would really like to chat.' "

"You will think of something. If not, he no make it."

"But…"

"He stay here, not for you. Stay *before* he meet you. So, he haf business here. If he think he no haf business— that too late, or hopeless—maybe he give up. Not much time. You figure it out, maybe we safe him. You *no* figure it out, and…"

I could actually feel her shrug across the line, so I said, "Okay, I'll try."

"Good. He good man. When he here before, the Dead share energy with him. As much as can. But not enough. He Full Dead, but he no full strength."

"What are you saying?"

"Souls must bank energy—each has finite amount. When Eric move into Sieg, he no have enough energy stored. He weak. Is easier for Sieg to absorb him. When he ejected, leave more energy behind. Is not much left. Dead cannot share more energy—need for themselves."

I swallowed. "If Stefan convinces him to stay, will he have enough energy to survive?"

"Perhaps."

"There must be *some* way for a soul to restore a depleted supply."

"*Da.* If willing to exterminate another soul, can take their energy. But must *completely* destroy other soul, so energy is loose. Then, can collect for self. What you think—Eric will want to do that?"

I swallowed again. "No." At least, I hoped not. "So what do we do?"

"Hope he has enough."

We hung up, and I saw I had a text from Torben to call him. He picked up right away.

"Nothing major. Just letting you know the Dioguardis are holding up their end of the deal. They designated one of their lackeys as a point person. Name's Olivia. She called this morning to let us know Nico and Rina are throwing everything they've got into finding Geordi."

"Which means what, exactly?"

"Everyone—*all* their soldiers—have dropped what they're doing to work on this."

My heart pounded, but for once, with *good* adrenaline pouring through me. I knew the Dioguardis would do anything to get him back. But the thought of hundreds, maybe thousands, of Mafia—*demon* soldiers—combing the planet for Geordi, was a balm to my soul. And their army worked *with* me for a change, rather than against.

I thanked Torben and hung up.

"That's good news," Liam said when I updated him. "Where to now?"

We had no other leads on Eric's life, and it seemed we'd found what we needed, if not how to resolve it. Plus, it'd been months since I left here.

"I need to check on my shop and the warehouse. This whole break-in business is concerning. If there even *were* break-ins."

Which would be weirder? That my apartment had been broken into multiple times, and all the police reports were lost? Or that it hadn't, and Jeannette lied about it?

Either way, I should check my other regular haunts, just in case, and thankfully, Liam didn't object to tagging along. When alive, he'd appointed himself my bodyguard, but now he couldn't protect me, except from other dead folk. Not that I needed protection, but it's nice he wanted to help. Plus, he made a decent sounding board. Not as good as Jason or Eric at challenging my thinking, but better than having to hash it out on my own.

We went to the warehouse first, and I unlocked and opened the roll door. Another weird moment, because the last time I did this was on the day I found the first rock. And yet, just like my apartment, all here appeared as I'd left it, including Vadim's three large shipping crates, still in the center of the space, their packing straw and wrapping cloths strewn everywhere.

I climbed onto a step ladder and peeked over the side of one of them, and Liam said, "I can pass through, and check if you missed anything."

"Thanks. That would be very helpful."

He searched each crate, but found nothing of interest, and everything else seemed in order, so I pulled the door down, locked it, and we drove to my shop. The mail, which I hadn't bothered to forward from here, had piled up below the slot in the door, but it was all junk, so I dropped it in the recycle bin, then peered around. I'd raised the shades and switched on the light, but the place felt dark and unused. Familiar, but...rusty. Like I'd woken it unexpectedly from a nap. Meaning no one else had been here recently, either.

I ran upstairs to check my office, while Liam examined the stock I had on display. The produce boxes I'd brought from the warehouse remained pushed against the walls, and I heard him using his ghost energy to poke around inside.

Up here also was undisturbed. None of it made sense. If anyone broke into my apartment—multiple times—then surely they also knew about my shop and the warehouse. Yet now it appeared none of them were breached.

I trotted back down the stairs in time to hear Liam grunt in surprise.

"What?" I asked, coming to stand by him at the register.

He gestured at a collection of books I had on a high shelf behind the counter. "Nothing. It's just—see that book there—the one with the funny symbol on it?"

He indicated an old leather-bound volume someone brought in years ago. I don't sell many books, but if I find one that might be valuable, I hang onto it, in case someone wants to buy it after all. Most of these just sit on the shelf, gathering dust. This one, however, I'd displayed in a stand, to show off its eye-catching cover— the "funny symbol" Liam had noted, a chain encircling a cypress branch and a crown, all etched into the leather and painted a still-vibrant red.

"What of it? It's a family crest. The book itself doesn't have anything interesting in it. It's literally the history of a land tract. Pretty boring, unless you're into that kind of thing."

"Do you know which family?"

"Yes—it's the Buonfiglios. They're rivals of the

Dioguardis. Mainly in Italy and farther south. Not as many in France, mostly because the Dioguardis kill them to keep them out."

In fact, this was the main reason I'd kept the thing in the first place. I found it amusing to put a book right over my head that basically said *screw you* to any Dioguardis who happened to visit my shop. Which, thankfully, weren't many.

Liam blew out a ghost breath. "Here's the thing. Did you notice the tattoos on Stefan's arms?"

I got a bad feeling in my gut. "Yes…but I didn't catch the details."

"He had a cypress on his right arm, and a crown and chain on his left. And he had a framed print on a shelf, of the exact same symbol as that book there."

Merde.

Chapter Eleven

"Keep your friends close, and your enemies closer."
~Sun Tzu, Chinese General & Military Strategist
(544-496 BC)

The café Stefan worked at hadn't been open long, but I'd been there a few times due to its proximity to my warehouse, and to the shops where I bought my daily food supplies. I don't recall seeing him, but I'm not that observant most of the time, so who knows? If I *was* more observant, I might have noticed the design of his tats right away, and put two and two together.

"So basically," Liam said as we walked through Les Docks toward the café, "Stefan is a mob member. Moreover, he's a rival of the group that murdered his aunt, Eric's sister, and Eric himself. And...Eric devoted his life to eradicating *all* organized crime, for obvious reasons."

I sighed. "Yes. That's it in a nutshell."

"What I don't get is why Eric didn't raise Stefan to be *against* the Mafia. Maybe if he'd been present in Stefan's life, his son would be a cop now instead."

I'd wondered that, too, until I did some more mental math. "Stefan's birth happened a year after Eric's sister died. I doubt he was thinking clearly then—sixteen, and just witnessed his sister's rape and murder? That'd do a number on anyone, let alone a kid. I'm guessing the

Buonfiglios approached him, thinking he'd join their cause to exact revenge, and that's when he met Elaine."

After leaving my shop, we'd stopped at La Bibliothèque de l'Alcazar, using one of the library's computers to access public records from twenty-two years ago. I'd found Stefan's original birth certificate, handily scanned and ready for download, from which I learned that Archambault must be Elaine's new married name, as her surname back then was Buonfiglio.

"My best guess," I continued, as we wove through the pedestrians crowding the walkway, doing their holiday shopping or meeting up with friends, "is that, initially, Eric considered their offer. Maybe they threw Elaine at him, or maybe not. Either way, at some point his moral compass took over and he realized he wanted a different kind of revenge. I'm not sure how the timing fits around the pregnancy, or if the Buonfiglios tried to force him to marry Elaine. But I bet his lack of involvement in Stefan's life wasn't entirely by choice."

"Do you think Stefan knows any of this?"

"Let's find out."

We'd arrived at the café, and I pushed through the door into the crowded shop. I spotted Stefan seated in a back corner, head down, writing in a leather journal. He was left-handed, so that's one thing different from his father. That and the tats and mob affiliation, but what the hey.

He'd exchanged his yoga wear for jeans and a plain black t-shirt, and as we got closer, I saw the tattoo designs were large and obvious, covering his forearms and up past his elbows. The chain and crown were gold and red, and the cypress branch resembled veins snaking around his arm. In my defense, I probably didn't register the significance because the objects were on opposite arms, instead of one unified crest. Still—hard to miss.

Stefan saw me and closed the journal, tucking it and his pen into a messenger bag slung over the back of his chair. Unfortunately, he'd chosen a two-top. Inconvenient for Liam and me, but reasonable for him, as he had no idea my invisible third wheel might like a seat.

Liam only said—loudly, but I expected it by now— "I'll look around. Take your time."

I gave him a surreptitious nod, which I hoped Stefan would take as a greeting instead, and sat in the vacant chair. "Thanks for meeting me. How was work?"

He lifted a shoulder, the gesture eerily reminiscent of both his parents. "Busy. Do you want anything? I can use my discount."

"I'm okay, but thanks." I studied him a moment, trying to decide what, if anything, I should reveal. Finally I said, "Were you born into mob life, or did you join more recently?"

His eyes widened. And then he laughed. "Both. As I'm sure you figured out, my mother's a native. But not my dad, obviously, so it caused a lot of drama when I came along. My mom kept hoping my dad would change his mind, and extracted a lot of promises from my grandfather that no one would kill him. Even after he— my father—became *un officier*, she held out hope. The family disowned her for a time, but she wormed her way back in."

"And you? When did you decide on a life of crime?"

He half-shrugged again. "When does anyone make a choice like that? I just sort of fell into it. My cousins are all in the Life. They'd invite me along to be their driver or whatever. It was fun, and the money's good. Helluva lot better than what I make here."

"Speaking of which—why *do* you work here?"

"My grandfather is big on respectability, and covering his ass. He insisted we all have legitimate jobs, so no one wonders too much how we pay our rent, or buy our groceries."

"Is that how your mom wound up working at the police department?"

His eyes widened again. "What are you—a private investigator?"

The thought didn't appear to bother him, but I said, "No. I really am just a friend of your father's. Something happened around the time of his death, and I'm trying to piece it together."

"Huh. Yeah, okay, whatever. My grandfather *is* the reason my mom works for the police, but it's complicated. She has...reasons...for being there."

That surprised me. If I read his broad hint correctly, he'd admitted Elaine was a mob plant, infiltrating the police at her father's behest. Which seemed improbable, as did his speaking so frankly with me about it in the first place.

"But surely they did a background check. They must know she's a Buonfiglio."

"*Oui, bien sûr.* But awhile back, they were sued over discriminatory hiring practices. My mother has no criminal record, and if they refused to admit her into the National Police School, it could have been a big scandal. The Buonfiglios have a *lot* of money, and even more expensive lawyers. So she got in, but they gave her a desk job. Which suits my grandfather. She reports to him, and can occasionally manipulate an evidence log or something. Nothing fancy, but it helps."

I sat back. "Why are you telling me all this?"

He thought a moment. "Don't know exactly. You're not a cop, and you knew my dad. You could probably find all this out anyway. It's kind of an open secret. I don't have friends I can talk with about my family—or my dad—so why not?"

His tone held a hint of wistfulness, and my gut said he'd be open to meeting Eric, if he thought he could. Plus, he apparently hadn't done worse than drive a getaway car so far. Who knew what his cousins were getting away *from*, but still. It gave him a veneer of innocence—a thin one, but it reassured me.

The next part could be tricky, though. He had to know of the Dioguardis. But did he *know* about them? Eric hadn't, until he died. But maybe for those actually in the Life, the demon stuff was common knowledge? Jason had never mentioned any other families *being* demons, so I assumed the priest who got the blood a thousand years ago was an aberration: Satan expected different results, and hopefully learned his lesson vis à vis giving his blood to just anyone.

I said carefully, "Do you know why your dad became a cop?"

"*Mais bien sûr.* The Dioguardis killed his sister, and instead of joining the Buonfiglios, he went toward the light."

Okay, then. But how to handle the rest of it, or convince him to help his father?

His cell phone rang and he checked the number, then made *excuse me a sec* noises and answered the call. "Hey—what's up?" I couldn't hear the other side of the conversation over the noise in the café, but after a moment, he met my gaze and grinned. "*Ouais*. I'm with her right now, Mom." Another pause. "No—it's fine. I can handle it." They had some more back and forth like this, and then he said, "Yeah, okay. See you there. Bye."

He set the phone down. "My mom wants to speak with you. She said to meet her in fifteen minutes. You up for it?"

****

"I don't like this," Liam said for the dozenth time.

While I tended to agree with him, we were in the Peapod with Stefan riding shotgun and Liam ghost-crammed into the backseat, so I couldn't respond. Besides, we were meeting Elaine in a public park, and as far as I knew, she had no personal vendetta against me. Her relationship with Eric ended decades ago, and if her new surname meant anything, she'd moved on. So hating the new girlfriend seemed unlikely. Plus, I was curious. Who wouldn't be, after all I'd learned?

I found street parking and we climbed out. The sun had burned the clouds off, and the temperature neared sixty degrees. We entered the park, following a paved path to its center, where Elaine sat on a bench, finishing a late lunch of sandwich, chips, and bottled water. She stuffed her trash into a paper lunch bag and made room on the bench for me and Stefan, but not Liam, of course. However, he took it in stride and went to stand near a bronze statue across from us, depicting some French Revolutionary War hero.

I sat next to Elaine, Stefan on my other side, and she said, "Thanks for coming."

She seemed calmer than back at the station, and didn't display any overt animosity, so I relaxed a little. "Sure. Obviously I'm curious, though—why am I here?"

She glanced away, watching the passersby. Probably this was Buonfiglio Best Practices, checking her surroundings for threats. Or maybe she wanted to hide her expression.

Finally, she said, "Actually, that's what I'd like to know. Why are you here? How did you track us down, and for what reason?"

A fair question, but it lacked an easy answer. How much should I reveal? Did I want to win her trust, thinking she'd help me somehow? Or should I hedge, in case she sought intel to use against me? Either way, I should keep my eyes open.

But I couldn't see an advantage to completely lying, so I said, "I didn't. Track you down, that is. I was searching for something to do with Eric, and I knew his last address. I figured I'd give it a shot. I had no idea who Stefan was, until he told me."

She leaned around me to shoot a look at Stefan. "You *told* her you're Eric's son?"

"*Ouais*. Why not? What can anyone do about it now? He's dead, so…that's it."

Now she shot *me* an unreadable look, before sitting back.

Liam narrowed his gaze. "What's she up to?"

My thought exactly, but again, I couldn't respond beyond an eyebrow raise.

Liam grunted acknowledgment. "Don't tell her too much—she might be trying to trap you or pump you for something she could use with her family. No idea what, but be careful."

I gave a slight nod, which neither Stefan nor Elaine appeared to notice. She chewed her lip, thinking, and Stefan closed his eyes and soaked up the sun.

Abruptly, she said to me, "You're not a Dioguardi. But you...*know* about them, right?"

Shock doesn't begin to cover what I felt in that moment. Did *she* know about them?

"I, uh..."

She wrinkled her nose. "Don't pretend ignorance. I hear your nephew's missing."

Liam took a half-step toward her, and Stefan's eyes popped open. "Mom!"

"Be quiet." To me, she said, "Word is he's been kidnapped by a pretty...shady...character."

"*Don't tell her anything,*" Liam urged.

What could I say? What *should* I say? Did she know the Dioguardis were bio-demons, and Geordi'd been taken by a Demon from Hell? Or was she merely implying that the person everyone knew as Paolo was "shady?"

I said cautiously, "What, exactly, are you talking about?"

"The Dioguardis are so frantic, they're not being careful. Everyone knows he's gone, and who—or rather, *what*—took him. Plus, they're asking for help—which I can provide. For a price."

I swallowed. Liam vibrated with *don't talk* energy, but my gut said she knew *something*, or why bring it up? Maybe she used her position at the police department to find out about me and my "connections," however remote and unasked for. Plus the "*what* took him" was telling, since anyone ignorant of the supernatural aspects of this would never phrase it that way.

"What do you want?"

She smiled, triumphantly. "For starters, an intro to Nico and Rina."

I frowned. "If you know about me, you must realize I'm low on their favor-granting list."

"Not my problem. But anyone connected to them, sniffing around Stefan—*that's* my problem. Maybe you knew nothing of him before, but now you do, and that's an issue."

"How so?"

"Eric was a thorn in their side for twenty years. Even now he's…dead"—did I imagine the hesitation?—"they may want revenge. I can offer Buonfiglio assistance in getting their Crown Prince back, in exchange for…assurances, about my son."

"*Maman!*" The son in question didn't appear to want her interference. He launched into a string of French expletives *very* reminiscent of his father, but Elaine focused on me.

"So how about it? Get me an in with Lord and Lady Dio?"

I watched her a moment. What was her angle? Did she really want to help the Dioguardis find Geordi? And if so, why?

At last I said, "Why not approach them yourself?"

"Believe it or not, Rodolfo Gianpaolo Buonfiglio's daughter is even lower on their list of 'friends' than you are. I'm asking as a mother—Stefan needs closure with his father. I think you know where he is, and that's why you're here in the first place. I'll help you get what you want, if you get me what *I* want—what we *both* want: Eric and Stefan to have a second chance."

Stefan's jaw dropped. "*Mais bon dieu—qu'est-ce que tu racontes?*"

Liam remained similarly suspicious, if not as angry. "Don't trust her! Who knows what her game is? *Don't say anything* she could use against you."

While I agreed on principle, I did need to get Stefan on board. And I was curious, about what she knew, and how she thought it would help. I sidestepped the *Eric is dead but still hanging around* issue, saying, "What can you offer the Dioguardis? What's in it for them?"

"I understand what Rina is going through—losing her son, and now her grandson. My father has access to underground channels they don't." Her smile was ironic. "Not *those* channels, much to his chagrin. But he'd love it if the Dioguardis owed him one."

Stefan fairly popped with anger and confusion. "What the *hell* are you talking about?"

She compressed her lips at him. "Give us a minute alone."

"No. This is my life, and whatever the hell is going on, I deserve to know." He faced me. "He's alive, isn't he? I *saw* him in his casket, so what—they used a dummy? It sure as hell looked real, but it couldn't be, right? He just figured out how to get away from me permanently. Did he enter witness protection? Is that it? At least he could have had the guts to tell me about it, and say goodbye."

I shook my head helplessly. What on earth could I say to him? About any of it?

Elaine said gently, "Your father *is* dead. But…there are things you don't know, and before I tell you, I need to talk with Hyacinth here—alone. *Please*—just a minute or two."

His jaw clenched, but he rose and essentially stomped down the path, disappearing into the park. Without being asked, Liam followed him. Elaine half-rose, then sat again, sighing.

"He's only twenty-two, and he's lived through a lot." She met my gaze. "Okay, cards on the table. You must realize how pissed I am at Eric. He abandoned us when we needed him the most. My family wasn't helpful, either, until I groveled my way back in. Stefan grew up with all that hanging over him. I didn't want him in the family business, but he sees it as a *va te faire foutre* at his father. And he's more reckless every day, now he thinks there's no father to say *fuck you* to. I'm worried that having nothing to push against, will make him push too far."

I blew out a breath. "Fair enough. *If* I had a way to give Stefan closure, it might even be something I'd want to do. But how do I know you're really going to help find Geordi, instead of planning some sort of inside attack on the Dioguardis?"

I couldn't believe I'd raised the issue. A few days ago, I'd've been happy to *help* anyone wanting to destroy them, regardless of motive or affiliation. But now...I needed them. More and more, I realized my minions and I could never save Geordi on our own, not with such a high-level Demon involved. Even his lackey, Chrétien, was more than enough demon for me. Plus, we'd made a deal, and my sketchy code of honor said that didn't include stabbing the Dioguardis in the back at the first opportunity. Especially as it seemed they were sincerely playing nice. So far.

Elaine's eyes glinted in the low sun. "You can never be totally certain we won't ambush them. But my grandfather has pledged his aid. And as a show of good faith, I can tell you we've narrowed down Marchosias's location to a *very* small region—which we control. Promise you'll help me, and I'll tell you right now where we think he is, *and* promise the Buonfiglios won't attack any Dioguardis found in the region, during negotiations."

Chapter Twelve

"The apathy of the people is enough to make every statue leap from its pedestal and hasten the resurrection of the dead."

~William Lloyd Garrison, American Abolitionist
and Social Reformer
(1805-1879)

"T'es sûre?" Sabine asked through Yvo. "He is no longer in Germany?"

"Yes. Elaine said the Buonfiglios began doing their own research as soon as the Dioguardis put the word out. Their intel shows Marchosias is somewhere in the Mediterranean region, most likely Greece or Turkey, both of which are controlled by the Buonfiglios. Elaine says her family will commit to a truce of sorts with the Dioguardis, and throw their resources into finding Geordi or helping get him back, however they can."

I still didn't totally trust her on this, but I already knew the Dioguardis had huge channels in Sicily, France, Switzerland, and Germany, but limited reach farther south. And it made sense that her father would offer his aid, to get the Dioguardis under his thumb. Plus, she'd actually named Marchosias, indicating her family's "resources" did solid work.

Sabine crackled faintly over the line, and Yvo translated. "Yes. Ve suspected Marchosias vould haf moved Geordi by now, but haf been searchink here, too, to cover our bases. If he is not in Germany, ve can shift our efforts elsevhere, and see vhat ve come up with."

"Sounds good."

While I had to be physically near the Dead in order to hear them speak, we'd figured out that—*duh*—Sabine could hear me perfectly well on speaker phone, saving Yvo half his translation duties. He gave me a quick rundown of how the demon-hunting-and-recapture efforts were going—not great, but not terrible, either, and Michael's sub-angels were helping anyway—and we hung up.

It was late afternoon, almost dinner time, and Liam and I were back at my apartment. After Elaine dropped her bombshell about Marchosias, she'd gone in search of Stefan, presumably to drop another bombshell on him, about his father being "Dead" rather than "dead."

I wished her luck on that one. Stefan was already angry. Finding out his dad hadn't actually left the planet, and *still* hadn't tried to connect with him, probably wouldn't improve the situation. But that was her side of our bargain, and therefore, her problem.

Meanwhile, I might as well assume she'd eventually convince Stefan we weren't all nuts, and plan accordingly, so I checked for flights from Marseille to Denizli, Turkey. I would've preferred driving, but it's thirty-plus hours by car, and only five by plane to Antalya, the nearest major airport, even with a stopover in Istanbul. I'd have to rent a car, and find a hotel for a night or two, but flights were frequent and cheap, so I tossed my phone on the couch and sat back.

Liam hovered nearby, equally at a loss for what to do next. He couldn't even make travel arrangements, as he'd done when a living minion. But his ghostliness gave him one advantage, in that he could observe without being, er, observed, as he'd done when Stefan stomped off. Plus, Elaine obviously hadn't seen or heard him, likely meaning she wasn't a demon herself. Which I had no reason to suspect, but given her "special knowledge," verification seemed smart.

After we finished our chat, she'd followed her son down the park path, and I'd followed her, figuring Liam would come back that way when he saw her. A minute later, he appeared on the path, heading my way.

We were alone in this part of the park, so I asked, "Find anything out?"

He shook his head. "Not really. He's at a fountain back there, blazing. It's a few yards from the edge of the park, and there's a satellite police station across the street."

Marijuana isn't legal yet in France, but I guess if you've joined the Mafia specifically as a *screw you* to your father the cop, lighting up in public has its appeal. And it was an example of the "recklessness" Elaine described. But would learning the truth about Eric, and maybe seeing him again, make things better…or worse?

Liam said, "What did Elaine say after I left?"

We headed for the car, and I gave him the details, then waited as he processed. When I first met him, I thought of him as "muscle" the Burkes had hired to do their bidding, not ask questions. But in fact, he's more of an introvert. He needs think time, and when he gets it, he frequently finds angles I've missed.

He'd stayed quiet during the drive home, and while I called Sabine and Yvo, but now he said slowly, "I don't get Elaine's stated motive. If the Dioguardis wanted to go after Eric through his son, why wouldn't they have done it already? While he was alive? They killed his sister, right in front of him. Why tiptoe around his son?"

"I wondered that, too. But if Eric really had no involvement in Stefan's life, maybe everyone thinks he wouldn't care what happens to him? Maybe that's even *why* he stayed away. Plus, we don't have a lot of options here. I think Nadezhda's right, and whatever kept Eric here originally is the only thing that will make him fight to stay again."

Even his feelings for me didn't seem strong enough. Not to say he doesn't *have* them, but clearly an unacknowledged son he's had for twenty-plus years would be a bigger draw than the half-dead, soul-sorting *petite amie*—or whatever I am to him—he's known a mere three months.

I continued, "So, we need Stefan, and Elaine is giving him to us. Whatever her reasons, I don't think we can care too much about them."

"I hear you. But what if those reasons come back to bite you in the ass later?"

I sighed. "They probably will. But until then, I'm going to keep moving forward."

With that in mind, I grabbed my phone and texted Jason that we needed to talk. Hopefully, he hadn't gone back to being so pissed about Flore that he'd ignore me, but if he did, I could maybe ask Bala to help with Elaine and the Dioguardis. As noted, she's another member of the Super Secret Sect who are against the main family. But she's clearly important to them, as witnessed by Rina *and* Nico rushing to her side at the hospital. However, I didn't need someone I trusted to make the intro, just someone who could.

A knock came at the door, and Liam and I jumped. I rose to answer it, which is when I realized my new door didn't have a peephole. Isn't there a law about that— something tenant-safety-related? Maybe Jeannette had to order a door fast, and planned to add the peephole later.

Liam frowned. "I don't like this. Does anyone know you're here? Anyone *living?*"

"You don't like anything. But if it makes you feel better, I won't open the door unless I know the person on the other side." I said loudly, "*Quoi? Qui est-ce?*"

A woman's voice said, "*C'est moi*—Jeannette."

I blew out a breath and opened the door. She'd changed from the floral muumuu to a polka-dot one, also pink, and wore the same feathered mules from last night. She'd added a pink mohair cardigan in deference to the pre-evening chill, and her glossy hair was swept up into a French twist with pink butterfly clips on either side, her face glowing fresh and smooth under the breezeway's flickering fluorescent lights. Would it be a compliment if I commented on it? Or an insult? Like, *you look great* now, *but before…ugh.*

While I dithered, she gave me a warm smile. "Hyacinth! It is so good to have you back. I forgot to ask last night how long you plan to stay?" She gestured at the door. "As you can see, I had to replace it. The contractor is coming the day after tomorrow to drill *le judas* and paint. If there is a time you'll be out, that would, of course, be easier."

"Careful!" Liam interjected loudly, making me jump, and Jeannette glanced over my shoulder before snapping her gaze back to mine.

Had she heard Liam? Or merely reacted to my startlement? I wouldn't necessarily know if he started "breaking through" to the Living, because I can hear-slash-see him all the time. And yet… What else would make her glance in his direction, at the exact moment he spoke?

She waited expectantly, so I said, "Erm, not sure yet. I'll be in and out, most likely. The contractor can come any time. It's not a problem."

Now I was on hyper alert. Did I imagine the disappointment that flickered in her eyes? She peered over my shoulder—openly, this time—and said, "I see you've settled back in. I didn't like having the place empty for so long. *C'est très dangereux.*"

"Well, Xaviera's gone a lot, and it's never bothered you. Which reminds me—did she forget to tell you this time? Her plants need watering."

Jeannette seemed momentarily confused, then shook her head ruefully. "How silly of me—I keep forgetting. There's been so much going on. I don't know where my mind has gone."

"That's okay—I can do it. Speaking of being away, do you think you could find the originals of the police reports you filed after the break-ins? I'd love to see them."

"I'm so sorry, *chérie.* I mailed you the only copies I had."

"Oh," I said, trying to sound disappointed, not like I knew she was lying. "Well, that's okay. I'll just go down to the police station and request new copies. Which one did you file at?"

"Oh, who knows? I can't even remember to water Xaviera's plants, let alone which station investigated the break-ins. I didn't go in, you understand. The officers came here."

That actually made sense, and paved a way for her to redeem herself. If she'd called the burglaries in, and the police—*if* they weren't mafiosi or demons in disguise—never filed the reports, then she hadn't lied. Plus, it was highly possible the post office lost the mailed copies, not her. On the other hand, the only evidence that anyone *had* broken in was my new door.

All at once, I had a mild inspiration. "Okay, never mind. The databases are all connected anyway, so I'm sure I'll find them. And actually, I will be gone for a few days again."

Liam couldn't stifle a grunt of warning, but this time, Jeannette didn't appear to hear him. "But *chérie*—you just got home. Why leave again so soon?"

"I need to cancel my lease in Zürich. It's in a building called Les Bonnes Nuits. Cute, right? Anyway, it's cheap, but it's costing me enough that I really need to move my stuff out and cancel. It will only take a couple of days. I might leave tonight or tomorrow, or I might wait another day. I have business somewhere else first, and I don't know how long it will take."

Liam moved into my line of sight, making cutting motions with his hand and fairly crackling with frustrated amazement at my sudden forthcomingness.

Jeannette said, "Of course. Would you like me to take care of things while you're gone?"

It seemed an odd offer, considering I had no plants or pets, but I only said, "Not for me, but how about this? I'll water Xaviera's plants today, and maybe you can check on them whenever the contractor comes to deal with the door? I should be home a couple days after that, and can take over plant duty again then."

"Of course—an excellent plan. Come see me before

you leave, to confirm."

She bustled back down the stairs, and I shut the door and faced Liam. "I know. You think I'm crazy. But if she does have anything to do with the break-ins, or made them up for some weird reason, her knowing I'll be gone could trick her into making another move. Plus, I just gave her enough info to figure out where my Switzerland place is. If it's suddenly broken into, after I just told her about it, that tells us something. Not sure what, but better than nothing."

Liam popped his neck and rolled his shoulders. "Not a bad plan. But...how will you know, if either place is breached?"

"I can fly home from Turkey via Zürich, and stop in. I really do need to get my stuff back. I'd drive there first, and then fly to Turkey, but it adds seven hours to the trip just for travel time, and I get the sense from Nadezhda that Stefan and I need to get to Eric as fast as possible."

Liam's eyes narrowed. "*You* can stop in—not we? Where will I be during all this?"

I chewed my lip. "We-ell, I thought if you stayed here, you could report on anything that happens, whether it's just the contractor finishing the peephole, or if someone breaks in, or..."

He glared at me. "No. Not going to happen. I'm coming with you."

"Liam."

"What?"

"I'll be fine in Turkey. You can't help me with that. But you can help here, since no one living will know you're hanging around. And if anyone breaks in who's also dead, or a demon, you'll be able to tell me that, too. It would be really helpful to know what's been going on, because right now, I have no idea. And *something's* sure as hell hinky."

He did another neck pop. "Fine. You're probably right, but—"

"—you don't like it," I finished, and he grinned sheepishly.

"Yeah, okay, being dead has made me more suspicious. I mean, my job was to be suspicious, but now it's on overdrive."

"I know. Same thing happened to me, when I started parenting Geordi."

My fear must have shown on my face, because he said, "Hey—it's okay. We'll get him back. And Chrétien—and pretty much everyone else—swears Marchosias hasn't even told Geordi he's been kidnapped. Kid's probably playing video games and eating too much sugar."

"I know. It's just—"

My cell phone rang with a local number I didn't recognize. I swiped to answer, and Elaine's voice greeted me. "I told Stefan everything. I doubt he believes me, but I gave him your address—*il arrivera tout de suite*. I am sure he expects you to affirm his belief that I am nuts, so it is up to you now, to make him believe us both."

"Okay, thanks." I paused. "Just to confirm—what, exactly, did you tell him?"

"That his father died in August, but not all who die pass on to the Afterlife. I said Eric stayed on Earth, but his soul is damaged, and this may be Stefan's last chance to see him. I mean, his real, final, no going back *ever* last chance, before Eric is gone for good."

Her level of knowledge surprised me. "Who told you all this?"

She was silent a moment. "You'll think I'm crazy. Even with what you know, this is pretty far out there. Eric came to me in a dream last week. I've always believed in ghosts, and psychic powers and such. We fought about it when we were dating. He's so logical and concrete. Or he used to be. *Sans doute*, dying opened him up to new possibilities. Anyway, he thought me silly. But I've had a few experiences. Nothing big—my grandmother visited me after she died. Didn't say anything, just hovered by the bed before moving on. That kind of thing."

My knee-jerk reaction was, yeah, that's a bit woo-woo. But who am I to judge? Probably Grandma figured out how to make herself visible but didn't want to scare anyone, so "kept it simple, stupid." Who knows? She might even still be hanging around here somewhere.

"Okay, assuming I believe you…tell me about the dream, and why it isn't *just* a dream."

"Because in it, he told me of you."

Liam saw my shock. "What is it? What did she say?"

I made shushing motions at him, saying into the phone, "What do you mean? If that's the case, why didn't you say anything when I showed up at your counter?"

"He did not show me a picture or anything. *Ce n'était pas comme ça.* But he spoke of you. He said he had met someone who showed him he is worthy of love."

I couldn't hide my disbelief. "*Eric* said *that?*"

She laughed, and I found myself warming to her. It was weird, having this shared experience of "Eric" with her. I don't have many exes, and had certainly never been friendly with *their* exes. So hearing a different perspective on my current so-called *petit ami* was…nice.

Elaine said, "Not in so many words. But he had a

lightness he lacked before. He never said your name—he only referred to you as *son ange*. We never had pet names, but I am guessing this will convince you of the truth of my words. *Oui?*"

I swallowed. "Yes. It does." Elaine could never have found that one out, unless Eric himself told her. "But…why did he come see you? I'm not jealous—really—but if what you say is true, and he's dream-walking, or whatever, why haven't I seen him?"

She hesitated. "I think he is making amends, going down the list of people he believes he has wronged, or failed in some way. I think Stefan is next, and then you. *Et puis…*"

I swallowed again. "And then he'll let go, and it will be too late."

"*Oui*. After you left the station, I realized you must be the *ange* in question. *J'étais toujours en colère*. But I love my son. *Tu comprends*—you love Geordi as your own, and like Rina, you will do anything for him, *oui?* Well, I will do the same for Stefan. I believe the only thing that will prevent his going to a place from which he can never return, is the prospect of a relationship with his father. So, if that means helping you save Eric, that is what I will do."

I exhaled. "Okay. Thanks for telling me all this." Outside, I heard heavy footsteps coming up the stairs from the next floor down. "I have to go—I think Stefan's here."

"Of course. Call if you need my assistance with convincing him. Good luck."

She hung up just as someone knocked on the door. Except this time, it was a hard pounding, and a booming voice said, "Hyacinth—child—are you in there?"

Chapter Thirteen

"Faithfulness to the past can be a kind of death above ground. Writing of the past is a resurrection; the past then lives in your words and you are free."
~Jessamyn West, American Author
(1902-1984)

I opened the door for Michael, devoutly hoping Stefan would wait a few more minutes before showing up. Although come to think of it, finding a ginormous archangel on my doorstep might go a long way to convincing him Elaine and I told the truth.

Today, my erstwhile "boss" wore sandals with wool socks, boat-sized jeans, and a black turtleneck, and had topped it all off with a literal "raspberry beret." He waved at Liam inside the apartment, then grinned at me. "Hyacinth! How goes the search for your nephew?"

I stepped aside, and he squeezed through the door and into the apartment, which shrank with his bulk in it. Liam gave me a nod, then took himself out and down the stairs. Unlike some of my dead minions—*cough*-Jun-*cough*—Liam's an atheist, and therefore not on Michael's to-do list. But "not having to hide" and "shooting the breeze with an archangel" are two different things, so I'm sure he left out of concern for his own mental health, as much as from tact.

I said to Michael, "Uh, making progress, I guess. It

would go faster if you could help."

"I know, child. I am sorry. Truly."

"But isn't that your *job*—dealing with demons and their misdeeds?" I couldn't keep the frustration from my voice, but he only lifted a massive shoulder.

"It is complicated. Geordi is not in any material physical danger at the moment. He is safe, and Marchosias will keep him that way. Otherwise, he has nothing to bargain with."

"But…" I trailed off, because it all seemed so illogical.

"Child. If a demon hurts someone, or performs a host of other evil acts, then yes, it is my job to stop them. And that happens a lot, on top of my other duties. I have a finite amount of resources, so for now, I must focus those elsewhere. For instance, on tracking down the demon hordes who escaped from Hell a few weeks ago, during that other matter."

He meant the battle at the cave, an unsubtle reminder that he was already cleaning up one mess for me. Even so, I had to try again. "But he's my *nephew*—in the hands of a Hell Demon!"

"Well, if you put it that way, child, Lucifer is my brother, and demons are his children—*my* nephews and nieces. And therefore, my family. So, unless Marchosias's antics escalate, I will not interfere. Besides, you said you are making progress?"

It would be fruitless to argue, and anyway, he had a point. Just because I worked for the guy didn't mean he owed me any magic-wand-waving favors, even if he *could* help.

He saw my capitulation and shifted gears. "Speaking of my other duties—and yours—I am here because another shard has been found, and I need you to retrieve it."

I tried to tamp down my excitement. This could be good, since we needed one of his rocks to bring Nick back. But of course, he couldn't know that, so I wiped all miscreant thoughts from my mind.

"Okay, where is it?"

"Switzerland, near Zürich."

Now *that* was a stroke of luck. "That's great—I'll be going there in a couple of days."

He thought a moment, then nodded. "That will be fine. There is not as much urgency with this one. It is actually being held for you."

I blinked. "By whom?"

He flashed one of his wicked grins that meant, like Jacques Rousseau, he enjoyed toying with me. "That is not important. The person who found it suspects its significance and will keep it safe until you can verify it. If it is mine, wonderful. If not, we will seek the next one."

"Okay. Sounds good. I'll go get it ASAP."

He watched me, and I worried I'd laid on the agreeableness too thickly. Would he suspect I wanted the rock for myself? Surely not. I'd never given him any indication I was interested in the shards, beyond my duty to retrieve them for him.

Then he said, "There is one more thing. I notice you are not finding souls to sort as frequently as before."

I opened my mouth, then closed it again. He was right. I'd been too busy to notice, but I hadn't needed to sort anyone since we were in Germany.

My reaction must have assured him I hadn't shirked my duties on purpose, and he relaxed. "Ah, well. Perhaps this is how it goes. But Hyacinth—I know you discovered there are other sorters besides yourself. You must understand, it is a very small number. Half a dozen at most, with several near retirement. If you do encounter any souls, I expect you to adhere to our bargain, and help them."

"Of course," I said, trying not to sound miffed by the professional slur.

He smiled. "Just checking. You have kept a few souls from me."

"Yeah, uh, sorry about that. They didn't want to go with you, so I sort of thought that counted as not believing in you."

"Sort of," he agreed. "But do not make a habit of it. I am not an enforcer. I help the souls who need or want my aid. But you are here to help me. Do not forget it."

He turned to leave, but I said, "Wait—while we're clearing the air—there's something I've been needing to ask you."

He paused, and I swallowed. Did I really want to poke the bear? He'd already forgiven me for several transgressions. But I'd been avoiding the conversation for too long, so I dove in. "What is your relationship with Vadim? You said once that you helped with his final journey. But he's an atheist, and clearly didn't pass on to any Afterlife, so what did you mean?"

He waited a beat, then said slowly, "Vadim is…unique. He is useful to me, due to the connections he had while alive, and even more for those he has forged in death. He performed a service for me a number of years ago, before he died. When *that* event occurred, he asked me to repay the favor by making him Full Dead, as you are wont to call it."

"That's it? He did you a solid, so you sealed his deadness for him?"

"Yes. Is there anything else? I have things to do, and I imagine you do as well."

I heard a new set of feet stomping up from below and shook my head. "Nope. That's it."

He nodded and exited through the open door, then vanished. He hadn't explained anything, but I should really ask Vadim, since he'd been my friend and partner for many years.

Stefan's head appeared at the top of the stairs, with Liam, silent and unseen, coming up behind him. He stomped onto the landing and glowered at me.

"Where the fuck is my father?"

****

We reached Denizli just before dawn. Fortunately, Elaine ponied up Stefan's share of the travel costs, because my bank account was dry. My minions had been withdrawing cash from accounts set up by the Burkes to fund their nefarious schemes—the logic being that we could use that same cash, to *defeat* those same schemes—but I didn't like doing that too often. So far, we hadn't drawn unwanted attention, but it was only a matter of time.

Unfortunately, my next option was Lily's and my Swiss account. But when last in Zürich, I'd promised to deliver my car for an appraisal, *after* the bank manager already disbursed funds using it as collateral. While I'd be in the neighborhood for the latest rock retrieval, I wouldn't have the car. And I still hadn't remembered to order a copy of Lily's death certificate, to prove I now had sole ownership of the joint account. Without that, I doubted Herr Gutzwiller would peer down his long nose and say, "Sure. No problem. You lied about your car, but I'll let you take more money out now, without your sister's permission."

Yeah—not likely.

So I gritted my teeth and grabbed my credit card, to pay the one-way fare, getting Stefan and me to Antalya with only a short layover in Istanbul. We'd packed light—no checked bags—so we headed for the car rental desk. If we'd had more time, I would've found a junker lot, like the one where Jason, Geordi, Eric and I had rented a so-called "car" when we first came to Marmaris three months ago. It was barely held together by duct tape and rust, but was practically free.

However, we didn't have time now, so I pulled out the credit card again, while Stefan hovered sullenly beside me. The attendant's gaze flicked from him to me. She probably thought him my "companion," given our obvious—yet not-parental—age difference. The whole thing freaked me out. Stefan looked so much like Eric, even with the tattoos and piercings, that I kept wanting to talk with him as if he *were* his father. He sounded similar, too, but of course he spoke the language of youth, whereas Eric had always acted like an old soul.

In any case, I read somewhere that acrophobia is more about being afraid you'll throw yourself over the cliff's edge on purpose, rather than falling accidentally. This was like that. Stefan rested squarely in the zone of a "stepson" for me, as the offspring of the man I'm—sort of—dating. Therefore, the thought of being romantic with him was "icky." But he *exactly* resembled my very sexy boyfriend, who I missed terribly. So, to keep myself from accidentally-on-purpose throwing myself off the cliff, I avoided interacting with him as much as possible.

Not too difficult to do, since he was still pissed at the world in general, and at me very specifically. But it did make traveling more uncomfortable than it could have been, and I half wished Liam had joined us after all, to act as a buffer for my confused emotions. But he had work to do in Marseille, so here we were.

I got my card back, and we boarded the shuttle to our newly rented Renault Clio. The thing was a manual, and bright orange to boot, so stealth was out of the question. Not that we needed to cover our tracks. As far as I knew, no one cared about Eric, except us. The demons all fought over Geordi and might keep tabs on me for that. But as long as they knew I hadn't found him yet, I expected they'd keep their distance.

Same with the Dioguardis, although now I thought about it, the Marseille branch, at least, might be interested in Eric's whereabouts. Oh well—too late now. We'd never tried to hide his location in the first place, so if they cared, surely they would've acted by now.

We climbed into the tiny car and I put it in gear, heading northwest toward Denizli. The drive takes just under three hours, and we left Antalya at around four a.m., so dawn hadn't quite broken when we found the hotel Jason, Geordi and I stayed at previously. I'm a creature of habit. What can I say? We checked in and headed to our rooms—different ones, on a different floor, but same concept of a tiny bathroom between them, accessed by connecting doors on either side.

By the time we got settled, it was past eight, and officially daybreak, but the clouds and rain made it not noticeably lighter from the hour before. It was also cold, so I added a fleece-lined jacket to my turtleneck and jeans combo, before joining Stefan in the hall.

He wore jeans and another short-sleeved t-shirt, the Buonfiglio tats fully on display, covering his trimly muscled forearms. He lounged against the wall, taking a deep drag of the fat joint in his hand, holding the smoke in, then exhaling slowly.

"That is some good shit," he said, offering it to me.

"Thanks, but I'll pass. You know, Turkey's very strict about drugs. Minimum sentence for possession—even just weed, and even for foreigners—is two years."

He took another pull, a clear *fuck you* aimed right at me—his estranged father's *petite amie*, and therefore, the Enemy—then casually stubbed the joint out on the wall, like it was all his idea. He tucked the remainder into a small metal case that held a few more rolled joints plus matches, then dropped the case into his messenger bag, which he slung over one shoulder. Airport security must have chosen to assume they were roll-your-owns, not illegal cannabis.

I gave myself a mental shake—not my business. "Do you have a coat? It's freezing out there."

He shot me a *you're not my mother* glare, before slipping back into his room and reemerging with a lightweight hoody over his arm. "Whatever. Let's get this over with."

He sounded skeptical. Who could blame him? He'd seen Eric's corpse in its casket, then watched with hundreds of witnesses as it was buried at La Cimetière Saint-Pierre. Now Elaine and I claimed that did not, in fact, mean Eric had left for good…yet. It was a lot to process.

Since nothing I said would help, I headed downstairs and out to the street, and he followed silently. We got in the car, and I drove to the ruined city of Hierapolis, where we parked and paid our admission, then aimed for the section of "town" where Nadezhda had indicated she'd be waiting. She resided somewhere in the ruins—I had no idea where, or how she managed not to get caught and evicted by the officials who ran the place, but somehow she did it.

The Hierapolis site is near the city of Pamukkale, which is known for its terraced hot springs and "white waterfalls" cascading down the nearby cliffs. These are actually limestone that has hardened over time into the current formations, comprising the "Cotton Castle" Geordi drew on the comics in the paper on Malta, which led us to Nadezhda in the first place.

The ruined city itself is larger than you'd expect, with several temples, an amphitheater, various churches, and the necropolis, made up of twelve hundred graves, tombs, and tumuli, of varying sizes and socio-economic statuses. It also includes the newly rediscovered Plutonium, where I'd found the second of Michael's rocks back when all this started, and where now, if all my dominoes fell into place, we'd pull Nick out of Hell.

Unfortunately, the cavern leaks poisonous gases. Ancient texts say that temple priests—high on ergot, the Greco-Roman equivalent of LSD—led animals in to die, while escaping harm themselves. People back then paid beaucoup bucks to witness these "miracles," keeping the temple in business, but modern site officials thought they'd rather not have a bunch of dead tourists on their hands and walled it off.

But I'd needed Michael's rock, so as a non-breather, unlikely to be affected by the gases, Eric had insisted on going in instead—yet another example of all he'd done for me, and why I had to be there for him now.

We found Nadezhda on the same low tomb she'd occupied the day she first showed me the Plutonium. She looked as rotund as ever, like a ripe tomato with stubby legs dangling halfway down the tomb's side. In deference to the rain, she'd added a wool shawl to her nineteenth century peasant dress, draping it over her head and shoulders. However, her petite feet remained bare, despite the cold. Her face split in a wide grin when she saw me, and she cackled.

Stefan sucked in a breath. "Is she for real?"

"Yes. Your weed isn't *that* good."

He gave me the side-eye, and I wondered if seeing Nadezhda would convince him that, since everyone around him regarded all this insanity as normal, it actually might be.

She hopped down, wasting no time. "Hyacinth—is good you come. You Stefan?"

"Uh...*ouais*."

"Good. Eric need see you—remember why he stay. Come now. I take you."

She waddled off in the direction of the hill where Eric had been made Full Dead, and I followed her, with Stefan trailing more slowly behind us.

Nadezhda said to me, "Is too bad you no come at night again. But this time of year, not so many tourists. Is fine—no one will interfere. But Dead no like coming out in the day."

Stefan said, "What's she talking about?"

We rounded the low hill we'd been climbing and I pointed to a large open area, about halfway up the next rise over. "That."

Stefan stopped and his jaw dropped, which I took to mean the Dead were visible to him.

There, on the hill across from us, a naked, unconscious Eric was tied, spread eagle on the ground, exactly as he'd been when first made Full Dead. Except today, several bonfires burned nearby for warmth, since according to Nadezhda, severe illness drains a spirit's energy, making them feel the cold. I assumed these were some type of ghost fire, so as not to alert the Living authorities, but as per usual, I couldn't tell. Either way, a hundred or more souls milled around him—men, women, and children, all garbed in the fashions of their eras, often with the wounds that killed them still evident on their ghostly forms.

I think this more than anything gave Stefan pause. No doubt he expected Nadezhda and I would bring him to a vacant, lonely location, and "pretend" Eric had showed up, allowing Stefan to maintain his sane and rational position that this was all bunk. Instead, finding this many souls here—and Eric himself—rearranged his brain. I could see him trying to work out the special effects required to fake a scene of this magnitude, and utterly failing.

A few souls broke from the crowd and came to greet Nadezhda, then peered at me. They drew back, muttering *Destroyer* in various languages, before shifting focus to Stefan. They registered surprise at his resemblance to Eric, and jostled to "touch" him. I knew from my living minions that this would feel like cold jello against his skin, or a push of icy air that breached the surface cells and went into his arm. He pulled away in shock, frantically turning to me as, for once, the sanest person in range.

"*Putain—qu'est-ce que c'est?*"

"They're dead," I said matter-of-factly. "They're

solid for me, but my minions—the guys I work with— gave me tips for you. I would've warned you, but you didn't believe your mom or me, so I figured you wouldn't listen. Anyway, they're making themselves visible to you, and Nadezhda made it so you can see your father." I paused. "You *can* see him over there, right?"

I gestured at the naked form on the hill, swallowing my own fear and desperate need to go to him, in favor of getting his son on board ASAP.

Stefan gulped and glanced where I pointed, then quickly away again. "*Ouais.* I see him. He's…dead? He looks so…not dead."

Actually, to me, Eric appeared closer to death than ever before, including when he was healed the last time. But I took Stefan to mean Eric seemed "real," and not like a ghost.

Nadezhda finished chatting with her friends, and broke in with, "*Da*—he dead. He slip away—think he no have reason to stay." She examined Stefan's face. "Is right? Or wrong?"

The struggle to sort his emotions showed in Stefan's every feature. "I…"

"Hey," I said as gently as I could, when my own emotions were screaming, *Help him, you bastard—you can save him, so just do it and figure the rest out later!*

I touched Stefan's arm, feeling the tension in his corded muscles. "This isn't easy, and I get why you're mad. You have every right to leave—to abandon him, as he abandoned you. But if you do that, you'll *always* feel abandoned. Stay and help him, so *you* can abandon *him*, but later, when he's aware of it. Don't do it now—he'll completely miss it."

Stefan gave a startled laugh. He scrubbed a hand

over his eyes, then faced the hillside. His chin jutted with determination, and he stomped over the hillocks and grasses, the Dead parting before him like a gray Soul Sea. I followed, and Nadezhda cackled and followed me.

We stopped in front of Eric, and Nadezhda produced a ghost blanket from somewhere which she draped over him for modesty. I resisted the urge to drop down—to cradle his beloved head and tell him it would be okay.

It will *be okay,* I thought. I said it over and over again in my mind, a mantra I hoped he'd feel, and that he sensed my presence, and found it comforting. But in point of fact, this was not about me. It was about Stefan.

Eric's son regarded him dispassionately, then said in a low voice to me, "What do I do?"

I sent Nadezhda a questioning look, and she said to Stefan, "Say whatever you like—is your relationship. But if you want him to stay, start with that."

He swallowed, Adam's apple bobbing, then dropped to his knees near Eric's head. He spoke earnestly, too low to hear, so I hoped he hadn't just told Eric off. Then he made the sign of the cross on the ghost cloth covering Eric's chest—guess Nadezhda had made it "touchable" for him—before kissing Eric's brow, and my heart clutched. There was such hope and longing in his face, but I didn't think he'd like me knowing about it, so I glanced away.

A moment later, he returned to my side, saying to Nadezhda, "What now?"

"Now, we wait."

Chapter Fourteen

"Thus that which is the most awful of evils, death, is nothing to us, since when we exist there is no death, and when there is death we do not exist."

~Epicurus, Greek Philosopher
(341-270 BCE)

Nadezhda said it could take a while, so after I went to Eric myself and kissed him and told him he couldn't leave me, we retreated, letting the Dead surround him again. They didn't appear to do anything specific, instead acting like a family gathering at the bedside of an ill loved one, hoping for a miracle.

Either way, Stefan and I clearly weren't needed for this part, and the "doctors" could probably handle things better without us getting in the way, so I extracted a promise from Nadezhda to call if anything changed, and we hiked back down the hill.

Stefan seemed a lot more subdued now, and I peeked at his profile as we walked. He had that determined set to his jaw that Eric often got, and after a few minutes, he finally spoke.

"That was...interesting. When—how—did you discover you could see the Dead?"

"It's a long story. But it's only been a few months."

"And my dad—where did you meet him?"

"Also a long story." I stopped, and he waited

solemnly. "Okay, you deserve to know the truth, but I'm taking a risk by telling you this. I met your father the night he died, *after* it happened, because it's also the night that I…died."

His eyes widened. "*T'es morte?*"

"Not exactly. Kind of. I've been brought back to life, but it's different than your father or the souls you saw today. They're what you'd call ghosts. They can pass through objects, or even people who are in their way, whereas I can't. I'm alive again—fully, with a solid body and everything. But I was dead for a while, and after that, I got my super powers."

"Which are…?"

"The Dead are real for me. It's not just that I can see and hear them. They're solid, like they still have their bodies. Even their clothes feel 'real' to me. I actually can't tell them from the Living most of the time."

"Huh."

I was feeling winded. I hadn't exactly been exercising regularly since I died, and all this hill work—plus the blatant honesty—really took it out of me. "Do you mind if we sit for a bit? If you'd like to talk more, that is."

He thought about it. "*Ouais*, okay, sure."

We found a flat tomb low enough for easy mounting and made ourselves comfortable. The rain had stopped, and the day was warm and muggy, and I wished I'd brought a water bottle. Stefan's hair curled damply around his face, making him look feral, and much less like his father. Nearby, I heard some type of insects buzzing lazily, a hypnotic humming that made me realize how long I'd been awake, after no sleep on our flight.

But I might never get another chance like this with

Stefan, so I took my jacket off and said, "Any more questions? You must be curious about all this."

He said bemusedly, "I still don't believe it's real. I mean, I *saw* my dad's body being buried. But I also just saw his…ghost…or whatever that was, tied to a hill. He felt…" He shook his head, clearly at a loss. "Kind of solid, but kind of…vaporous? Like a thick fog, except…resistant, when I touched him. I didn't go straight through. It was…weird."

No kidding.

He looked troubled. "But it isn't like that for you…?"

"Nope. If I poked your dad's arm, and then yours, it would feel exactly the same to me."

"Are you his *petite amie?*"

"Uh…we haven't exactly labeled anything. But I care about him, a lot. He's important to me, and like you, I don't want him to leave without knowing how I feel."

I thought he might deny my implication that he needed his father, but after a brief bout of indecision, he gave in and nodded. I also thought such a direct question deserved one from me in return. Sort of a modified, un-negotiated tit-for-tat.

"What about you? How did you wind up in the Life, with the Buonfiglios specifically?"

He reddened. "I told you—it just sort of happened."

"No, it didn't. You made a choice. You and your mom were outsiders for a long time. Plus, I doubt you'd be invited along on random crime-sprees, with everyone knowing who your dad is. I think something happened, and you asked to join up. What changed?" I watched him, then inspiration hit. "You contacted him, didn't you, and he rejected you?"

He was silent, staring into the near distance at the grassy hillocks. At last, he said, "My whole life, I wanted a relationship with him. I'd see his picture in the papers now and then, and imagine him showing up at my football games. I worked so hard at it, I even played elite for Olympique Marseille. I thought if he just knew me, he'd want to be in my life—that I could impress him with my athletic skills, or...whatever."

What could I say to that? My own parents had died so young, I never got to the stages of either pushing them away or seeking to regain their attention. Stefan by contrast had spent his whole life in limbo, simultaneously hating his father *and* wanting to earn his love, a never-ending cycle of push-pull. That would mess with anyone's psyche, let alone a kid's.

He continued, "Finally, a few years back, I tried to meet with him. He agreed but never showed, and my grandfather found out. He threatened to cut my mother off for good, and end my dad's protections. I asked to join up, to prove our loyalty, and my grandfather agreed."

He held something back, I was sure of it. I thought it through, and then my stomach and heart both sank. "Your grandfather tricked you, didn't he?"

Stefan studied the Buonfiglio crest, branding his arms. "*Oui.* He wanted my father killed, and used me to do it. He had me find an apartment in Dioguardi territory, knowing that every time my cousins came to visit—invading their turf—it would piss the Dioguardis off more. After a while, on a night when they'd be sure to hear of it and retaliate, he had us stir up trouble. And then..." His eyes clouded and he cleared his throat. "Then he sent a message to my father, supposedly from me. Eric rushed to stop the fight, and…they shot him. He died, because of me."

I swallowed my own sorrow, knowing there were no words that could take away his pain and guilt. "Were you there? When it happened?"

He looked away, shamefaced. "I stayed in the car—the getaway driver again. I didn't even find out he'd died until the next day. But whoever pulled the trigger, it's on me."

"No, it's on your grandfather."

"Perhaps. But I was the method of delivery. I've even wondered since then if he intercepted my message to my father—the first one—and that's why Eric never showed."

The wistful hope in his voice was unbearable. I wanted to say, *Of course that's why—if Eric knew, he would have been there.* But I doubted it would help, since Stefan *had* been the one to reach out initially, and either way, felt responsible for the outcome.

He cleared his throat. "Anyway, my grandfather can claim he kept his promise to my mother, because my father just got caught in the crossfire. He can even say he only tried to help me, by alerting my father to the danger I was in. It's really messed up."

"Does your mom know any of this?"

His lips twisted ironically. "*Non.* She believes I joined up to stick it to my dad. Which isn't that far off. But she doesn't know my grandfather threatened her livelihood, or orchestrated my dad's death. I'd appreciate it if you don't tell her, but I know I can't stop you."

I debated with my conscience, then said, "If it helps, a Dioguardi killed your dad, not one of your cousins. He didn't actually mean to. Your dad shot him in the arm, while he—Paolo—aimed only to wound. Paolo's arm jerked up and he accidentally killed your dad after all."

He said sharply, "Paolo Dioguardi killed him?"

Drat. "You've heard of him?"

"Only marginally. My cousins used to call him the weakest link. I never understood why. But now, after talking to my mother... Is he one of the, uh, special ones?"

Drat, and more drat. Had Elaine told him about the demon side of this, too? Of course she must have, and I should have thought to clarify that with her. But what should I do now? Lie like hell, or admit the truth? Then again, maybe knowing that Paolo—the real one, not the Marchosias version—was a bio-demon would actually yank Stefan back from the criminal ledge he was poised on.

"Yes. He's *special*, like most of the Dioguardis. Seriously—they're a bad group, and your mother's wish to meet with them isn't the best plan."

He lifted a shoulder. "She has her ideas about what's best for me, and I've got mine."

Something in his tone set my fictional arachnid superhero senses tingling. "Really—Paolo didn't mean to kill your dad. It was a terrible accident. Eric understands that—neither you nor Paolo is to blame."

"Maybe. But it all started with me. I just wish I could fix it somehow."

Nothing I said would help with that, so we fell silent, lost in our own thoughts. I understood the guilt he carried, but I think he felt better for having told someone what happened on his end. It also explained a lot of the anger, both at his dad and at himself. What would Eric think if—*when*—he woke up and found out? Or maybe he already knew.

The sun broke through the clouds, further warming the air and making me drowsy, and the humming sounds grew louder. It was an odd time of year for insects to be active, and also mildly annoying, when I just wanted to drift off for a nap. Plus, if it turned out to be a wasps' nest, I didn't want to get stung.

I said to Stefan, "Do you hear that? Where's it coming from?"

He listened a moment. "Hear what?"

"The insects. Humming. They sound like—"

Merde. I hopped off the tomb. "I have to go get something. Be right back."

He frowned and also jumped down, once again channeling his father. "*J'irai avec toi.*"

I started to tell him no, but then thought, why not? He was already enmeshed in the Crazy Life of Hyacinth Finch. Not quite a minion, but he'd probably follow me, regardless, and at least he'd be an extra pair of eyes.

"Fine. But if I tell you to leave, you leave. *Ça va?*"

He nodded and I headed around the back of the tomb we'd been sitting on, tracking the low vibrations I'd finally realized had nothing to do with insects, and everything to do with one of Michael's rocks. Which could be a real boon, since I needed one of his and one of Satan's, and had thought I'd "borrow" the one awaiting retrieval in Switzerland. However, it would be hard to hide that one from Michael, since—*duh*—he knew about it.

But this one... With luck, he'd never find out. At least, not until after I'd used it.

Stefan watched curiously as I moved among the sarcophagi and family graves prevalent in this section of the necropolis. I probably resembled a hound dog on the trail of something good. But as we drew nearer, and the vibrations grew stronger, my heart sank. We rounded a fallen marble column and found ourselves at the walled off entrance to the Plutonium. I put my hand against the stones under the arch, and sure enough, the vibrations were strongest here.

"Crap."

"What?"

I sighed. Stefan had told me lots of very personal stuff, and I thought I could trust him. Or maybe he just looked too much like Eric. What the hell—I needed the shard, and he had nothing better to do. He might as well know what I did.

"I need something on the other side of this wall. Unfortunately, the passage is full of poisonous gases. That's why it's walled off. Your dad went in for me last time, but he's obviously incapacitated now, and we don't have time to wait."

"Poisonous gas? How do you know?"

"It's common knowledge. Birds used to fly in and drop dead, before they closed it up. In ancient times, temple priests would put on a big show, driving bulls inside, who would also drop dead. Then the priests would drag their bodies out, to show the crowds. The spectators thought the priests had special powers, but I think they just weren't inside long enough to be affected."

"And what you need is farther in, necessitating a longer stay?"

"Exactly."

He studied the entrance. "I'll do it."

"You can't. Did you not hear the part about

171

poisonous gases, and great big bulls dying?"

"I'll be okay. I think what's really going on is the gases are heavier than the air, so they're sinking low to the ground. The bulls would have their noses down, so would breathe much more of the fumes than the priests, whose noses would be at a higher level."

I stared at him, and he grinned.

"I don't do a lot of drugs, but I know some shit about them. It's just chemistry. I was really good at that, *lorsque j'étais au lycée.* I even thought of going to college to become a chemist, before my life took a different turn."

He caught my eye and reddened, reminding me how young he really was. He had his whole life ahead of him. He didn't have to stay in the mob or do anything else he didn't want to.

He gestured at the walled up arch. "Anyway—we can remove a few of the bricks, and I'll climb through and get what you need."

"If what you say is true, I could just go in."

"You're shorter and lighter weight. Remember the birds? Smaller bodies mean less resistance to the gases."

"But—"

"*Ça suffit!* It is decided. *Et puis*, I have done *some* drugs. My tolerance is higher than yours."

So much for not acting like Eric. They both had a savior complex a mile wide, as near as I could tell.

Stefan picked a pointy stick up off the ground and moved to the arch, where he began scraping at the mortar between the bricks. Apparently, no one had noticed my previous break-in, as the padlock from the interior grate lay right where I'd tossed it three months ago, on the dirt filling the bottom half of the arch.

I found the brick I'd removed before and pulled it out, and Stefan dropped the stick and found two stones, one sharp, the other heavier. He placed the pointy one at the join of two bricks and used the other as a hammer. It was pretty ingenious, and a few minutes later, we had an opening large enough for a six-foot-tall, twenty-something, stoner mob guy to climb through. He heaved himself up and over the bottom half-wall, and I experienced a pang.

Eric might be unconscious, on the verge of leaving the Earth for good, and seem completely indifferent to his carbon-copy adult son. But I suspected that if said son died on my watch, or anything else unthinkable happened, it would *not* go well for me when Eric woke up.

Stefan saw my expression and smiled, a little sadly. "I will be okay. But if I do die, I'll come back and haunt you."

Crap. Was this a suicide mission? Did he think if he died, he could connect with his father on that plane instead? He stepped away, and I cried out, "Wait—stop!"

Too late. He'd already vanished inside, armed with his phone flashlight and nothing else. While we worked, I'd told him what to look for, and where. It felt closer in than the last one, a straight shot down the main tunnel. But I hadn't thought to try connecting with Stefan's thread before he left—if that were even possible—so I had no sense of his location or how he fared.

In any event, I heard his footsteps returning after only a minute or two, and I swallowed my disappointment. He couldn't have found the rock in such a short time, which meant I'd have to figure something else out, like going in myself.

However, when he came into sight, he grinned, holding up a good-sized specimen, slightly larger than his hand, rough-edged and medium gray, with lighter streaks throughout.

I said, "You found it? That fast?"

"*Ouais.* It was closer in than you thought."

He passed it to me, and I immediately recognized the vibrations. He pulled himself back through the arch, and set to work replacing the bricks, and I thought, *It can't be this easy.*

Or maybe Eric's natural cynicism had finally rubbed off on me—one clear area where he and Stefan differed. Stefan might not be sunshine and light all the time, but he wasn't cynical.

My cell rang and I swiped to answer without checking the caller ID, hoping it would be Nadezhda. Instead, Torben's voice greeted me across the line, saying without preamble, "Olivia called. Thanks to the Buonfiglio aid Elaine arranged, the Dioguardis put feelers out in the south, in addition to their own territories. They think Marchosias will respond within a few days."

My heart thudded, and I couldn't decide if I felt reassured, because we might have a real shot at getting Geordi back soon, or terrified, because Geordi's demon Mafia family was making nice with a loose-cannon Hell Demon—*and* their Buonfiglio rivals.

Reading my thoughts, Torben said, "This is a good thing. We have to make contact with Marchosias. And the Dioguardis have the means to do it, especially with Elaine's family's help."

"Whereas we don't."

"Exactly. And they're being really upfront,

checking in twice a day. I think Jason's right, and even though they hate you, if they're keeping their promise about this, they'll keep the one about you being in Geordi's life."

Some of the tension eased out of me. I might hate them as much as they did me, but their involvement in this just made sense. Without them, I wouldn't know where to start, or how to negotiate Geordi's safe return. And Torben was right: They had zero reason to keep us informed about any of this, except that they'd promised they would. So maybe the Demon Mafia Code would hold after all. Fingers crossed that the *non*-demon Buonfiglio Code would, too.

"Okay, thanks. That helps."

"No problem. Also, one more thing—Jun found one of Satan's shards right here in Paris. Ulrich and I are working on a plan for extraction. We should have it in a day or two."

"Really? That's great." Stefan seemed engrossed in repairing the brick wall, but I stepped farther away just in case. No need to enlighten him quite yet, about the whole King of Hell aspect to this. "You're sure it's one of Satan's?"

"Positive. Now we just need to find Rachel, and a Michael rock, and we're set."

I turned the new shard over in my hand. "About that... I just found one of Michael's here in Turkey. Like, literally a few minutes ago."

Torben was silent a moment. "This feels too easy."

"Yeah, but... You were searching for Satan's shards, and it's my job to find Michael's. Maybe it's not that weird that we both succeeded so fast?"

"Maybe."

My cell buzzed with a text from Nadezhda.

"I've got to go—there might be news about Eric. And I still have to go to Switzerland and get Michael's other rock. Which also feels like too much Cosmic Good Karma. I mean, one shows up in Zürich, where I need to go anyway? *And* I find one here? *And* you get one of Satan's?"

Torben actually laughed. "You know, maybe it's just time for your luck to change. You've been on empty awhile. Maybe the universe is making up for that."

"Maybe," I said, echoing his earlier skepticism.

"Either way, enjoy the win. But if we suddenly find Rachel dropped into our laps, now *that* would be suspicious."

We hung up, and I opened Nadezhda's message, which read, *Come quick. Big problem.*

So much for my Cosmic Karma.

Chapter Fifteen

"Most people would die sooner than think; in fact, they do."

~Bertrand Russell, Welsh Polymath
(1872-1970)

"He *stole* a *body?*" Stefan stared at Nadezhda and me like he'd returned to his earlier assessment that we were bonkers. "What—how—I can't even begin to believe it. *My* father—*Monsieur le Bon Flic*—the goodest good cop *ever*—stole another human's corpse?"

Given Eric's own admissions about what he'd done in the service of justice, I doubted he was the goody-two-shoes Stefan thought him. But I probably shouldn't further shatter his son's illusions just yet, so I kept my mouth shut.

Nadezhda just nodded. "*Da.* Is why he sick now. The body he borrow, it absorb him. Now part of him, he part of it—part of the man he borrow. They intertwined, maybe forever."

I said, "So now we need something of *Sieg's* to save Eric?"

"*Da.* But not for make Sieg stay—for make him *go*. Make loosen hold on Eric. Is not like Sieg a whole person, is only bits of him remain. We kill bits, or make let go, Eric maybe survive. If not..." She shrugged—or tried to—it barely made a ripple near her neck.

Stefan still struggled with this new knowledge. I would've kept the corpse-hopping from him, but Nadezhda let the cat out of the bag with no warning. So much for things being "easy."

I blew out a breath. "Okay. I'll call my guys in Paris. They worked with Sieg, and maybe know something. Or at least they can do some research. How…" I swallowed, then steeled myself. "How much time do we have?"

Nadezhda gave it due consideration. "Maybe…few days? He better now—fighting to stay. Visit from son help. But Sieg very strong. Smashed to bits by man who eject Eric, but parts survive, like roots of plant. Keep growing, worm inside, then like weed, kill host."

Stefan gulped and paled. If he only knew how crowded it actually *was* inside Sieg's body, with Rachel also hiding there. But she had put protections in place so Eric wouldn't notice her, which had likely kept her out of the absorption process that now destroyed him.

I checked my phone—decent cell coverage. I stepped aside and dialed the Central Office, aka Torben. He picked up right away, and I explained the situation.

He let out a stream of German that sounded very impolite. Then he said, "None of us knew each other well, but I'll see what I can find out. Also, forgot to say earlier that we came up with nothing on the supposed break-ins. So either your landlady lied about them, or lied about reporting them. Either way, she lied."

I said thanks, and we hung up. If only I could touch base with Liam, but that was the Big Flaw in my plan to post him as a spy. I'd learned over the past months that the Dead *can* travel with the Living, or together in groups, where they can essentially share the energy "costs." Like how Vadim and his friends brought Eric here. But when solo, it takes a lot of their energy to breach a one- or two-kilometer radius. Dito had only managed it with the aid of the ghost lavender he'd taken, which amped him up. So another thing the rest of the world gets mostly right is that ghosts will stay near the place where they died: stuck in their home, or on the lonely stretch of road where they were hit by a car—or at the diner where they had a heart attack from eating too much sausage and bacon.

Speaking of which, Stefan and I never ate breakfast, and I couldn't remember if I'd had dinner yesterday, not counting the snacks I'd brought on our food-less economy flight to Turkey. I hated to leave Eric, but Nadezhda waved us off.

"Go. You no help here. Go home to France. You find something, you call. If I can, I take care of it here. Meanwhile, Dead will do what they can."

"They can help?"

"*Da*. Maybe. They try. They like him—maybe no hate you so much anymore, too."

She cackled and we left, making our way back to the car.

****

By the time we got back to the hotel, which we hadn't needed to check into in the first place, it was barely midday. I found a direct flight from Antalya to Zürich departing in a few hours, so we checked back out and stopped for food at the nearby store where Jason had once gotten Geordi his favorite "sugary slugs," otherwise known as apricot delight.

He—Jason—hadn't responded to my text on behalf of Elaine yet. Maybe he'd had second thoughts about helping me after all. I couldn't focus on it now, though, so I loaded up on car-friendly munchies, such as böreks and baklava, while Stefan found a meat wrap for himself, and bottled coffee for us both. I also added a box of sugary slugs to my stash of things I'd give to Geordi, *when* we got him back. Then we paid and hit the road.

Turkish speed laws being basically nonexistent, we made it to the airport in record time and returned the car. After an uneventful flight, and with the time change working in our favor, we landed in Switzerland at six-thirty. We could have used the U-Bahn—Zürich's light rail system—to get around, but the address Michael gave me was far enough away to make driving better. Plus, I wanted to stop at my apartment on the way, so I pulled out my credit card again and rented a cheap, fuel-efficient silver VW Up so small that Stefan barely fit in the front seat.

Geordi and I hadn't been in Zürich long, before haring off to Germany, so none of the landscapes felt familiar. And when we climbed the stairs to my first floor flat, I felt like a visitor, not someone coming "home." I inserted my key in the lock, and a few of my neighbors' doors cracked open, as they wondered who invaded my vacant apartment. I'd been gone four weeks, after living here less than six, so who could blame them for being curious?

I heard a noise from the passage behind us and glanced around to see Monsieur Renaud standing by his door at the top of the stairs. As the only other tenant I'd gotten to know here—an older man, with a grandson Geordi's age—he'd been kind to us, loaning Geordi books to read, and making friendly conversation whenever we met.

I smiled tentatively, but it took a moment before he

recognized me and moved toward us. "Hyacinth? Is it really you? *Qu'est-ce qui se passe?*"

"*Oui, c'est moi.* Just here to get my stuff, and then I'll be moving out, back to France."

Stefan frowned. "Who are you talking to?"

I gave him a *duh, that guy* look, when the penny dropped faster than usual, and I turned to Monsieur Renaud. "You're dead? What happened? You were perfectly healthy when I left!"

I sounded like an idiot. People die all the time, and we weren't even *that* close. But I already felt overwhelmed by all the crap hurtling my way: Eric, Stefan, and Sieg, plus Jason, Bala and Dito, and then the two shards we'd just found, plus the one I'd come to get. And the apartments, both here and in Marseille, with accompanying break-ins—or not, depending. And my car, the Dioguardis, my new deal with Jacques Rousseau. And above all: *Geordi.*

Despite my efforts to guide my own destiny over the past few weeks, I felt even *more* like a pinball, being constantly thwacked by some new and unexpected flipper, forced to go in an entirely different direction than planned, and always—*always*—banging into new challenges, while trying not to hit the bottom and drop into darkness forever.

Monsieur Renaud and Stefan watched me with varying levels of concern—the one for my emotional state, the other for my sanity—and I took a deep breath, then blew it back out.

"I'm sorry," I said to Monsieur Renaud. "Give me a sec."

He gave a very Swiss-French half-shrug. "I am in no rush. Take all the time you need."

The doors up the hall were closed again, so evidently the looky-loos had either recognized me, or hidden themselves at my outburst.

I faced Stefan. "Okay, you know about the Dead now. The ones Nadezhda helped you see in Turkey have decided to stay on Earth. Either they aren't religious, or their religion supports an Afterlife here rather than in Heaven or its equivalent." He nodded cautiously—so far, so good. "Well, there are also those who die who *don't* stay here. Are you Catholic?"

France is the sixth largest Catholic country in the world, and not to stereotype or anything, but the Buonfiglios are from Italy, which is the fifth. *And* they're Mafia, so I felt fairly certain Stefan's family, if not he himself, was among the ten percent of regular Mass goers in the nation.

He nodded again.

"So—you know Archangel Michael? He's my boss. When I'm not saving your father and hunting rocks, I sort souls for him. There's a dead guy here, and I need to help him on his way."

Stefan jumped at that, peering around nervously and stepping aside, though he hadn't been that near to Monsieur Renaud in the first place. "*Vraiment?*"

"Yes. You can't be here when I call Michael down, so…"

Crap. I'd just realized the Plutonium shard was loose in my carry-on, which I'd brought up from the car so I could pack it with whatever items I wanted to collect from my apartment. But if Michael sensed the rock and took it, along with the one he'd asked me to retrieve, I'd have none.

Math: Yet another pinball flipper, throwing me off-course.

Well, I'd have to cross my fingers and pray.

I opened my door, then handed Stefan my carry-on. "Go—take this as far away as you can get in ten minutes. Give me another fifteen, then come back. Don't let anyone see what's inside, and if you can, find something to block it."

Like his father, he was quick on the uptake. He only took the bag and said, "Like what?"

"I don't exactly know. Maybe iron or other elemental metals might help?"

Monsieur Renaud said, "I have an iron safe in my apartment, but my door is locked."

I repeated what he'd said for Stefan's benefit, adding, "I have, uh, ways of getting in, but I don't have my, uh, tools with me."

"Not a problem," Stefan said, removing one of his piercings—a black pearl on a long, thin pin—and moments later, the door was open.

Monsieur Renaud recited the safe combination, which I gave to Stefan, and he disappeared inside with my carry-on in tow, while Monsieur Renaud and I returned to my apartment. As in Marseille, nothing seemed out of order or rifled through. Not that I'd left much here to rifle. Marseille is the only place I've lived long enough to accumulate "stuff," and this flat was pretty barebones: an open area comprising kitchenette, dinette, and living room, tiny *salle de bain*, and one bedroom that Geordi'd used, while I slept on the couch, and Eric took the floor.

I said to Monsieur Renaud, "Did you happen to notice anyone lurking around, or going in or out of my place, since I've been gone?"

I'd mostly asked just to cover my bases, so it surprised me when he said, "*Oui. Il y avait une femme*— brown hair, in a pink dress. She had *une silhouette généreuse.*" He paused dreamily, then cleared his throat. "She said she was *une vieille amie* of yours. I had another engagement at the time, so I do not know if she broke in. But she was definitely lurking, as you say."

Brown hair? Pink? Jeannette? *Here*? Before I'd even told her about the place? She'd certainly given no clue that she already knew of it, so I had to admire her poker face. But it made me doubly glad I'd left Liam behind, and even more anxious to check in with him.

"Okay, thanks. Not to rush you or anything, but— you're Catholic, right? You believe in God, and want to pass on to, uh, wherever you go next?"

He gave a self-deprecating smile. "*Oui.* I am prepared for my final judgment, whatever it may be. I have done my best. That is all one can do."

Okay, then. I thought, *Michael*, and there he was.

Granted, the holidays loomed, and it's a good bet Michael celebrates Christmas. But even so, his ensemble was one for the books. For starters, he sported a bright green long sleeved t-shirt emblazoned with a Santa hat-wearing baby, encircled by the slogan, *Jesus Puts the "Christ" in Christmas*. Then he'd added red corduroy pants—the kind with hammer loops and tool pockets on the sides—and his favorite footwear: ginormous sandals, over red and green striped socks. And all of it was topped off by the largest, fluffiest Santa hat I've ever seen.

Good thing Stefan had absented himself or he might think he'd gotten some really dicey weed. Even Monsieur Renaud looked stunned. But since Michael had literally appeared from nowhere, he recognized the presence of an angel, and bowed his head, awaiting his fate.

"Child," Michael said to me. He glanced around as though visiting an old haunt he hadn't seen in awhile. Essentially this was true, as he'd come here on several occasions, under the pretense of being an uncle to Geordi on Lily's and my side of the family.

He regarded me expectantly, so I said, "Philippe Renaud. Definitely up."

"Ah." He made the sign of the cross over Monsieur Renaud. "Come, my son. I will show you the way. Hyacinth—you will retrieve the rock now, yes?"

"Yes."

Did I imagine it, or did his eyes narrow suspiciously? I wiped my thoughts and gazed back steadily. I should know by now that deceiving Michael— an *archangel*, and my boss—was a dumb idea. Especially for something as big as this. I told my conscience I'd fork over the shard after we used it, re-righting my moral compass again, but it was still a huge risk.

If he suspected anything, he didn't call me on it. He only said, "Very well, child. I will return when you have retrieved it."

A moment later, he and Monsieur Renaud were gone, and I sagged onto an ancient kitchen chair at my equally ancient chrome and yellow Formica table. Even "honest" encounters with him left me simultaneously drained and on edge. For one thing, I doubt I'll ever feel comfortable being a Sorter. I mean, who am I to judge whether someone gets the reward of Heaven, or is tortured in Hell for all eternity?

But I did get that sense about most new souls, Eric

being a rare exception. It was a conundrum, like being a great assassin who hated killing people. And yet I felt obligated to use my talents, in part because I'd agreed to do just that, in exchange for staying on Earth with Geordi. Except now it seemed he would've been safer with the Dioguardis after all. Probably they would have spied Marchosias in Paolo right away, and whisked Geordi off to safety. Instead, I'd *begged* Jason to include Paolo on the mission to take Geordi to Bala's island home.

I dropped my head in my hands, but only for a second. Then I stood and went around the apartment, grabbing only what I couldn't replace, and piling it on the table. Entering Geordi's room gave me a pang, but it didn't take much to clear it out, due to its entire contents being books borrowed from Monsieur Renaud. I filled a grocery bag with these and took it down the hall, knocking on the door and waiting for Stefan to answer, presumably after checking the peephole.

Which reminded me of Jeannette, and her possible visit here, and my urgent need to do six things, in half a dozen places, all at once.

I set the bag of books on the dining table. "Rock?"

Stefan went to the safe and retrieved it. I saw stacks of cash inside, not noticeably diminished, and thought Eric would be proud of his son in this respect, at least.

Plus, evidently the iron *had* prevented Michael from detecting the rock. Meaning it would probably block his demon nephews and nieces as well, not to mention Satan. Lily's safe is also iron, so I made a mental note to store all current and future magic rocks inside it, just in case.

We went back to my flat and Stefan helped me stuff my things into my carry-on. I shut and locked the door, and we headed down to the basement to give the landlady my key. Frau Blauch glowered when she saw me, but brightened when she learned I'd moved out for good. I didn't request a refund on the rent, so by the time we left, she was all smiles.

And that was it. Another chapter of my life, however small, closed.

Stefan stayed silent as we headed for the car. He smelled of weed, so he must have used his alone time at Monsieur Renaud's to light up. I wondered if Eric knew about that? Neither of us is a prude, but if Stefan did it to escape, instead of as an occasional fun buzz, it could be a problem.

I gave myself a mental shake. Not my business. I barely knew him, and had no clue what drove Eric to abandon him. Yet at the same time, I considered him a new minion. Argh. I had to stop collecting strays. They only further complicated my already too-complex life.

But baked and silent though he might be, it felt…nice, having him around. He didn't have to tag along with me to Switzerland—he could have flown straight home from Turkey. I'd agreed to take him to Eric—*check*—and arrange for Elaine to meet the Dioguardis—*in progress*. But he hadn't objected, and had proven himself useful by first retrieving, and then concealing, the rock. Plus, if anything untoward happened to me in this next phase of our trip, at least Stefan could tell someone about it.

The address we sought was in Zug, a chi-chi lake town thirty minutes south of Zürich, so we headed in that direction, arriving just after nine. We could have waited and gone in the morning, but I needed to get at least *one* thing settled. Besides, the whole house glowed with lights, cars crowding the street, people milling across the lawn. Obviously, the owner was throwing a party.

I parked the VW two blocks away and peered down at my ratty turtleneck and jeans, then at Stefan's t-shirt and tie-dyed sneakers. "Did you bring anything fancier?"

"Nope."

"Neither did I."

Oh well. I unbuckled and opened my door, and Stefan said, "Mind if I sit this one out?"

I paused. "Sure. No problem. Just don't go anywhere. I'll be right back."

With so many people around, I felt safe. But after just acknowledging gratitude for Stefan's presence, I was suddenly solo again. Maybe he wanted more alone time with his weed. What did I care? As a rental, the car had probably been used as a hotbox before.

I climbed out, then walked to the house and up the wide front steps, approaching the open double doors. No one paid me any heed, so I stepped inside. The entry was breathtaking—bigger than Dioguardi Central, and more subtle in its Wealth. I saw important—*read: valuable*—paintings, priceless vases filled with richly scented flowers, and of course, *objets d'art* everywhere.

My sticky fingers twitched, but I told them *no*, and moved farther in, searching for the host. I'm not sure where the distinction lies, but everyone I saw gave off "guest" vibes. They all wore Rich Folk Garb—expensive bling on the women, dark colors on the men—and clustered together, using the glasses in their hands to gesture with as much as drink, while chatting in that fake-friendly way people do at social gatherings. In my experience, the host usually wanders the party, checking in at each group before moving on to the next. But as near as I could tell, *I* was the only one wandering anywhere, besides the servants.

I finally caught the attention of one of these, a man carrying a tray of appetizers. "*Excusez-moi, où est l'hôte?*"

He shook his head, which I interpreted to mean he didn't speak French. I did my best in German instead, which made his expression clear, and he rattled something off while pointing at a nearby curved staircase. I nodded my thanks and headed up.

It was quieter upstairs, as no other guests had gone off-book and left the main floor. But hallways branched out everywhere, and if the servant had given specific directions, I hadn't caught them. So unfortunately, I'd have to go door to door. The thick carpet muffled my steps, and no one answered at the first five rooms I tried, but I heard voices at the sixth. I felt very intrusive, but Michael had said the host expected me. So I took my courage in hand and knocked lightly.

The conversation abruptly stopped, and after a pause, the door opened on a woman in her seventies. She had white hair curling softly around her pale face, and she was tiny—well under five feet tall. She wore a pleated lavender chiffon dress with three-quarter sleeves, matching hose, and lavender patent leather shoes that had to come from the children's section. A corsage of night lilies on her shoulder gave off a heavy perfume, and she wore a huge pear-cut diamond ring on her left ring finger, with matching large teardrop diamonds at her ears.

Her bright brown eyes regarded me inquisitively. "*Kann ich Ihnen helfen?*"

A movement came from behind her, by the gold silk

drapes—a man, about her age, balding, portly, and wearing a black tux with the tie loosened and his top two buttons undone. He caught my eye and reddened. A four-poster bed stood against one wall, the lights were dimmed, and a fire crackled softly in the walk-in fireplace. Clearly, I'd interrupted something, er, special.

I said, "*Je suis désolé, mais je ne parle pas allemand. Parlez-vous français?*"

The woman nodded. "*Oui. Puis-je vous aider?*"

The man tugged his tie the rest of the way off, and I said, "I'm really sorry—I can see I'm intruding."

She frowned. "No, it is fine. I am not busy. But I do need to return to my guests, so…?"

"I really don't want to disrupt your, er, plans."

"I do not understand. I have already said I am not busy, so please, state your business."

I'm a direct person, but this felt like a delicate situation. Still, I needed the rock, so I gestured at the man and blurted, "What about him? I can come back later, if you prefer."

Her eyes widened and she gasped. "You see him?"

Crap. I turned to the man. "You're dead?"

But it was the woman who answered. "Of course he is, dear. And I have a job to do. But I believe you can stay for it, if you like. You must be Hyacinth. I am Lavendel von Kantz."

Chapter Sixteen

"For I know the plans I have for you...plans to prosper you and not to harm you, plans to give you hope and a future."

~Jeremiah 29:11
(Bible, NIV)

Michael grinned, enjoying his little joke. He wore the same clothes he'd had on an hour ago, and had greeted Lavendel warmly when she called him down. The man, Walther, was a neighbor who'd been dressing for her party when he had a heart attack and died. He'd showed up at the party anyway—why let a little thing like death ruin your plans?—and when Lavendel realized what had happened, she'd brought him up here to process.

She gave Walther's deets to Michael and said, "He should go up."

Michael nodded. "Of course. But first..."

She gave a nod herself, moving to the door. "I will fetch it. I will return in a moment."

She left, and Michael said to me, "You see, child—you are not as alone as you may think. There are not many like you, but there are a few. I thought it might be good for you to meet one—perhaps network a little."

"Lavendel's a sorter? But she can't sense the rocks? So how did she get one?"

"It came from a soul she sorted a while ago. The details are not important, but after I took the man away—he went down—she noticed the shard in his things. I would have verified it myself, but I have been busy. And besides, I wanted to give you an introduction."

I wrinkled my nose. "Wasn't it dangerous, leaving it here? What if the demons found it?"

He lifted a massive shoulder. "She is a sorter. The demons would have no reason to suspect her of having anything of interest. I felt safe, and so did she."

Lavendel reentered the room, bearing a green velvet-wrapped bundle which she handed to me, before going to stand with Walther, who waited patiently by the windows.

As soon as I touched the wrappings, I felt the vibrations, and obviously, so did Michael. He gestured eagerly for me to unwrap it, which I did, and ceremoniously handed it to him. The whole thing felt redundant, but whatever. At least I already had another of his rocks—in the car, barely a block away. But Michael didn't appear to notice it, so maybe his radar only worked over short distances? Or this shard's vibrations masked the other's?

He placed it lovingly in the pouch at his belt, then faced Walther at the window. "Come, my son. I will show you the way."

Lavendel gave Walther an encouraging wave and he stepped forward. Michael touched his arm, and he got that trusting look all souls got, no matter where Michael was taking them. A moment later, they were gone, and I sagged with relief.

Lavendel said, "Would you like to sit on the bed for a moment?"

I almost said no, then thought, why not? I sat, and she hopped up to join me, barely making a dent in the cream silk duvet, her feet dangling well above the floor.

"I remember when I first became a sorter," she said. "So exhausting. But one does get accustomed to it, as time goes on."

"You mean there's no escape?"

She laughed. "I am afraid not. At least, not until you are old, like me, and ready to retire."

She didn't seem ready to slow down any time soon, but what did I know? Either way, she must be one of the sorters Michael had mentioned, who'd be leaving the "profession" soon.

I said, "Do you mind if I ask you something?"

"Of course, dear, go right ahead. I believe that is why Michael brought us together. He is not oblivious. I am sure he has noticed you are struggling."

That surprised me. Not so much that Michael would have noticed, but that in such a short acquaintance, *she* had. "You think I'm struggling?"

She studied me a moment. "Maybe that is too strong of a word. But yes, I can see the process is not natural for you. For some sorters, they would judge everyone around them, alive *or* dead, just for fun. But for you— and me—it is not in our nature. I believe you are more of a—how do you say it?—a live and let live person."

She'd hit the nail on the head with that one. But I had other things to discuss. I'd never met anyone else like me, other than Nadezhda, who I still found intimidating. By contrast, Lavendel seemed open and frank. Or maybe it was her size. It's hard to feel threatened by someone resembling a tiny a white-haired sparrow.

I said, "I noticed you didn't touch Walther."

Her brows rose. "Ah—you are one of those. It is very rare. But to answer your question, no, I cannot touch the Dead, only see and speak with them. I have never met anyone who could do that, until now."

"I have."

"Really? How fascinating."

"I'm not actually sure if she was ever a sorter, but she absolutely can touch the Dead. So can I. In fact, they are so real for me, I can't tell them apart from the Living most of the time."

"That must be very confusing for you."

"Yeah."

She didn't offer any advice, but just having my feelings affirmed helped. I blew out a breath and rose off the bed, and she dropped down to the floor beside me.

"I have to go," I said. "But…maybe we could stay in touch? It would be nice to hear your perspective on some of this stuff."

"I would like that."

I took out my cell phone and she recited her number while I entered her into my contacts. Then I sent her a text, so she'd have my digits, and she walked me downstairs and out onto the porch. I thanked her and wished her well with her party, then headed down the steps and up the dark road to the car.

The streetlights were spaced far apart, and I hadn't parked under one. So I didn't notice until I was right next to the car that the front passenger seat was vacant. In fact, *all* the seats were. I frantically yanked open the hatch—Stefan's bag was missing, and mine lay open, the contents strewn all over.

The *remaining* contents, that is. Stefan had

absconded with the rock.

Merde.

He couldn't have gotten far on foot. I jumped in the car and buckled up, wondering where he'd gone—and *why*? I hadn't told him the shard's significance, just that it belonged to Michael, and he hadn't expressed any interest in it. Plus, he could have just taken it while at Monsieur Renaud's. So what had happened in the last thirty minutes, to make him want it? And again—for what purpose?

I pulled away from the curb and headed up the block. I had to find him, to get the rock back, and also because, as noted, I felt responsible for him. No matter what Mafia family wedge lay between him and his father, I couldn't face Eric knowing I'd lost his only son.

Shit. The Buonfiglios. I slammed on the brakes at a stop sign, thinking fast.

Stefan's family were rivals of the Dioguardis, but not demons. Stefan clearly hadn't known any of the supernatural stuff, until Elaine and I told him. Plus, Elaine had said the Dioguardis weren't being "careful" in their search for Geordi, and *she* knew he'd been taken by a Hell Demon. If she'd told Stefan, he might suspect that a powerful relic belonging to Archangel Michael would be of interest to his family, in their quest to beat the Dioguardis.

Merde and double *merde*.

Had he played me all along? Had Elaine asked me to take him to Eric, to insert him into my life, so they could pick the right moment to pounce? Was *that* why she wanted an intro to the Dioguardis—to attack from within, after all? Or to get an even bigger hold over them somehow?

I peeled away from the stop sign, peering at the houses around me, and down any side streets I passed. *Where are you, damn it?*

I should have asked why he wanted to wait in the car. Although with his resemblance to Eric, no matter what excuse he made, I probably would've believed him.

Damn, damn, and *more* damn.

Stefan taking the shard might not be so bad on its own. But the domino ramifications of having to find *another* rock Michael didn't know about, led me straight from *no way to resurrect Nick,* to *Geordi's out of my life forever.*

I would *not* let that happen, no matter who Stefan's father was.

Think, damn it. He'd probably stick to the main road, to get as far away as fast as possible. However, he'd want to remain hidden, so he'd probably walk on the lawns or near the houses, keeping to the shadows. But…what was his destination, or his end goal?

I pulled over again, trying to force rational thought back in, so I wouldn't waste more time. If I'd already lost him, I should save my energy for something else—like locating another rock, and then using it to bash Stefan's lying head in when I found him, Eric's son or not.

Or should I search a little longer? Maybe he'd gone to the airport, or more likely, the train station. For that matter, he had his phone. He'd probably called an Uber by now and skedaddled that way.

Lavendel likely had connections who could help me, if the size of her home gave any indication of the status and wealth she enjoyed. But now that I'd calmed down, I realized pursuit would be futile. Stefan was long gone, and I'd never catch him. I took out my phone and dialed

Torben, and he picked up right away, cutting me off before I could speak.

"Hyacinth—are you coming back? We have Satan's shard, and Olivia says Marchosias agreed to meet with the Dioguardis. She doesn't know what they're offering, but is confident it will be enough. I told her you'll pull Nick out at the Plutonium, and she's going to propose it as a good central location for the exchange. If the Buonfiglios uphold their promise to not interfere, we should be good to go."

Thank God. I didn't dare hope too much—there were still way too many things that could go wrong. But Marchosias considering the Dioguardis' offer was a huge start.

Torben continued, "Now, we just need to find Rachel and get her to Turkey, with our rock and the one you found."

I swallowed. "About that… I kind of lost it. That's why I'm calling."

The line was silent. Then he said, "How?" I told him, and he swore. "Why do you think he took it?"

"My best guess is as an offering to the Buonfiglios. He mentioned needing to prove his loyalty, and I think he saw this as too good an opportunity to pass up."

"Makes sense. I'll see what I can find out."

"Thanks. And while you're at it—"

"I'll search for another shard."

"Thanks. Again. Any progress on Sieg, and what might make him let go of Eric's soul?"

I heard his regret through the line. "Sorry. He kept to himself, or spent time with Rachel. She really had a grip on him. Believe it or not, he was mostly normal at first. Not nice exactly, but I wouldn't have thought he'd go so far in the other direction. She really pushed him."

"What about her journal? Maybe she made notes about him in it."

Torben whistled. "I never thought of that. When we combed it before, we weren't focused on Sieg, and might have missed something. I'll get Jun on it. He's read more of it than anyone else."

"Good. I'll go pick Liam up in Marseille, and be back in Paris, probably late tomorrow."

"Not necessary. Ulrich or Jason can take the train and get both Liam and your car. Then you can come straight back here from Zürich—save you the extra eight hours of driving."

My heart clutched at the casual mention of Jason. I should've known he wouldn't ditch me, even after what I'd done. "Jason's there?"

"Not right now, no. He went home an hour ago, but he should just stay here. He's been over every day, after visiting Bala at the hospital. It's been very helpful. He has specific knowledge and a skill set that we—Ulrich and I, and even Jun—don't have. Between him and Dito, we've learned a tremendous amount."

So, being Jason, he'd gone so far beyond "not ditching me" that he'd been working with my minions this whole time. I closed my eyes, so overwhelmed with gratitude I couldn't breathe. If only he were here now. Maybe he would have suspected Stefan's motives.

But…would I have listened to his warnings?

Probably not.

I sighed and opened my eyes again. "Okay, that would be great. Jason should probably go. He knows where I live, because he lived there, too. Which reminds me…"

I told Torben about Jeannette's possible visit to my place in Zürich, and he said he'd see if he could find travel records or any way to prove it was her or not, and we hung up.

For the hell of it, I dialed Stefan's number. Maybe he'd just pick up and say he took the rock so Michael wouldn't sense it so close by. No dice. I tried Elaine, but got her voicemail. I thought about calling Nadezhda, but if Eric's condition had changed, she would have called me.

I opened the link for Jason's contact info, staring at his number. Should I?

Packing up my place here, I already felt alone and adrift. But Marseille didn't feel like home anymore, either. For a long time after I left the States, I'd drifted on purpose, enjoying the freedom of being able to pack up and go at a moment's notice. But now...

I just felt unsettled, not free. And though not really alone anymore, I hadn't known my minions long. Most of the time they felt like coworkers: friendly ones you'd eat lunch with, and see on the weekends occasionally, but not close, despite the fact that we lived together.

And the hardest part of all this was that the giant Geordi-sized hole in my life grew wider daily. As the last remaining member of my tiny family, he brought desperately-needed sunshine and light into my solo existence, and the prospect of losing him forever yawned before me like a cavernous dark canyon I'd never climb out of.

And the only other person who knew what that felt like...was Jason.

I hit the call button, my heart abruptly thundering like a jackhammer. I shouldn't call—I should hang up and just talk to him when I got back. I should—

Too late. He picked up on the first ring. "Hyacinth? Sorry I didn't call you. We've been busy here."

I couldn't tell from his tone if he thought my call good, bad, or neutral. And suddenly, I couldn't think of anything to say. The tears welled up, and I must have made a noise, because he sucked in a breath.

"What is it? What's wrong? Are you hurt?"

I shook my head, then realized that of course he couldn't see me. I forced a calming breath. "N-no. It's just—Geordi, and Stefan, and—"

I started to cry harder, because I *so* needed to talk about my fears for Eric, and how much I needed him. But it was patently unfair to do that with Jason, who I *also* needed.

Someone must have told him who Stefan was, because he just said, "Hey—it's okay. We'll figure it all out. Geordi will be safe, and we'll get him back. I promise."

Just hearing him say that helped. "Thanks. It's just…" I sniffled, then dashed the tears from my eyes. "Stefan took the shard we found. So now I have to get another one, and I d-don't know where I'll f-find one…"

There was a pause while he processed. "Stefan—Eric's *son*—stole it from you?"

"Yeah—it's all my fault. I couldn't help it. They look so much alike. I know he's not Eric, but I projected his father's honorableness onto him. Big mistake. I should've realized that if he'd even consider joining the Buonfiglios, his moral compass must be skewed. Plus…" I swallowed. "I think I used him as a substitute for Geordi."

He was silent a moment. Then he said softly, "I get

it. I miss him horribly, too. And…I miss you."

I fought to keep the tears down, and lost. He sat quietly on the other end, not talking, just being there while I cried. He deserved so much more than what I'd been giving him. And a huge part of me wanted to *give* him more. But I didn't know how, or if I even could.

Finally I said, "I'm better now. I'm sorry. I guess it all just got to me."

"I know. Are you okay to drive? I can stay on the line if you need me to."

"I'm okay. I just need to get home now."

Home.

All at once, that word meant something: Paris, Lily's place—*my* place. And…Jason. My feelings for Eric hadn't changed. He would always be part of me—a piece of my heart.

But with sudden clarity I realized that when I thought of being settled—anchored safely in my crazy new world—I thought first of Jason. And Jason had put himself—his personal safety, his feelings, everything— on the line for me, time and again. I'd never had anyone, ever, do that for me, that I could recall.

Not even Eric. His feelings for me *were* genuine, no question. But… As Jason always said, Eric had his own agenda—his own goals, that he didn't always share with me.

But now I realized—Jason's agenda *was* me. He might put Geordi absolutely first, and he might disagree with me—a lot—but only when he thought what I did would be detrimental to my safety, or to Geordi's. If that's not…love…then what is?

"I…miss you, too."

There was a long pause. Then he said, "Good."

I bit my lip and sniffled again. "I'll see you tomorrow."

"Yes. You will. Torben called—Ulrich is picking me up in the morning to drive down to Marseille. He offered to take the train, but if we both go, I can drive your car back, while he and Liam ride in Lily's. Plus, I feel like I should talk with Jeannette, since I know her pretty well. I'll see you after that."

We hung up, and I sat a moment, taking in what I'd just done. It felt…good. Like my heart expanded, my eyes opened, and my world brightened, filling with hope and promise. I inhaled, then exhaled slowly.

Then I opened the maps app on my phone, typed in Lily's address, and headed for home.

Chapter Seventeen

"The safest road to hell is the gradual one—the gentle slope, soft underfoot, without sudden turnings, without milestones, without signposts."

~C.S. Lewis, British Author
(1898-1963)

Elaine called the next morning with the Buonfiglios' demands. I wasn't far off—they didn't want to bargain with the rock. Not exactly, anyway. They wanted me to turn them into demons, and then they'd return it. So basically, they were holding it for a ransom I couldn't pay.

I'd driven all night, stopping only for gas, and arrived at Lily's—it might be my home now, but it would always be *her* place—after four a.m. My living minions were early risers, and Ulrich was already up and making coffee when I walked in. My dead minions didn't sleep much, so Jun and Dito were also up, working at the dining table. I'd been too tired to do more than greet them before crashing for a couple hours' sleep, which ended when Elaine's call woke me.

I said now, "Are you nuts? I can't do that. Only Satan can make demons."

Elaine remained unruffled. "Hell Demons, yes. But blood demons, like the Dioguardis—that is different, *n'est-ce pas?*"

203

"True. But you must know the blood *came* from Satan originally."

"Even so, there must be some way to get it now—extract it, and give it to us."

"There's not, and you can keep the rock. I'll find another one."

"That is not a good idea. If you do not meet our requirements, we will tell Michael you kept this one from him—*and why.*"

I sucked in a breath. Stefan no doubt told her the Michael part. But how had either of them learned of the plan to bring Nick back? Were the Dioguardis being so incautious that *they'd* let it slip? Rina was a very desperate mother-slash-grandmother, but hopefully not *that* reckless.

Or maybe Elaine was bluffing. I said, "I don't know what you're talking about."

"Is that so? Let us just say that your boss may be very interested to know you are planning to *take back* one of his deliveries, and not from the Good Place."

Crap. Not bluffing, then.

"I still can't do what you're asking. Even *if* I could lay hands on their blood, it's diluted. The first infusion happened thirty generations ago, in the twelfth century. Even the strongest Dioguardis don't have much now. It wouldn't be enough to, uh, convert your whole family."

"Not them. Stefan."

I froze. "No. No, no, *no*. I am not making Eric's *son* into a *demon*. Stefan can't possibly want this—is it his grandfather, forcing him into it?"

"No. He wants this for himself."

That couldn't be right. How had I so misjudged him? Unless Elaine was mistaken—but I didn't think so.

I even detected a hitch in her voice, like she wasn't as on board as she claimed.

"But you don't want it for him. Do you?" She hesitated, and I pushed ahead. "So why are you helping him? Do you have *any* idea what it's like? Does *he*? I can tell you, it's no picnic. He might not be a Hell Demon, but he'll be a Hell *magnet*. Maybe more so than the Dioguardis—they at least had Satan's consent. Who knows what this will do to Satan's rage level? There was a married couple—they wanted Satan's powers, to do his work on Earth. So you'd think he'd be all over it. Nope. He literally *turned them inside out.* Is that what you want, for your *son?*"

I stopped, waiting while she considered what I'd said. It might not make a difference, but I had to try. And it was all moot anyway, because I couldn't do it.

Finally, she said simply, "I cannot stop him. I thought seeing his father would bring him back from the edge. But instead, it pushed him over."

I shook my head in disbelief. "I can't reconcile what you're saying with how he acted in Turkey. Certainly not like he'd been called to the Dark Side. In fact, he seemed genuinely interested in helping me. I don't get it."

"*Moi non plus.* But here we are. He has the shard, and if you do not help him—even if you do not want it back—he will find something creative to do with it. And it will not be good."

Merde. She had a point: Stefan was smart and resourceful, and if I didn't meet his demands, perfectly capable of issuing a *fuck you* to me, by being "creative." Anger at his father had driven him to join the mob. What would anger at me, thwarting his current Demon Life Goal, make him do?

I said, "Can you stall him a little? I need time to find out if it's even possible. I'm not saying I'll do it if it is, but I just don't even know."

"I'll try, but he already bought train tickets to Paris. We'll be there tonight. When he wants something, he's very impulsive. Not at all like his father's careful deliberation—Stefan acts when an idea strikes him, and thinks about it only later."

Which might explain why he'd taken the rock in the first place. Maybe he hadn't planned it. Maybe while hotboxing in the rental car, it occurred to him in a flash that he should become a demon by stealing an archangel's relic from my luggage in the back.

I said, "Do you still want an intro to the Dioguardis? In light of this new development?"

"*Oui*. If Stefan is successful, he will be a new type of bio-demon. They will not be happy when they find out. But my family will keep our promise to help get your nephew back. I am hopeful that aid will be valuable enough for the Dioguardis to agree to Stefan's continued safety."

Oh well. At this point, the formerly insurmountable task of getting Elaine an in with the Dioguardis now felt laughably easy and unimportant, compared to making her son a demon.

"Okay, I'll work on it," I said, and we hung up.

It wasn't quite eight yet, and I considered going back to sleep. But I'm mostly a morning person, and Elaine's call had keyed me up.

For one thing, Jason would be dropping by sometime today. In the cold light of a drizzly late November dawn, my emotional revelations of the night before weren't so clear. I did still have feelings for Eric, but...I acknowledged my feelings for Jason, too. I just didn't know which were stronger, or if Jason really felt the same for me. Being glad I missed him and saying he'd see me today didn't exactly equate to a declaration. Maybe I'd just been overly emotional, projecting feelings onto both of us that weren't based in the reality of our situation.

Either way, I had a few hours before he returned from Marseille. But it also meant I couldn't ask him about the Dioguardi blood, since that was an in-person conversation.

Then I remembered Dito. He probably knew as much as Jason did, about the likelihood of Stefan becoming a demon.

I pushed myself out of bed and into the master bathroom. When I arrived home, I'd finally switched from the guest room to Lily's. It was silly to avoid it, and she'd want me to have it. Besides, I'd been asking my minions to sleep on the couch or the floor for too long. They're a bunch of ex-military dudes, and while very respectful and polite, as noted, basically strangers. Having my own private bathroom, and leaving the guest bathroom to them, made way more sense.

But as with my revelations about Jason, it now felt weird to wake up in Lily's bed, surrounded by her things. Even the bathroom vanity was littered with her cosmetics and other personal care products, which she'd no doubt used the morning before she kidnapped Geordi and fled to me, only to die after all at the hands of the Rousseaux.

I swallowed my grief and guilt, then returned to the bedroom and opened the top drawer of her dresser. Without looking inside, I emptied the contents onto the bed, then repeated the process with the other drawers, on down to the bottom. I found old shopping bags in the closet and stuffed everything into them before I lost my nerve, then brought them all out to the front door. I'd slept in my clothes—a bad habit I'd picked up in recent weeks—but they weren't too wrinkled, so I decided moving Lily's stuff *out* of the dresser was enough for now. I'd move my stuff *into* it later.

I didn't see Torben anywhere, but Jun and Dito remained at the dining table, the two volumes of Rachel's journal open before them. Even Eric slept sometimes, or did the ghost equivalent of it. But Jun and Dito rarely did. Perhaps because they were more committed to the Spirit World? Maybe Eric's unfinished business kept him too tethered to Life, and therefore, to the habits of the Living.

Pushing random speculations aside, I went to the kitchen, found the coffee still warming on the machine, and poured a steaming mug. I added cream, then went back to the dining room and sat next to Jun, across from Dito.

"How's it going?"

Both of them had mastered the use of ghost energy enough to flip the journal pages by themselves, freeing my living minions—aka Torben and Ulrich, as they were the only ones here with me in France—to do other things.

Jun answered, "I think we're onto something. There's a lot in here about Sieg. She really manipulated him, and describes it blatantly. She basically groomed him to be her safe house."

"How so?"

"For starters, she isolated him from his family. Although the Burkes did that to all of us, to some extent."

I'd never even asked my minions about their

personal situations. They'd offered to help, and I'd accepted—grudgingly, no less. Maybe not as bad as Rachel, but at a minimum, I'd been pretty thoughtless. The living ones, especially, must have families to get back to.

"I'm sorry," I said.

"For what?"

"Everything she did to you, and for what I'm asking of you now. You don't have to stay, you know."

Jun actually laughed at that. "*I* asked *you* to keep me here, remember? And anyway, what she did to Sieg was far worse than what she did to the rest of us. She made him believe his family plotted against him, and—of course—she could save him. And in case you're wondering, yes, she seduced him sexually, too. Actually, in every way—physically, emotionally, mentally. She made him see her as the only thing between him and utter destruction, and if he didn't do everything she asked, essentially, the world would end."

"Wow. That's…disturbing."

"It fit with his own inclinations. She chose well. Anyone else might have been more difficult to convince. However, when she told him he might have to kill himself to let her spirit into his body, he did push back, at least a little. This is all from her perspective, of course, so she writes that she easily re-convinced him. But I think he'd started to question her, and at the end, he wasn't as gung-ho as she thought."

Dito nodded agreement. "I'm reading her second journal now, and she says he tried to get in touch with his former fiancée. She—Rachel—pretended to be the fiancée and texted back that he was worthless and should kill himself."

"Jeez."

I'd only seen the violent living Sieg, or the version with Eric's spirit—and Rachel—in residence. So I really had no idea who he'd been as a person, before the Burkes came into his life.

"Any idea what might make him let go and move on?"

"Not yet," Jun said. "We really need someone who knew him well."

"His fiancée?"

"Maybe." He sounded doubtful. "I think the rift was too great. I'm not sure she could help him let go and move on. She might just piss him off and make him want to stay."

Dito added, "Love and hate. Same coin and all that."

I wondered if he referred to Bala. Which reminded me of Jason, and *his* relationship with her. But it also reminded me why I came to talk with Dito in the first place.

"On a different topic—how much do you know about Dioguardi demon blood biology?"

"A fair amount. We all do—it's required at our school. What do you need to know?"

"How diluted is it now?"

"Hard to say. I think you already know some of us get more—or less—than others. For instance, Paolo had very little. Jason, too, but more than Paolo. And it manifested pretty late in both of them, which also usually means a lower concentration."

I couldn't recall if he knew about Jason taking the Rousseaux's powers, but it seemed likely, so I asked cautiously, "Would it make a difference if the demon's powers were, uh, enhanced at some point?"

He considered. "Maybe. Or the addition could dilute the blood further. Want to tell me what you really want to know? It would help me answer more accurately."

I cleared my throat. "If, say, someone has a high concentration and, uh, donates blood or something, could it make the recipient a demon?"

His brows rose. "Are you asking for a friend?"

"Kind of. Look, without getting too far into detail, can you just tell me if it's *theoretically* possible to make a brand-new strain of bio-demons, using current Dioguardi demon blood?"

He thought a moment. "Obviously, the question has come up before, but there's no definitive answer. Some say it's possible, if the blood is taken from a powerful young demon. Early adulthood at the latest. The older we get, the weaker we are. But others say no way. For example, Bala needed a transfusion. There's no Type Demon blood, so she got 'regular' blood."

I hadn't considered that. "Will it make her less of a demon?"

"No. Which is why some say that, similarly, giving demon blood to non-demons won't affect them. Although, if the demon also shares their powers during the transfusion, it might work. Still, we don't usually donate blood, just in case. Wouldn't want a bunch of random bio-demons roaming around."

"Okay. So it might be possible, or it might not."

Not exactly helpful, but maybe I could string Stefan along—maybe even give him "regular" blood instead, and get the shard back before he figured it out.

Dito said, "Anything else?"

"Yeah. Are there other demon families out there? Or are the Dioguardis the only ones?"

He watched me silently, then finally shrugged. "It's possible. Likely, even. Similar to the question of life on other planets. It would be stranger if there *aren't* other families. But bottom line, I've never heard of any." He paused. "Except for you and Geordi."

I swallowed. It was all so confusing. *Was* Geordi a demon? How could he be, when according to Jason, neither Lily nor I—nor our parents—were? But if not demons, then…what were we?

Either way, it appeared no other *known* demon families existed. Which is no doubt how Nico and Rina, distant cousins—very distant, but still—wound up marrying each other, to keep the blood from getting further diluted. But maybe now Rina'd become concerned about inbreeding, and the Satan connection, and so had targeted Lily to "freshen up" the bloodline.

The elevator opened and Torben stepped out, carrying cloth bags heavy with food. He greeted me, then headed for the kitchen. I thanked Dito, then joined Torben as he unloaded various meats into the fridge, making my mouth water and my stomach rumble.

He eyed me up and down. "Thought you might need this. I'll cook the sausages now, and we can have the rest for dinner."

I opened my mouth to argue, then thought, what's the point? I might as well embrace it and move on. "I may have a lead on retrieving the rock, but to be safe—any luck finding a backup?"

"Actually, yes."

I stared in surprise. "You're kidding. That's great."

Maybe I wouldn't have to pretend to make Stefan a demon. Although the threat remained that he'd tattle to Michael, or do something else fun, just to spite me. But

Torben frowned.

"Yes. Kind of. It's just…weird, that it showed up right after I started searching for it."

That *was* weird. Combined with the easy retrievals of both the Plutonium shard and Satan's, it seemed far too fortuitous for my usual bad luck. "Where is it?"

He grimaced. "Even weirder. It's downstairs, in an apartment on the first floor."

"Say…what now?"

"You'll have to verify it, of course. But there's a collector with a safe full of artifacts he's found over the years. Our intel shows very high potential that he has a 'special' stone, uncovered in Africa last week. The safe is iron, which may be why you haven't noticed the vibrations."

My gut clenched, channeling Liam. "I don't like this. It's all *way* too easy."

"Yeah, that's my take, too. But if it *is* Michael's, you have to get it back regardless, don't you?"

He was right. I needed to recapture any and all items bearing Michael's powers, no matter how "easy" the job, or how suspect their sudden appearance.

And anyway, it had to be just a coincidence. This building was full of wealthy tenants, and my clients in Marseille had taught me not to be surprised by basically any crazy thing the rich elite did, including collecting rocks and storing them in iron safes.

Besides, I still had to *get* it from the man. And the last time I'd thought someone a "harmless collector," I'd wound up trapped in the Burkes' dungeon.

Torben had finished putting away the meat, so I said, "Care to join me for a field trip?"

"Sure. Why not? Might as well get it over with."

We told Jun and Dito the plan, then rode the elevator down to the first floor and headed for the apartment in question. A middle-aged man in a crisply ironed suit answered our knock. He was about my height, with a ring of dark hair circling his otherwise bald head, and a stomach just going to paunch.

"*Puis-je vous aider?*"

I gave him my best *I'm a normal person* smile. "Good morning. Sorry to bother you so early. I just moved into the penthouse suite, and I heard through the grapevine that you collect rocks."

"The penthouse?" His mildly curious expression brightened, and he smiled. "You must be Lily's sister. Hyacinth, right? Please, come in."

He widened the door, and Torben and I followed him into a spacious entry, and from there, to an apartment almost as large as Lily's, and equally well-appointed with expensive furniture, wall hangings, and the requisite *objets d'art*.

"I am Pierre Chambert," he said. "I have heard so much about you. I am very sorry for the loss of your sister."

He held out a hand, and I let him clasp mine warmly. "Thank you. This is my friend, Torben."

They shook hands as well. Then he said, "Are you interested in one of my rarer pieces?"

"Maybe. We, uh, heard you recently came back from Africa."

He beamed. "Of course. I found a lovely specimen."

He removed a red silk wall-hanging from above the sofa, revealing a large safe. He dialed in the combination and opened the door, and I immediately felt the vibrations. The iron safe altered it somehow, but it was clearly a "vibrating rock," and therefore, one I needed.

Pierre reached inside and pulled out a medium-sized, irregularly-shaped stone, with streaks of lighter grey—almost silver—throughout. He handed it to me, and the vibrations intensified, a thrumming bass that made me nearly drop it in surprise at how much the iron had blocked it.

"What do you think?" he asked. "Beautiful, *n'est-ce pas?*"

"Yes, it's lovely," I managed over the intense shaking.

Torben frowned in concern, but I gave a slight shake of my head.

Then Pierre said, "Take it. It's yours."

I stared at him. "Are you sure? But—why?"

"I have lots of rocks. Think of it as a gift, in honor of Lily. She was a good friend. I play cribbage, so every week, she'd bring down her own board, a beautiful triangular one from the seventeenth century that belongs in a museum. She said art should be enjoyed. So, we enjoyed it. Now, it's my pleasure to give her sister a token of our friendship."

"Thanks. That's very…generous of you."

And weird. Beside me, Torben's frown deepened, and I could almost hear both him *and* Liam saying, *I don't like this.* Me, either, but what could we do?

My cell rang, and I pulled it out. "Sorry—let me just see who this is."

Jason's number showed on the screen, so I made another apologetic noise and answered the call. Before I could greet him, he said, "We have a problem. A big one. Jeannette isn't Jeannette anymore. She's Rachel."

Chapter Eighteen

"As dead flies give perfume a bad smell, so a little folly outweighs wisdom and honor."

~Ecclesiastes 10:1
(Bible, NIV)

By four-thirty, Jason, Ulrich, Liam and Rachel-Jeannette had driven up from Marseille and were crowded into Lily's—*my*—apartment. When I'd gotten over the shock, making more apologetic noises at Pierre for leaving, plus grateful ones for the gift of the rock, Torben and I hightailed it back to the penthouse, keeping Jason on the call, even in the elevator.

"You know," he'd said through the line as we rode up, "it's kind of good news. We needed to find her, and now we have."

"But she *stole another person!*"

"True. But—well, we're bringing her up to Paris. With Dito's help, I think I can...extract...her from Jeannette."

The elevator opened into the apartment and we exited. Torben had gotten the gist from my half of the conversation, and updated Dito and Jun, while I said to Jason, "Safely?"

"I think so. Not being a demon, Rachel wasn't as...thorough...as she could have been. But she must have improved her technique since Sieg. I think

Jeannette's alive in there somewhere."

That was something, anyway. "How will you get her up here? And—are you restraining her? How?" Silence. I swallowed. "Do I want to know?"

"Hyacinth. You've known about me for months now. I've managed not to flaunt it—to rarely use my powers, and try to act 'normal' around you. But it's who I am. Even more so, after…"

He trailed off, and I said, "I'm sorry. I know it's my fault. You would never have taken the Rousseaux's powers, if not for me."

"It's not your fault. I did what I had to, to save *all* of us, not just you."

I fought down the lump in my throat. Because this was one of the biggest sacrifices he'd made. Maybe not *only* for me, but still—I couldn't blame him for being more of a demon, when *I* drove him to it.

"Okay," I managed. "What—how—"

"I've essentially cuffed her. I used the spell Claude used when he controlled Eric at their villa. It's…part of me now. All their spells are, and the powers to use them. Not full strength, but enhanced enough that I can control her indefinitely." He hesitated. "You may as well know—I also made it so she can see the Dead. She and Heinrich really had no clue what they were doing, and she can't see them on her own, just hear them occasionally. So, for convenience…"

He waited while I processed the implications of him openly using the Rousseaux's powers.

"Okay," I said finally. I wanted to say so much more, but not in front of the others, and not on the phone.

"I'll see you soon," he promised, and we hung up.

Forget restraining her. I'll never understand how he

crammed her into Lily's car, even if it is a hybrid SUV. She certainly wouldn't have fit in the Peapod, which Ulrich wound up driving instead, with Liam riding shotgun. Even so, she must have taken up most of the SUV's middle row, where Jason had put her, rather than having her next to him for the whole trip.

Now that I knew Rachel was flying the plane, the brightness in Jeannette's eyes looked more like maniacal fervor. And I assume possession by a psychopathic spirit improves hair and skin quality, accounting for the reverse-aging I'd noticed.

"Why?" I asked after Jason got her into the apartment. "Why take over my landlady?"

Her restraints weren't visible, so whatever "spell" Jason had used, I hoped it held. She wore another pink muumuu, chiffon this time, and pink ballet flats, but she'd changed her pink nail polish for black. She smiled, and with the pretense over, it was Rachel's dreamy-evil grin, and I shuddered.

"To await your return," she said, clearly enjoying my revulsion. "I even staged the recent break-ins at your place. I thought you'd *have* to come home when you heard, but it turns out Jeannette never filed the police reports, even for the ones last summer. She's quite lazy, but motivated by vanity. Not having a body is boring, so I offered her the gift of youth, and she let me in. I've been in her for a while. I was about to give up and try something else, when you finally showed up."

"How did you even get to Marseille?"

She lifted a shoulder. "Hitched a ride—and then another, and…"

Eww. But it confirmed what Yvo had said, about the corpse near where she'd crossed over from Germany.

And it didn't look good for Jeannette's prospects, since Rachel hadn't left that person alive, or, most likely, any of the others she'd "borrowed." Hopefully, Jason could somehow manage it. Even if Jeannette had been dumb enough to invite Rachel in, she didn't deserve to die for it.

Liam said, "She let herself in to your place a few times after you left. She didn't take anything, just wandered around, but I got suspicious. So one time when she came upstairs, I went down to her place and snooped around, and I found something."

He gestured at Jason, who handed me a small journal. Its pages were covered in Rachel's spidery scrawl, mixed with news clippings on the deaths of Geordi's parents, and his subsequent kidnapping by his aunt—me—also MIA. Skimming, I learned that *apparently*, Lily and Nick had "reconciled" and gone on a "second honeymoon" when their car "hit a tree." Then I got greedy for Geordi's trust fund, and skipped town with him. Who knew?

"So," I said to Liam, "you figured it out, but had no way to tell us."

"Exactly." He shook off his obvious frustration. "I waited, figuring you'd come back soon. But if Jason and Ulrich hadn't shown up when they did, I would've tried to find my own way back here. I didn't know what she might do, and I didn't want her to escape again."

"Now that you have me," Rachel said, "what will you do with me?"

She didn't seem concerned about her capture, so she must have a few machinations left up her muumuu sleeves. Her convoluted mind being at least as creative as Stefan's, whatever she had planned couldn't be good.

But once we gave her to Satan, that would be it. This time, he'd make *sure* she was obliterated.

I checked in with my moral compass: Did I feel guilty about this in any way?

No, I decided, I did not. I'd feel worse about killing a sugar ant I found on the kitchen counter, because he was just going about his ant business, earning an honest ant living. But Rachel was both pure evil and a necessary domino in the Nick Resurrection scheme, which I *had* to accomplish if I wanted to stay in Geordi's life. So, Satan could have her.

I only said, "You'll find out soon enough."

I turned to find Jason watching me, expression unreadable. Clearly *his* moral compass pointed in a different direction. Would we always have rifts like this between us? Couldn't he see I had to do *whatever* it took, for Geordi's sake?

Jun had been watching Rachel closely, ever since she walked in, and now he narrowed his eyes at her. "She's up to something."

"Of course," Ulrich said. "She always was. I don't see why death should change that."

"True. But whatever it is, I think she *wanted* us to catch her."

Rachel laughed, bubbly and carefree. "Jun—it's good to see you. I'm sorry I had you killed. You understand, right? You were becoming a nuisance. Of course, back then, I thought death more…final…than it actually is."

She scanned the room, filled with my minions, most of whom were formerly *her* minions. Then she spied Dito. "Well hel-*lo*, handsome. Who are you?"

He ignored her, saying to me, "Jun's right. I don't

know her, but from reading her journals, I know she'd never accept being captured, unless it's all part of her master plan."

I asked Jason, "She's secure? She can't escape?"

He nodded—no hesitation. Which made me feel worse, because he clearly didn't approve of my plans, but he'd still helped.

"I've got her tethered. She can't leave Jeannette, but she can't harm her, either. Essentially, she's imprisoned in Jeannette's body, until we let her out."

I faced her. "You heard him. So what is it? What makes you think this is all going your way?" I paused, struck by a piece of the puzzle I hadn't noticed before. "And why were you waiting for me in the first place? If you wanted revenge, why not kill me when I showed up?"

Her smile went slow and seductive, and she leaned closer, as though sharing an intimate secret. "Because I have a present for you. I can provide what you need, to make Sieg let go of your ghost friend."

Crap. "You're bluffing. It's a trick, so we'll release you."

She made a *tsk*-ing sound. "Hyacinth. You're smarter than that. Sieg is *mine*. He would do *anything* for me, including dying and giving me his body. So when Eric moved in, Sieg—the tiny remaining remnants of him—knew what to do. He immediately chipped away at Eric's soul, absorbing him one piece at a time. Those bits are now part of Sieg. Without their return, Eric can *never* be whole again, and eventually, he'll fade to nothing. But one word from me and Sieg will relinquish them. Give me Sieg's remnants—let us both go, together—and your friend—the man you *love*—will be saved."

****

Jason gripped my shoulders. "It will be all right."

We were in Lily's—now my—room, while I desperately tried not to have a panic attack. I wasn't succeeding.

"How? If she's telling the truth, she can save Eric. None of my guys have found anything useful—even Sieg's family wouldn't have any influence on him. But without her, we have nothing Satan wants—she's our only bargaining chip, to make him give up Nick. And if I can't bring Nick back, the Dioguardis will take Geordi from me, *forever.*"

Even just saying the words made my stomach roil and I shook again, my hands and feet going numb, head spinning. Plus, Jason's jaw had tightened at the mention of my morally awful plan to doom Rachel's evil spirit, in order to bring back Nick's not-much-better one. And I hadn't even told him yet about Stefan wanting a Dioguardi Demon transfusion. What would he think of me when he knew? I'd lost Geordi, and was losing Eric—I *couldn't* lose Jason, too.

He always could read my emotions. His expression softened, and he pulled me close. "It will be all right," he repeated. "I promise."

I hiccupped into his chest, letting myself feel safe in the warmth of his arms. "How are you so certain?" I pulled back. "And how are you so damn nice all the time?"

He smiled, a little sadly. "How is it that you find niceness so unusual, you need to comment on it all the time?"

I opened my mouth, then shut it. As usual, he had a

point. "I guess I just don't think I deserve it. From you, especially."

His brows rose. "Why?"

A simple question, with no easy answer. His eyes were dark, our bodies pressed together. I shook my head, helpless to express my feelings—for him, but also my guilt over what I continually put him through. His gaze lingered on my mouth, and then he kissed me.

It started out slow and gentle at first, but it felt so good—so *right*—that I made a noise in the back of my throat. He rightly took that as encouragement, and kissed me harder, his mouth moving over mine as I opened to him, his hands stroking my arms and back, pulling me tighter until our bodies touched everywhere, his full hard length pressing into me.

He walked me to the bed, pausing when I bumped it with the back of my legs. With evident effort he broke the kiss, his eyes hot and dark.

"Hyacinth—this is terrible timing. And I know you have feelings for Eric, but I *swear* that, whatever happens next, I will help you save him. *Whatever* you decide. But you need to know—I've wanted this for a long time. And if we don't stop now..."

He waited, watching me. I couldn't help it—I needed him, needed *this*, in ways I couldn't explain, and didn't want to overthink. I lifted a hand to caress the firm lines of his jaw, and he closed his eyes.

"*Hyacinth...*"

I dropped my palm to his chest, waiting until he met my gaze again. Then I said, "Yes."

He groaned, leaning down to capture my mouth again, this kiss ripe with promise as he pushed me backward onto the bed. I pulled his shirt up and over his head as we fell, and discovered his hand had found its way under my sweater and into my bra, caressing and teasing my breast even as I slid *my* hands over the hard muscles of his chest to tease his own nipples.

Somehow his jeans were off, but then, so were mine—my sweater, too. I was mostly naked, on Lily's bed, with Jason mostly naked on top of me, and a room full of minions plus Rachel mere meters away. And it still felt *right* and *good.*

He rolled us over, putting me in the driver's seat, so to speak. He'd never force me, but even more, he'd want no questions later, about this being one hundred percent mutual. He'd been patient for so long, I wouldn't have been surprised if he gave up on me—on this—altogether.

Thank God he hadn't.

I deepened the kiss, pressing into him, letting him know how much *I* wanted *him*. His fingers slid inside my underwear, and I gasped when he touched me. I felt his smile under my mouth, but then I did my own exploration, and he sucked in a breath.

"*Jesus...*"

He was ready—we both were—and moments later our remaining clothes were out of the way and he slid into me—or I slid onto him. It was definitely mutual, and amazing and crazy and like nothing I'd ever experienced. He pulsed his thread into me, entwining it with my own, and I hadn't felt it—felt *him*—like this in so long that the sensation overpowered me, like I literally couldn't tell where I ended and he began.

We moved together, slowly at first, then faster and more urgent, saying with our bodies all the things we couldn't say with words. Then suddenly we were up and over, wave upon wave cascading between us, his mouth capturing my cries of pleasure, to mingle with his own. And it went beyond the physical—the emotional release was too much, and I collapsed onto him, sobbing, but with relief at having finally shared something so incredible and intimate with him. And at the same time, feeling uncertain about Eric, and what this might mean, going forward.

He understood, and caressed my back. "Shh…it's okay. I'm not going anywhere."

"But—"

"No buts. And no regrets."

I lifted myself up, gazing down at him. "That was…"

He grinned. "Good. *Very* good. But I know you—you're already feeling guilty. I'd be lying if I said I didn't want anything more than sex from you. Because I do. But for right now, today, this can be just sex. I won't make any demands…yet."

I said, "It's not just sex for me, either. But…"

"*No buts.*" He pulled me down into a long, slow kiss that promised more—of this, of him, of a future, together. The picture was *so* tempting—and rife with complications.

He was right. I did feel guilty, about Eric maybe dying, fully and forever, *while* I lay in bed with another man. But also about Jason, who I could still hurt terribly, intentionally or not.

More than that, he was right to question why I found his support—or niceness in general—suspect. Why *didn't* I deserve that? And what if I couldn't get past it?

Maybe I had no regrets. But I had a lot of "buts" to process.

Not right this second, though. For these few

moments, I let myself enjoy being with him, feeling him inside me—not just physically, but also his thread, warm and happy and satiated. We kissed lazily, shutting out the real world a little longer, before we had to face the problems at hand.

Chapter Nineteen

"He is no fool who gives what he cannot keep to gain what he cannot lose."
                    ~Jim Elliot, American Christian Missionary
                                                  (1927-1956)

Even though we'd just had amazing sex, and I could still feel the soft glow of Jason's thread, like a gift left behind, to remind me of what we'd shared—even with all that, when I told him of Stefan's demands, he blew a gasket.

Okay, it was Jason, so his version of gasket-blowing was to calmly and irrefutably explain why I was nuts, with lots of jaw clenching and lip compressing thrown in.

"No," he repeated now, yanking his jeans on in the angriest way imaginable for an even-tempered demon. "Even *if* it were possible, have you considered that if Nico and Rina find out, it would *completely* negate your deal with them?"

Merde.

I actually hadn't thought of that. Obviously, the Dioguardis would take it as a personal attack, if I helped a rival mob faction gain demon powers. Elaine herself had pointed that out, but I hadn't extended the connection to *Nico and Rina will be pissed at me personally.*

I pulled on my own jeans more slowly, considering my limited options. "If I don't do it, Elaine says Stefan will find something 'creative'—meaning 'bad'—to do with the shard. He's smart, and now that he knows about the supernatural stuff, I wouldn't put it past him to bargain with it to become a Hell Demon instead. Which is worse, right?"

Jason's jaw ticked. "Yes. It's worse. But you *can't* do it—they'll lock Geordi up forever. They'll turn him against you, so that even if you find a way to see him, he'll hate you."

"Then I'll make sure they never find out."

He watched me for a beat, still shirtless—*hoo-boy*— then shoved a hand through his sex-mussed hair. "God damn mother-fucking-shit-to-hell. You're going to do it with or without me." He blew out a breath. "What, exactly, is your plan?"

I hugged my ratty sweater closer. "I don't know. I thought maybe I could give him regular blood and pretend it's from a demon. Then when nothing happens, I can say, oh well, I tried, now give me the rock."

It sounded lame as I said it, and Jason shook his head. "You just said Stefan is smart. He'll never fall for that, *and* he'll want proof of results before forking anything over. Next?"

"I guess...try to find some demon blood somewhere? Dito said there's no definitive answer about whether it will work. Plus, it's very diluted now, right? So even if I give Stefan actual demon blood, it might not convert him. But if he *knows* it's real, maybe he'll honor our deal, regardless of the results."

"Where are you going to get demon blood?"

My face heated. Because of course, the only living

bio-demon I knew—besides random Dioguardi peons—was him. I could have asked Bala, but not until she recovered, and I *definitely* couldn't ask Nico or Rina.

He blew out another breath. "I'll do it."

"No—I can't ask that of you. I'll find another way, or—or I'll tell Michael. Surely in a situation like this, he could find the time to intervene."

"You can't," he said flatly, reaching for his shirt. "If you call Michael down into the middle of this, he'll wonder how Stefan ended up with the shard in the first place—why you didn't immediately return it when you found it. More than that, he may find out why you need it. Have you considered that?"

I nodded miserably. "It's one of the threats Elaine made—that she or Stefan would tell Michael I'm trying to bring Nick back." I sat on the bed, dropping my head into my hands.

What could I do? What choice did I have?

He finished pulling on his shirt, then came to sit next to me. "Hyacinth, I said I'll do it. I promised to help you, and I won't let you down. I don't agree with your methods, but if you're going to do it, at least I can help with damage control. Maybe."

With him so close, I wanted to slide into his arms and seek comfort, reassurance—*anything,* to make this all bearable. But yet again, a chasm had opened between us. Maybe the sex was a bad idea—too much, too soon. No matter what he said, he had to be regretting his choices, when I was clearly so morally bereft.

"Hey." He tilted my chin up. "I'm not going anywhere. Remember what I said? I'll help you, no matter what. But I know how your mind works, and right now you're thinking the worst. Mainly about yourself.

But you're a lot like Eric—you have your own moral code. I may not agree with it, but it's one of the reasons I…"

Seconds ticked by. My heart pounded, and my palms slicked with sweat, and his mouth quirked sadly.

"Okay, not now. Just know that I'm here for you—*all* of you. Even the parts you don't like about yourself. You make me crazy, in both the best way possible, and the worst way imaginable. But let's not lose sight of the bigger picture. Getting Geordi away from Marchosias is top priority, and while Nico and Rina agreed to work with us because you extorted them, we need them more than they need us. So, I'll donate blood to Stefan, and we'll go from there."

I couldn't even express the depths of my gratitude. Both for what he'd offered to do, and for what he'd stopped himself from saying. If the sex might be too much, the emotion definitely was.

His eyebrow lifted in ironic acknowledgement of what I felt, but couldn't say out loud. Then he angled my face, giving me one long, slow, gentle kiss, filled with promise and hope, his thread glowing stronger and brighter than ever inside me.

But…could I accept this from him? Or would I forever feel guilty for constantly chipping away at his moral code? Just in the time he'd known me, I must have destroyed a dozen of his most dearly held principles. At some point, they'd all be gone. Would his feelings for me evaporate then, too?

Most likely, yes. But as always, what choice did I have?

Someone knocked at the door, and I started guiltily, but Jason grinned, looking once again like a carefree, sex-satisfied demon. "Relax. We're consenting adults, and it's nobody else's business, anyway."

"Easy for you to say. I have to live with them." I cleared my throat. "Uh, come in."

The door opened, revealing Torben and Liam, neither of whom acted repulsed or even surprised to find Jason and me on a bed whose sheets were decidedly rumpled. Maybe they didn't know why. Or maybe they did. Jason was right—again. It shouldn't matter. But for all my declared independence, it appeared I cared more what others thought than I realized.

Weirder—I cared what *they* thought. My minions, who not long ago would have killed me on their former bosses' orders, but whose good opinion now mattered to me.

I felt my face heating, but Torben only said, "You done in here? Liam and Jun have been working on Rachel, and they think she's right. She *can* save Eric, and she might be the *only* one who can."

I blew out a breath. "Okay. What's the plan? Just tell me, and let's get going."

Liam said, "It's pretty barebones. We take Rachel to Turkey, she convinces Sieg to let go of Eric, and…we let her go."

I could tell the words left a bad taste in his mouth, but I *had* to save Eric. "We can always find her again later."

Liam grimaced. "Maybe. With luck."

"Like, immediately. Even if we give her a head start, it doesn't mean we can't recapture her the next day. Maybe we can track her somehow—make it easier to get her back this time."

Liam perked up at that, and I turned to Jason.

"Before I leave for Turkey—"

"*We* leave. And I know what you're about to ask. So yeah, let's get it over with. Call Elaine and make the arrangements. We can stop by to see Bala in the hospital and snag a phlebotomy kit while we're there."

I stared at him. "You know how to use one? Is there *anything* that stumps you?"

His lips twisted, and his expression filled with everything raw and unresolved between us. I looked away, to find Liam and Torben watching us thoughtfully. Which felt worse than if they'd been judgmental. *I* didn't want to think about my relationship with Jason, let alone have anyone else analyzing it.

I said to Torben, "Could you ask Dito to come in here? I have something to do, and I need him for it."

Torben clearly had more questions but knew I wouldn't answer them. Instead he said, "Sure. But first, there's something else you should know. There's been chatter on the dark web. We've been monitoring it, for the rocks, and just because." He hesitated, then shrugged. "You might as well know. A few minutes ago, Ulrich came across an auction that mentions a 'prize so valuable, even Satan can't afford it'—posted by someone calling themselves Paolo."

Oh God—

Jason gripped my arms, his eyes hard and almost black. "*Don't go there.* We *will* get him back. Do you understand me? We knew this would happen. Marchosias *wants* us to react—to get so afraid, we can't function, and will cave to all his demands. *Don't let him get to you.*"

"But—"

"*No.* Listen to me—he used Paolo's name

232

specifically to fuck with us. You have to stay calm. I know it's hard, but put your trust in Nico and Rina. They have the numbers, both in resources to bargain with, and if that fails, soldiers—hundreds of Dioguardi demons, maybe thousands. And *all* of them will give their lives to save Geordi. Plus, the Buonfiglios are involved, now, too. You can't do anything right now—you have to stick to your own plans."

I forced down the bile, the nausea, the absolute and utter terror brought on by Torben's simple words. "I know you're right, and nothing's changed. It's just—if he's being so blatant, *naming* Satan—he's not just screwing with us, he's screwing with Satan. He's so confident, he doesn't think he has to be careful. And that might mean…"

I couldn't put those fears into words, but as always, Jason understood. He pulled me close, and I let him hold me, observers be damned.

"Marchosias won't hurt Geordi. If he's damaged in *any* way, even slightly, he loses value. Plus, now we have something to work on. If we can determine where the post originated from, that would be huge. I'll get the details from Ulrich and share them with Nico and Rina. I know how scary this is, but it's progress."

Progress. My nephew mentioned in a dark web auction by the Hell Demon who kidnapped him was "progress."

I managed a nod, and he let me go, and I pretended I wasn't more scared than I'd ever been in my life. Not just about this—about all of it: Rachel, Eric, Stefan, Geordi. Even Jason, and our relationship.

If this was progress, we should all be terrified.

****

Elaine said to meet her and Stefan at le Cimetière du Calvaire, Paris's oldest and smallest cemetery, which is only open once or twice a year to the public. It's even harder to be buried in. You have to be a descendant of someone "in residence," and presumably, share one of the eighty-five graves already in use, as there's zero room for expansion.

Evidently, the Buonfiglios are one of those families. Lucky—?—for us. Also odd, since they're Italian. But then maybe that explained why the Dioguardis—who are Sicilian—couldn't completely force them out of France, since they'd been here for eons.

In any case, before we left, I raked around in Lily's closet for the cribbage board that had fallen out earlier. It must be the one Pierre had described. How many triangular cribbage boards could Lily own? And the fact that she'd shared it with him—"enjoying" a piece of priceless art—reminded me again how much I missed her. But worrying about Geordi was worse, so I focused on what I could do, not what I couldn't.

Jason raised an eyebrow when I brought the game board out, so I explained about Pierre's generosity. "I want to give this to him on our way out, to remember Lily by."

"I'm sorry."

I looked at him in surprise. "For what?"

"That Lily got caught in the middle of all this, and that you lost your sister."

I swallowed. Should I ask if he knew Nick targeted her specifically? Everyone kept insisting the Dioguardis were the only demon family, but there had to be *some* other supernatural dynasties out there, or else how would Rina have known targeting was even possible?

In the end, I didn't say anything. What difference would it make now, if Jason knew or not? We had enough between us in the present, without dragging in the past.

So I said, "Thanks," and left it at that.

There wasn't much else to do, to get ready. How *did* one prepare to make the unacknowledged son of one's ghost *petit ami* into a demon? Using the blood of the demon with whom one had just had sex, thereby cheating on said *petit ami*? Miss Manners—or her French equivalent—probably didn't have a rule about this, so I'd have to make it up as I went along. Again.

Rachel, according to Jason, couldn't escape or do anything awful, even without his physical presence. But I wasn't taking any chances, so I put her in the master bathroom—which had no windows, and we were on the top floor anyway—and surrounded her with several pieces of Lily's best cast iron cookware.

Jason started to crack a joke, then thought better of it. "You know, you may be right. We never did figure out why the drug she gave me didn't work, or why the iron in the Black Gate in Germany 'cured' you and Geordi. Either way, it can't hurt."

Rachel just smiled her evilly winsome smile, like she had it all in the bag, and sat on the closed toilet seat. "Hurry back."

I shut and locked the door, then got Jason's help in dragging the dresser over to barricade it. Then Jason, Dito and I got in the elevator, while Torben, Liam and Jun stayed back to plan Misguided Mission Number Two: Return to Turkey, Part Deux.

We rode down to the first floor and headed for Pierre's door, when abruptly, a wave of ice sliced the air around me. I twisted to find Jason and Dito both white with shock and grappling with a joint shield big enough for all three of us and then some—a literal wall of ice—the most powerful shield I'd ever felt either of them make.

My palms slicked and my gut clenched. "What is it?"

Jason ground out, "Demons. Very strong ones."

"*What? Here?*"

"Not now," he managed, though it was clearly an effort.

Dito also shook, his face slicked with sweat, and I thought, if just the remnant of a demon did this, it must be a very bad one, indeed. Jason inhaled, then exhaled, and his shield eased up, though not completely.

"They're gone. But they were here recently—within the last few hours."

"So…around the time Torben and I came down to get the rock?"

"Yeah. I wonder why they didn't take it themselves? Satan will be pissed about that."

"Maybe they got here after I left? And since I'd already taken it from Pierre's iron safe to Lily's, they couldn't tell where it went?"

"Maybe…" He sounded doubtful.

"What? Just tell me. Clearly you think something else is going on."

"It's just…odd. Like they came, and then left again. I'd think if they were after the shard, they'd take more time. Why come here, just to say, oh well, too bad, so sad? And…"

His hesitation scared me even more. I did a little lip compressing of my own at him, but it was Dito who spoke up. "What Jason doesn't want to tell you is it wasn't just *a* 'very strong demon.' It was several, all of them Kings of Hell, and all of them carrying."

Ignorance is bliss. I didn't know how scared I should be, because I had no clue what he meant. Sadly, that innocence couldn't last. "What are you saying, exactly?"

"That Satan sent his best capital-D Demons, *and* he gave them special powers. *His* powers. He would never do that, unless the job was so important, he had to."

My heart pounded, but I clung to my naïveté like a drowning woman to a life preserver. "I thought he gave his powers to his demons all the time."

Jason said tersely, "Nope. A little here and there, maybe, but not like this. These Demons had so much of his powers that they feel *like* him. For him to use that much of his energy—essentially, it means either his prison is drastically compromised, or he's so confident it will be shortly, he's being incautious. Either way, it's bad—for us, the world, everyone."

"But…they're gone now? And we have *some* time?"

He inhaled and exhaled again, and I felt his shield recede some more. "Yes. But not much, so let's offload the board and get on with it."

Somehow, I managed to take myself in hand and knock on Pierre's door. He took so long to respond, I thought he'd gone out. And when he did answer, he initially didn't recognize me.

But after a moment he said, "Of course—Hyacinth. I am so sorry. I am not myself today. Retirement does that to one, *n'est-ce pas*? I spend all day lost in my own thoughts, so that when a visitor arrives, I forget how to be social."

He'd seemed alert earlier, but maybe now he'd been

napping. I handed him the cribbage board. "Lily would want you to have this. Thank you for the rock, and for being her friend."

He accepted the board, clearly confused again. "Rock? Yes...of course. But did I tell you of my cribbage matches with Lily? How strange that I do not remember."

"It was very early. Torben and I weren't fully awake yet, either. Not enough coffee."

He nodded gratefully, clutching the board close. "Thank you for this. It is nice to see you again—both of you. Come see me again, soon."

He included Jason in his magnanimous smile—but not Dito, of course—and we said our good-byes and left, Pierre shutting his door softly behind us.

"That was weird," I said to Jason as we took the stairs down to the ground floor. "Especially since you and Torben look nothing alike."

Jason said, "Yeah, it's almost like..."

He hesitated again, and I glanced back. "What?"

He shook his head in disbelief. "I'm not trying to keep anything from you, it just makes no sense. It's like...one of the Demons possessed Pierre *during* your first visit. But..."

I froze. "If that's the case, why *give* me the rock? I mean, Claude gave up one of Michael's, so he could use Satan's to get his brother out of Hell. But if these were Satan's top envoys, why do the exact opposite of what their boss wants?"

Never mind that this was exactly what I did, by keeping the very same rock from *my* boss.

"I have no clue," Jason admitted. "But if a Demon *that* high-level is so flagrantly going against Satan's wishes, with Satan's own powers in him…"

Dito finished his thought. "It makes no fucking sense, *at all*. And it means we have a big fucking problem. Because if we use this shard to get Nick out, Satan's going to notice. He might even come down harder on us, just because he's pissed at his Demons. We'll have to hope Rachel is enough to appease him, and that his prison holds until we're done."

I got a really bad feeling in my gut, because this time, I thought I knew what he meant. But just to be safe, I killed my ignorant, innocent naïveté once and for all. "Why?"

Jason said, "Because a side effect of bringing anyone out of Hell—not just Nick—is that we have to open Satan's prison. Literally, we have to unlock the door to pull Nick through. So Satan will have one golden opportunity to slip out himself—and maybe leave whoever we send in behind, trapped there forever."

Chapter Twenty

"All we who are dead below
Have become bones and ashes, but nothing else."
                                    ~Epitaph of a Roman Cynic
                                    (3rd century CE)

It's not that the severity of the situation didn't impress me. Or that I was blasé about letting Satan out of Hell, and maybe leaving one of our guys behind. I just couldn't stop to agonize over it. We *had* to get to the cemetery to meet Elaine and Stefan, and any way I approached it, we had to stick to the plan to take Rachel to Turkey, use her to save Eric, and then somehow exchange her for Nick, even after initially letting her go.

At least everything would be close by, in one general location. Too late to pick a different Hell gate, but I couldn't decide if the Plutonium being larger and better-known would make it easier for us to get in and back out, or more dangerous in the long run, because it gave a better prospect of escape to Satan. There *must* be a way to keep him trapped, because my only other option was not getting Nick out, and losing Geordi forever.

I guess I'm selfish, because the risk of Satan being freed seemed smaller than that of Geordi being raised solely by the Dioguardis. There's at least some justification there. The Dioguardis, while not Hell Demons, are the equivalent version on Earth. Them having sole access to Geordi's powers had to be nearly as bad as Satan unleashed on the world.

Besides, maybe we could somehow extract a promise from Satan to play nice during the exchange. I shuddered, remembering the *feel* of him on Barnacken—how he'd touched my essence, probing, assessing—and then let me live. It sickened and nauseated and terrified me. But maybe—just *maybe*—I could use that connection and ask him not to leave while we were there. Jason had said demons were required to abide by their promises. Satan might not be a demon per se, but surely honor among thieves and all that.

Now, as we approached the cemetery, I had to shift focus. We'd stopped at the hospital and found Bala much improved. Dito was embarrassed by his behavior, but she was so happy to see him that he managed an apology and they kissed and made up. Figuratively, but still.

Jason didn't act any different in front of her. After what we'd shared, I'd expected him to hem and haw a bit, but nope—nada. So maybe he'd told the truth about there being nothing between them. On his part, anyway. I couldn't help noticing that Bala's eyes cut to him often, but she always looked away before he caught her.

Prior to the fight with Marchosias, she'd been a smartass, pressing my buttons and flirting with Jason at every opportunity. Now, she'd sobered. Her injuries were serious—the doctors had used the phrase "life-threatening" many times. So maybe the experience rearranged her priorities, making her realize what—or rather *who*—she really wanted.

I didn't know how I felt about that. My own feelings were confusing enough. But I was grateful for everything she'd done, trying to save Geordi, so if she loved Jason, maybe they should get a shot at making it work. She couldn't be *more* messed up than me, and he deserved a chance at real happiness.

Dito gave her hand a squeeze, then Jason leaned close and said something low in her ear that I didn't catch. Her eyes widened, and she faced me. "Are you nuts?"

Guess he'd told her the plan. "Maybe. If you have a better idea, I'd love to hear it."

"Nope." Her gaze shifted to Jason and softened. "Be careful. Sharing your blood—your powers—*with* the Rousseaux's in you—who knows what that could do."

"True," he admitted. "But even I can't see another way at this point."

She turned to me again. "He's only doing this because *you* asked him to."

Jason cut in, "No, she didn't. I offered."

Bala snorted. "Same difference. You're doing it *for* her. Why?"

The directness of the question showed she already knew the answer, and Jason reddened. "It's…complicated."

"Yes," she agreed. "It is. Have you told her the risks—like what could happen if you drain too much of your powers? Either into Stefan, or just from the process itself?"

I frowned. "What does that mean?"

"Nothing," Jason said levelly, his focus on Bala. Something passed between them, and her eyes flickered black. Then her shoulders slumped and her irises faded back to blue.

"Whatever. But she's not one of us. Keep that in mind, while you're doing her *favors.*"

That stung, but it wasn't anything I hadn't already thought about myself, and until I put out all the current bonfires in my life, I couldn't focus on figuring out where I did fit in, so we said our good-byes and left.

We found an unlocked supply closet, and I stood outside the door, while Dito went around a corner to stand watch there. Jason slipped inside to grab what he'd need for the blood draw, coming out again moments later, before anyone happened by.

Something about it—the fact that he was *stealing,* from a hospital—gave me an attack of conscience, and I said, "You really don't have to do this. Bala's right. It's too risky, and—"

He took my hand, squeezing it. "Bala's a worrier. It has nothing to do with you."

"Tell me what happens if you drain your powers."

"I won't."

"But—"

"I *won't.* I'll be fine. I want to help you, so will you just *let* me, for once?"

I glared at him. "Stop being so damn—"

He put a finger on my lips. "I swear to God, I'm not being *nice.* Niceness might be the last thing on my mind right now."

His thumb caressed the side of my mouth, and I fought to maintain control, to not lean into him and take what he so blatantly offered. "We have to go…"

He blew out a breath and stepped back. "Fine. I said I wouldn't press you. I just…I can't help it, sometimes. I need you to know this isn't a fling for me, and it scares the shit out of me. *You* scare the shit out of me."

Weirdly, I felt better knowing he wasn't as self-assured and in control as he generally acted. He stuffed the phlebotomy kit inside his jacket, and we went around the corner, retrieved Dito, and rode the elevator back down to the car.

It was well past supper time now, and very dark out. The cemetery is on a hill, under the watchful eye of the Sacré-Coeur Basilica, and is so small and un-publicized that even many Parisians don't know it's there. We parked and Elaine let us in at the gate, then led us through the maze of unlit graves to the family mausoleum where Stefan waited inside. Like most structures in the cemetery, it had been built of stone, the exterior carved in largely religious designs, with the Buonfiglio name in Roman letters above the open iron door bearing their crest.

We stepped into the cool, silent interior, and found Stefan kneeling in front of one of the drawers, praying. Which seemed off, when he hoped to become a demon. Unless he prayed *to* them, for help with the transition. Either way, it was heartbreaking—on the one hand, so much like his father when I'd seen him pray that it took my breath away. But on the other, his closed eyes and clasped hands pointed up his youth and vulnerability.

Jason shut the door behind us, casting the tomb into total blackness, then powered on a lantern he'd brought, throwing reasonably bright light into the four corners of the small space. I tried not to think of the symbolism— that I was sealed in a mausoleum, in Paris's oldest cemetery, in the dead of night, with a century or more's worth of Buonfiglio mafiosi bones all around me. I forced in a breath, telling the panic to recede, *or else*. It did. Mostly.

I said to Elaine, voice low so I wouldn't disturb Stefan, "Are you sure about this? Is *he?*"

She gave a half-shrug. "He will do it, with or without our help. And he is prepared to do something even *more* drastic if we don't help, so *ouais*—I am as sure as I can be."

"But are you *okay* with it—with what he'll be, if this works?"

She watched her son for a moment, the love she felt shining through her expression. But there was sadness, too. "*Les enfants* must go their own way, and make their own choices. I am proud of him, for what he wishes to do, even if I would prefer he choose a different path."

While we talked, Jason had set out the phlebotomy kit and a pile of alcohol wipes. He removed his jacket and tied his left arm above the elbow with a tourniquet band. He cleaned his skin with a wipe, made a fist, then tore the wrapper off the needle, attached it to the tube, and the tube to the bag. He made another couple of fists, positioning the needle at his nicely popping vein, and I glanced away, trying not to think about it.

Unfortunately, my gaze landed back on Stefan, which only made me feel worse.

Dito said quietly, "She's right. It's not your decision, and whatever happens, it's on him."

I took a deep breath, surreptitiously nodding my thanks. Although, given what Stefan hoped to do, both he and Elaine should get used to the Dead hanging around. But hey, the longer I delayed the further destruction of his innocence, the better.

He'd just finished his prayer. He crossed himself and kissed the crucifix he wore, before tucking it back inside his t-shirt and rising to his feet. Not praying to demons, then.

He was a puzzle, for sure. And Elaine was *proud* of

him? None of it made sense, but who am I to judge? Michael resurrected me to work *for* him, not against, as I did now. As Dito said, I had my own problems. I couldn't keep shouldering everyone else's.

I peeked at Jason just as he slid the needle back out, the phlebotomy bag now filled with his dark red, demon-rich blood. He secured the bag and took off the tourniquet, then faced Stefan and said flatly, "Where's the rock?"

He sounded really unhappy. Maybe this would be the thing that pushed him away for good, despite what he kept saying to the contrary. He'd said I scared him. Well, *I* scared me sometimes. Especially at times like this.

Stefan regarded us both suspiciously. "How do I know you're really a demon?"

I stepped forward. "Stefan, this is Jason. He's a Dioguardi."

Stefan's eyes popped. "No shit? How'd you get him to come here?"

I blew out a breath. "Look, you'll never hear me say this again. But…not all Dioguardis are bad. He's on…our side."

I'd almost said "my side," but if anything, Jason was on Geordi's side—the real reason he'd agreed to do this.

Stefan said, "Okay, I'll buy he's a Dioguardi. But that's no guarantee he's a demon. No rock without proof."

My jaw clenched. It was a reasonable request, but I just wanted to get this over with. I started to tell him off, when all at once *white-hot heat* surrounded us, burning my skin, my clothes so hot I wanted to tear them off. I gasped and Stefan instinctively shoved his mother behind him, both of them looking around wildly for the source. Meanwhile, Dito appeared neither surprised nor uncomfortable. But as a ghost, maybe he didn't feel it?

Lightning flashed, sound *cracking* our eardrums and ricocheting off the walls of the tomb, my whole head throbbing, the brightness searing my eyeballs, completely blinding me. Then just as fast, it vanished, replaced by an icy wall of coolness that was both soothing, and equally terrifying, in its sheer power.

When I could finally see again, Jason stood nearby, flexing his arm and shaking his hand out. Stefan wiped his eyes, streaming with tears from the heat, while Elaine collapsed onto the flat-topped ornately carved sarcophagus that took up most of the tomb's floorspace. And Dito stood as before, arms folded across his chest, one eyebrow lifted at Jason, whose own eyes were just fading from pure black to their normal baby blue.

Jason said to Stefan, "That good enough for you?" He caught my gaze on him, and his expression saddened. "I told you I've been holding back. This seemed like a good time...not to."

Elaine jumped up and tugged Stefan's arm. "*Mon chou—t'es sûr?*" She turned to Jason, clearly terrified, like it had *just* occurred to her what her son intended. "Please—take your blood and go. I—I'll give you the rock. I'll—"

Stefan removed her death grip from his arm. "*Maman.* You'll do no such thing." He faced Jason, tense with determination. "We had a deal. And yes, that's proof enough for me."

He pulled the duffel he'd brought to Turkey from behind the sarcophagus, raking around in it and coming up with what I hoped was a clean white t-shirt, covering a hard, lumpy object. He handed it to me, and I immediately felt the humming. Maybe the mausoleum walls muted it before, or it just hadn't felt like "speaking" until now. To be safe, I shook the shirt loose. Sure enough, it held the stolen shard. I rewrapped it and dropped it in my purse.

Jason sent me a questioning glance, and I nodded. All systems were go.

He said to Stefan, "Do you know your blood type?"

"B positive."

"That works. I'm O positive. Which arm?"

"I'm left-handed, so…I guess my right?"

"Got it."

Jason sounded calm enough, but I recognized the tension in his shoulders. I opened my mouth to stop him—to say there had to be another way. I took a step forward, and Dito touched my arm. "This isn't your decision, either. Let it be."

Jason sent me an ironic look, then said to Dito, "Okay, you're up."

Stefan frowned in the direction Jason had spoken. "Who are you talking to?"

I sighed. "Better get used to it. There's a dead demon here. Another Dioguardi—Dito. He's going to help you and Jason with the…procedure."

Elaine blanched and sat back down on the sarcophagus, but Jason said to her, "You'll need to move. Stefan—you'll want to be lying down for this."

Elaine shook her head. "Please, Stefan—"

"*Maman*. You know why I want—*need*—to do this."

Her mouth worked like a fish drowning on land, desperate to find her way back through this terrible mess. "I know, but he wouldn't want this for you. He—"

Stefan gently tugged her up. "It doesn't matter. It's the only way."

She was crying. The "he" in question must be her father, but if so, why wouldn't he want this? Despite what she'd said, I still believed this had to be a ploy by the whole Buonfiglio family, to out-perform the Dioguardis. I knew less about Elaine's family than I now did about the Dioguardis, but I doubted they were a "kinder, gentler," more moral Mafia.

However, maybe demonhood crossed a line for them. It would for Eric, when he found out. I pushed the thought away. Like Stefan, I believed this to be the only way through my own mess. I'd never find my way "back," but maybe whatever was "forward" wouldn't be *so* awful that the ends didn't justify the means.

Stefan set his mother aside, then lay down on the sarcophagus. "I'm ready."

"No, you're not," Jason said, echoing the words he'd uttered the first time he showed his powers to me, when we were trapped in the Rousseaux's villa in Turkey. He caught my eye, and an awareness passed between us. He spoke to Stefan, while regarding me steadily. "But it will be all right in the end. One way or another."

He pulled four lengths of rope from the same bag that had held the lantern, and passed them to me. "Clean his arm with one of the wipes, then tie him down with these, while I talk to Dito."

They stepped aside, plotting Demon Transfusion strategy, and I grabbed a couple of the alcohol wipes and approached Stefan. He seemed utterly calm, which was good, because my heart pounded like gangbusters. I tore both wipes open—might as well be thorough—and held his right arm up, using my phone as a flashlight, and trying to see through the cypress branches to where his veins might be. Which is when I saw the old needle tracks.

My gaze jerked to his, and he shrugged. "It was a few years ago. I used, I got clean, it's over." He paused. Then, in the spirit of total honesty, he added, "Except for weed, of course."

I couldn't help it. I smiled. This was the Stefan I knew: open and upfront about himself and his past. It could've been a lie, but I didn't think so. "Why are you doing this?"

"I told you—to become a demon."

"But *why?*"

He studied me a moment. Like Eric, he had an awesome poker face, and I couldn't read his thoughts, or his secret agenda. Which Eric also sometimes had. Jason would say *always*.

At last he said, "It's a means to an end."

He looked away, and I gave up and finished wiping his arm. There weren't many tracks, from what I could see through the tats, so he likely hadn't used long, or recently. I grabbed a piece of rope, noting handy iron rings placed at the sarcophagus's corners, probably for easy lid removal when a new corpse had to be added to the pile. I tied Stefan as securely as I could, then stepped back.

Dito and Jason finished their confab and moved to the sarcophagus, and Jason removed the used needle from the phlebotomy bag's tube, replacing it with a clean needle and catheter. He tied a length of rubber above Stefan's elbow, then palpated his arm until he found a nice vein. He inserted the catheter, then flicked a glance at me and Elaine.

"You should probably wait outside."

"No," Elaine and I said in unison, and surprisingly, he didn't argue.

"Well, I tried."

He did something with the catheter-needle-bag combo, and his blood began flowing into Stefan's arm. He stepped back, and he and Dito closed their eyes, just as they turned black.

And then...

The white fire came back, except it was *more*— more hot, more violent, more blinding and deafening and shattering. It doubled, then tripled, and I lurched away, trapped by the tomb's suffocating stones. From inside my bag on the floor, the rock woke and started shrieking, adding to the cacophony, though I'm probably the only one who heard it. Its energy joined the demons', circling the dark space, seeking an outlet, or...an inlet, like it wanted to crawl *into* Stefan, crazy as that sounds.

Worse, suddenly the bones in the drawers around us, and in the sarcophagus below Stefan, *vibrated* with the demon energy flying around the room. I felt them in *my* bones—a throbbing, pulsing power that liquefied me from the inside out. I fell against the nearest wall of drawers, my back supported by it, held there by fear, unable even to slide to the ground.

I no longer saw with my eyes, but with my mind. As his blood flowed from the bag, Jason's powers, guided by Dito's, latched onto the catheter, also entering Stefan's arm. His veins lit up, red, then orange, then yellow and white with fire and heat and *power*. I sensed Jason's thread, mingled with his powers, and the rock's, too, thrashing to connect with the rich demon blood flowing from the bag.

251

And then I sensed something else—something far worse—the *Rousseaux's* powers. Mixed with Jason's as they were, he must not be able to separate them. I'd used those powers myself, just a small drop, and the connection was instantaneous, the urge to take a sip—to *use* that evil demon energy for something, *anything*— had boiled my blood with desperate desire.

Oh God. Now Stefan would be forever bonded to them as well. I cried out, knowing I couldn't stop it— that the time for realizations was long past. Elaine screamed as well, but we didn't make a dent in the roaring vortex of sound consuming us all.

The blood moved faster now, way faster than a normal transfusion, taking minutes rather than hours. Through my mind's eye I knew the bag had more than half emptied, Jason's powers now a river of energy that would overwhelm Stefan, if it didn't outright kill him.

He thrashed wildly on the stone slab, but his bonds held. The bones below and in the drawers pounded to be let out—like a pressure cooker, they were about to burst, clamoring for the source of the powers that filled them with renewed purpose. Somehow, I knew if they broke out, they'd destroy anything in their path. They felt *evil*—hot with furious desire to commit unspeakable acts against the Living.

Without conscious thought, I untwisted my own thread and formed it into an icy silver web of light that I cast toward the drawers and around the sarcophagus. I pulled the loose end, tightening the net around the bones, and felt their dismay at being thwarted.

Jason and Dito jerked in surprise, and the blood flowing into Stefan faltered. Even the rock pulled back as though startled.

"What are you doing?" Jason asked, his voice strained as he fought for his own control.

"Holding them back!" I shouted, not knowing if he heard or understood.

Either way, a moment later, fresh power surged from the two demons, and the blood flowed again. A few drops leaked from where the needle poked Stefan's vein, sliding down his arm and falling onto the web I'd made. It burned like acid, white hot pain shooting through the threads straight to my heart. I gasped and lost control of the web and the bones shrieked with victory, pushing to tear through. The rock vibrated wildly, but I couldn't tell if it wanted to help me, or help the bones.

Jason's consciousness twisted toward me again, but I straightened and grabbed the threads, forcing myself to not let go, despite the burning heat of his powers coursing through them, and Dito's, the Rousseaux's, the rock's—and now *Stefan's*, too.

It was working.

The bones rattled harder, their vicious energy trying to get out, and I used all my strength to hold the web tight.

With extreme effort, Jason ground out, "*Almost there…*"

His swirling powers curled together, forming a single thread that funneled down to the needle and into Stefan's arm. Jason made a cutting motion, "snipping" the thread, and the ends shrank to nothing, one side back into Jason, the other into Stefan.

Instantly, my sight returned and the white-hot heat vanished and the bones were silenced. The rock gave one final wail, and then its energy, too, retreated. I released the web, feeling my thread slide coolly back into me. Did

I imagine that it seemed different—altered, somehow?

I shuddered. I'd be worried if I *wasn't* changed by what we'd done.

Across the tomb from me, Jason had collapsed to the ground, shaking and white, slick with sweat. I took a half-step toward him, but Dito got there first, kneeling and checking his pulse. He glanced at me, his eyes already fading back to blue. "He'll be fine."

I let out the breath I'd been holding. Thank God—he'd survived. I don't know how. If I'd thought anything he did before was terrifying, this was beyond comprehension. My heart cracked with the knowledge that he'd done this for *me*. Maybe for Geordi, too, but still—he could have died. We *all* could have.

Especially the one who'd had to receive all that demon power.

Elaine had thrown herself across her son, weeping uncontrollably. He was pale, his eyes closed tight, but he appeared to be breathing normally. Another miracle. I found a pocket knife in Jason's bag and cut Stefan's bonds. He stirred and stretched, dislodging Elaine as he sat up and opened his eyes.

They were completely black.

Chapter Twenty-One

"While seeking revenge, dig two graves—one for yourself."
~Douglas Horton, American Protestant Clergyman
(1891-1968)

Crazy as it sounds, Jason, Dito and I ditched Elaine and Stefan at the cemetery and went home to pack. I couldn't change any of it now, and besides, we left him in good hands. If ever there was a time to need one's *maman,* this was it.

I did wait for his irises to fade back to green, though. Eric would never forgive me for this, no matter what. But if I left Stefan permanently "powered up," it would be *so* much worse.

Also, once Elaine recovered, I extracted a promise that her father would abide by his word and help the Dioguardis as much as possible. The whole experience had clearly sobered her, and I thought she'd lost interest in playing games with demons. Plus, now that Stefan had unsanctioned Dioguardi blood in him, helping Geordi was her only guarantee they *might* not come after her son in a murderous rage. Jason agreed to facilitate a meet and greet for her, and we left, arriving home very late.

However, my minions had already made all our travel arrangements—naturally—and were ready to leave whenever we were. Rachel remained secured in the bathroom, humming tunelessly in Jeannette's off-key alto, but otherwise, it was business as usual.

I added our newly retrieved rock to the iron box that had formerly held Rina's letter, where my minions had placed the other two—the one of Satan's they'd found, and the one Pierre gave us. I also dropped Geordi's scarab, the dove feather, and the *porc-épic* into it for good measure. Ulrich sealed it up so it wouldn't open in transit, while Torben presented me with a quasi-official laminated badge proclaiming I worked for Interpol, and a folder of paperwork that looked suspiciously like the one we'd used to gain admittance to the military base at Sennelager.

Reduce, Reuse, Recycle: An important tenet of the Modern Day Relic Hunter.

"What's this?" I asked, though I already had a good idea.

"You're transporting a dangerous criminal from Paris to Turkey. She'll be shackled—physically—so you'll need special treatment during boarding, on the plane, and in customs."

Guess we wouldn't be staying under the radar. Not that we could anyway, iron box notwithstanding. Any Hell Demon worth their salt must know we'd been collecting shards, if not why. And that I'd recently been to Turkey. Its multiple gateways to Hell, plus Eric's presence, made it a no-brainer as our destination. But the whole thing reminded me of Germany, and my first minion-bloated venture: I travel light; they do not.

I sighed and took the papers and the badge, stuffing them in my bag. "Anything else?"

"Nope. We're on the red eye, so we need to leave for the airport in an hour."

I went back to Lily's—*my*—room and exchanged the Marseille-Turkey trip contents of my carry-on for fresh New-Turkey trip items. Rachel heard me through the bathroom door and cooed a greeting, but I ignored her and went into the spare room, hunting through the closet until I found a black pantsuit I'd left here ages ago. It wasn't too moth-eaten, so I added a white blouse and sensible loafers, then checked myself in the full-length mirror.

Agent Hyacinth Finch looked at least as official as her fake badge, so I called Jason and my minions into "my" bedroom, and we moved the dresser away from the bathroom door. I lifted a questioning eyebrow at Jason, and he said, "I've got her secured. She can't escape."

He was pale from our ordeal, but seemed to be holding up, so I nodded. Torben and Ulrich opened the door and added hand- and ankle-cuffs to Rachel's demon shackles. Unfazed, she just waited until they were done, then rose and followed us through the apartment and down to the garage. Three living men, plus me, Rachel-Jeannette, and two ghosts would never fit in the Peapod, so we opted for Lily's SUV, which seats seven.

We made it to the airport without incident and split up. I doubted Interpol agents had entourages, even if half of mine weren't visible to the Living, so only Jason stayed with Rachel and me. He had his very own quasi-official badge-plus-suit—he looked *really* good in it—so we flashed our fake papers at various security checkpoints, and a short while later, boarded the back of a plane bound for Turkey.

Somewhere near the front, Torben, Ulrich, Liam and Jun also sat. Luckily, the plane wasn't full, so the two Dead didn't have to double up on either of the Living, but Jason and I were crammed on either side of Jeannette in the last row, by the bathrooms. Probably Interpol's budget didn't extend to first class tickets for "dangerous criminals" and their guards. But regardless, *my* budget didn't, so it was a moot point.

A little while after that, we took off, arriving in Antalya seven hours later, just after dawn. Jason managed to doze during the flight, but still appeared exhausted when we landed. I pushed down my anxiety—he knew his own capabilities. Surely he would've said something, if donating his blood-plus-powers to Stefan could cause permanent damage.

He caught my eye. "Stop worrying. I'm just tired. I'll be fine—really."

Rachel-Jeannette smiled seductively. "Not your usual energetic self? How...disappointing." Her gaze traveled down his body, lingering on his lap, and he narrowed his eyes at her.

"Give it up. The spell holding you won't loosen. It's self-maintaining at this point."

Her mouth curved higher, conveying *are you sure about that?*, and I swallowed my doubts. "Self-maintaining" sounded good, and her needling was just that: her attempts to get under our skin and cause trouble. So the best plan would be to simply not let her.

We deplaned and showed our paperwork to anyone who asked for it. The heavy iron box-of-rocks raised eyebrows at the x-ray machines, but I'd refused to check it into cargo. So Torben had added hazmat stickers to the outside, and the top paper in my fake folder claimed it contained radioactive evidence, indicating airport security should *back off and leave it alone*. Or words to that effect.

It did make me wonder what crime Rachel was supposed to have committed, but it had the desired effect of causing everyone to hustle us through, in the interest of leaving work on time instead of drowning in bureaucratic red tape. So in short order, we met up with my other minions who'd rented a big black SUV, similar to the ones we had in Germany. At least we didn't need two this time.

Torben drove, with Ulrich—once again looking moody and guilt-ridden—in the front passenger seat, while Jason and I took the middle row, and we put Rachel-Jeannette in the back with Liam and Jun. I set the iron box at my feet, and Torben pulled away from the airport, heading for Hierapolis, where we arrived three hours later by mid-morning.

Rachel seemed content that we'd release her as promised and made no attempts to escape or even annoy us again. The shards were also quiet, thankfully. I'd been afraid Satan's would cause a ruckus on the plane, despite the iron blocking it, but so far, so good.

In fact, the whole thing started to feel doable—like we could actually pull it off. Maybe, as Torben said, my luck had finally changed.

We parked and got out. We'd made it to Turkey, where we'd save Eric, get Nick back, and find Geordi. It was chilly, but the sun peeked out. My minions had my back, and I literally felt the weight of my worries floating off on a breeze of optimism.

I should have known better.

****

Nadezhda circled Rachel-Jeannette, inspecting her like a farm animal at an auction. She didn't go quite so far as to lift her arms or check her teeth, but it was close.

At last, she stepped back, nodding decisively. "*Da.* She know how make Sieg let go, save Eric. But—you are certain consequences are worth it?"

I nodded. It sickened me, but I couldn't let Eric's soul die, and despite my questionable morals, I also couldn't renege on my promise to release Rachel in exchange for her help.

"Okay. Is your decision. Come—this way."

She led us through the maze of tombs, but not to the same hill as before. I'd told her that ultimately, we needed to be near the Plutonium, so she'd moved Eric to a flat open area formed by the Roman ruins near the walled-up arch. The mid-morning sunlight streamed over the surrounding hills, and cracked slabs covered most of the ground, but she'd found a grassy spot to tie him down.

This late in the year, and so deep in the center of Hierapolis, I'd seen no living tourists, and even the crowd of souls watching over Eric had thinned somewhat. Those that remained parted to let us through, and when we reached him, I sucked in a breath. He was gray, his ghost skin translucent and loose on his formerly fit frame. When I bent to touch his unconscious form, I noticed his pseudo-breathing had almost entirely stopped. He was covered in a fine sheen of ghost sweat, and he shivered violently, even under the pile of ghost blankets heaped on top of him.

I lay down, resting my head in the crook of his neck, hot tears sliding down my cheeks. "Eric—*please*—you have to hang on. We're going to save you. I *promise.*"

I felt Jason's eyes on me, and unconsciously, my thread tried to connect with his. It was horrible of me, but I needed him, to get me through this. My own thread felt tired, or changed somehow, from the experience at the tomb. And when I reached out to him, I sensed...hesitation. Would he reject me now, in this awful moment? Had I *finally* found the thing that would make him leave me?

Beneath me, Eric stirred, throwing off the blankets, and I shot up, adrenaline whooshing through me, hoping to see those jade eyes opening and regarding me cynically at any moment.

Instead, angry red welts appeared all over his exposed ghost skin, and when I touched one, it seared my fingers with unimaginable heat. I gasped and jumped back—the spots were expanding, heat radiating outward, well above his still form.

"What's happening? Why is he doing that?"

Nadezhda frowned and pulled the remaining ghost blankets away. "I do not know. Is very strange. But I think we have no time for talk. Must do this now, or will be too late." She said to Rachel, "Come. You take Sieg now, make leave Eric. Do as promised."

Rachel said sweetly, "Of course. That's what I'm here for—to take back what is mine. And Sieg is most definitely *mine*. There's just one *teeny, tiny* thing." She faced Jason. "You'll have to release me now. Your holding spell stops me from...communicating...with Sieg."

"No," I said, "absolutely not. That wasn't part of our deal. Help him first, and *then* we let you go."

"Suit yourself. You're the one trying to save the *man you love*, not me. But maybe this will change your mind."

She stepped closer to Eric, and the red spots *boiled up,* reaching toward her, his ghost skin literally bubbling like mini volcanoes about to erupt. She stepped back, and they subsided.

"You see? *That's* the bits of Sieg that are joined with your lover. They've been hiding, but when they felt me, they surfaced, wanting to be with me—my own true love. If they can't, they'll destroy *your* lover from the inside, burning his soul, like his own personal internal Hell."

Jason watched us, expression unreadable, and my stomach clenched. Rachel's barbs about Eric being my "love" were clearly designed to drive a wedge between us, but she needn't have bothered. We'd made our own.

Even so, he said quietly, "I promised I'd help you, and I swear, that hasn't changed. I don't think releasing her is a good plan, now *or* later. But it's your call."

Her arm inched closer to Eric, and the boils on that side bubbled up furiously, their heat so intense—even at this distance—that I gasped. "Okay—unshackle her."

Her eyes lit with triumph. "Your demon spell *and* my hands and feet."

I swallowed, but nodded miserably at Ulrich. He found the keys and removed her hand- and ankle-cuffs, then stepped back. Not too far, though, I noticed. He felt my gaze and met it, then shifted his focus back to her. But not before I caught the shame in his expression. Maybe in his mind, stopping Rachel's escape would atone for his failure to protect Geordi. In any case, the more eyes on her, the better.

Jason moved to her. "If you try *anything* beyond getting rid of Sieg, you'll regret it."

"Is that so? I guess we'll find out."

He shook his head, like he couldn't believe he had to do this. Then he closed his eyes, standing very still as…nothing happened. Nothing noticeable, anyway. I don't know what I expected, but now that I knew how powerful he was, I assumed I'd feel it when he "activated" those powers.

However, *something* changed, because Rachel heaved a sigh, like a great weight had been lifted from her. She closed her eyes and raised her face to the sun, soaking in its weak, early rays. Liam and Jun moved subtly closer to her, but she either didn't notice, or didn't care.

I pulled my sweater tighter. "Get on with it. Make Sieg leave Eric, or we re-shackle you."

Her eyes popped open, looking dreamy. "Of course. As I said, I'm here to get what's mine, and I intend to do just that."

I couldn't decide if her confidence meant she really could, and would, pull Sieg from Eric, or that she had a different plan, and this was all a ruse to distract us.

She rotated in a slow circle, smiling winsomely at Liam and Jun—man, I wished I'd never seen that smile—then taking in the amassed souls, waiting a respectable distance away, plus Nadezhda, my other minions, and me. Her glance landed on Eric, and she tapped her cheek, like a surgeon deciding where to make the first cut.

Her knowing gaze flicked to mine, and I got a bad feeling in my stomach. "Hyacinth. Thank you *so* much for bringing me to Sieg. I never could have found him on my own, and our reunion will be so much sweeter, because *you* made it possible."

Without warning she flung her arms wide, rose onto her toes, and whirled like a giant ballerina, moving faster than I would've thought possible for Jeannette's size.

Her muumuu flew out around her, transforming her into an enormous pink toy top, spinning faster and faster, a blur of chiffon, her large thighs tapering to slimmer calves as she twirled on the tips of her pink flats.

Before any of us could react, she froze. She teetered, eyes rolling back into her head, then fell hard on the ground. And then I felt it—a cold, foggy ooze seeping from Jeannette's motionless form, *away* from Eric, and I had my answer.

"*Stop her—she's escaping!*"

Liam and Jun dove toward the fog, trying to contain it, but it simply passed through them. Jason and Dito joined them, their eyes going black, and for once, I was unequivocally *glad* they were demons. Whatever they did, the fog came up short, hissing in dismay. It swerved, but couldn't penetrate their barrier, and they herded it back.

Torben ran to Jeannette's body and checked her vitals, while Ulrich's face showed his anguish and shame at failing *again*, and his indecision as he tried to work out how to help. He grabbed a ghost blanket from the pile beside Eric, unfurling it and waving it at the fog from this side, also forcing Rachel toward Eric, and away from us and Jeannette.

Torben said to me, "She's alive—barely."

All at once, Eric thrashed against his bonds, the boils bubbling like hot lava, the unbearable heat reaching out for Rachel's cool fog. Oh God—Sieg *did* want to join her. Eric's spirit would be shredded by the force of Sieg's remnants—they already stretched him into a grotesque, twisted shape—a mass of putrid-green-redness, bloated and swollen with hatred.

"*Help him!*" I shrieked, not even sure who I

addressed. Most of the Dead had backed away, not wanting to get involved. Nadezhda watched the unfolding events, also not interfering, so I unleashed my helpless rage and anguish on her. *"Don't just stand there—do something!"*

"Wait," she said calmly, and I took a half-step forward, my fear so strong, I wanted to grab her and shove her at Eric.

Then something flickered near the corner of my eye and I froze. As Sieg reached for Rachel, her fog jerked back, seemingly in distaste. But his boils strained, bulging outward until one broke free with a loud *hiss-pop*! I dove toward them, but someone grabbed me, pulling me back as I thrashed almost as much as Eric.

"Let me go!"

"Hyacinth!"

It was Jason, but in my terror I only flailed harder. "No! We have to help—"

"It's not what you think. Look at him—see what's *really* happening."

His utter certainty—plus his six-foot-six iron grip on me—forced me to pause and do what he asked. And then I saw what Nadezhda and Jason both had already seen: Yes, Sieg's boils pulled at Eric's soul, but as they popped free, they left behind clean ghost skin—healthy and pink, not red—not even gray.

Moreover, as they floated away, they coalesced into a hot steam that grew to the size of Rachel's fog, then swirled toward her...and she backed away. But Dito stood behind her, maintaining whatever spell he and Jason had used to herd her forward. Her heavy fog couldn't float more than a few inches above the ground, and she thinned and stretched, trying to escape. But

Ulrich waved his ghost blanket harder, moving closer to Dito, so that they formed a box around her, with Eric on one side, Liam and Jun also brandishing ghost blankets on the other, and the Sieg Steam closing in from the front.

In seconds, he reached her, and I *felt* him—he didn't want to "become one with her." He was *enraged.* Like hot oil on cold water, when they touched, they exploded, his spray sizzling my skin even as her fog froze me. Ulrich launched himself at them, spreading the blanket wide to smother the fire, except their conflagration already bloomed to bonfire-size.

Suddenly, Nadezhda noticed him and waved her arms frantically, shrieking, "*Ne!* Stop!"

Instinctively I ducked, and Jason curled himself over me, flattening us both to the ground, just as a sonic *boom!* thundered off the hills around us. The earth shook and Jason pressed down harder while unidentifiable things fell on and around us. It lasted moments—maybe seconds—and then just as fast, ended.

Cautiously, Jason pushed himself up, and when he deemed it safe, rolled off me, coughing in the clouds of hot ash smothering the hillside. I coughed, too, gasping for breath—there'd been an awful lot of Jason on top of me—and trying to focus through the burning smoke searing my eyes. When it finally cleared, I saw my minions, Nadezhda, and the Dead, mostly where they'd been before, except, like us, lying or sitting on the ground.

I crawled to Eric, reaching him just as Nadezhda bent and cut his bonds with a knife from her skirt pocket. The boils were gone, and even through the remaining ashy haze, I saw his complexion had vastly improved.

His pseudo-breathing was shallow, but steady, and he stirred as Nadezhda re-covered his—still naked—lower half with a ghost blanket. This time, his eyes did open, their jade depths even older than before.

"*Mon ange.*" His voice sounded hoarse and weak. "You are here."

"Yes. You scared me so badly—please don't ever do that again."

"You scared me, too," a male voice said, coming around a nearby Roman brick wall. "But not in the way *ton ange* means."

It was Stefan, followed closely by Elaine. His eyes flickered black for a fraction of a second, before returning to the same ancient gray-green as his father's.

His father, who went white with shock at the sight of his estranged son. He struggled to sit up—abruptly looked very woozy—and fainted.

Chapter Twenty-Two

"My life closed twice before its close;
It yet remains to see
If Immortality unveil
A third event to me...."
~Emily Dickinson, American Poet
(1830-1886)

Elaine stared at Eric as though, quite literally, seeing a ghost. She approached slowly, dropping to her knees on his other side. She reached out hesitantly, her fingers brushing into his cheek, and quickly withdrew her hand. "Is he...?"

Nadezhda waddled up. "He okay. Just surprised."

That was the understatement of the year. She stooped and slapped his cheeks, and Elaine's jaw dropped. She whispered to me, "Is she dead, too?"

"No."

I'd answered automatically, my brain whirling with so many things, I couldn't form a coherent thought. Eric *just* came back to me, and now he'd find out I made his son a *demon*. Plus, I couldn't see Jason behind me, but I knew he watched us, and my heart cracked, because either what I'd shared with him meant I'd cheated on Eric, or what I did now hurt Jason.

Both, in fact.

Then my brain clicked on a detail having nothing to

do with either of them. "Where's Ulrich?"

Torben glanced up in surprise, then looked around, as did my other minions. But Nadezhda lifted a shoulder in her version of a shrug. "He no make it."

"He... What did you say?"

"I try to stop him. He take blanket, cover fire-fog. But is ghost cloth. I make so Living can touch, when you"—she gestured at Stefan—"visit before, then forget to unmake it."

My mouth worked like a fish. "What..."

"Ghost cloth not real cloth. Made of energy. Sieg is all rage, all hot oil. Rachel, ice water. Explode when energies meet. Ulrich throw ghost cloth on fire-fog— more energy. Not smother—make *bigger*. Too big. No outlet, so—implode. Sieg, Rachel, Ulrich, no survive. But on plus side, Eric absorb their energy—replenish his stores. He better now."

Ulrich...was gone? And...

I lurched to my feet. "*Rachel* is gone? Like, obliterated, dead for good, *gone*-gone?"

"*Da.*"

Oh God—our bargaining chip. I turned to Jason— he'd disapproved of the plan from the start, but now that my next domino had vanished, taking with it our best hope of getting Nick back and forcing Nico and Rina to keep their promise, his horror mirrored my own.

"Fuck," he said simply. "It's my fault. I shouldn't have loosened the holding spell, even a little. I thought I could control her, but I couldn't. I'm...weak...from earlier."

"You tricked her?"

"I tried. I loosened the spell enough that she wouldn't notice the tiny bit still holding her. We all knew she was up to something. I think she planned all along for you to bring her to Sieg. She didn't know where Vadim took Eric, and she wanted whatever energy or powers Sieg had left for herself. Plus, like the other Dead, she couldn't travel easily on her own. So she took over Jeannette, and waited for you to show up." He lifted a shoulder helplessly. "I'm sorry. I really thought I could re-shackle her in time to make the trade for Nick."

Stefan frowned at us. "*Qu'est-ce qui se passe?*"

Dito dragged a hand through his hair. "I'll go in anyway. Maybe if I just tell Satan she's gone—"

Whatever Nadezhda had done to make the Dead visible and audible to the Living evidently extended to Dito, and Elaine gasped and went white with shock, while Stefan—who could see and hear Dito on his own now—jerked back. "*Satan?* You're going to talk with *le diable?*"

I'd had just about enough of him—of everyone, and everything—and rounded on him.

"It's *your* fault Jason's powers are depleted and Rachel escaped. You *asked* for this—*you*. No one forced you, and now you're part of it. Did it *never* occur to you that demon blood *comes from Satan?* That by taking it— *and* Jason's powers—you'd be forever linked to *Hell?* You *demanded* I make you a demon. I didn't want to, but I did, and now you have to *get over it and live with the fucking consequences.*"

"*Mon ange.*" Eric's voice was deadly quiet. I froze, then slowly faced him. He'd managed to sit up, half-covered by the blanket, his bare chest rising and falling with the effort at maintaining control. "You did…*what*…to *my son?*"

Oh God. "I…"

His green eyes hardened. "Leave. Now. I never want to see you again."

Stefan stepped forward. "Don't blame her. She's right—I made her do it."

"It's true," Elaine interjected quickly, startling Eric, who clearly hadn't noticed her until now. "*Vraiment.* She would have refused, but he forced her to do it."

Eric's lips compressed. "Is that so? And…did *you* try to stop him?"

"He…" She shook her head miserably. "*Non.* I did not understand. Hyacinth tried to warn me, but I didn't listen."

Stefan's own eyes hardened. Not black, mercifully, but with barely suppressed "normal" rage. "What do *you* care? You've *never* been part of my life, so why the self-righteous act now?"

Eric held his gaze for a long moment, then broke eye contact, dropping his head shamefacedly. "It is not that simple."

"Isn't it? I'm *your son.* Not *once* in twenty-two years did you try to see me." His jaw clenched and his hands fisted at his sides. "I don't know why I came. I should have known better."

I was still too much in shock to think straight, but Jason broke in, "Why *are* you here?"

"We followed you from the cemetery. I thought I could…" Stefan slumped. "*Ça ne fait rien.* I was mistaken."

Torben and Dito had been quietly conversing while the rest of us, including Nadezhda and the Dead, focused on this, but now Dito cleared his throat. "Sorry to interrupt, but Olivia texted Torben. Nico and Rina made arrangements to meet Marchosias here. He's going to accept their offer. We need to bring Nick out *now,* or the deal with you being in Geordi's life is off. If we can't do it, they might even move the exchange somewhere else."

Elaine scrambled to her feet, going to her son and tugging his arm. "Please—let's go. You see—it will never work. Let's leave—go home—before—"

But Stefan straightened. "*Ici?* Paolo—Marchosias—will be here? Today?"

"Please," Elaine pleaded. "It is not worth it. Can you not see that?"

He ignored her, looking at me. "He is the Hell Demon who has your nephew. *Oui?*"

Eric jerked back in shock. "*Mon ange*"—guess old habits died hard—"*de quoi parle-t-il?*"

I swallowed. "It's true. Marchosias escaped from Hell, before Barnacken. He's been in Paolo a long time. Remember Geordi's scarab? It was protecting him, like he always said. Probably shielding him, too. But he gave it to me, to protect me. And as soon as he no longer had it, Marchosias took him. Dito's dead now, and Bala's in the hospital. The Dioguardis are negotiating with Marchosias to release Geordi, but—" The nausea roiled and I choked down my anguish. "—unless I bring Nick back to life for them, I'll never see him again."

Jason said coolly, "What she isn't telling you is that we had a plan. Remember how tight it felt inside Sieg? Rachel was hiding in there with you."

Eric blanched. "Rachel survived? Satan did not destroy her?"

"Yes. She escaped, but we caught her, and were going to trade her to Satan, for Nick. We needed one each of Michael's and Satan's shards to pull him out, and we had them—until Stefan *stole* one, then forced Hyacinth to make him a demon, in exchange for its return."

He squatted in front of Eric, keeping his voice level, but I knew the cavernous rage he held back. "So, thanks to *your son,* she roped me into sharing my blood—my *powers*—with him. It took too much out of me, and now Rachel—the *one* bargaining chip we had with Satan—is *gone.*"

Eric regarded his son, confusion and disbelief in his every feature, and Stefan said dispassionately, "*C'est vrai.* I took the rock, to get what I wanted. But now…" He faced Jason, his eyes slowly going black. "Now, I can help you get what *you* want. If I am the cause of your weakened state, I am sincerely sorry, and the least I can do is use my new powers, to ensure the safe return of Hyacinth's nephew, right here, today, as planned."

Jason rose, eyes narrowing. "What are you saying?"

"*Simplement* that, if we pool our powers—yours, mine and Dito's—perhaps we can pull Nicholas Dioguardi out, without offering Satan a trade at all." He raised a hand, palm out, then made a fist. The veins in his forearm bulged orange, then red, then went as black as his eyes. He released the fist and lowered his arm, and his veins receded again.

Elaine had started to cry. She opened her mouth, but Stefan shot her a quelling look and she gulped and stepped back. He returned his gaze to Jason, who watched him, considering.

At last Jason said, "You realize that removing Nick from Hell goes against everything your grandfather wants, which is absolute power in the north also, not just down here. Giving the Dioguardis their son and heir back only increases their power, and will piss him off."

Stefan lifted a shoulder. "Despite what you all think,

I did not become a demon to help my grandfather do anything. I had…other reasons." He turned to me. "I have been exploring my new abilities. You said I would be a 'Hell magnet,' and I believe you are correct. But that goes both ways—not only can Hell suck me in, but *I* can pull things *out*."

Sudden hope flared and I said to Jason, "If that's true, then Dito can still go in. His powers are enhanced by being dead—it doesn't *have* to be you or Stefan. Right?"

Jason shook his head slowly. "Unfortunately, because I made Stefan, our powers are linked in ways mine and Dito's aren't. Essentially, Stefan's powers *are* my powers—we're bonded, and more powerful together than apart. Plus, because Dito's dead, and would literally only be spirit-walking through Hell, he's not as effective as a so-called magnet."

I started to ask what he meant, when abruptly, the ice of a demon shield sliced the air around us. It came from Dito, white-faced and struggling for control, as two figures rounded the ruins to join us: Jacques Rousseau and his latest demon pet, Flore. They stopped a few yards away and his mouth split into a yellow-toothed wolf's grin.

"I believe I can help as well. As you know, I have an…in, with Hell. I can once more offer protection on your journey, and assist with the…negotiations."

At his arrival, the souls who'd been milling around suddenly remembered they had prior engagements, and dispersed in all directions. Nadezhda, while not seeming impressed by Jacques—even if he *was* Bael of Hell— also decided she'd had enough fun for one day. She retrieved a pile of men's clothes she'd laid out on a tomb and placed it near Eric, then waddled off without a backward glance.

I felt Dito's shield like a cool bubble of safety, protecting my remaining minions and me, plus Eric, Stefan, Elaine and Jeannette, who remained unconscious on the ground nearby. I didn't sense Jason's shield, though, and I tried not to dwell on how weak he might actually be.

Jacques took in our defensive postures. "I assure you, my offer of aid is sincere." He said to Flore, standing slumped and vacant-eyed beside him, "Tell them, my pet."

Weirdly, his presence snapped me out of my shock-stupor. All my years of dealing with rich asshole clients kicked in, and I was on solid ground again. "What's she got to do with it?"

Jason said tightly, "He's suggesting Flore enter Hell with Stefan and me. Demon pets have all their master's powers. Not to use on their own, but their masters can literally use *them*, like puppets. So, without going into Hell himself—and risking his own safety—Jacques can send Flore in to do his dirty work. Then, if we fail, Satan will annihilate us and her, not Jacques."

"No," I said immediately. "Absolutely not."

I already felt guilty about letting Flore commit herself to Jacques's whims for the next five centuries. I couldn't have Satan destroying her in Jacques's stead *also* on my conscience.

Jacques said politely, "It is not a request. The two young demons here both have my powers in them. *We* are bonded, just as they are. I cannot control them fully out here, but in Hell…"

He lifted a shoulder, his implications clear, and my

stomach dropped as I saw the confirmation on Jason's face.

"No…"

"*Oui.*" Jacques regarded me thoughtfully. "*Bien sûr…you* have my powers in you, as well. Don't you, *ma chérie?*"

I stared at him. Because of course, I *had* stolen powers from the Rousseaux once before—a tiny drop, when I retrieved that first fateful rock for Michael. And though the pull then was instantaneous, I hadn't thought about it much since, because it hadn't seemed to affect me. Except… Now he brought it up, the power abruptly awakened, coursing through me like fire, burning me from the inside out, and I gasped.

He only lifted an eyebrow at me. "You see, Mademoiselle Finch? That is what it feels like, when I can only *partially* use my powers through you. Imagine the pain if you were in Hell."

He made a cutting motion, and the fire receded and I sagged back.

"Claude told you we were linked." His eyes flicked to Jason, then Stefan. "All of us. And so, you will enter Hell to retrieve Nicholas Dioguardi *with* my aid, or…not at all."

Eric struggled to stand, holding the blanket wrapped around his waist. "*Non*—I forbid it." He included both me and Stefan in his glare—although not Jason, I noticed.

Stefan didn't even bother to scowl back. He just said to Jason, "Can you think of another way?" Without waiting for an answer he knew wouldn't come, he continued to me, "Or can you live without ever seeing your nephew again? With the Dioguardis having *total* control over him? If you can't bring Nick back, they'll meet Marchosias somewhere else, and you will *never* see Geordi again—not today, and not even from a distance."

I swallowed. "I'll go, instead of Flore. This is my mess, and I'll handle it."

"*No.*"

So many of them said it at once—Jason, Eric, Stefan—even Jacques—a cacophony of negatives. But Jason reached me first, gripping my arms. "You can't."

"I *have* to. Don't you see? This is all on me. I have to be the one to take care of it. Flore may have made her own dumb choices, but it's my fault she succeeded." I said to Jacques, "If I have your powers in me, too, I can go instead, right?"

Jason shook me, hard. "*Listen to me.* We can't *both* go. Who will be here for Geordi?"

"*Mon ange,*" Eric broke in. "He is right. It is too dangerous. If you both go into Hell, and do not return…"

I let out a sob of mingled frustration and terror. "It *has* to be me. I can't put this on someone else. I—"

Jun stepped forward, saying to Jason, in his normal calm cadence, "She doesn't understand." He faced me. "It's not like when I spirit-walked in Hell. Whoever goes now will need to *physically* enter Satan's Kingdom— mind *and* body—and soul. I went for recon only, to observe and gather information. To be the Hell magnet Stefan describes, the magnets must be near the soul they're pulling out."

"No…"

Jacques lifted a shoulder negligently. "In any case, it is not up to you. *Oui,* I could send you into Hell in Flore's stead, but I will not. Who can say? Perhaps Satan will take her on himself, as a consolation prize. Then she will be a full Hell demon much earlier than planned. But either way, her companions will be these two young demons, not you."

This couldn't be happening. I looked at Jason. How weak was he? Would he even survive this? My fears must have shown on my face, because he raised his hands to cup my cheeks.

"It will be all right. I swear it."

"But—"

"No buts. And whatever happens, no regrets." He released me and turned to Dito. "You'll stay with her and Geordi."

It wasn't a question, and Dito simply said, "Of course."

Jason's glance flicked to Torben. "Where are the rocks?"

I tried to come up with an argument—anything to stop the inevitable—but Torben moved to the jumble of carry-ons we'd stashed nearby, while Eric reached for the ghost shirt Nadezhda had left for him. He yanked it on with one hand, the blanket in his other, and spoke to Stefan.

"*Non.* Whatever is between us, you cannot do this. Please—I beg you, *mon fils*—"

Stefan said quietly, "You have no right to call me that. *Ever.* I am *not* your son, and I never will be."

Eric went white and Elaine took a step toward him, hesitating, then faced her son instead. "Please. For *my* sake—don't do this."

"*Maman.* I am already a demon. There is no going back. I don't have the knowledge to do what they want on my own, but I have the powers to help. *Ça suffit.* It is decided."

Torben returned with the iron box and unlocked it, holding it in such a way that only I could see inside. He shot me a meaningful look, which I interpreted as a warning to not let Jacques see the scarab, feather, or *porc-épic*. Probably wise, given the scarab, at least, appeared to have anti-Hell Demon powers.

I reached for one of the rocks, palming the scarab as I did so, then dropping it into my hoody pocket while setting the rock ceremoniously on the ground. I repeated the process twice more with the other trinkets and shards, noting that the three rocks were all roughly the same size and coloring, so they must have come from the same portion of the original slab.

Which seemed almost as weird as how they'd all showed up, right when we needed them. But whatever. At this point, I was way beyond caring *how we*'d gotten them.

Jacques's eyes lit with excitement. "*Mais c'est merveilleux!* How did you manage to find *three* of them?"

I stuffed my hands casually into my pockets, gripping the scarab in my left, and the feather and coin in my right. "Just lucky, I guess." Who knows? Maybe it was even true.

"Most excellent. This will provide more than enough power to pull your man out."

"Why?" I asked bluntly. "And no more bullshit about taking Satan's toy from him. What's the real reason you're helping us?"

Jacques's grin only widened. "Ah, but Mademoiselle Finch, *c'est pas des conneries*. By taking Satan's 'toy,' as you say, I can send a message—demonstrate what he is up against."

Jason's gaze shot to him. "Shit. It's a power grab."

I frowned. "What do you mean?"

"Jacques is sending Flore into Hell, imbued with his powers, in a bid to overthrow Satan and rule Hell himself."

Jacques shrugged. "Does knowing this change anything? Our agreement is already sealed, *n'est-ce pas?*"

I opened my mouth, then shut it in defeat. At least if Jacques attacked him, maybe Satan would be too weak to come after us, for what we were about to do.

"*Bon,*" Jacques said. He turned to Jason, Stefan, and Flore. "Come. It is time."

I stepped forward and grabbed Jacques's arm, his overwhelming heat burning my hand, even through the sleeve of his white suit. "Wait—make it so I can see them when they're gone. I know you can—*please.*"

His expression was impassive. Then his eyes flicked black, and my veins caught on fire.

"Hyacinth!" Jason said urgently, taking a step toward me.

"*No,*" I said, just as urgently. "You're right that we can't both go in, but please—I have to see what's happening. I…"

I trailed off miserably. Eric stood nearby, now fully dressed. He might hate me forever for what I'd done to Stefan, but at least I'd saved him. I felt his thread, tenuous, but whole again, and for that I would be forever grateful. But even if Eric and I were finally over, I still might never resolve everything with Jason that made *our* relationship impossible. And either way, I couldn't bear not knowing what happened to him.

Slowly, he nodded. Then he bent and kissed me.

I don't know if it was our shared Rousseaux powers or what, but the kiss felt electric—not in a sexy way, but literally, like his thread and mine channeled together into a huge power surge. I gasped, and he broke the kiss, whispering low so only I could hear him, "Whatever happens now, I'll always be a part of you."

Then he turned and raised his hands over the shards, Stefan copying him. Jacques waved Flore forward, and she went to them automatically—a puppet, just as Jason had described.

Jacques tugged me aside, his powers in my veins liquefying until they burned lava-hot. I just had the presence of mind to shove my hands into my pockets again and grab the scarab, feather, and *porc-épic*, before Jacques's, Jason's, Stefan's and Flore's eyes all went black, and my own eyesight vanished, replaced by a darkness that went beyond black, into a deep void that engulfed me, inside and out.

And then I saw into Hell.

Chapter Twenty-Three

"The soul sees written over its head, you are damned forever. It hears howlings that are to be perpetual; it sees flames which are unquenchable; it knows pains that are unmitigated."

~Charles Spurgeon, English Baptist Preacher
(1834-1892)

Unbearable heat, absolute blackness. He had no memory of getting here—either the rocks sucked him in, or more likely, Jacques opened the Plutonium. That must be it. While he'd tried to use the shards, he didn't have the connection to them that Hyacinth did, and couldn't access their powers. Or maybe he was just still too weak.

He shoved the thought away and assessed the situation. He sensed Stefan on one side of him, Flore on the other. But there was no sight, no sound, only the empty void. Jun hadn't mentioned this in his description of his journey into Hell, but maybe Jacques's demons had already been waiting for him, before he arrived.

As though the thought conjured them, a fiery path appeared, glowing bright enough for Jason to see two formless demons ahead of them, leading the way. Flore had already fallen into step behind them, but Stefan hesitated. While close to Jason in physical age, Stefan's demonhood was in its infancy.

Come.

His voice didn't work, but the thought reached Stefan, and he steadied himself. Good. For this to work, Stefan had *to function. Jason's own recovery was taking longer than anticipated, and he wouldn't make it through without Stefan's help.*

He had to. For Geordi. And for Hyacinth.

The memory of her face when she'd said she needed to know his fate stabbed him. It would be better if she didn't. Even if he survived, she should never see what happened in here—no one should. But he couldn't stop her—he never could. Her convictions were absolute. And at least if he died, she'd be spared wondering how.

Plus it gave him strength, knowing she watched his progress—that she cared enough to travel with him, even if from afar. And she did *care. She just didn't understand those feelings. Who could blame her, when her whole life had been spent in foster care, and then moving around Africa and Europe? She had always been in charge, relying on no one but herself. Even her sister, consciously or not, had looked to her for support. Now, when he or anyone else tried to help—to be "nice"—the feeling was so alien and unrecognizable, it made her uncomfortable.*

He forced the thought of her away. To survive—to return to her, and show her what sharing a future together could mean—he absolutely could not feel *right now.*

The demons led the way down the endless path slowly. Or maybe impatience twisted his sense of time, the never changing scenery dragging him into an infernal monotony from which he'd never escape.

But eventually—hours or days or minutes later—they came to the great open space Jun had described. As he'd said, there were no visible fires, but the heat grew exponentially—so unbearable, it became a part of Jason, his skin melting, his eyes hot coals. As before, Jacques's demons refused to travel past the edge of the room, instead shaping their formless voids enough to point toward the center, where an even darker Presence sat atop a massive gray-white throne.

Maybe Hyacinth's moments of hysteria were rubbing off on him, because all at once he felt like Ebenezer Scrooge, with the silent, unyielding Spirit of Christmas Yet to Come pointing at his own grave, demanding he face his future.

Hyacinth. Geordi. They *were his future, and he needed to know they were safe. He couldn't bear a life without them—or bear the thought of them trying to survive the Demon World without his help. Hyacinth's tunnel vision made her reckless. Like Rina, she would literally do* anything *to protect Geordi, or anyone else she felt responsible for. She even thought she understood the consequences, but in reality, none of them could control any of this.*

He steeled himself, then led the way into the vast room, flanked by Stefan on his left, Flore on his right. They approached the throne openly—stealth would be pointless. Satan had probably noticed Jun, and chosen not to care. But their current mission couldn't be secret, so they boldly crossed the flat ground until the throne and its occupant were mere meters away.

The Presence was as formless as Jacques's demons, the deep black void He presented far more terrifying than if He'd chosen some monstrous shape. On one side of the void, an iron handcuff floated in midair, a long chain snaking down from it to another cuff around the meaty wrist of Nicholas Dioguardi. He seemed none the worse for having been shot in the head and then passed into Hell, to be chained to Satan for eternity. In fact, he looked better *than he had in Life, so Satan must be* very *enamored of him, indeed.*

If he recognized Jason, he gave no sign. Not surprising, since Jason had been careful to keep himself separate from the main Dioguardi branch. All his work had been in the peripherals, while Paolo, Dito, and Bala had infiltrated the inner Family, trying to rectify the harm the Dioguardis had perpetrated. And still did.

Nick's eyes lit with excitement when he saw Flore, the length of his chain allowing him to just reach for and grab her hands. "Shit—you did it." He faced the Presence, pulling her around with him. "Master, she's here. I told you she'd do it."

Jason's gut clenched. They were expecting *Flore? This couldn't be good.*

****

I gasped, and my mind's eye flew to Jacques. "Did you know about this?"

His own shock was so obvious, I had my answer. His powers in my veins surged and I felt his anger and frustration—but also his futility. He tried to control Flore—to draw her back, and when that failed, he focused his rage on Jason and Stefan.

"*No*—" I began, but here, too, I felt his total impotence.

Until he turned that rage back on me. "*Ta gueule!* Something is wrong, and Mademoiselle Finch, *you* of all people should be very afraid. If things do not go as I planned, your friends will *not* escape. Certainly, *I* will not aid them, and neither will my demons."

Eric's thread surged with his own rage. "*Non.* Stefan will return, or I will kill you."

I honestly don't know if he spoke to Jacques or me, but either way, Jacques simply sent a tiny bit of his powers in Eric's direction, freezing him in place as he'd been in Turkey, outside the Rousseaux's villa.

What should I do? What *could* I do?

The rocks—their whole purpose was to pull Nick from Hell. Surely I could use them to pull Jason and Stefan out as well—or if it came to it, instead. I sent my thread to the shards—they felt…odd. But it was my only hope, though I had no clue how to begin.

Desperately, I pictured their energy, trying to manipulate it, to make a "Hell magnet" of my own that would pull the two demons and Nick back to Earth, without Jacques figuring out what I did. My hands still clutched the trinkets in my pockets, and I noticed the coin growing warmer—not overly hot, but I felt each individual carved quill against my palm. Tiny threads reached out from them, joining the rope I'd made by combining my thread with those of the shards, and I felt its pull increase subtly.

Then I heard a Voice in the back of my mind—the same one that spoke on Barnacken—and my focus jerked back to Hell and the events unfolding before us.

****

"EXCELLENT. YOU HAVE DONE WELL, MY SON."

The chain jerked, yanking Nick forward, dragging Flore with him, so that they fell at the throne's foot. The Presence stilled, assessing, probing—first Nick and Flore, then moving to Stefan and…Jason.

He felt the Presence taking his measure, followed

by...not surprise, exactly, but...thoughtfulness.

"AH. A DIOGUARDI DEMON." The focus returned to Stefan. "AND YOU AS WELL. BUT NOT BY BIRTH. THERE WILL BE CONSEQUENCES FOR THAT—FOR TAKING WHAT IS MINE, WITHOUT MY PERMISSION. BUT FIRST, YOU WILL TELL ME WHY YOU HAVE COME."

Jason clenched his fists and opened his mouth, but Stefan spoke first.

"We are here to make a trade. One of your demons, Marchosias, has taken a child and is holding him for ransom. Another of your demons, Bael, has imbued Flore with his powers and plots to overthrow you. In exchange for giving you this information—for warning you of his scheme—we ask that you give us Nicholas Dioguardi, to take back to Earth and facilitate the child's return."

Jason felt his jaw drop. Stefan knew Jacques was Bael? And what the fuck was he doing—telling Satan of Jacques's plan to steal the throne?

Without warning, the Rousseaux powers coursing through his veins went dark. And then he knew—Jacques had abandoned them, protecting himself and leaving them behind.

Hyacinth—could she see this? Did she know Jacques had ditched them? His heart cried out to her, but he ruthlessly cut it off. At least he could stop her from feeling his thread, and experiencing whatever pain and torture he had to endure.

The Presence regarded Stefan for a long moment. "WHY SHOULD I GIVE YOU MY MOST LOYAL SON? WHAT PURPOSE WILL SENDING HIM TO EARTH SERVE ME?"

Stefan remained standing tall—Jason gave him props for bravery. Or maybe it was stupidity. Either way, he answered calmly.

"He is a Dioguardi—the son and heir. And it is his only child that Marchosias has taken, which I'm sure you know. Without Nick, the child's aunt—who I believe you also have an interest in—will lose access to him. Give us Nick, so that Hyacinth and Geordi can be reunited."

What. The. Fuck.

Before Jason could process any of the dozens of questions flying through his brain—How did Stefan know about Satan and Hyacinth? How were they connected? And would it be enough to make Satan relinquish Nick?—Flore stood and faced the throne. Her eyes brightened, her shoulders straightened, and she spoke in a clear, firm non-demon-pet voice.

"Master, we did all as you decreed. I am here and ready. Use me as you planned."

Nick also pushed himself up, standing in front of the Presence, although he seemed less certain than Flore about whatever was happening. Even so, his voice didn't waver.

"I am also ready, Master. Send me back to Earth, where all the powers of the Dioguardis await you. The porc-épic *is calling. Generations of Dioguardis who bear your blood—Hell's blood—are reaching out across the ages. Your prison gate is unlocking—opening—pass me through, and all will be as we planned."*

Jason felt it then: a subtle shift in the cavern's air. Not a "cool" breeze exactly, but a movement—a current that caressed his skin with a less-hot warmth, before passing behind him, to flow up the path. Up, and back— back—farther back, until eventually, it would go…out.

Hyacinth must be using the shards. An inevitability, but still a shock to know *Satan's prison had been unlocked, that the door cracked open, and not just for his demons—for* him. *He* couldn't *escape—surely his bonds would hold.*

But…what did the porcupine coin have to do with it?

The Presence on the throne rose, and abruptly the lightly caressing air became a vortex of heat and energy, both dark and the absence of darkness, sucking any light in the room into a river of power, a White-Light Brick Road, leading straight from Hell to the unsuspecting world above.

"YES. IT IS TIME."

The Presence descended the throne, stopping before Flore and Nick. Flore stood strong, but Nick cowered, and the presence laughed—a roar of triumph and joy.

"FEAR NOT, MY SON. YOUR REWARD SHALL BE ETERNAL HONOR. BUT TELL ME—IS YOUR BODY WAITING ABOVE?"

Nick cringed. "Yes, I feel it. It—it's not quite at the gate. It's—"

"NO MATTER. IF YOU FEEL IT, IT IS CLOSE ENOUGH.. I AM VERY PLEASED WITH YOUR EFFORTS. NOW, LET US SEND YOU BACK TO YOUR FAMILY, SO I MAY REPLENISH MY POWERS AS PLANNED."

Without doubt, something awful *was about to occur. If Satan fed off the Dioguardis' powers, could he break free after all? But how would he get them? Could he send Nick across the Light Road, then pull him back the same way, bringing new stores of powers directly into Hell? And what of Flore's role in all this?*

Jason had to warn Hyacinth, even if it meant she felt his pain after all. Frantically he sent his thread out, to tell her—anyone—*what was happening.*

Too late—something sliced his thread in two—a Power so great, so absolute, he might never recover—it might end him, here and now.

And that made him one of the lucky ones.

****

I screamed. Jason's thread—it reached out—and then vanished. Not retreated—just *not there* anymore. Jacques jerked back and normal eyesight returned, everything so bright, I couldn't see—but then—

The rocks—the three I'd placed on the ground—they'd formed a large triangle, out of which *gushed* white light, so blinding and terrifying and powerful it knocked me to my knees.

Hatred.

Evil.

Vengeance.

And then I knew—realized what I should have long ago: The rocks were *all* Satan's. He'd wanted us to find them—had told his demons to plant them where we'd notice them. And I'd used them exactly as he intended, to open the gate to Hell—not just a crack, but *wide* open.

The *porc-épic* burned my palm, its threads suddenly far from benign or protective, and I took it out and hurled it away. *What had I done?*

Jason.

My soul screamed for him, but the light was too powerful, the Hell Gate belching hot winds and greasy smoke and lava blobs that became demons, forming their temporary shapes just enough to scatter in all directions.

Michael—surely whatever bonds he'd used to trap

Satan in Hell in the first place couldn't be broken simply by unlocking the gate, or it would have been done before.

Wouldn't it?

Everyone else had also been knocked down by the roaring vortex of light. I twisted, searching the faces for Jacques. If he wanted to take down Satan, now would be the time to act.

But he was gone—no sign of him anywhere.

And then with a resounding *roar*, the earth inside the triangle crumbled, vanishing into a limitless pit below, and I scrambled to keep from falling over the edge.

****

The rocks above ripped Stefan away from the throne. Them, and something else. His gaze flew to Jason, struggling against the vortex—he had to help— Jason was weak because of him—they were all right about that, even if they didn't understand why he'd done it.

But he couldn't help. He'd stolen Jason's strength, but even so, it wasn't enough to stop the vacuum. The shards sucked him out—he couldn't see, but he felt Nick being pulled through also. If he could just throw a line to Jason, surely their momentum, his and Nick's together, would pull Jason out, too.

"Here!" he yelled, unsure if Jason could hear him, let alone react.

He made a fist, balling his powers into it, and hurled them in Jason's direction. He gave as much as he could—his own agenda paled compared to this. But try as he might, he couldn't give all *the powers back. They were part of him now, forever entrenched.*

Still, maybe they would be enough to save Jason— or for Jason to prevent Satan from succeeding at whatever he'd planned.

*Then Stefan was falling—*up*—through dirt and other organic matter, until the Earth spewed him out and dropped him, coughing and choking, to land on the hillside a few meters from his father. Eric stood rooted in place, wild-eyed and frantic, struggling to move as he watched the vortex from Hell threatening to suck Hyacinth down forever.*

She scrambled near the edge—too close—Stefan had to get to her—but he couldn't stand—he'd given too much back to Jason, and though he'd recover, it wouldn't be in time…

****

*Jason caught Stefan's powers—*his *powers—and fell to the ground, clinging to them, a lifeline in the horrific insanity around him. He couldn't see in the light-absence-blackness-void—couldn't hear above the thundering roar—but he knew Stefan and Nick had been sucked back to Earth by the power of…*

Satan's *shards.*

How wrong they'd been. Not in their original interpretation—it made sense that a combination of Michael's and Satan's powers could resurrect Nick. But they'd been wrong to believe they'd found any *of Michael's rocks—or Satan's—by accident. And while the yin-yang of opposing powers might be strong, placing three of the* same *stones together had created a magnetic attraction amplified beyond belief.*

And they were still active. Maybe he could "ride" them back out himself. He managed to stand, turning to where the path should be—but it had disappeared. And he was weak. Too weak. He shouldn't have dismissed Bala's warning, but there had been no other way.

He felt the Presence behind him—it filled with pleasure at his predicament—at the blame he heaped on himself, and the utter subjugation that he now must face.

But when it spoke, full realization dawned, and he fell to his knees in shock and horror, weeping for what they had done.

****

Stefan lay where he'd fallen, breathing hard. I scrabbled farther from the edge of the pit, just as it spewed forth another shape—Nicholas Dioguardi, his newly dug up corpse covered in black dirt and hot oil and the grime of Hell.

He landed on his knees, falling forward onto his hands, coughing, retching, vomiting black-orange hot lava. Then he wiped his mouth and sat back. He saw me and grinned and the bottom dropped out of the world.

"HYACINTH. IT IS GOOD TO MEET YOU IN PERSON AT LAST."

Chapter Twenty-Four

"To Paradise…Satan could never find the way Until the peacock led him in."
~Charles Godfrey Leland, American Writer
(1824-1903)

Oh God—what had we done? Brought Nick back—but with *Satan* hitching a ride.

Ohgodohgodohgodohgod.

Michael—he had to help with this. I closed my eyes, but before the thought got out I felt Him—Satan—His power surging toward me, cloaking the message, and my eyes flew open.

"THAT IS NOT A GOOD IDEA, HYACINTH. IF YOU INVOLVE MY BROTHER IN THIS, THERE WILL BE CONSEQUENCES—FOR ANYONE POSSESSING DIOGUARDI BLOOD, AND THEREFORE, MY POWERS."

He never took his gaze off me, but suddenly Stefan jackknifed, clutching his stomach as his veins went fiery red, and he coughed and choked on the dark red blood streaming from his nose and mouth. A moment later, the spasm ceased, and he fell back, gasping for breath.

Elaine stumbled to him, as Eric fought like a madman to break Jacques's controlling spell, still in effect, even with its maker gone.

But Stefan shook his head. "Will be…all right. My

fault…"

"*Non*," Eric said. "It is not your fault. It—"

With Elaine's help, Stefan pushed up to a sitting position and managed a glare at his father. "*Si. C'est…ma faute…pas celle de…quelqu'un d'autre.*"

Satan-Nick just stretched his arms high, then shook the dirt and oil from his body like a dog shaking itself dry. And when he spoke, his voice sounded more like Nick's, as though he were settling in. "Whoever is to blame, you have my powers—my *blood*—in you. I said there would be consequences, but I am not ungrateful for your warning about Bael. So, if Hyacinth does not call down Michael—or *any* of my brothers—I will let it slide. For now."

I swallowed. What choice did I have? Besides, if Satan wreaked havoc here on Earth, Michael would notice on his own. Maybe he'd think I should have told him first, but screw it. I'd had one too many impossible choices recently. Add this one to the list and move on.

But, my conscience whispered, *it's* Satan. *Think what he can do, even in a short time.*

I pushed the thought away. I *couldn't* let Satan torture Stefan, or by extension, Eric.

"Okay," I managed, and saw the triumph in Satan-Nick's eyes. But also something else.

Was it…relief? *Holy shit.*

I said, "I *saw* you in Hell with Nick, before you, uh, moved in. You talked about the Dioguardi powers being at your disposal, so you could *replenish* yours."

His eyes narrowed, going *almost* black, and then…fading back to blue.

And I had my answer.

"You're weak—you escaped Hell, but you're low

on gas." And then it clicked. "Flore. You gave *her* your powers—Michael's prison contains *them*, not necessarily *you*. So you swapped her like a pawn at the end of a chessboard, making her a Queen—of Hell."

I don't know how I had the chutzpah to say any of that—to *Satan*—but I knew I was right, thanks to the utter fury in his expression. With a casual wave of his hand, Stefan jackknifed again, and this time, his blood-vomit came out black and thick, streaked fiery orange and oozing grimy smoke. Elaine threw herself across him, sobbing, and Eric fought so hard to go to them, I feared he'd break himself in two.

"*No!*" I shrieked, and Satan-Nick smiled.

"I may be weakened. But I am not powerless."

"Okay," I gasped. "Okay—I won't call Michael down. Just please don't hurt Stefan—none of this is his fault. *Please.*"

He made a fist and Stefan's body slumped. Then with a wave, he broke Jacques's spell and Eric ran to his son, kneeling and caressing his back as Elaine did, murmuring encouragingly. Who knows how Stefan felt about it, but he was too weak to resist, so there's that.

Satan-Nick said to me, "You see. I can be reasonable, despite what my brother thinks. And I am appreciative of your efforts in regards to that other matter, though I would have preferred to destroy her myself." His gaze flicked to Jeannette's unconscious form, forgotten in the chaos. "Ah, well. It's the thought the counts." He turned back to me. "I know you set up a meeting with the Dioguardis here, today. And the oh-so naughty Marchosias. When will they arrive? I have business to discuss, with both of them."

A movement came from behind me—Torben

approaching hesitantly. It must be obvious what had happened, but just to be safe, I said, "It's Satan. He hopped into Nick as we sucked him out, and put Flore on the throne in his place. Jason—" I choked, then forced the words out anyway. "Jason got stuck behind."

Torben only nodded. "I know. We'll get him back." He inhaled deeply, then blew the breath back out, before facing Satan-Nick. "The Dioguardis are here. They've been waiting for Hyacinth to bring Nick out. Obviously, they noticed when his body disappeared, and made their own assumptions. Olivia—our contact—texted that they're on their way over, and Marchosias will be here soon, as well."

Thank God. The Dioguardis were keeping their promise to me.

But…I hadn't exactly brought *Nick* back, had I? He might be in there somewhere, but it wasn't *him*. Would they honor our deal? They *had* to.

Besides, they had Satan's blood in them. Surely they'd be okay with having him in Nick's stead. Like maybe it would be a big honor for the King of Hell to choose *their* son as his vessel, and they'd be thrilled to share their powers with him?

I thought of Rina being less fond of the Demon-Hell business than her husband, and decided *probably not.* But even if she tried to back out, Nico had also agreed to our deal. Surely he'd be all over Satan's plan—it might even make him less angry at me.

"Excellent," Satan-Nick said, throwing a warning glance at all of us—me and Torben, Stefan, Elaine and Eric, and Jun, Liam and Dito. "No one says *anything*. Do you understand? If anyone tells Marchosias I am present, I will end you, and your entire families. Remember that weak is a relative term, and I am still an archangel, though my brothers would prefer otherwise."

His gaze landed back on me. "Especially you, powerful though your nephew is—the only family you have remaining. I will kill him without a thought if you reveal what has happened." He watched me, and as on Barnacken, I felt his probe—my mind, my heart, my soul—and his malicious smile widened. "Ah—your friend, trapped in Hell. *He* is your family, too. Perhaps I should instruct Flore to end him now, as a precaution."

I gasped, falling to my knees. "*No*—I swear, I won't say anything. *Please* don't hurt Jason—or Geordi."

He regarded me for a long moment. "That will be up to you. But understand that I need something from the Dioguardis, and if they know I am stuck in their Prodigal Son, they may be less inclined to share it with me. Which reminds me…"

He peered at the smoking, blackened hole, mostly filled in now. I tried not to picture Jason trapped below, at the mercy of Satan and the new Queen of Hell. I felt the weight of the earth separating us, a vast, suffocating grave, and choked down my terror.

He *would* come back—he'd promised. But…was Bala right? By helping me—*again*—had he damaged himself beyond repair?

Abruptly Satan glared at all of us. "Where is the *porc-épic?*"

What the hell?

"I don't know," I said. He raised a hand and I scrambled up. "Wait—I threw it—over there somewhere."

"*Find it.*"

I gasped and started to move, but Torben interjected,

"On it," motioning to Liam and Jun, and the three of them began methodically combing the ground for the small black-and-blue coin.

Everything moved too fast—I couldn't think clearly, but I managed to wonder why Satan wanted the coin? Right *now*? Did it have protective powers that would shield his presence from the Dioguardis and Marchosias? If so, did it have to be in his actual possession to work?

I had no time for more—footsteps approached from the other side of the ruin closest to us. And then a warm breeze funneled down from the other direction, whistling over the hills and the tumbled, grass-covered bricks of the broken walls, caressing our skin before dancing away to swirl around the tombs and tumuli crowded nearby.

Satan-Nick shuddered as it passed him, saying to my minions, "*Find the coin now.* If you don't, I will take you to Hell and torture you for centuries—and *then* end you."

Moments later, the Dioguardis rounded the ruin, led by Nico, belligerent as ever, with Rina close behind, coiffed to perfection and dressed in another pale wool pantsuit. They were followed by what had to be a whole mess of Dioguardi cousins, based on their black hair, blue eyes, and general "demon Mafia goon" vibes. Eric moved subtly closer to Stefan, who lay on the ground, weak and recovering, while my other minions kept their heads down and continued their search.

One of the Dioguardis—a woman in her thirties with straight black hair and blue cat-like eyes—gave a slight wave to Torben with her smartphone. Olivia, I surmised. Torben nodded back, which was all very civilized, and at the same time, bizarre, under the circumstances. But it reminded me that the "goons" I kept referring to were just people, born into a family unlikely to encourage escape, whatever their own individual wants and desires.

Very civilized and rational of *me*. But the bulk of them were still gung-ho demon mafiosi, so I'd better remember *that*, first and foremost. I checked, but saw no eyes going black. Evidently, no one suspected Satan's subterfuge yet, so I tried to relax and focus on next steps.

Speaking of which, Rina saw her dearly departed "son" and rushed forward. "*Nicky!*"

She flung herself at him, and Satan did a fair impression of Nick's asshole indifference, similar to his father's: He shrugged her off. So much for the happy reunion. But Rina appeared satisfied. She stood next to him, caressing his arm and glowing with happiness. Even the weird waxy texture of his embalmed skin didn't seem to bother her.

As with Dito's return, Nico was less impressed. He scowled at Nick, then deliberately transferred his attention to me. "Get on with it. I didn't make fucking nice with Rodolfo Buonfiglio to stand around waiting. Where the fuck is Marchosias?"

Satan must be able to access Nick's memories, and understand the subtext, even if I couldn't. I mean, your deceased son comes back from Hell, and you don't even say hi? What's up with that? Or maybe indebting himself to Elaine's father just pissed him off too much to focus on anything else. That had to hurt—not that I cared how Nico *or* Stefan's grandfather felt. More power to both Families if, after this, they finally wiped each other out for good.

Before I could respond, the warm breeze circled through us once more, then stopped and became Marchosias in Paolo's form, holding Geordi's hand at his side.

"Tata!" Geordi squealed, breaking free and running to me, and I grabbed him, holding him tight and crying so hard I worried I'd scare him.

I couldn't help it. Like Jason, I'd been shoving my terror so far down that now I actually held Geordi in my arms, all the fear and rage and heartbreak broke the dam and burst forth.

Paolo-Marchosias watched us, the glint in his eyes telling me I'd better be careful, or this would still go south. As far as Geordi knew, he'd spent the last several days with Paolo, a favorite cousin. If he thought it odd that Paolo had started using his demon powers openly, he gave no sign, just pulled back and grinned at me.

"I missed you *so* much, Tata."

"Me, too," I managed thickly, swallowing back the sobs, and dashing at my tears.

He frowned, channeling Jason as much as ever. "Why are you crying?"

"I'm just so happy to see you. Are you okay?" I gulped. "Did—did you have fun?"

It was an absurd question, given what had really transpired, but Geordi just said happily, "Yes! We played video games, and did other stuff, but don't worry, Paolo made me eat good food. Sometimes. But we also had candy and cookies and cake. Is that okay?"

I laughed in spite of it all. He really had no idea of the danger he'd been in. "Yes. That's fine. Treats are okay, as long as they're just treats, not the norm."

Paolo-Marchosias cleared his throat, and I sniffled once and pulled myself together, straightening and gripping Geordi's hand so hard, it probably hurt, though he didn't complain. He glanced behind us at my minions, who combed the ground for the *porc-épic*, then at his resurrected "father." At least, I assumed he recognized Nick. Hard to say, since after Lily initiated the divorce, Geordi'd had no contact with him.

Either way, he must know *something* was up, if only because Nick's body, though in good shape, didn't look quite "alive" yet. He appeared pale and blotchy, his skin matte in some places, shinier in others. Geordi showed no concern, one way or another, and only pressed against my side, regarding Satan-Nick and his grandparents solemnly. However, Rina was so focused on "Nick," she barely acknowledged Geordi, and Nico maintained his scowling belligerence, as per usual.

Marchosias said to Rina, "I believe we had a deal. Are you prepared to pay the ransom we agreed on?"

She swallowed and stepped forward. She seemed…scared, and my heart raced. As noted, I have no great love for the Dioguardis. But in the entire time I'd known Rina, I'd never seen her afraid. What, exactly, had they agreed to trade, for Geordi's safe return?

Nico glowered at his wife, then at Marchosias. "Yeah, I'll pay the price I offered. I don't renege on my promises."

He directed this last comment at Rina, but she ignored him, focusing on Marchosias. She took a calming breath, straightened her spine, and nodded once.

"Yes." Then she faced me. "Where is the *porc-épic?*"

Absurdly, Satan-Nick and I now exhibited near identical levels of confusion. I'd recovered my powers of reasoning, and thought I knew why Satan wanted it. He'd mentioned being "stuck" in Nick, so I assumed he couldn't "perform" in his current state, but also couldn't leave Nick's body. Since the porcupine quills represented generations of Dioguardis who bore his blood and his powers, I guessed the coin would facilitate sucking those powers back into himself. Then he'd probably use them to crush Marchosias, and anyone else he deemed "naughty."

But why did *Rina* want it? Did she intend to use it herself, to further tap into Satan's powers, and perhaps thwart Marchosias? Surely not. She wouldn't endanger Geordi—and everyone else present—so stupidly. Would she?

And yet, she had no idea Satan was here, or that he'd been weakened. She believed him safe in Hell, and as powerful as ever. Maybe, despite not being Pro-Satan-Hell-Demon, she thought to call in a "favor?" Enhance her own demon strength to get Geordi, without paying the ransom after all?

Her steely gold gaze skewered me, so I said, "Somewhere nearby. I tossed it, just before—uh—Nick came back." Buying my minions some time, I added, "How did you know I had it?"

She sniffed derisively. "I gave it to Nicky for protection. As I'm sure you guessed, it has Dioguardi powers—*my* powers—in it, so I always know where it is. Generally, not specifically."

Nico frowned at her. "What's this about?"

She compressed her lips, and his eyes went black. After a tense moment, she decided it wasn't worth the fight. "I want Geordi to have it, right here and now. A guarantee, that nothing like this"—she threw a glance at Marchosias—"will *ever* happen again."

Something in her answer felt off, but I couldn't figure out what. Then Liam stooped and snatched something from the ground.

"Found it!"

He held it up triumphantly, and in another odd moment, I realized it must truly be of similar composition to the scarab, because he could hold it exactly as a living person would, without using his ghost energy to levitate it.

Rina held out her hand, and after checking with me—I nodded—Liam approached and dropped it onto her open palm. Satan-Nick's eyes narrowed, clearly wondering what she intended, and Nico's scowl deepened. He started to speak, but with a flick of his wrist, Marchosias silenced him. Nico's eyes bugged out, and his mouth worked, but the only sounds he made were a muffled grunting. Which only enraged him more, but he was helpless against a Hell Demon's spell, and we all ignored him.

Marchosias said to Rina, "Begin. I am waiting."

Rina nodded again and inhaled deeply. She closed her hand around the coin, and her gold eyes went black, and the air around us fractured—flashed hot—flashed cold—then hot again. Her eyes were gold again, then they closed, her arms jerked up and her hair flew straight above her head as though sucked by a vacuum. The warm breeze returned, but now it came *from* her—a roaring hot wind—it surrounded us, pulling the Dioguardi cousins and Nico to the ground, their arms and hair jerking up as though they, too, were caught in a vacuum.

I threw myself over Geordi, pushing him down, watching helplessly as light streamed through the fingers of Rina's hand holding the *porc-épic*. Then with a thunderous *crack!* the light arced out toward every

Dioguardi peon present, and I curled tighter around Geordi though I had no idea how to protect him.

The light reached his cousins—they *screamed* when it touched them—and the loudest, most agonized sound came from Nico. His veins glowed black, then red and orange, then went white, and he heaved and twisted, like he wanted to crawl out of his own skin. Marchosias watched him, then carelessly flicked his wrist, breaking the spell.

"You *bitch*," Nico snarled at Rina. "*What have you done?*"

But she was going through her own rainbow-vein crisis. Her palm opened, and the *porc-épic* fell from it, and she sagged to her knees. The grasses under the coin sizzled and smoked, oily black with a terrible stench, and the wind became a tornado—it circled up-up-up, sucking the light back out of the Dioguardis, leaving them unmoving, strewn across the ground. Then it funneled down-down-down, straight into Marchosias. Paolo's body thrashed wildly, and then he, too, dropped to the ground, unconscious.

All at once, the hot air rose again and vanished, leaving us in stunned silence.

Moments—seconds—eons ticked by.

I moved cautiously off of Geordi. He seemed none the worse for wear, and I started breathing again. Stefan pushed himself to a stand, ignoring both Elaine's and Eric's attempts to stop him, and went to Paolo's unconscious form, his expression intense. Eric followed him, keeping a respectable distance, while Torben knelt by the Dioguardi peon closest to him—Olivia—and checked her vitals, and Elaine took a deep breath and began doing the same with the fallen forms near her.

Nico regained consciousness first, coughing and spluttering, pushing up onto his hands and knees. He crawled to Rina just as Elaine helped her to sit up.

"*What the fuck was that?* You've gone too far this time, Rina. I swear—if you reneged on our deal with Marchosias, *you'll* be the one to pay for it, *not me.*"

He raised his hand, palm out, and I flinched, waiting for his eyes to go black, and for the blast of his righteous fury to slam into his wife. But...

Nothing happened. And abruptly, his fury became...terror?

He stared at his palm wildly, then at his wife. "*What did you do?*"

She sat back, arms resting loosely on her knees. She looked relaxed—and relieved, as though a great weight had been lifted from her. "Traded our powers for Geordi's return."

It was like she'd spoken a foreign language, and Nico couldn't compute. "Our...powers. Mine...and yours? For a *child?*"

"No."

Relief etched his features, and he started to sag back. But then she leaned forward, speaking succinctly, relishing every word.

"*All* our powers. Every last Dioguardi is no longer a demon. Marchosias has it all—this ends now. We're human, like everyone else."

Chapter Twenty-Five

"It is easier to forgive an enemy than to forgive a friend."

~William Blake, English Poet
(1757-1827)

The Dioguardis who were conscious enough to hear Rina's words murmured in shock and examined their own palms, expressions stunned as they realized that they were, indeed, powerless. My gaze flew to Satan-Nick, who appeared as dumbstruck as his "father."

And a bubble of hysteria rose inside me, because without realizing it, Rina had just destroyed Satan's power source, leaving him impotent and stuck in her son.

I stood, pulling Geordi up, and he tugged my hand. "Tata, Dito…"

I glanced down at him, but before I could discover what he wanted, Stefan rose and rounded on Rina. "They're no longer demons—*any* of them?"

His own eyes suddenly went black and I gasped. "But *you* are…"

He jerked back in surprise and his eyes went jade-gray again. He raised his own hands, flexing his fists, then nodded slowly. "Yes…I guess I am."

Nico shoved himself up to a stand, and unable to articulate his fury at his wife, aimed it at Stefan instead. *"What the fuck are you talking about?"*

307

Stefan met his scowl dispassionately. "I made a deal with one of your demons—Jason. He shared his blood and his powers with me. So technically, I'm a Dioguardi demon now." He paused, eyes flickering black, then jade again. "I should say, *still.* Even if the rest of you aren't."

Rina went white and rose to her feet. "No—that isn't possible. I traded *all* our powers to Marchosias. There are *no* Dioguardi demons left."

Geordi looked curiously around at the assembled crowd. "Tata, where's—"

Crap. He'd probably noticed Jason's absence. But one, I didn't want to upset him, and two, the last thing we needed was anyone focusing on him right now. So I gave his hand a warning squeeze, and he subsided.

Dito cleared his throat and stepped forward. "Actually, there are." His eyes also flickered black, before going blue again.

Rina shook her head. "I don't understand. I used the *porc-épic*—it pulled our powers out, generations of it, and sent it to Marchosias. He sealed it off—we *can't* access it anymore."

Dito said simply, "I think I know what happened. Yes, the *porc-épic* pulled all the Dioguardi demon powers, out of all the Dioguardis. But…Jason doesn't just have Dioguardi demon powers." His gaze met mine. "Does he?"

Oh God.

"No. He also has the Rousseaux's—Hell Demon powers. And you helped with Stefan's transfusion, so now you do, too. And…" I turned to Stefan. "So do you."

Eric staggered as though struck. "*Mon fils*—you are linked to a *Hell Demon?*"

Before Stefan could respond, Satan-Nick, who'd

been watching and listening as events unfolded, said bluntly to his "mother," "Why? Why would you do this?"

She met his gaze levelly. "Because it needed to be done. It was the only way—we had something Marchosias needed, that he couldn't get anywhere else. He has ambitions—we needn't go into what they are—"

Satan-Nick narrowed his eyes. "Yes. We do. Tell me *all* of it."

She frowned. I had to assume the "Nicky" she knew wouldn't be so inquisitive. Certainly the one I'd known had only been interested in being a rich playboy, not in anything to do with—God forbid—work. But clearly he wouldn't let it go now, so she continued.

"He didn't share the details with me, of course, but my understanding is he wants to overthrow Satan. He's not the only one—other Hell Demons have similar goals."

"Which ones?"

The question clearly confused her. "Does it matter?"

"*Yes.*"

Briefly, I wondered if my promise not to out Satan extended to warning him that he'd better act more like Original Nick, or he'd out *himself*. But it wasn't really my business, so like the rest of my minions and the Dioguardis, I kept my mouth shut and prayed for safe passage out of this fiasco.

Rina recovered her equanimity. "Oh, I don't know. Bael—Jacques Rousseau—and his brother, obviously. Maybe others. Marchosias is no fan of theirs, so I think he wanted our powers to defeat them *and* Satan. I needed you back, and Geordi, so…we made a deal."

"But at what cost?" Satan-Nick asked softly. To her,

maybe it sounded gentle. To me, it was deadly.

She only shrugged. "We've been demons for a long time, and what has it gotten us?"

Nico broke in, snarling, "Wealth—power—the fucking *lifestyle* you're accustomed to."

She glanced at him. "I don't care. Without my son and grandson, none of that matters."

His confusion was almost comical. "But...you chose Lily for Nick, specifically because of her heritage. You said it would strengthen our powers..."

Her smile went brittle. "I lied. Yes, I knew of Lily's family, but I also knew *she* had *no* powers. I figured by the time you learned the truth, it would be too late." She turned to me. "Unfortunately, I didn't know that you *did* inherit the family gifts—or that Geordi would get them, too."

I stared at her uncomprehendingly. She'd wanted Geordi to *not* be a demon? To essentially begin the process of de-demonizing the Dioguardis?

Nico growled, "Are you telling me my fucking grandson no longer has the blood, either?"

Rina's eyes gleamed with malice. "Yes. I see you get it now. There are *no* Dioguardi demons *anywhere*, anymore."

Geordi said, "Tata, Jason—"

Quickly, I squeezed his hand again—too late. Satan-Nick's gaze flicked to him, and my stomach dropped. Which would be worse? That his actual father might take renewed interest in him? Or that *Satan* would?

Satan-Nick regarded him silently for a moment, then glanced at the assembled crowd, giving those of us in the know another silent warning. But when he addressed Rina, he sounded more like Original Nick again.

"Well, then, I'm glad you brought me back. I was never a fucking demon in the first place." He faced his "father," eyes glinting triumphantly. "A fact *you* never let me forget. But things are different now." He flung an arm around Rina's shoulders, side-hugging her defiantly. "It's the dawn of a new age for the Dioguardis, *Dad*. None of *you* are demons anymore. But *I've* been to Hell and back, and soon enough, I'll have more powers than you ever dreamed of."

Oh God—what did *that* mean? Could he somehow extract powers from Jason or Stefan? Or Dito? Or did he have some unknown pipeline back to Flore, and his stores of powers in Hell?

Then he looked at Geordi again, and renewed terror settled low in my gut.

"Come here, son," he said quietly. He telegraphed another warning at me, and I gave Geordi's hand a reassuring squeeze.

"Go. It's okay. I'm here."

Geordi walked slowly to Satan-Nick, who knelt before him. I don't think anyone else could feel it, but I felt Satan's probe, like he'd done to me—twice now—assessing Geordi inside and out. After a moment, Satan-Nick rose, expression unreadable.

"Go back to your aunt," he commanded. "You can stay with her for now."

Rina gasped in shock, but sudden sweet hope soared within me, and Geordi ran happily to my side, flinging his arms around me while I held him tight. Did this mean—*could* it be possible—that after all this time, Geordi *was* no longer a demon? And therefore, safe from all the factions who'd wanted him for his powers?

He had no Rousseau powers to protect him, but he

also hadn't seemed to be affected by the *porc-épic.* Then again, I'd thrown myself over him. If his powers were "vacuumed" out the way his cousins' had been, I wouldn't necessarily have seen or felt it. But Satan had just *given* Geordi to me, which had to be because he no longer possessed anything Satan wanted. Especially demon powers, since as noted, Satan's tank was on empty.

He *was* still a Dioguardi, though, and Rina grabbed Satan-Nick's arm. "What are you doing? We agreed to share custody. We—"

"Enough. My son is useless to me now, thanks to you."

She looked like he'd slapped her. "But…"

"I said *enough.*" To me he said, "Geordi stays with you. But I see him when I want, or…" He lifted a shoulder, the message clear. Beside him, Rina made a small desperate noise, and he relented. "And his grandmother gets to see him, too."

I swallowed. "Of course. Uh…thank you." I hesitated, but I might never get another chance. "In exchange for upholding our, uh, *agreement*, I have a, uh, small favor to ask."

He narrowed his eyes. I wasn't really in a favor-asking position. But I *could* say screw the consequences and out him at any moment, and for whatever reason, he wanted to maintain the Nick fiction. So he said, "Go on."

My heart pounded and my palms were sweaty. "Can you use your, uh, connections in Hell, and bring Jason back to Earth? Alive and unharmed?"

Surprise flashed in his eyes. Then calculation. I'd taken a big risk, reminding him of Jason's existence. But that *had* to be less awful than Jason being trapped in Hell, forever.

He only said, "I'll consider it."

I bit back another plea. He hadn't refused, and I had to be satisfied that I'd at least started the conversation. Without another word, he stooped and retrieved the *porc-épic* from where Rina had dropped it. He tossed it once and caught it, then put it in his pocket.

Rina swallowed. "I—Geordi—"

Satan-Nick said quellingly, "I need it more than he does. Don't you remember, *Mother?* You gave it to me, since I'm not a demon, to protect me from anyone who might be against us." He looked meaningfully at Nico, then back at Rina. "Or…from Satan himself, even."

The hysteria bubble rose again—had he really given her such a broad hint? He caught my eye, ironic acknowledgment in his expression. But also another warning, and I forced the bubble down again.

To her credit, Rina waited a few more seconds before dropping her eyes in acquiescence. "Of course. Whatever you think is best, Nicky."

"Damn right," he said. Then, with a commanding glare at his cousins, he moved away from his former prison's gate, in the direction from which the Dioguardis had come.

Rina followed him, as did the others—including Olivia—who'd all recovered physically, if not "demonly." But Nico stood rooted to the spot a moment longer. He'd shown no great love for Geordi, but now he examined his grandson speculatively, before glancing at his "son's" retreating back.

He took a step in that direction, then paused and turned to me. "You think you've won. You're wrong. We had a deal, and whatever my goddamn son thinks, you'll honor it."

With that, he walked out of sight around the ruins, leaving me by the gaping blackened Hell hole, surrounded by my minions, with Geordi once again safe-safe-*safe* in my arms.

****

After all that, none of us knew what to do next. The first order of business, logically, was to clean up the mess—hide the blackened earth under clean dirt and loose grass, and probably call Michael down to give him the damn rocks. Though how I would explain finding *three* of them—all Satan's—I had no idea.

But when I stooped to pick them up, I no longer sensed their threads. Had sucking Satan-Nick from Hell drained their powers? It seemed likely, but I didn't feel capable of that level of decision making just now. So I put them back in the iron box for safekeeping.

Jeannette had finally stirred, and after some pretty good fake hysterics, copped to the fact that she'd invited Rachel in. For one thing, she couldn't hide her sudden ability to see and hear the Dead, and then she figured out we all knew the truth anyway. Elaine, who'd had basic medical training at the Police Academy, checked her over and decided her only lasting wound would likely be embarrassment. She now lay propped against a ruined wall, recovering.

Meanwhile, Eric hovered uncertainly near Stefan, who'd stayed silent and thoughtful ever since realizing he was the last living Dioguardi Demon, not counting Jason, stuck in Hell. But now I noticed Stefan mainly studied Paolo, who, while he'd regained consciousness, still sat on the grass with his head down, avoiding the rest of us.

Stefan caught me watching him and gave one of his Eric-adjacent Gallic half-shrugs. "I wanted to kill him. That's why I took Jason's powers, and why I went into Hell. I knew if you couldn't bring Nick out, the Dioguardis and Marchosias—and therefore, Paolo—wouldn't show up. I needed him here, so…I offered to help you."

My jaw dropped, and he grinned, not quite the old Stefan again, but close.

"Becoming a demon had nothing to do with my grandfather, despite what you all thought. I had some foolish idea that if I avenged my father's death, it would earn his love. *Quel putain de cliché, n'est-ce pas?* But now…" He regarded Paolo pityingly. "I can't do it. You said he never intended to kill Eric. But at first, I didn't care. Paolo is a Dioguardi demon, *and* he invited Marchosias in. I figured both of those were reason enough for him to die. And yet…"

He trailed off, and I finished for him, "You've realized he's just pathetic, and not worth what it will do to you, if you go through with it."

Paolo flinched at my words, but refused to look up, and Stefan gave a sad half-smile.

"*Ouais. Et puis*…I have come to understand that nothing I do will *earn* my father's love. I either have it…or I don't." His gaze moved from me to Eric, and I saw the unbearable hope in his eyes.

Eric's jaw clenched, and he faced Elaine. "Your father thinks I am dead. So, it is time you learned the truth. Both of you," he added to Stefan, then included me in his glance. "*Et toi, aussi.* Whatever you have done—whatever is between us in the past, or comes next—you must understand the reason we are all at this point now."

He shoved a hand through his hair, and leaned against a nearby wall. By unspoken agreement, Elaine, Stefan, and I—with Geordi clinging to my side—found similar seats, getting comfy for his Big Reveal. My minions, as usual, were handling clean-up duties. Mainly Torben, as the only living one remaining, but Dito, Jun and Liam did their part, picking up bits of ghost rope, or folding the remaining ghost blankets, and tidying other "dead" detritus left behind. So I sat back, and Eric began his explanation.

"It is both very simple, and very stupid, and I regret it every day. I make no excuses. It is only that—" He gave a firm shake of his head. "*Bon.* Elaine, when you said you were pregnant, I was stunned. But also *happy*— I swear to you. My sister's death, the path I finally understood was mine to follow—I knew what I must do. *Eh bien,* my grief over Thérèse was mitigated by the thought of a new life being born: *my child.*"

His eyes shone with unshed tears, and a suspicious sheen brightened Stefan's eyes as well. Elaine cried openly, saying, "If all that is true, why did you abandon us?"

"Because," Eric said simply, "your father told me if I did not, he would demand you get an abortion, and if you refused, kill the child himself, after its birth."

Elaine looked as shocked as I felt. And disgusted— horrified—grief-stricken. "But…we're Catholic."

"And yet, this was his threat. He expected me to join the Buonfiglios, to exact revenge for my sister. I did not realize it then, but he had groomed me. He put us together—you and me—hoping we would marry. When I told him I would fight the Dioguardis from the right side of the law instead, it enraged him. I believe he would have killed me then and there, except he is a very twisted man. He understood that, though only a boy myself, I wanted this child—"

He faced Stefan. "I wanted *you*. He knew that raising you in his family, and forcing me to watch from afar, would be a far worse torture than killing me outright. And he was correct. Not a day has passed since you were born—since I learned I had a beautiful, perfect *son*—that I have not wished myself with you. I thought, perhaps, when you were grown...*mais non.* Your grandfather made it clear he would kill you without warning, were I to attempt any contact."

He choked and looked away, shamefaced, then forced himself to meet Stefan's gaze again. "Nothing can make up for what I have done. I should have found a way, despite his threats. And if you doubt me, I understand. But I could not face your life being ended, before it began. And so, I stayed away. But I did not stay ignorant. I have watched you from a distance, and I hope that now, perhaps, I can be in your life. In whatever way you will allow."

Tears streamed down my own cheeks. So much tragedy in Eric's life—I couldn't bear it. First, the loss of his sister, which I certainly understood, since the loss of my own still carved a raw, open wound on my heart. But then to lose his *son*—able to see him from afar, but never to be with him—poured pounds of salt in that wound.

Of course he believed Elaine's father. He'd seen his sister's death—been forced to witness it by the Dioguardis who killed her. He'd pay *any* price to save his son from that same horrific fate, even if it meant giving him up forever.

My heart cracked with the knowledge of what he'd

sacrificed, and I wanted so badly to go to him and hold him while he wept. But this wasn't my story, and it was Stefan's reaction that Eric—and the rest of us—awaited with bated breath.

Stefan stared at Eric so long, I feared he might not respond at all—that he'd just turn on his heel and leave, abandoning his father as he'd planned all along. But then he shoved a hand through his hair and blew out a breath.

"That goddamned, motherfucking *prick*."

Chapter Twenty-Six

"All is well, provided the light returns and the eclipse does not become endless night..."
    ~Victor Hugo, French Novelist and Playwright
    (1802-1885)

"What now?" Torben asked. "Apart from getting Jason back. I know *that's* top priority."

Geordi and I had left Eric alone with Stefan and Elaine, to give them space to process. It would take time, but I was hopeful that, even with Eric being a dead cop, and Stefan in the mob—*and* now a demon—they could mend their *other* fences, and have a relationship going forward. I didn't know how I—or Elaine—fit into the picture, but Eric had his son back, and Stefan had his father, which was all that mattered.

I said, "Yes, we *will* get him back, if it's the last thing I ever do in my entire messed up life *and* death." I exhaled. "But I don't think we can do anything about it right now. Satan—"

I stopped and shuddered. Speaking of him in casual conversation like this felt surreal, but what the hey. He was out, and I couldn't do anything about *that* right now, either.

"Anyway. Satan said he'd consider it. Which, at first, I interpreted as he can help, but may not want to. But now I wonder—if he gave his powers to Flore, is he

319

even in charge anymore?"

Torben whistled. "Good call. When we get home, I'll research what happens when an archangel gives away his powers." He paused. "I assume we'll return to Paris at some point...?"

I didn't answer right away. Instead, I watched Geordi, lying in the grass nearby, hunting for bugs. *Home.* Mere days ago, that meant Paris—and Jason. And it still did.

I shifted my focus to the Guilliot-Buonfiglio trio. But...I had feelings for Eric, too.

No—I *loved* Eric. But I'd come to realize it might not be the same kind of...love...I felt for Jason.

Even that tiny admission terrified me, because who knew if what Jason and I had could survive everything between us, if—*when*—he came back from Hell? Like that didn't present a big enough obstacle on its own.

Elaine cried and hugged Stefan, and Eric felt my gaze and glanced up. He studied me, no doubt correctly reading my expression, because his own filled with irony. Then it softened, and a rare smile lit his face, his eyes glowing with it.

Mon ange, he mouthed at me, then gestured at Stefan. *Merci beaucoup...*

I nodded, then looked back at Torben. "Yeah, I guess. I mean, we're down a living man. Two, counting Ulrich." I hesitated. "Are you...okay? About all that?"

Torben lifted a shoulder. "I'll cry later. Promise. But we all took a risk when we joined the Burkes. Some of us knew what we were getting into, and signed up anyway. Others didn't, but that's no excuse. We should have investigated better, so that we *did* know. Ulrich tried to rectify some of the fallout. He wouldn't have regrets, so while I'll miss him, yeah—I'm okay. Besides, Yvo and Sabine might come to Paris, with Leopold. I guess Michael's subordinates have been helping them round up the escaped demons, and they don't need to be in Germany anymore."

Liam had been resting against a low wall nearby, but now he straightened. "Sabine's coming to Paris?" He caught my eye and reddened. "And, uh, the others?"

"Guess so," I said.

Jun had also been standing by, listening and thinking as usual, before jumping in. Now he said slowly, "I don't think Satan *is* in charge anymore. We will need to verify, of course, but if Michael's prison is there to contain Satan's powers, and he gave them to Flore to facilitate his escape, I don't think he can access them, or force her to use them in ways she doesn't want to."

"So," I said, "Flore isn't just Queen of Hell. She's the new *Satan?*"

"Yes. But there's more. I think Satan had another reason for all of this."

He hesitated, and I said, "Spit it out."

"Of course. We know that Jacques Rousseau wanted to overthrow Satan and steal his powers, to become King of Hell himself. I think when Satan swapped with Flore, he gave her the Rousseaux's powers as well. As in, they are seriously weakened, if not no longer Demons at all."

My minions never failed to amaze me. "How? And how do you even know any of this?"

"I gleaned a lot when researching my abilities for Rachel. And it makes sense. While you were looking into Hell, I watched Jacques Rousseau. Something happened before he left that enraged him. I have seen enough demons using their powers to recognize the signs. He tried to do something, and failed. And that is when he vanished. I believe he ran from Satan, whose retribution he feared."

"I still don't get it. If Satan can just take the Rousseaux's powers, why not do it before?"

Dito broke in. "Remember, Satan's powers were tethered in Hell, shortening his range and weakening his impact, and the Rousseaux have been out awhile. But when Jacques sent Flore into Hell, he had to imbue her with his powers, so she could execute his plan to overthrow Satan. All Satan had to do was reach up that power line, give it a yank, and Jacques's powers would be sucked right down it, out of him, and into Hell."

I said slowly, "So if Jacques's attack really had been a surprise, he might have succeeded. But Satan knew about it—both that Flore was coming, and who'd be empowering her—even before Stefan told him. He planned the whole thing."

Jun said, "Yes, that is most likely the case, though I haven't figured out how."

I groaned. "Nick. Satan used him from the start—contacted Flore through him, planting the idea that she should become a demon and find a way into Hell. Satan probably even knew *our* plans, and who I'd ask to convert her. Together, she and Nick made the perfect through-line to the Dioguardi powers, which Satan needed to survive out here, and to the Rousseaux, who he wanted to punish."

Torben whistled again. "So Satan drains the Rousseaux's powers and gives them with his own to Flore, thinking he'll be ten times more powerful out here with all that Dioguardi juice in him—maybe even so strong, he can control Flore remotely. Instead, Rina gives his lifeline to Marchosias, leaving him trapped in her jackass son. But on the plus side, Jacques—and probably Claude, as well—are no longer a threat. To us or Satan."

I frowned at Dito. "But if Satan issued a recall on Rousseau powers, and they're what protected you and Stefan—and maybe Jason—" I swallowed and pushed the fear away again. "—from Marchosias's appropriation of *Dioguardi* powers, then how are you all still demons?"

Geordi pushed up from his position in the grass a few yards away. "Oh—I helped with that."

I stared at him. "You did…what?"

He came to stand with us. The sun had warmed considerably since we arrived, and he wore a light hoody, covered in grass and dirt, with equally dusty jeans and sneakers. His black hair was mussed, and there were dirt smudges on his nose and cheeks. He resembled any other almost-eight-year-old boy, but my heart clutched with fear.

"I helped—I protected you, and Uncle Dito, and the man who looks like Eric."

He pointed at Stefan, now coming to join us, followed by Eric himself, and also Elaine. From their expressions, they'd heard Geordi's words.

"Protected us how, exactly?" I managed over the jackhammering of my heart.

"I tried to tell you before, when you were talking with Daddy, and Grandma and Grandpa. Paolo said Dito and Bala tried to hurt us, and that's why we had to hide, but I think he made a mistake. So when I saw you and Dito—and the other man—were in trouble, I used my scarab. And your feather."

"My…feather? How…"

I couldn't form the words, but I pulled it and the scarab from my pockets. They appeared unchanged—the same black onyx as ever—but Geordi nodded happily.

"I told you my scarab was magic. And Paolo taught me how to send my powers out into other things. Not a lot—he said we had to be careful, so no one noticed us."

I bet, I thought, casting a cynical glance at Paolo, still sitting by himself because my minions treated him like the pariah he was. Obviously, Marchosias had needed to be cautious, so as to not draw unwanted attention. But he'd needed to assess Geordi's abilities, while also fearing Geordi might catch on and use those same powers against him. He'd walked a fine line, but I had zero sympathy for Marchosias *or* Paolo at this point, and refocused on Geordi.

"Anyway," he continued, "he didn't know it, but when he showed me that, I saw you. You were sad, but you had the feather and my scarab, so I sent my powers into both of them."

"You saw me? How—when?"

He shrugged, an unimportant detail in his young mind, though it seemed wildly important to me. Although, after what Rina had done, maybe not as much anymore.

"I just did, Tata. So anyway, when we got here, and Grandma used Daddy's coin—"

I interrupted, "You know about that, too?"

He gave me one of his *well-duh* looks. "Of course. Daddy showed it to me when I was little. He said it belonged to my ancestors, and it would make me strong. When Nadezhda gave me my scarab, I saw it was like the coin, so I knew it had to be magic. But when Grandma used the coin, it felt funny."

"How so?"

He considered, then finally said, "I don't know. Just kind of…wrong. So since I put my powers into the scarab and feather before, I thought maybe I could use them now. I knew you had them, so I made sure they kept you safe, and then I saw Uncle Dito and the other man were in danger from the coin, too. So I added them to my powers. And Jason, too, of course."

"*Jason?* You…felt him?"

Oh God—if Geordi had felt Jason, all the way down in Hell, his powers must have been stronger than *any* of us realized. And Marchosias now controlled that power. I simply couldn't face it—the implications were too terrible. And yet I *had* to, because whatever Marchosias had planned, it likely meant utter destruction and chaos, for us and everyone else.

But before I could process any of it, Geordi said, "Yes—I still do."

"*What?*"

He frowned, a young carbon-copy of the cousin in question. "Of course, Tata. I can always feel other demons—just like they can feel me."

For a fraction of a second, his words didn't fit together in my mind, their meaning lost in a disconnected jumble. Then they dropped into place.

"*Other* demons? You're…still a demon?"

"Of *course,* Tata. What else would I be?"

****

"Did you know?" I demanded of Dito. "Did you know, and not tell me? I—"

"No," he interrupted. "And keep your voice down, unless you *want* him to hear you."

We'd moved a safe distance away, leaving Geordi

happily face down in the dirt again, searching for bugs under Elaine and Torben's watchful eyes. Fortunately, he didn't seem too concerned about Jason being trapped in Hell. In Geordi's mind, there was nothing Jason couldn't do, so obviously, he'd be back soon. If only I could be so sure.

Stefan had stepped aside with Dito and me, and Eric followed him. I doubted he'd let Stefan out of his sight again for a long while, but especially not now. Paolo also had finally raised his eyes and started to stand, but Jun and Liam moved to block him, and he sat back, defeated.

The fear and nausea rose again, and I leaned against a stone tomb, seriously afraid I might be sick. This couldn't be happening—I'd barely begun to think Geordi *wasn't* a demon anymore—that Rina had given his powers away, too. She'd said *all* the Dioguardis were no longer demons, and Geordi had no Rousseau powers in him, so…

I jerked upright again. "How? *How* is he still a demon? He wasn't infected by the Rousseaux, or near Stefan during the transition. So why weren't his powers sucked out, with all the other Dioguardis'?"

Dito said calmly, "Because he's not a Dioguardi demon. Remember? You said so yourself."

Oh God. I *had* said that, a few weeks back, when Jason and I discussed Lily's and my background, and I'd finally understood that if Nick had no demon powers—wasn't even a "carrier"—anything Geordi inherited *had* to come from our side. Probably through our mother.

But even with that realization, Jason had pointed out that…

"He *is* still a Dioguardi, though. Wherever the power comes from, he's the Dioguardi Heir—the *one* living Dioguardi remaining, with any powers at all."

"Except for Jason," a voice said quietly, and we turned to find Paolo standing nearby, Liam and Jun hovering apologetically close behind.

"Sorry," Liam said. "He insisted, and I didn't know how far we should go to stop him."

My first thought was, *As far as you need to.* My fear for Jason, my impotent rage at learning Geordi had become an even *bigger* prize than before—it all coalesced and I wanted to aim it at Paolo until I'd filleted him into tiny bits that could *never* hurt my nephew, ever again.

"Please," he said quietly. "I know I did a terrible thing, and you can never forgive me. But if you let me, I can help make it right."

"This will *never* be right," I managed over the bloodlust roaring through me. "You *invited a Hell Demon in.* To enhance your *own* powers, not for any noble reason like helping anyone else. It was a selfish, self-serving act, and because of you, Jason is trapped in *Hell.* And now the Dioguardis *and* Satan are powerless, and everyone will want Geordi even *more.*"

The sobs were about to overtake me. I couldn't deal with this—the horrifying facts bombarded me from all sides, cold and ruthless, turning me into a blubbering, terrified ball of desperation. And the one person who could always shake some sense into me—forcing me to focus and move forward—had been ripped from me, maybe forever.

Eric touched my arm. "*Mon ange.* It will be all right."

I wanted to ask him *how*, but too much lay between us, with him taking over Sieg, and what I'd done to

Stefan, and everything else. But more than that…he wasn't Jason. The realization hit me, both expected and a total shock. Was this it? Had I made my choice? The knowing irony in Eric's expression said I had, whether *I* admitted it or not.

Paolo spoke up again. "I understand that you hate me. But it will never be as much as I hate myself. And I *can* help make it right, at least as far as Jason goes."

I compressed my lips. "Go on."

"I'll go into Hell and bring him back out for you."

I stared at him. "How? You're not a demon anymore, either. Are you…?"

He shook his head. "No. Marchosias took all my powers, long before Rina did her thing."

"Then how are you going to get into Hell, and get Jason back out?"

He glanced at Stefan, who slowly nodded.

Eric's gaze whipped between them. "*Non*—I forbid it. I—"

Stefan looked back at him levelly, and Eric's shoulders slumped.

"I am sorry. I have no right. But more than that, it is your decision. And perhaps this will not mean much, but…I believe you are stronger and more capable than your grandfather or anyone else knows. I am proud of you, and if you do this, I will support you." He smiled tentatively. "But I will also worry, until you are safe again."

Stefan's mouth quirked up on one side. "I'll allow that." He faced Paolo. "How do I know this isn't a trick, to somehow steal my powers and use them against us—or Jason?"

Paolo lifted a shoulder. "Make me a demon pet. You

have the Rousseaux's powers in you, and therefore, access to all their spells. Like Jason, they are a part of you now. Dito can show you. Make me a pet, so that I can use your powers, but not control them."

I cut in, "What about Flore? Can't she do what Satan did, and reach out from Hell, to yank those powers away from Stefan, through you?"

"Flore is not the one who granted those powers to Stefan. Jason is. Satan could take the Rousseaux's powers, because he is the one who made all Hell Demons. So in theory, Jason could use me to take his powers back from Stefan. But that would cut off his escape route." He regarded me seriously. "And he would *never* cut off his only way back...to you."

My heart surged, my breath caught. This could work—we could save Jason and bring him *home*—to me. My utter relief and joy must have shown on my face, because Eric caught my eye. Something unspoken passed between us—not conscious on my part, but at last, he gave a Gallic half-shrug.

"*Mon ange*—I believe I must leave you now." I gasped, and his lips twisted ironically. "Not in that way. But I must go to Marseille. As you discovered, I have unfinished business there, and it is where my son will eventually return. *N'est-ce pas?*"

Stefan nodded, and Eric's gaze flicked to Elaine, before meeting mine again. "I am sorry, *mon ange.* But I must go where Stefan is. And...I believe this is what you want for now, as well—what is best for us both."

I swallowed, throat closing over my tears. Then I managed a miserable nod. "I'm sorry—for making Stefan a demon, and for—for—"

I couldn't say the words that would make this final.

But he understood.

"*Bon.* It is decided. Perhaps we will meet again. I hope we do. I…" He paused, his expression filled with regret. "Or…perhaps not. But you will always be *mon ange.*"

He took my hand, then leaned in to give me a quick, soft, kiss. I felt his thread, warm with happiness, but tinged with sorrow. Then it receded slowly, until it was gone.

"*À bientôt…*"

He walked over to Elaine and murmured something to her. She reeled back, looking wildly at Stefan, who straightened and said, "I'd better go speak with her. She should leave, before my grandfather finds out what happened. And she shouldn't be here for this, in any case. Neither should my…father."

I could tell the word felt foreign to him, but I also sensed his wonder and pride that he finally had a father. One that might want to stay and support him, whether Stefan himself wanted that or not.

He went to his parents, and I faced Paolo again. "This better not be a trick. If *anything* you do further endangers Jason, or Geordi—or Stefan—or *anyone* else, I'll kill you myself, with my bare hands, and then I'll give your corpse to Jacques Rousseau and your spirit to Satan, and they can torture you for the rest of eternity."

Paolo only nodded sadly. "I understand. I deserve worse."

A thought struck me, and I demanded of no one in particular, "Does *Satan* know? That Geordi has powers? He checked him—I felt him probing Geordi. But he let him go—*gave* him to me. Why?"

Dito said, "Maybe the scarab really is a shield, and

it blocked Satan from sensing Geordi. And maybe the feather helped. Liam could hold the coin, and all three seem to be made of the same material. Maybe they really do have powers, somehow."

I pulled them from my pockets again. They looked the same—no sudden glowing lights or even rock-like vibrations, to suggest they were anything but ordinary trinkets. And yet... I had felt something from the coin. And they were all types of onyx.

I sagged with relief. "That must be it—Satan must not know. So all we have to do is keep him from finding out. And make sure Geordi never goes anywhere without *both* the scarab and the feather."

"Obviously," Dito agreed. "But first, I think we can use them now, for something else."

"What do you mean?"

"Remember what the seller at the gem show told you? Dove feathers bring clarity, and will free you—or someone you love—from the bonds that keep you apart."

I exhaled sharply. *Clarity.* I had that now. I knew who I loved—who I couldn't bear to be separated from—who I'd fight for, with every last piece of myself, no matter what.

Did I imagine it, or did the feather abruptly grow warm in my hand after all, filling with bright, *good* energy?

"And the scarab?"

"You know something about Egyptian artifacts—that's one of your specialties, right? So you should know that scarabs represent protection, as Geordi always said. But they also facilitate resurrection. I believe if you are holding both the scarab and the feather, imbued with Geordi's powers—Jason's blood relative—and if you were to send your thread through them, with Stefan and Paolo, into Hell…"

"We might be able to pull Jason out," I finished for him.

Stefan rejoined us. "I told Eric I did not want him here for this—it would be too distracting. He will hitch a ride back to Marseille with *ma mère et* Jeannette."

I watched as Eric bent to help Jeannette up, then, with one final look in my direction, he placed a hand at Elaine's elbow and the three of them turned to leave. I stopped myself from following him. He *had* to go—he understood that Stefan needed absolute focus for this to work. But my untidy emotions cried out to him—my onetime lover, my friend.

I swiped at my tears and faced Stefan.

He said to Dito, "*Bon,* I am ready. Tell me what to do."

Moments later, Paolo was Stefan's demon pet, and they began the long dangerous trek into Hell. My eyes were shut tight, my hands clutching the two stone talismans. I couldn't see into Hell this time, so I focused everything inward, concentrating on my thread, preparing as best I could to help in any way possible.

And I prayed harder than I ever had, ever in my life, except when I'd prayed for Geordi's return. That had worked out—this had to, also.

Please bring Jason home to me. Just…please…

A word about the author...

Kerry Blaisdell is the bestselling and award-winning author of the acclaimed Dead Series, including DEBRIEFING THE DEAD and its sequels, WAKING THE DEAD, DAMNING THE DEAD, and BURYING THE DEAD, which InD'tale Magazine recommends for "fans of shows like 'Constantine' or 'Supernatural.'" She also writes award-winning Romantic Suspense (PUBLISH OR PERISH, a Publishers Weekly BookLife Prize Quarterfinalist) and Historical Mystery.

She has a B.A. from U.C. Berkeley in Comparative Literature (French/Medieval English), and a Master's in Teaching English and Advanced Mathematics from University of Portland. Kerry lives in the gorgeous Pacific Northwest with her family, assorted animals, and more hot pepper plants than anyone could reasonably consume.

To connect with Kerry online, join her Facebook Reader Group (https://bit.ly/kerryskin), or subscribe to her Very Occasional Mailing List (https://www.subscribepage.com/kerrysvoml) and get TWO free downloads!

Thank you for purchasing
this publication of The Wild Rose Press, Inc.

For questions or more information
contact us at
info@thewildrosepress.com.

The Wild Rose Press, Inc.
www.thewildrosepress.com